A Long Way From Warsaw

A Novel of World War II Poland

Margarita Morris

Published by Landmark Media, a division of Landmark Internet Ltd.

PROLOGUE

Highgate East Cemetery, London. September, 2005

A sudden breeze rustles the leaves of the trees as his sister's coffin is lowered into the ground. At least the rain has held off, although he brought an umbrella with him just in case. He's lived in London for so long now, he's used to the vagaries of the English weather. As the priest intones the familiar words 'earth to earth, ashes to ashes, dust to dust', Jan reaches into his breast pocket for his wallet and takes out the photograph he always carries with him. Next to his heart.

The black and white image has seen better days. It's badly creased and there's a hole in the middle. But the faces – his parents Emeryk and Maria, his sister Anna, his older brother Lech, and himself as a skinny eleven-year-old – smile at him and he remembers that day as if it were yesterday. The twenty-second of August 1939.

He's the only one of the family left now.

This photograph is his most treasured possession.

It was Anna's idea to take the photograph, even though news of Lech's mobilisation had come so suddenly and time was short. He remembers her fixing her beloved Leica to the tripod with quick, expert fingers and setting the clockwork timer so that she could also be in the picture. There was only time for one shot, so it was a good job everyone was looking at the camera with their eyes open.

At the time it seemed like a bit of a lark: posing for a family photo before Lech went to see off those pesky Germans who were snapping at Poland's borders like a pack of overexcited gundogs. At least that was how it had seemed to Jan, as an eleven-year-old boy. He hadn't understood the real threat from Nazi Germany. But how many people had? Hitler had cut such a ridiculous figure with his stiff-arm salute and his pathetic moustache that looked as if it had been drawn under his nose by a child with a black crayon.

But looking back now, he can understand the anguish his parents must have felt, seeing their eldest son going off to war. Thank goodness Anna had the foresight to capture that moment when they were all still together. For the last time. Was it a premonition that caused her to suggest the photo? She was always the insightful one. Jan, like most eleven-year-old boys, took his family for granted. It was a happy home and he had nothing to complain about except his mother nagging him to be home in time for tea. Now he takes nothing for granted. Your loved ones can be snatched from you in a heartbeat.

As if sensing his thoughts, his wife slips her arm through his and he turns to her, giving her a grateful smile. On his other side his son and daughter stand with their spouses and his three, soon to be four, grandchildren. Following Anna's example, he's taken so many photographs of his family over the years, the spare bedroom is stacked high with photo albums. No, as an eleven-year-old he could never have imagined all this. All this joy and sorrow.

'…through our Lord Jesus Christ, who will transform our frail bodies…' The voice of the priest breaks through Jan's thoughts. Anna's body was certainly frail after what happened to her. She never fully recovered. A drop of water lands on his hand and he realises that he's crying. Crying for his sister, crying for his family, crying for his friends. Crying for his lost childhood.

As the mourners prepare to leave, Jan lingers for a moment longer by his sister's grave.

'You saved my life,' he tells her silently now. 'If you hadn't taken this photograph, I'd have died a long time ago.'

Then he puts the photograph back where it belongs, next to his heart.

PART ONE
MOBILISATION
AUGUST 1939

CHAPTER ONE

Anna leans her bicycle against a tree and walks down to the water's edge, her Leica slung around her neck on its leather strap. A family of ducks – mother, father, and five ducklings – is bobbing on the lake near the shore and she wants to capture the moment before they disappear.

She crouches down to get a better angle, lifts the camera and peers through the rangefinder to focus the lens. The Leica was a present from her parents on her eighteenth birthday and she's still getting used to it, experimenting with the aperture and shutter settings to get the best results in different lighting conditions. Today she slipped out of the apartment before anyone else was awake and the light has a clean, fresh quality to it which she hopes will make for a good set of photographs. She's been in Stare Miasto, the Old Town, photographing the old houses with their ornate façades, the churches and the Royal Castle, finishing with a detour through the Krasiński Gardens on her way back to Królewska. She presses the button and hears the satisfying click of the shutter before a breeze ruffles the surface of the water and the ducks paddle away.

She straightens up and returns to her bicycle. Sounds of the city waking up reach her from beyond the edge of the park. She's stayed out longer than she intended. Her mother will be getting breakfast ready. She mounts her bicycle and sets off in the direction of home.

For some reason that she can't explain, she pedals faster than usual. She tells herself it's because she doesn't want her mother to worry. But later she'll admit to herself that there was something she couldn't quite put her finger on. A certain tension in the air. A sense of time running out.

At the apartment block on Królewska she runs lightly up the stairs to the second floor, the feeling of urgency intensifying all the time. An unfamiliar smell – cologne mixed with tobacco – warns her that someone has just climbed the stairs ahead of her.

As she rounds the corner, she sees a man – a policeman, in fact – standing outside her parents' apartment, his fist raised, about to knock on the door. What can he possibly want? She shivers, despite having just cycled fast in the warm sun.

'Can I help you?' she asks, climbing the final flight of stairs. She's surprised at how calm her voice sounds, when her heart is thumping against her ribcage. She clutches the camera like a talisman as if it has the power to ward off whatever is about to happen.

Level with him now, she sees he's holding a slip of red paper. This cannot be good news. But these are not normal times, as her father keeps reminding them. War with Germany is a distinct possibility.

'Does Lech Nowak live here?' The policeman breathes heavily and beads of sweat stand out on his brow.

'He's my brother.' But he won't be up yet, she thinks, not given the time he crawled in last night.

'Please give him this.' The policeman thrusts the piece of red paper into her hands and then takes the stairs to the ground floor two at a time. Stunned, Anna leans over the banister and sees the top of his head disappearing out of the door.

She slips into the apartment, pausing in the hallway to

read the piece of paper. Her breath catches in her throat. It's a mobilisation order for her older brother. Lech is a reserve officer in the artillery. He's to report immediately to the Light Artillery Regiment in Warsaw.

'What's that you've got there, love?' Her mother appears from the kitchen carrying a fresh loaf of bread through to the dining room. 'Did I hear you talking to someone?' Maria is wearing her old house dress, the one she wears when she's planning a day of baking.

Emeryk emerges from his study, his brow furrowed. 'What is it, Anna?'

Anna hates to be the bearer of bad news. But having intercepted the policeman, it's now her responsibility to inform her parents of their eldest child's fate. Mutely, she hands the slip of paper to her father. Maria rushes to her husband's side and together they bend their greying heads over the mobilisation order. Anna watches, helpless. She should have told the policeman there was no one by the name of Lech Nowak living here. She could kick herself for her stupidity.

Maria lets out a cry and runs back to the kitchen. It's her sanctuary, her place of refuge. But her father remains where he is, his face impassive apart from a slight contraction of his brow.

'I've been expecting this for some time now,' he says.

Before Anna can respond, Jan tears out of his room in his pyjamas, barefoot, his hair tousled. 'What's going on?'

Only Lech is still sleeping through this drama which concerns him.

Maria reappears, her eyes red and puffy, and attempts to draw her youngest son into an embrace, but he pulls away, embarrassed by this outpouring of emotion and motherly love.

'I'll wake him up.' Anna goes to Lech's door.

She knocks and calls his name. When there's no answer, she opens the door and peers into the gloom. The reek of stale tobacco, alcohol and male sweat assaults her nostrils.

Much as she loves her brother, his personal habits can be trying. 'Lech, you need to get up.'

He's lying on his front, his head turned sideways, one half of his face pressed into the pillow. A bare arm hangs over one side of the bed, the fingers trailing on the floor. Dead to the world. Losing patience, Anna marches up to his bed, switches on the bedside lamp and gives his shoulder a firm shake. 'Lech, you have to wake up!'

'Whaaa!' He comes to with a start, staring at her with bloodshot eyes. 'Anna! What the hell? You frightened the life out of me.'

'Time to get up.'

'Why, what's happened?' He rolls over onto his back and squints at her, shielding his eyes from the light with one hand.

'Your papers have arrived.'

'What papers?'

'You've been called up.'

'Called up?' he repeats slowly as if he doesn't understand the meaning of the words.

'It's your regiment,' she articulates slowly. 'You have to report for duty.'

Realisation dawns on his face. He sits up suddenly, then clutches his head and falls back onto the pillow with a groan.

'Late night, was it?' She crosses her arms and tilts her head to one side, raising her eyebrows at him. She can't resist an opportunity to tease him, even on a day like today.

'Be a good sister and fetch me a glass of water and an Aspirin, would you? I just need a minute.'

Taking pity on him, she does as he asks and when she returns, he has at least managed to sit up in bed. But he looks a fright, his hair sticking up in tufts and dark smudges under his eyes. Heaven help us, she thinks, if Poland's future depends on the likes of her brother.

He takes the Aspirin and knocks it back with the water. 'Thanks.' He gives her a rueful smile, acknowledging that he might have over-indulged last night. 'I'll be along in a minute.'

Anna returns the Leica to her room, then goes to help her mother with the breakfast. If this is to be Lech's last meal before setting out, she knows Maria will want to make it a special one. Heaven forbid that Lech should be called upon to defend his country on an empty stomach.

Maria has already covered the table with her best linen tablecloth. Anna helps her put out fruit preserves, slices of cold meat, cheese, boiled eggs, fresh butter and bread rolls. By the time they've finished, it's a breakfast fit for a king.

'So where's this mobilisation order?' Lech finally appears, washed and dressed, and wearing his military uniform. The uniform has transformed him from a hungover layabout to a respectable Polish officer and Anna's heart swells with pride. She passes him the piece of paper which Lech studies carefully.

'Are you going to fight the Germans?' asks Jan, his eyes lighting up. He has changed out of his pyjamas into his shorts and shirt. 'Is there going to be a war?'

'Hush,' says Maria, carrying a pot of coffee into the room. 'This is not a game.'

'I'm sure it's nothing to get excited about,' says Lech with his usual casualness. 'Probably just a limited mobilisation. Show Hitler how well prepared we are. Then he'll think twice about crossing the border.'

Jan looks disappointed, but Anna hopes Lech is right. Lech has always been the optimistic one, breezing through life with a carefree attitude that she envies. She can see from her father's face that he doesn't share Lech's optimism, but he won't want to say anything that will worry his wife.

'Now, everyone sit down and have something to eat.' Maria claps her hands together. 'We are going to eat together as a family before Lech goes away.' She bustles back into the kitchen, but not before Anna has seen her surreptitiously wiping her eye with the back of her hand. She returns with the bread knife, saying brightly, 'Now then, who would like bread?'

It seems to Anna that this breakfast has the solemnity of a Last Supper. This could be the last time they will all be together for a while. The thought makes her throat constrict and she has to force herself to swallow. But then she looks at Lech who is liberally spreading butter on a thick slice of bread, and wonders if she isn't being a little melodramatic. Maybe Lech is right after all? He could be home in a matter of weeks, days even. When the Germans see that Poland has amassed a serious defence, they'll back off. At least that's the theory. Her father, she notices, is eating very little, his brow set in a frown of concentration. She has no doubt that he understands the situation far more than any of them, certainly more than Lech who hardly ever bothers to pick up a newspaper or listen to the radio.

Anna catches Lech's eye across the table. She wants to ask him what he really thinks about the mobilisation order. He seems unconcerned, but is that just bravado? He winks at her. Is that supposed to be reassuring? She doesn't feel reassured.

'Don't forget to take plenty of warm underwear with you,' says Maria as she pours Lech a cup of black coffee.

'Honestly,' says Lech, laughing, 'it's August, not the middle of winter. I'll be going to the Polish countryside, not Siberia.'

'You don't know how long you'll be gone for,' says Maria. 'It will be autumn soon and the weather can change suddenly.'

'I'll be back in a couple of weeks. We'll show the Germans what we're capable of, then it will all be over.'

'Are you going to shoot the Germans?' asks Jan. 'Have you got a gun? Can I see it?'

'That's enough, Jan,' says Maria. 'We do not talk about shooting people at the breakfast table.'

Jan's shoulders slump and he picks at his bread, scattering crumbs over the edge of his plate.

After breakfast, Lech goes off to pack and Anna helps her mother wrap up food parcels for him in the kitchen: a half loaf of bread, a whole sausage, four ripe apples, some cheese wrapped in muslin. A meat pie. It reminds her of family picnics in the countryside: swimming in the lake, ball games, her father reading a book, her mother setting out the checked picnic blanket. Lech calling her to come into the water – 'It's lovely and warm' – and then laughing at her when she shrieks with the shock of the cold.

'Will he have room for all this food?' she asks. 'There's enough here to feed half the battalion.'

'I don't want him to go hungry,' says Maria. 'You don't know what sort of rations they'll get.' Her tone suggests she doesn't trust the Polish Army to look after its young men, at least not the way a mother would.

Lech appears in the doorway with his kitbag slung over his shoulder.

'I hope you've left room for all this,' says Anna, indicating the huge pile of food. She catches his eye and a look of understanding passes between them. She wants to laugh – she can see he does too – but they control themselves, not wanting to offend their mother who means well. Anna helps him squash the bread, sausage, fruit, cheese and meat pie in amongst his clothes. 'Don't eat it all at once,' she jokes.

'I'll try not to.' He lifts his bag off the table. 'I guess I should be going.'

So soon? Anna has to stop him, even if just for a minute or two. She has an idea.

'Wait.' She runs to her bedroom and grabs her camera. Then she takes the tripod down from the top shelf in her wardrobe. Thank goodness she didn't use up the whole roll of film this morning. Returning to the living room, she says, 'Gather round everyone, I'm going to take a picture.'

'But my hair's a mess,' says Maria, tucking loose strands behind her ears. 'I haven't had time to arrange it this morning.'

'It doesn't matter,' says Anna. She just wants a picture of everyone before... before what? Of course this isn't going to be the last picture of them all together. But it seems like a moment that should be preserved. 'Everyone stand over there.' She points to a place in front of the sideboard where the morning sun is shining on the wall. She can be quite bossy when the occasion demands it. Whilst they shuffle into position and arrange themselves, she fixes the camera onto the tripod, checks the focus, and makes sure everyone is in the frame. Lech is standing between Emeryk and Maria, a head taller than both. Jan is in front of his older brother, pulling faces at her. She sets the clockwork timer – one of the features of this model of camera – then moves quickly to stand next to her mother.

'Smile!' she orders as the timer ticks down.

There's a flash of light and a click of the shutter as the camera captures the moment. There, it's done! She hopes everyone was looking at the lens with their eyes open. There isn't time to take another shot.

After the excitement of the family photograph, the atmosphere is subdued. Even Jan has calmed down, perhaps understanding for the first time the seriousness of the occasion. It isn't every day that your big brother is called up.

Emeryk shakes Lech's hand before drawing him into an embrace. 'God bless you, son.' The words catch in his throat and he wipes a tear from his eye. 'I'm sure you'll do Poland proud.'

Maria holds her eldest child tight as if she never wants to let him go. She plants a kiss on his forehead and murmurs that she loves him.

Lech ruffles Jan's hair. 'See you soon, soldier,' he says. 'Look after everyone for me.'

Jan nods solemnly, for a moment seeming much older.

Finally Lech turns to Anna and hugs her tight. 'It'll be all right, sis. I'll be back soon.'

'I hope so,' she says, her throat tight and her heart full.

And then he's gone, the sound of his boots echoing in the stairwell.

CHAPTER TWO

Once he's out of the apartment and striding down the street, Lech breathes a sigh of relief. He's always hated long-winded goodbyes. The photo was a nice idea, but he felt foolish being the cause of so much fuss. It was all too emotional, as if Anna wasn't expecting him to return. Ever. She can be fanciful sometimes, letting her ideas run away with her. Lech refuses to think like that. He'll be back home before the leaves start to fall.

If he's honest, the mobilisation couldn't have come at a better time. Now he won't have to worry about being sacked from the bank. Since leaving university he's struggled to find a career he actually enjoys. He hates being cooped up in a windowless office all day. Come to think of it, it wouldn't be a bad thing if he was away for a month or two. Give him time to think about his future and what he wants to do with his life.

He nods a greeting to their neighbour, old Pan Woźniak, who has popped out to buy a newspaper and is making his slow, doddering way back to the apartment building.

'Good morning, young sir,' says the old man. His eyes flick to the canvas kitbag on Lech's shoulder and he stands as straight as his aged frame will allow. 'I see you have been called upon to defend our country. May God be with you.'

'Thank you,' says Lech. 'But the Polish army is well prepared.' He doesn't expect they'll need the intervention of the Almighty.

'Hmm.' Pan Woźniak sounds unconvinced. 'Anyway, I mustn't hold you up. Good day to you!'

'And the same to you,' says Lech. 'And give my regards to your wife,' he adds to the old man's retreating back.

Why is everyone so worried? The whole point of this mobilisation is to show Herr Hitler that the Poles are not going to be a pushover like the Czechs. Anna thinks he doesn't pay any attention to current affairs, but even he noticed when the Nazis marched into Austria and then Czechoslovakia. He's not a complete idiot. But the difference between those countries and Poland, is that Poland will put up a proper fight. Poland is well-prepared. Isn't that what the newspapers and cinema newsreels have been saying all summer? Smiling schoolchildren and factory workers posing for photographs beside brand new tanks built with the funds they raised. Posters of infantry columns marching beneath the protection of a sky full of Polish planes, the captions declaring that Poland is strong, united and ready!

He takes a deep breath, filling his lungs with the early morning air, and exhales loudly, adjusting his kitbag on his shoulder. His mother has packed so much food, it weighs a tonne. He'll share it with the other men on the train – always a good way to win friends.

At least his hangover is beating a hasty retreat, thanks to the Aspirin and the three cups of strong black coffee he drank at breakfast. How many glasses of vodka did he have last night? No idea. He remembers the bar was crowded and smoky with darkened windows and a live band. And the singing. He remembers the singing. Patriotic songs about Poland that grew increasingly belligerent as the evening wore on. And the woman he danced with. My God, how could he not have remembered her! He feels a stirring in his groin as he recalls her curvaceous figure and tumbling dark curls. He never knew her name, and doesn't know what happened to her. But if last night was his last night of freedom for a while, then what a way to spend it! He doesn't remember how he got home. Probably one of his friends put him in a taxi. Yes, that will have been it. And then he slept the sleep of the dead until Anna woke him this morning. He winces at the thought of his sister seeing him like that – crashed out and stinking of old cigarette smoke and stale alcohol. Anna would never behave like that.

At the barracks he joins a long queue of men waiting to report to the duty officer. More keep arriving all the time. Eventually it's his turn. The duty officer studies Lech's mobilisation order, stamps it and gives him a train ticket to Oświęcim, ordering him to depart immediately, all in the space of about thirty seconds. Then he orders the next man in the queue to step forward.

Lech takes his ticket outside. Now that he has an actual destination it all seems so much more real. Oświęcim. He's never been there, but thinks it's a small town on the German border. An inconsequential sort of place in the normal run of things, but of strategic importance if the Germans decide to invade. And it will be up to Lech and his fellow soldiers to keep the good people of Oświęcim, and the whole of Poland, safe. For a moment, Lech feels the very real responsibility thrust upon his young shoulders. Then a group of reservists emerge laughing and chatting, and he realises he needs to get a move on if he's going to get to the train station in time.

Hundreds, if not thousands, of men are converging on the central station, their kitbags a sure giveaway of their true purpose. Practically every man of the right age in Warsaw seems to have been called up. So much for a secret mobilisation. This is something much bigger than Lech imagined. There was a rumour a couple of days ago that France and England had warned Poland against a full mobilisation, fearing it would provoke Hitler into action.

But it's obvious that Hitler doesn't pay any attention to the softly-softly approach. He only understands displays of physical force. In a perverse way, Lech rather hopes that Hitler *will* be provoked. Just let that little Austrian upstart try invading Poland. Then he'll see what's coming to him.

Lech pushes his way through the mass of bodies milling about outside the station, seeking a familiar face in the throng.

'Hey, Lech!' He hears a voice he recognises and looks to see where the sound is coming from. 'Over here!'

A hand shoots up above the heads of the surrounding men and sure enough Lech spots the blond head of his friend Aleksander. They were at school and university together. They've known each other for as long as Lech can remember. Aleksander stumbles through the crowds and clasps Lech by the arm.

'Am I glad to see you here!' says Aleksander. 'I thought you weren't going to make it.'

'I only just arrived. What's happening?'

'They're sorting us out, starting to board the trains. We should get a move on if we don't want to be standing all the way to Oświęcim.'

They squeeze onto a carriage, the seats already taken. Aleksander dumps his kitbag on the floor and sits on top of it. Lech does the same.

'Did you get away all right, this morning?' asks Aleksander.

'Yeah, not too bad.' Lech doesn't mention the family photograph, knowing it will sound sentimental and portentous. 'How about you?'

Aleksander pulls a face. 'Mum wasn't happy, but she put a brave face on it. She'll be all right in a day or two.'

Lech nods his understanding. Aleksander's mother is a widow. Aleksander is her only child.

Doors slam, a whistle blows, sooty steam belches from the funnel. As the train jolts forwards there are ebullient shouts.

'Let's send Hitler packing!'

'Crush the German threat!'

'Poland will never be defeated!'

Lech joins in at the top of his voice. The energy and enthusiasm of the men on board is contagious. It's impossible not to be swept up in the general mood of optimism. After months of growing tensions, the situation in Europe worsening, at last they are going to do something about it. None of them knows what the future holds, but they're such a vigorous bunch, it's impossible to imagine them defeated.

CHAPTER THREE

Maria lights three candles, one for each of her children, beneath the statue of the Virgin Mary. She touches the fingertips of her right hand to her forehead, chest, and each shoulder in the sign of the cross and bows her head. She has come to the Church of the Holy Cross to pray for Lech, for his safe return, but she can't seem to find the words to express what she feels in her heart as a mother. She lifts her eyes to gaze at the statue of Mary, her namesake, who stands with her head bowed and her hands outstretched, a look of sorrow on her youthful face. Maria feels so helpless. Did the Virgin feel the same when her son was taken away in the garden of Gethsemane?

A mother's first instinct is to protect and nurture her children, and this is what Maria has always done. As a baby, Lech cried to be fed every hour of the day. He grew into a boy who loved to climb trees and was always getting into scrapes, coming home with muddied knees and torn trousers. Anna was quieter, more contented as a baby. Her artistic talents were apparent from an early age. She was always drawing – people, houses, landscapes, animals. That's why they bought her the camera for her eighteenth birthday. And then seven years after Anna was born, Jan appeared, unplanned and unexpected, a gift from God just when she thought she was too old to have any more children.

Maria has been blessed, she knows that. Emeryk is a good man, even if he spends too much time with his nose in a book and his head in past centuries. And she's not done a bad job of bringing up her children, even if she says so herself. There's always been food on the table and clean clothes for everyone to wear. Maria believes in practical expressions of love, such as sending Lech off with plenty of food. She wonders if he took her advice and packed warm underwear. Probably not, but what can she do? He's an adult now, she realises, with a pang. And he's going to fight for his country. *Mary, Mother of God,* she mutters under her breath, *keep all our sons safe. And our daughters too. Amen.*

At the sound of footsteps on the stone floor she turns to see Father Piotr approaching, his hands hidden in the wide sleeves of his cassock. The elderly priest baptised all of her children and never forgets a face.

'Good day to you, Pani Nowak.' His lined face is careworn, but the fire in his eyes still reveals the inner depth of the man, the calling and conviction that made him devote his life to the church. Maria admires that sort of commitment. 'I hope I am not disturbing you.'

'Not at all, Father Piotr.'

He glances at the candles. There are many others besides Maria's. You can feel the heat they're giving off. 'A great many supplicants today, I see.'

'It's the mobilisation,' says Maria. 'My eldest son, Lech, has been called…' Her voice trails away.

'Hush, my dear,' says the elderly priest, laying a hand on her shoulder. 'This is a difficult time for a mother, seeing her child go off to defend his country. But we must trust in God's goodness and grace.'

'I know,' says Maria. 'But if only there was something I could do myself.'

'God has a part for all of us to play, even if we can't see

what it is yet. Be patient and in time all will be revealed.'

'Thank you, Father.' Maria feels herself standing a little bit taller, her sense of purpose restored.

'God bless you, my child.' He makes the sign of the cross on her forehead. 'There will be difficult times ahead, but with His grace, we will prevail.'

*

Anna takes her camera and cycles back to Stare Miasto, hoping to see her friend, Wanda. She wants to use up the film so she can get it developed. If there's a war, who knows if you'll be able to do everyday things like develop rolls of film?

The roads are busier than usual. Whether it's because of people returning to Warsaw after the summer or leaving the city fearing the outbreak of war, it's hard to tell. Groups of uniformed reservists head towards the train station and she scans the faces, hoping to catch a glimpse of Lech. But he left hours ago and is most likely long gone by now. Where will they send him? She hopes, for her parents' sake, that he remembers to write home occasionally.

How different everything looks now compared with this morning. Then – if she had given it any thought – the world was full of possibilities. Her adult life was just beginning. In the autumn she would be going to college to study art. She was ready to fall in love, have her heart broken, console herself with books and music, travel. But now everything feels suspended. There are no more certainties, except the relentless tread of time. The long, hot summer is going to break. There's going to be a storm.

In the narrow streets of Stare Miasto, she hops off her bicycle and walks to the restaurant on Freta where Pan Lewandowski is clearing the tables. He does the best meat stew and dumplings in the city and the air is rich with the aroma of spices and herbs.

He greets Anna with a warm smile. 'Are you looking for

Wanda? She's upstairs.'

Anna thanks him and climbs the stairs to the flat above the restaurant where the Lewandowski family live.

'Hi, it's me, Anna,' she calls as she nears the landing.

Wanda rushes out of the living room. 'Anna! I'm so glad to see you.' She throws her arms around her friend.

Wanda is a vivacious red-head with a face covered in freckles, and green eyes that always seem to be dancing with amusement.

'Do you want to go for a walk?' asks Anna. 'I have a roll of film to use up.'

'Sure,' says Wanda. 'I'm working in the restaurant this evening, so it would be good to get out now.'

They stroll around Nowe Miasto with its elegant seventeenth- and eighteenth-century façades and Anna takes a couple of pictures.

'Lech was called up this morning,' she says. 'It was such a shock, just out of the blue like that.'

'Oh, Anna!' Wanda clutches Anna's arm. 'I'm so sorry. Where are they sending him?'

'No idea.'

'Do you think he'll be all right?'

'I hope so.' She knows Wanda is sweet on Lech, not that Lech has ever noticed. 'He thinks he's going to be home in no time. You know what he's like.'

'You don't sound convinced,' says Wanda.

'Do you think there's going to be a war?' This is not the usual sort of conversation they have. Usually they talk about the latest fashions and boys at school.

'Well, if there is,' says Wanda, 'then I'm jolly well going to make the most of the last days of summer. And you should too.'

Anna laughs. 'Okay, go and stand over there. I've got one shot left.'

Wanda poses in front of the white, domed church of St Kazimierz, her head held high, hands on her hips, a huge smile lighting up her face.

Anna looks through the viewfinder, adjusts the focus and presses the button.

There, she's used up the roll of film. She'll make sure to get it developed before Herr Hitler causes any trouble.

*

Jan is bored. His father is in his study with his history books. His mother has gone to church to light a candle for Lech. Anna has gone out again with her camera. What does she find to photograph all the time? When she suggested he find a book to read, he scoffed at the idea. How can anyone sit and read when there could be German planes flying overhead any minute?

If only!

He stares out of the window at the cloudless blue sky above the rooftops, but there's nothing to see except a lone pigeon that lands on the gutter of the building opposite. After the excitement of the morning when Lech was called up to join his regiment, Jan expected everything to change. He thought there would be soldiers on the streets, tanks and military vehicles manoeuvring in the squares. Junkers flying overhead. He longs to see a German plane blown out of the sky. But nothing is happening. Yet.

The clock on the mantelpiece chimes the hour. Three o'clock. Tea isn't for another couple of hours. No one will miss him if he slips out for a bit. He puts his shoes on and lets himself out of the apartment, closing the door quietly behind him.

The courtyard is deserted save for a black cat that watches him with a disdainful air before disappearing into an open doorway. He kicks a stone, hands in his pockets, wishing that he was old enough to go off and fight like Lech. He hates being the baby of the family.

'What are you doing?'

He jumps and turns around. Weronika has crept up on him without him noticing and is standing there, hands on hips, staring at him. He hates it when she does that. She lives with her parents in an apartment on the other side of the courtyard. Her father is a doctor in the hospital, a fact that Weronika never tires of telling people.

'Nothing.' Jan wishes now that he'd stayed inside.

'Don't lie. You were kicking that stone.'

At school, Weronika is something of a know-it-all.

'Why did you ask if you already knew what I was doing?' Jan is pleased that he managed to think of a come-back. Normally Weronika leaves him feeling tongue-tied. Maybe she's not so smart after all.

'What I meant, obviously, was, *why* are you doing that?'

Jan rolls his eyes. She always has to have the last word in any argument. And now he can't think of a good reason for kicking the stone. It seems like a silly, childish thing to do. But Weronika doesn't have an older brother like he does. That's one thing he has over her.

'Lech was called up this morning,' he says, proudly. 'He's gone to fight the Germans.'

At this, Weronika raises her eyebrows and cocks her head to one side so that the two thick braids of hair either side of her head hang at odd lengths. Jan had expected her to be full of awe and admiration, but instead she appears to be considering this new piece of information with scepticism.

'My father,' she says, 'thinks that Poland's situation is hopeless. He says the Germans will destroy us.'

'No!' shouts Jan. 'That's not going to happen.' How can she even think that? It's such an unpatriotic thing to say. A betrayal of their country.

'I'm only telling you what Papa says.' She looks taken aback as if he's slapped her.

But Jan is shaken because she's planted a seed of doubt in his certainty of Polish victory. Maybe they're not as invincible as he thought. Her father is a clever man, a doctor as she keeps telling people. What if he's got a point? And then another thought strikes him. What if his own parents think the same thing, but are just keeping it to themselves so as not to worry him? Suddenly Jan's world, which until now had felt so solid, feels a little less certain. And the war hasn't even started yet.

'I'm sorry,' says Jan. 'I didn't mean to shout.'

'Yes, you did.' Her look softens 'I think your brother is very brave,' she adds.

It's the first nice thing she's ever said to him. Really, Jan can't make her out. Girls!

'Thank you,' he says, aware that it's his turn to make amends.

'So what are you going to do if there's a war?' asks Weronika.

'Me?' What an absurd question. They're both too young to do anything, more's the pity. If he was older, it would be a different matter entirely.

'Don't you want to do something to help your country?' She makes it sound like a challenge.

'Of course I do, but I don't see what I can do. We're only eleven, remember?'

'So what? If the war goes on for a long time, which Papa thinks it might, then I'm going to train and work as a nurse as soon as I'm old enough. There'll be lots of wounded people to look after.'

Jan hopes that he's never wounded and needs looking after by bossy Weronika. Aren't nurses supposed to be kind? He thinks she'd make a terrible nurse. But what she said about the war going on for a long time interests him. Lech thought it would all be over in a matter of weeks, if it even got going in the first place.

'In that case,' says Jan, 'I'm going to join the army as soon as they'll have me.'

He's obviously said the right thing because Weronika claps her hands together and her face bursts into a big smile. For a scary moment he even thinks she might kiss him, but she quickly regains her composure.

'That's wonderful,' she says. Her mother calls her then

from an upstairs window overlooking the courtyard. 'I have to go now. But I'll see you around.'

As Jan heads back inside, he feels as if he's grown a couple of inches taller. Did he really just make a commitment to fight for his country? He doesn't even like Weronika, but it felt good when she smiled at him.

*

The journey, which started out with so much hope and enthusiasm, has turned into a long, weary slog. Lech wipes the sweat from his brow for the umpteenth time. Even though they've got all the windows open, it's like a sauna in the carriage. The singing stopped a long time ago when voices became hoarse and throats became parched.

The brakes squeal and he's jerked sideways as the train grinds to a halt at yet another station in the middle of nowhere. He's lost count of the number of stops they've made. He had no idea there were so many small towns and villages, each with their own poky little station.

The train jolts as yet more carriages are shunted onto the end. The platform is clogged with more soldiers – peasants who look as if they've come straight from the fields, their weather-beaten faces set with dogged determination. They're less enthusiastic than the Warsaw crowd were, as if they'd rather not have been called away from the all-important job of bringing in the harvest.

Women of all ages – mothers, girlfriends, wives, sisters – throng the platform too, hugging their men and crying into handkerchiefs. Thank God his own mother didn't insist on accompanying him to the train station. He wonders what his family are doing now. He hopes to God they're not wailing like these peasant women who can't seem to hold themselves together. Anna is stronger than she thinks. Jan is too young to really understand the seriousness of the situation. As for his parents, they've lived through bad times in the past, the Great War, no less, and he has no doubt they'll pull through this present crisis. They are survivors, his family. He feels a lump forming in his throat and coughs to clear it. This is no time to be getting all sentimental. There's a hiss of steam and they are moving once again.

The day drags on as the train rolls through flat countryside, past fields ripe with wheat, and orchards heavy with fruit. He shares his bread and cheese with Aleksander and the other men sitting nearby. Someone gives him a ripe peach in return. With full stomachs and little fresh air in the train, the men start to doze, heads dropping onto chests.

In his dreams he's a child again, running through the fields, climbing trees, playing in the stream. There's Anna calling to him and Jan, still a baby, crawling on the grass. Then he's a teenager, chasing after girls, staying out late, smoking his first cigarette. His mother fussing over him, worried about him. His father telling him he needs to decide what he's going to do with his life. Find a direction, that's what he has to do.

A nudge in the ribs and he's startled awake.

'Wakey, wakey,' says Aleksander. 'We're here.'

Embarrassed, Lech wipes a drool of saliva from the corner of his mouth. He has been known to talk in his sleep, so he hopes he didn't say anything that would betray the anxiety he's feeling in the pit of his stomach. But no one is paying him any attention.

Around him the men are standing up, hauling their heavy kitbags onto their backs. He scrambles to his feet before someone tramples on him, but his legs are stiff from sitting all day in a cramped position and he has to stamp on one foot to bring it back to life. He peers out of the window but it's dark and there's little to see.

One by one, the men jump down from the train, wearied from the early start and the long journey. All Lech wants to do is lie down in bed and get some proper sleep. Hitler can invade tomorrow, but please God, not tonight.

*

That evening Anna takes her father a cup of tea in his study. He's usually to be found shut away in this small room with its comforting smell of leather and old books. In the corner, a Chopin Nocturne plays quietly on the gramophone.

Emeryk is bowed over his desk, his head in his hands, reading something that he has written. An academic paper, most likely, judging from the history books and notes strewn across the desk's surface. She looks in vain for a clear place to put the cup of tea.

Emeryk pushes aside a pile of papers and Anna puts the cup down. She turns to go.

'Stay,' he says, removing his reading glasses and reaching for her hand.

'I don't want to disturb you.'

'You're not. I haven't done any useful work for the last two hours. I don't seem to be able to concentrate. I keep reading this piece I wrote on the 1795 Partition of Poland, but the words just keep going round in circles.' He pushes the papers roughly to one side. 'I fear history is about to repeat itself.'

Anna slips off her shoes and sits in a leather chair, tucking her legs under her. She has always enjoyed a special, close relationship with her father, as if she's the only one of his three children he can have a proper conversation with. He used to tell her stories before they moved on to discussing weightier matters. Lech has never had the patience for discussions about history and politics, and Jan is at that awkward age: too old for stories but too young for current affairs.

'When Lech was called up this morning,' says Emeryk, taking his mug of tea in both hands and blowing gently across the steaming liquid, 'it reminded me of my own days back in 1914.'

Anna waits for her father to go on. He's never talked much about the war when he was conscripted into the Austro-Hungarian Army. Did he believe in what he was fighting for, or did he simply find himself at a certain time and place in history? This was back in the days of empire, before the birth of the Second Polish Republic, the only version of Poland that Anna has ever known. But the Republic is only twenty-one years old, only three years older than Anna herself, and suddenly it seems a fragile thing. What's two decades in the life of a nation? No more than the blink of an eye.

'At the end of the last war,' says Emeryk, 'the Treaty of Versailles was supposed to settle the question of European borders once and for all. But Germany resented the settlement and as a result ill-feeling has been smouldering for the last twenty years. And now Germany has a megalomaniac in charge who has poured petrol on the powder keg of resentment to further his own lust for power. I fear Europe is going to explode.'

Anna suddenly has a vision of Europe in flames, fanned by a small Austrian in jackboots with a toothbrush moustache. It would be comic if it wasn't so terrifying.

To hear her father speak these words is chilling. He's rarely wrong on these matters. As a professor of European history at the university, he has followed recent events with more understanding than most. The annexation of Austria in March '38 and the German occupation of the Czech lands exactly one year later showed just what Hitler was capable of. The horror of *Kristallnacht* in Germany in November '38 when Jewish shops were smashed and looted, synagogues set on fire, and German Jews fled for their lives, struck a note of terror into the hearts of all right-minded people. Anna and her family are not Jewish, but they know Jewish families in Warsaw; they shop at Jewish stores; they have Jewish friends. Emeryk has always argued against the ghetto benches reserved for Jews in Polish universities. And this summer when Hitler and Stalin signed a non-aggression pact, her father predicted that nothing good would come of it.

In the light of his desk lamp, she notices for the first time that he's starting to look old. His hair is turning grey and there are permanent worry lines etched on his forehead. He closes his eyes and pinches the bridge of his nose between finger and thumb.

'You think Hitler will want to take back the lands granted to Poland after the last war?' she asks. He's explained to her before how parts of Upper Silesia and the province of Poznań were ceded to Poland. A strip of land known as the Polish Corridor gives Poland access to the Baltic Sea next to Danzig, but it cuts East Prussia off from the rest of Germany, a situation which a fanatic like Hitler is hardly likely to tolerate.

'It will be more than that,' says Emeryk. 'Hitler won't stop until he has wiped Poland off the map of Europe.'

'He can't do that!' she protests. 'Our army will fight him! And what about France and Britain? Haven't they promised to come to Poland's aid? They won't let Germany destroy us.' Surely the situation can't be so utterly hopeless.

He acknowledges her protest with a smile. 'We have fought and won in the past,' he says. 'In 1920 we saw off the Soviets and gained our freedom.'

'So we can do it again, right?'

'God willing,' he says. 'But I fear it will not be easy.'

PART TWO
INVASION AND THE BATTLE FOR
WARSAW
AUGUST - SEPTEMBER1939

CHAPTER FOUR

Nothing has happened. Yet.

Lech and his fellow officers have fallen into an easy routine. A week of army drills, excursions into the countryside on horseback, evenings filled with card games and light-hearted conversation. The threat of war seems even more remote than when they were first mobilised. The days are still warm and sunny, the countryside rich and verdant, the company convivial. At this rate, thinks Lech, he'll return to Warsaw fit and tanned, looking as if he's been on holiday.

There's still no sign of the Germans advancing over the border, which only reinforces the belief that Herr Hitler was bluffing all along. Or the Polish mobilisation has had the desired effect in making the Germans think twice. Optimism is the name of the game, and Lech is only too happy to play along. No doubt if he were at home his father would want to discuss contentious political topics that would dampen the spirits and sound the alarm bells. But Lech is not at home so whenever he hears his father's voice in his head, he dismisses it and focuses his attention on what is in front of him: friends, good humour and the tail end of summer.

It's well past midnight when Lech climbs into bed on the last day of August. He, Aleksander, and a couple of other fellows stayed up late playing a game of poker in which Lech was the resounding victor, consolidating a winning streak that has lasted almost since they arrived.

'You lucky bastard,' said Aleksander, punching him playfully on the arm at the end of the game. 'How come you always win? Are you sure you're not cheating?'

'Must be my exceptional talents,' said Lech, punching him back.

'Yeah, that and your modesty.'

'Of course.'

He's still buzzing from the high of winning, unable to sleep, when he hears Aleksander's soft snoring in the bunk next to his. He feels a surge of love for his friend. They've shared so many good times and now here they are, showing Herr Hitler how well-prepared Poland is.

As he drifts off to sleep, he wonders what they'll do tomorrow. There should be time for a horse-ride after the day's drills are over. He feels like exploring further afield and having a good gallop across the countryside. It's forecast to be another fine day. They should make the most of it before the seasons change.

*

A deafening roar and a series of earth-shattering explosions wrench Lech from the safe world of his dream where he has been galloping through a wildflower meadow, the sun on his face, the wind in his hair. Panic and chaos have erupted in the barracks, men running around, half-dressed, shouting orders. Disoriented, Lech tries to sit up, no idea what time it is or what is happening.

Is this war? Have the Germans invaded? He feels a childish urge to argue that he's not ready, like the games of hide-and-seek they played at school which started before he had found a good place to hide so he was always 'caught' before the game had properly got underway. *It's not fair.* But what had he expected? That the Germans would send a messenger to say, *We're on our way?*

Someone shakes his shoulder and he looks up to see Aleksander standing by his bed, already in full uniform.

'Get up,' shouts his friend. 'We're under attack from the *Luftwaffe!*'

'So Hitler wasn't bluffing?' But Aleksander has already turned away.

The realisation that this isn't a drill but is for real spurs him into action. He leaps from the bed, pulling on his uniform, his fingers fumbling with the buttons. Where are his boots? Why aren't they where he left them last night by his bed? He crouches down and sees that they've been knocked under the bed. He reaches for them and pulls them on hastily, the laces tangling themselves before he can do them up properly. After so much planning and preparation, he can't believe that the Germans have caught them on the hop after all. What a shambles.

Outside, the scene is already apocalyptic. Stuka dive bombers scream overhead, dropping incendiaries. They rain down from the sky like giant hailstones, igniting on impact. Fires are springing up everywhere, destroying buildings and equipment. Lech and the other officers dodge the shower of bombs as they try to organise the men into fighting units but it feels like a hopeless task. Everywhere is chaos.

And then the first shell lands, smashing into a building that is already in flames, throwing shrapnel far and wide, tossing bodies into the air like rag dolls. As he runs for cover, Lech can only think that German tanks must have crossed the border with lightning speed to have arrived so quickly in the wake of the *Luftwaffe*. How can the Poles possibly mount a meaningful defence in the face of this relentless onslaught? No one expected anything like this. The shock of it takes his breath away.

An order goes out to man the anti-tank guns. At last, something positive is happening. If they can get themselves organised, they might – just – stand a chance of fighting back. Give the Germans a run for their money. Lech leads a group of stalwart peasant lads who gamely fire shots in the direction of the approaching tanks, but they might as well be flinging stones with catapults and slingshots for all the good it's doing. And still the German tanks keep advancing and the shells keep falling, battering the barracks to smithereens. The casualties are already too many to count.

CHAPTER FIVE

'Come away from the window!'

Jan spins around to find his mother standing in the doorway, arms akimbo, fury written all over her face.

'I just wanted to see what was happening.' The distant rumblings of explosions on the outskirts of the city woke him at dawn. After all this time, he can hardly believe it. The war has finally started. He's been squinting into the bright, clear sky, desperate to see an enemy aircraft shot down by Polish anti-aircraft guns. He imagines the German plane exploding like a firework, or going into a tailspin and crashing to earth, smoke pouring out of its rear. Another far-off boom sends a shock wave through the air that rattles the window pane. He risks a glance outside, but there's nothing to see.

The air is rent by the howl of an air raid siren blasting from the loudspeakers that the government has installed on lampposts and above shop doorways. His mother grabs his arm and pulls him away from the window once and for all.

'Get dressed!' she says. 'Quickly now. We have to go down to the basement.' She runs from the room, calling for Emeryk and Anna.

With the siren wailing, the threat of danger suddenly

feels too close for comfort and Jan quickly pulls on his trousers and a jumper and joins the rest of the family who are gathered by the front door to the apartment. His mother is clutching a picnic basket in both hands as if they're about to spend a day by the lake.

Jan follows his parents and sister down the steps to the basement, joining the throng of neighbours, some of whom he's sure he's never seen before.

The basement is dingy and stuffy. It smells of coal dust and too many bodies crammed into the low-ceilinged space. There's an odd assortment of chairs, donated by the residents of the apartment block, and a couple of stained, old mattresses which Jan thinks are best avoided. The only light comes from a paraffin lamp in the centre of the room which gives off an oily smell, contributing to the airless atmosphere. There's even a bucket in the corner behind a flimsy curtain that someone has strung up on a pole. Jan would rather be hit by a bomb than take a pee in front of all these people.

'My poor knees!' exclaims old Pani Woźniak. 'I hope I don't have to go up and down those cellar steps too often.' Her husband helps her onto a wooden chair then sits down himself with a puff and a grunt.

The three young Kowalski children from the apartment across the landing burst into the basement like three small torpedoes and immediately jump on one of the filthy mattresses where they proceed to fight each other. Their weary-looking mother appears a few moments later, a squawking baby in her arms. Ignoring her other children, she settles herself on a chair and immediately unbuttons her blouse and offers the baby her breast. Jan looks hastily away, not wanting to be caught staring at his neighbour's boobs even though the sight fascinates him.

He spots Weronika on the opposite side of the basement sitting primly with her mother who looks like an older, bossier version of Weronika. Best to steer clear. Her father, Jan supposes, is at the hospital dealing with the casualties.

Weronika is probably hoping for an opportunity to practise her embryonic nursing skills. Jan hopes it won't come to that. She smiles at him, but he looks away, too embarrassed to smile back. The last thing he wants is for her to come over and start talking to him in front of his family.

'That poor woman,' says his mother, nodding in the direction of Pani Kowalska and her howling infant. 'Her husband's been called up. It can't be easy for her, coping with all those children.' She goes and sits beside Pani Kowalska who looks close to tears.

Jan peers at his watch in the dim light. They've only been down here twenty minutes, but it already feels like ages. His stomach rumbles and he looks longingly at the picnic basket. Would it be rude of him to start devouring its contents? Knowing his mother, she'll have packed enough to feed the five thousand. But no one else is eating, so he suppresses the urge. No one, that is, except for the Kowalski baby who has finally stopped crying and is sucking at the breast with slurping noises that make Jan feel even hungrier.

Pani Woźniak gets out her knitting and starts clacking away with her needles. Anna and his father are reading books, although how they can concentrate on a book at a time like this is quite beyond him.

This is not at all how Jan imagined spending the war, skulking underground like some terrified animal in its burrow, cheek by jowl with all these people. He hopes that Lech is having a better time of it, shooting lots of Germans. He closes his eyes and decides to see how far he can count before something happens.

He gets as far as two hundred and thirty-seven when his counting is interrupted by the ear-piercing shriek of a Stuka dive-bomber.

'Here they come,' says old Pan Woźniak in a resigned voice. His wife shakes her head but keeps knitting as if her life depends on it. Pani Kowalska's baby stops feeding and resumes its wailing as if in competition with the Stuka to see who can make the most noise. But the other three Kowalski children are suddenly stunned into petrified silence.

The dive-bomber sounds like nothing Jan has ever heard before. The shriek rises in pitch and volume, a massive crescendo, until it feels as if God is drilling into his skull. More planes join the first one, their combined sirens creating a hideous cacophony. A legion of demons released from the gates of Hell. Jan clenches his jaw and grits his teeth. Where are the Polish anti-aircraft guns? Why aren't they shooting the Stukas out of the sky?

When he can't stand it anymore, he stuffs his fingers into his ears and hunches down, trying to make himself as small as possible. No one moves, no one breathes, even the knitting needles fall silent, as everyone waits for the inevitable.

A series of explosions rocks the ground. The building shakes, as if lifted off its foundations. The paraffin lamp dies. Somewhere nearby there's a rumbling crash. Jan covers his head with his hands, fully expecting to be buried under an avalanche of falling masonry and roof tiles. He doesn't want to die. Not like this.

A few seconds pass before he realises that he's still alive. Slowly he removes his fingers from his ears and opens his eyes. His ears are ringing, but that's a small price to pay. By a miracle, the building is still standing.

'Hail Mary, Mother of God!' mutters his mother under her breath.

A shower of dust falls from the ceiling joists, but nothing else comes down. They've survived. There's a communal exhalation of breath and then everyone is talking at once.

'That was bloody close.'

'Reckon they've hit the factory.'

'Could have been us.'

Someone relights the paraffin lamp, illuminating all the ashen faces. The Woźniaks have their arms around each other; the Kowalski children are huddled together on the mattress, their eyes wide; his mother is comforting Pani Kowalska; Anna is brushing the dust out of their father's hair with her fingers.

Suddenly Weronika appears beside him, having crossed the short distance from the other side of the basement when he wasn't looking. He expects her to be carrying a first aid kit, but she's empty-handed.

'Were you scared?' she asks.

His instinct is to deny being frightened. It's not the sort of thing a self-respecting eleven-year-old boy admits to a girl. But he has the uncomfortable feeling that Weronika can see right through him. The truth is that the shriek of the dive-bomber terrified him witless. When the bombs fell, there wasn't time to be scared, only shocked. But now that the danger has passed, he finds to his dismay that he's trembling all over like a badly set jelly. Weronika can see his reaction for herself and she'll only call him a liar if he says he wasn't scared.

'Were you?' he asks, his voice sounding strangely hoarse.

'Of course,' says Weronika matter-of-factly. 'Who wouldn't be? But we have to stay strong despite our fears.' It seems like a very grown-up sort of thing to say.

She takes his hand and gives it a gentle squeeze. He should be mortified at this attention from a girl in front of his family and neighbours, but he finds he's strangely comforted and his shaking subsides a little. Maybe it wouldn't be so bad to be cared for by Nurse Weronika after all. But what about his promise to fight when the time comes? He's no longer sure he's got what it takes.

CHAPTER SIX

'Retreat! Repeat, this is an order to retreat!'

Lech can't believe what he's hearing. The order is being given to retreat, withdraw, get out, throw in the towel. However you want to put it, it seems like a shameful thing to be doing. But what choice do they have? The barracks have been demolished, their artillery destroyed, dozens of men killed already. Frankly, it's been a bloodbath, and the war is only a few hours' old.

Now it appears that the Polish strategy of defending the frontiers was more for show than because it was militarily the right thing to do. They're too thinly spread along the border with no hope of defending themselves against the German onslaught. And that is what it has been – a merciless onslaught of planes and tanks moving at lightning speed. It's galling to admit it, but the German war machine is simply bigger and faster than anything the Poles can offer in return.

The word on the ground is that they're going to conduct a fighting withdrawal to the east of the Vistula. *A fighting withdrawal?* Who do they think they're kidding? We couldn't defend ourselves when we were standing still, thinks Lech. How on earth are we expected to do so whilst we're retreating with our tails between our legs? For the first time he doubts the wisdom of the Polish generals.

Lech and the peasant lads have been manning the anti-tank gun all morning to no avail. The truth is, the Germans are better equipped. Their planes roar overhead with a speed that takes your breath away. The wailing of those dive bombers is enough to fry your brain cells. And as for their artillery power, it's an order of magnitude bigger than anything the Poles expected to be dealing with.

Absurdly he thinks of his younger brother Jan and how disappointed he'll be when he hears how quickly the border defences were overrun. Jan looks up to him, although Lech would be the first to admit he's not the greatest of role models with his late-night partying and drinking. But when it comes to defending their country, he wants Jan to be proud of him. But so far, even though he's done his best, he's achieved nothing. He feels as if he's let his family down, although the situation is hardly his fault. Suddenly his strength deserts him and he falls to his knees. He has a vision of himself being marched into a prisoner-of-war camp. It's over before it's even begun.

A hand grips his upper arm and drags him to his feet. 'Get up!' shouts a voice in his ear. 'We're leaving.' It's Aleksander.

'We're running away,' moans Lech. 'We haven't done any proper fighting yet. Why weren't we better prepared?' A burst of anger surges through him. Someone should take responsibility for this disaster and if not the Polish high command, then who else? Why didn't they have better intelligence on German preparations? Why didn't they provide better training and equipment?

Aleksander pulls him around roughly so that they're almost nose to nose. 'We haven't lost the war you idiot! We just need to regroup. It's a strategic retreat, not a complete surrender.'

'Sorry,' says Lech, pulling himself together. Aleksander is right as usual. Lech's problem, as he's been told many times, is that he's too much of a Romantic. He had dreams of a swift Polish victory and now those dreams have been shattered. He needs to get a grip. He never expected such sudden carnage, but Poland isn't defeated yet. Just because the Germans crossed the border in a blaze of lightning doesn't mean the war is over. They just need to regroup, recharge and redouble their efforts.

Lech follows him back to what remains of their barracks. The building was hit by a series of incendiaries which destroyed the roof and blew out all the windows. They gather the remnants of their belongings, the order being to take all guns, supplies and ammunition. Above all else, Lech makes sure he has his trusty revolver with him. He's kept it clean and well-oiled all this time. He's damned if he's going home before he's killed at least one German. He has to have something to tell Jan that will justify the misplaced pride his younger brother has in him.

*

They march through the streets of Oświęcim, the townspeople watching them in sullen silence. To Lech it feels like a march of shame, a public humiliation. He wants to apologise. *I'm sorry. We did our best but it wasn't good enough.* He trudges on, keeping his head down, not wanting to catch anyone's eye. He can't stand the disappointment in their faces.

Without warning a shot is fired and then another. Lech looks around in bewilderment and, to his utter astonishment, sees the barrel of a rifle pointing at him from the upstairs window of a town house. Who is shooting at them? Instinctively he reaches for the hilt of his revolver.

'It's the bloody *Volksdeutsche!*' says Aleksander.

Unbelievable as it seems, the people shooting at them are Polish citizens but of German descent. A bullet whizzes over his head and Lech ducks. The man next to him – one of the peasants who manned the anti-tank gun – takes a hit to the arm and cries out in pain. So now we find out which side people are on, thinks Lech. It hasn't taken these German Poles long to make up their minds. They've probably been looking forward to this day for a long time. Hitlerites, the whole lot of them. They must have cheered when the *Luftwaffe* flew overhead. If the Führer comes in person, they'll toss flowers into his path.

Uproar breaks out amongst the lower ranks. 'Arrest them!' 'Burn their houses down!' 'Kill the traitors!' Lech's fingers are itching to draw his revolver and shoot back. These people are not patriots and don't deserve the protection of the army. Good men died for nothing in the fighting this morning if this is how the army is repaid.

'March on!' comes the order from the senior officers in charge. 'Do not retaliate! Your orders are to march!'

Aleksander tugs at his arm and Lech lets his hand fall from the hilt of his revolver. They march on.

'They're not all traitors,' says Aleksander, once they're past the worst of the shooting. 'Not everyone here is a closet-Nazi. It's just a handful of households causing the trouble.'

Lech supposes Aleksander is right. Still, it's galling to walk away from such blatant provocation.

'The people of Oświęcim will sort out the traitors in their midst,' says Aleksander. 'There'll be reprisals, just you wait.'

At the train station they slump to the ground, exhausted and demoralised. No one is going anywhere in a hurry. They'll have to wait in the scorching sun whilst the track is repaired, however long that takes. They could be here all day at this rate. There's nothing to do except patch up the wounds of the men unlucky enough to have been hit by the *Volksdeutsche,* and wait. Lech is thankful he's suffered nothing worse than wounded pride and sorrow at their plight.

It's late in the day by the time the track is fixed and the train is ready to depart. The men climb on board. No one speaks. They're all too exhausted and disgusted with themselves, with their army, with their leaders. With their failure. Lech knows that every man is feeling the same deep-seated shame that he feels. He can see it in their downcast eyes, their downturned mouths, the way they look as if they just want to curl up and hide.

Lech sits beside Aleksander in much the same position they sat on the journey here ten days ago, but the difference between arrival and departure couldn't be starker. Then they were full of buoyant optimism and fighting spirit, if a little weary from the journey. Now they are battered and bruised, physically and morally. And that's not to mention the ones who haven't made it this far.

The train crawls towards Kraków, as if it is too ashamed to get up any speed and doesn't want to arrive at their destination with indecent haste. God knows what they'll find when they get there.

As day fades into night, the train is held up by one delay after another. Lech dozes fitfully. Every time he wakes, he hears muttered conversations and grumblings.

'What went wrong?'

'Why weren't we better prepared?'

'How could the Germans have invaded with such force?'

Theories galore, but no one has any real answers. Right now, Lech is too tired to care.

Aleksander nudges him and says he's going into the carriage ahead. There's someone he wants to speak to. Lech nods and stretches out in the space vacated by his friend, glad to have a bit of extra room. He leans his head back, closes his eyes and falls into a dream-state where Jan appears out of nowhere and asks, 'How many Germans did you kill?' Before he can answer, there's an ear-splitting screech of metal on metal. The train grinds to a halt. Then an explosion rocks the train, sending shock waves through the carriage. The men are on their feet in an instant. Through the window, in the grey light of morning, Lech spies a dozen or more enemy aircraft circling overhead like vultures, targeting the train. Another bomb explodes and everyone ducks for cover. Clouds of choking, black smoke stream past the window.

'They hit the carriage up ahead,' shouts a voice.

The carriage up ahead?

Where is Aleksander? Lech looks around frantically for his friend, but he hasn't returned. How long was he asleep? He has no idea.

'Out!' shouts a voice of command. 'Evacuate the train immediately!'

'No!' shouts Lech. 'We have to rescue them.' There's no way he's leaving this train without his friend.

He pushes his way past dozens of men heading in the opposite direction. They curse and swear at him but he doesn't pay any attention. His only thought is to reach the carriage up ahead and find Aleksander. But at the buffers between the carriages, he sees that the way ahead is a blazing inferno. Twisted metal blocks his path. Thick, choking smoke obscures his vision and threatens to suffocate him. He covers his nose and mouth with his left arm and feels his way with his right hand. He trips over the leg of a man lying motionless in the aisle and falls clumsily onto the floor, burning his hand on hot metal.

He scrambles to his feet and a voice behind him shouts in his ear. 'Evacuate now! That is an order from your superior officer! Out now, or I will have you shot for insubordination!' He can't see the speaker in all the smoke but the man has him by the arm and is dragging him back towards the exit. Lech is too disorientated by the smoke and heat to resist. The carriage in which he hoped to find his friend is a blazing wreck. No one could have survived the force of the blast.

Lech allows himself to be pushed off the train. Stumbling over the uneven ground, he follows the survivors as they run for cover to a line of nearby trees. 'I'm so sorry, Aleksander,' he weeps. 'I wanted to save you.'

At the edge of the forest he collapses onto his knees, his lungs burning from the smoke he has inhaled. Tears course down his face as he gasps for breath. He can't believe Aleksander is gone, just like that. And so many others, too. Good men who wanted to fight for Poland. The train carriages have become their coffins.

CHAPTER SEVEN

Anna helps her mother iron and fold the laundry into neat piles whilst they listen to the radio. Keeping busy is the best way not to become overwhelmed with worry, says Maria. But Anna judges her mother's anxiety levels by just how busy she's keeping herself. When they're not sheltering in the basement during the air raids, Maria is washing, tidying, dusting, and polishing the silver. The permanent worry lines on her brow reveal her true state of mind. What has happened to Lech? Is he still alive? The news from the front is not reassuring, whatever gloss the government tries to put on it.

They've had the radio on all day, eager for news, and yet dreading it at the same time. When they run into their neighbours on the stairs or in the bread queue the conversation is always the same. 'Have you heard about such and such a battle?' or 'This building has been bombed' or 'That hospital has been destroyed.' The human fascination with disaster seems to know no limits.

It's not all bad news, of course. The Polish garrison on the Westerplatte peninsula is still holding out, a beacon of hope amidst the tidal wave of destruction. But the Post Office in Danzig fell on the first day despite the valiant efforts of those defending it.

The programme they're listening to – something light and undemanding – is suddenly interrupted and the broadcaster says there will be an important announcement in the next few minutes.

Maria puts down the iron and rushes to Emeryk's study. 'Come and listen.'

Emeryk emerges from his study, book in hand, his reading glasses perched on the end of his nose.

Jan dashes out of his room. 'Have we won? Is it over yet?'

'Shush,' says Maria. 'Listen to the radio.' They are now playing a military march.

Anna folds the last tea towel, adds it to the pile, and joins her family around the radio which has pride of place on the mahogany sideboard. In these dark and uncertain times, it's a vital link with the outside world. There's a crackle of static and Emeryk fiddles with the knobs to try and get a better reception.

'Don't lose the station,' says Maria. 'We don't want to miss this.'

The radio announcer repeats his statement that there's going to be an announcement soon.

'Oh, I do wish they'd get on with it,' says Maria.

More military marches, then finally, the national anthem. Pride and foreboding swell in Anna's chest. Families across the whole country will be gathered around their radio sets, waiting with bated breath. The upbeat Polish national anthem with its spirited call to take up arms and defend the fatherland is followed by the more sombre British national anthem, its measured tones seeming to herald something truly portentous. The Marseillaise strikes a lighter note.

There's a brief moment of silence before the announcer speaks the words they've been longing to hear. 'Great Britain and France have declared war on Germany.'

'Thank God.' Maria clasps her hands together as if offering a prayer of thanks.

Emeryk sobs openly, the tears running down his lined face. He opens his arms to her and Anna allows herself to be wrapped in his tight embrace as her own vision starts to blur.

'Are the British going to shoot the Germans out of the sky?' asks Jan, his face aglow with excitement. He runs to the window and looks up as if he expects to see RAF planes swarming out of the clouds like avenging angels.

'Give them a chance to get here,' says Anna, laughing. 'England's not that close.'

'Come along,' says Emeryk, clapping his hands together. 'This is no time to be indoors. This is a time for celebration. Poland now has a powerful ally. We should show our appreciation of our British friends.'

Anna looks at her father in astonishment. What has happened to the university professor who spends his days closeted with his books? But then she understands. History isn't just something you read about. History is real, and sometimes you find yourself living it, here and now. History in the making, isn't that what they say? One day her father may write about this moment. But for now he wants to live it.

So they quickly don their shoes and coats and head outside, joining the thousands thronging Nowy Świat. A mass of humanity snakes its way northwards towards the Branicki Palace, the home of the British Embassy. Everyone joins in with hearty renditions of 'God Save the King', even if their English is not really up to it. People toss flowers into the air in joy and gratitude. It seems to Anna as if half of Warsaw has turned out to sing and cheer, buoyed up by the longed-for announcement. Poland no longer has to stand and fight alone.

From a distance they can just make out the Polish foreign minister on the balcony flanked by the British and French ambassadors.

Long live Britain! Vive la France! The mood is infectious. Anna's own heart is bursting with love for these staunch allies. She is sure that every Varsovian feels exactly as she does. Victory will be theirs. Lech could be home in weeks or even days after all.

But then the wail of the air raid siren cuts through the singing and cheering, destroying the euphoria and striking a note of terror into the party atmosphere. Stunned, as if someone has just poured a bucket of icy water over her, Anna stares at the cloudless blue sky from which death and destruction could rain down at any moment.

'Are the British here already?' asks Jan.

The British? No, that's impossible. She gathers her senses. 'Run!' she shouts as the crowd scatters in all directions, desperately seeking the nearest shelter.

CHAPTER EIGHT

They're not what you'd call an army. Not anymore. Lech finds himself with a rag-tag group of men from his battery, about thirty or forty in total. Really, they're just a group of individuals who have decided to stick together because what else can they do? A Captain Mazur has assumed control of the group and they continue eastwards on foot, obeying the original order to head towards Kraków. But what then? No one is sure.

Lech is numb from the shock of defeat and even more so from losing his friend. Lech wanted to recover Aleksander's body and give him a proper burial but there was no time and there were too many bodies. Now his heart aches for his friend, the only death that has any real meaning for him, even though there are hundreds more dead from his own unit alone, not to mention thousands across the country.

If it wasn't for Captain Mazur and the other men urging him on, Lech would gladly sit down by the side of the road and not walk another step. From what he can see, Poland is defeated, they just haven't accepted the fact yet.

It's painfully slow going. They pass through villages still smouldering from air raids, bodies littering the streets.

Traumatised survivors stream east, fleeing for their lives, clogging the roads. Household belongings are piled precariously on carts; young children cling to their fathers' backs like stick insects; babies are carried in their mothers' arms; old people press on doggedly with the aid of walking sticks, struggling to keep pace with the young.

They're two miles from the previous village, trudging behind a long column of civilians, past abandoned fields of destroyed crops, when the crowd freezes. People stare at the sky as a German bomber flies so low overhead you can see the nuts and bolts of its underbelly.

Lech and his fellow soldiers dive into the shelter of some nearby woods, but most of the civilians are too weighed down by children and possessions to move quickly enough. Shrieks of terror fill the air as bombs fall and the machine gun fires. The bastards, thinks Lech, targeting helpless civilians. The plane disappears as quickly as it came, as if the pilot and crew want to get back to Berlin in time for their tea. When Lech and the others emerge from the trees and make their way back to the road, a scene of carnage awaits them.

Captain Mazur orders them to help bury the dead. It's the least they can do, thinks Lech, since they failed to stop the German invasion.

*

They sleep by the roadside, using their packs as pillows, covering themselves with their coats. It's still just warm enough, but already there's a noticeable nip in the air at night. In the mornings, they are damp with dew. Soon it will be too cold to sleep outdoors.

The plan is to find a new army group to join. They have to stop this endless wandering and do some real fighting. But their hopes are continually dashed. Whenever they come across another fragment of Poland's broken army, the order is always the same. Keep marching! Keep heading east, away from the Germans. But where to exactly? Kraków, the original destination has been occupied. So too have Łódź and Kielce. Their options are running out.

Mazur looks helplessly at his band of men and points to the east as if to say, what choice do we have? We have to obey orders.

Is this what we've come to? Lech wonders. Surely the Polish Army can't be so decimated already that we're wandering around the countryside like a bunch of bandits. The thought crosses his mind on more than one occasion that if they are now bandits they should start behaving as such and attack some German bases. Guerrilla warfare, if that's what it takes. He puts his idea to a couple of the men.

'That would lead to anarchy,' says one of them. 'We have to trust that the Polish Government has a plan.'

Yeah right, thinks Lech. Some plan this is, walking east until we drop dead from exhaustion.

Poznań, Łódź and Kraków have all fallen to the Germans. There is no news yet of the fate of Warsaw, but Lech doesn't hold out much hope. He prays that his family is safe.

Rumours reach them that the Polish President and senior members of the government have escaped across the border into Romania along with the commander of the army. They should try to do the same, but really, it feels as if they've been abandoned.

Two weeks after setting out on foot, they arrive on the outskirts of Tarnopol. If they go any further, they'll be in Ukraine. They collapse in the shade of some trees, exhausted, dirty and unable to fully comprehend the extent of their failure. Sounds of a commotion on the road ahead drift their way, but Lech is too tired to care what it's about.

'I'll go and investigate,' says Mazur. No one offers to accompany him.

Fifteen minutes later their Captain returns, worry etched across his face. 'Now we've got a problem,' he says.

*

Jan thrusts the edge of the metal spade into the stony ground and presses down on the top with the heel of his boot. He meets resistance and gives the spade a sharp shove with his foot, refusing to admit defeat. This time he manages to dislodge whatever was causing the blockage and the spade sinks without warning into the earth. He loses his balance and topples forwards. He quickly recovers himself and yanks the spade out for another go.

'All right there, son?' The old man next to him in the line chortles. He has a face more wrinkled than a prune.

'Yeah, fine,' says Jan. He wipes a muddy hand over his sweaty forehead. If an old fella like that can dig, then so can he.

'Here, have a swig of this.' The old man offers him a water canteen.

Jan takes a grateful gulp and almost chokes. Vodka! His throat burns and his eyes water but he refuses to show weakness. He hands the canteen back. 'Thank you,' he gasps.

'That'll put hairs on your chest,' says the old man with a toothless grin.

Jesus, thinks Jan, is that what peasants drink out in the field all day? But now that he's got over the initial shock, the vodka is having a soothing effect on his aching limbs and tired muscles. Better not have any more though, or he won't be able to walk straight and his mother will go berserk if she smells it on his breath. She was already reluctant to let him join the civilian guard digging anti-tank trenches on the outskirts of the city. But when Anna said she was joining up, their mother lost the argument and had to let them both go. They travelled out on the tram, Anna promising to look after him. This is the most fun he's had in ages.

Everyone is standing shoulder to shoulder, digging for their lives. Rich and poor, office workers, shopkeepers, housewives, students, kids. If you can hold a spade then you're in. You can hardly tell who's who when everyone is wearing old shirts and trousers caked in mud. Jan, Anna and Wanda have been assigned to a stretch along a hillside on the outskirts of the city, near a nice, middle-class district with attractive villas. It wouldn't be so bad if it wasn't for the shriek of overhead planes and the thud of distant explosions. Elsewhere people are digging in parks and playgrounds, wherever there's a vacant patch of ground. It's a vast, communal effort and Jan is proud to be taking part. The German tanks must not be allowed to enter the city, must not be allowed to thunder down the elegant boulevards and ride roughshod through the narrow streets of Stare Miasto. The tanks must not be allowed to fire their guns on his family.

Jan gets back to work, not wanting to be seen slacking. Digging for hours on end is harder than he thought it would be, but anything is better than skulking in the cellar waiting for the bombs to fall, listening to Pani Kowalska's baby bawling its head off.

Anna and Wanda look like fishwives with their hair tied under grubby scarves and dirt smeared across their faces.

'We'll be like strapping peasant girls when this is all over,' jokes Wanda.

Anna grunts in reply.

He has to hand it to his sister though, she's got more balls than a lot of girls. And boys for that matter. He wonders how Lech is getting on. Jan was disappointed when the Polish Army failed to stop the Germans crossing the border, but he expects they're putting up a brave fight. The radio announcer reports each day on the number of enemy aircraft shot down over Warsaw. Over thirty and counting. Jan is keeping a tally. The radio plays snippets of Chopin's Polonaise in A Major, the 'Military', throughout the day as a way of telling the world that Warsaw is still standing, still fighting. Still hanging on by the skin of its teeth. A bit like me, he thinks, as he thrusts the spade into the ground once more. At least he'll have something interesting to tell

Weronika.

They work until the light starts to fade. They've done all they can for one day, digging a trench so deep that a tank would topple into it like a beetle stuck on its back.

As they plod home, they are forced to take detours around barricades constructed out of old furniture, overturned trams and paving slabs ripped from the ground. They are living in a fortress now and the city has become unrecognisable. Shop windows are criss-crossed with strips of paper to stop the glass from shattering. Sandbags are piled around the bases of important buildings. Litter and rubbish are piling up in stinking heaps.

Soldiers returning from the front lie in the streets, exhausted and discouraged. Jan gives each one a surreptitious look, afraid of seeing Lech in the glazed eyes and weary faces. But he's not there.

*

'The government has left the capital,' says Maria. 'They clearly think it's not safe here. We should go east.'

They have just sat down to eat their evening meal. Jan is starving and doesn't want to listen to talk of politics.

'Go east?' Emeryk puts down his knife and fork. 'Whatever for?'

'To be safe, of course,' says Maria.

'But where would we go?'

'To my brother's in Lwów.' She makes it sound as if she's already booked the train tickets and packed their bags.

'They don't have room to accommodate us,' says Emeryk. 'It's one thing staying with them for a week in the summer, but it's not a long-term solution.'

Jan thinks of his uncle's cramped apartment in the centre of the eastern city of Lwów and has to say that he agrees with his father.

'Besides,' says Emeryk, 'people are pouring into Warsaw from elsewhere. They must think that Warsaw is the safer place to be. I've heard stories of German brutality against civilians in the rest of the country.'

Jan stops chewing and looks from his mother to his father. They aren't a family that normally argues, but he can feel the tension rising between his parents over this issue. Anna, sitting opposite him, catches his eye. She has also stopped eating and is listening attentively.

'The evacuation of the government,' says Emeryk, 'has caused everyone to panic. It's an absolute scandal. At a time like this a government should stand firm and set an example to its people. Instead everyone who holds any sort of public office is fleeing across the Vistula and, like a bunch of lemmings, ordinary people are following them.' He resumes eating as if that is the end of the conversation.

Maria looks as if she wants to say something else but then changes her mind. Jan can see from the look on her face that this subject is not yet closed, but she will bide her time. They finish the meal in silence.

CHAPTER NINE

The Red Army has invaded Poland from the east. This is the news that Captain Mazur relays to his exhausted and demoralised band of men.

Lech hopes it's all lies and propaganda spread by the Germans to further undermine Polish morale, but Mazur says that radio broadcasts in Polish, Russian and Ukrainian have confirmed the fact.

'What are they saying exactly?' asks Lech.

'They're calling themselves our liberators,' says Mazur.

Cynical laughter greets his words. The men don't believe the Soviets' claim and Lech doesn't blame them. He picks up a pebble and tosses it angrily into the road. They've marched east for days to escape the German advance and all they've done is walk straight into the arms of the Soviets. Back in the summer the Soviets signed a non-aggression pact with the Germans, so whose side are they on now? Their own, most likely.

Up ahead, sounds from a loud hailer carry on the wind, but the voice is too indistinct for the men to make out what is being said.

'We should find out what's happening,' says Mazur.

Most of the men agree with him and start getting to their

feet, but Lech has misgivings. This could be a serious mistake. Do they really want to put themselves at the mercy of the Soviets who have never been a friend to Poland? Maybe they should just turn around now. But then what? Head straight back into the German lines? Hardly an attractive option. But neither is moving closer to the Soviets. They're exhausted, disorganised and without proper equipment, three things which certainly won't apply to the Red Army soldiers who are no doubt all fresh as daisies and armed to the teeth.

As his group walks towards the source of the announcements, Lech staggers to his feet and follows them. They've come this far together, he can't abandon them now.

They reach a large group of Polish soldiers, disparate bands who have all headed east. When he stands on tiptoe, Lech sees a long line of military trucks crammed with armed Russian soldiers and tanks bearing the hammer and sickle, in case anyone was in any doubt as to their nationality.

'Brothers! We are all Slavs!' The voice bellowing through the megaphone speaks Polish with the tell-tale sing-song intonation of a Russian. Listening to Russians speak Polish is normally a cause for mirth and merriment, but no one is laughing now. 'We are not Germans. We are not your enemies. Where are your officers? We wish to negotiate with you.'

A furious debate breaks out amongst the Poles. No one is short of an opinion or three.

'The Red Army is our only hope.'

'The Russians can't be trusted.'

'They'll partition Poland like they did before.'

'They'll fight the Germans for us.'

'Don't be ridiculous. They're in league with the Germans.'

'Stalin is no better than Hitler.'

Lech would prefer to have nothing to do with the Red Army and is surprised that this opinion isn't unanimous.

'Quiet!' The voice booming through the megaphone is

less conciliatory now. 'We haven't got all day. Send me your officers.'

A handful of senior officers, including Captain Mazur, gather together for a hasty conference. Lech imagines there isn't a whole lot to discuss. What options do they have? Eventually the most senior officer walks towards the Soviet tanks waving a white handkerchief. The Russian soldiers look on from the comfort of their trucks.

A hush descends on the Polish soldiers. Their fate is about to be agreed by a discussion between two men, but Lech suspects the Soviets have already decided the outcome of the conversation and that this charade is purely for show.

They wait in the blistering sun, parched and frustrated. Lech feels like a pawn in a game over which he has no control. More than anything he wants to be in charge of his life, but war has robbed him of all autonomy. The future is in the lap of the gods, or more accurately the hands of the Soviets. He rests his elbows on his knees, lets his head drop forward, and closes his eyes. Visions of the burning train fill his mind's eye.

'Men of the Polish Army!' Lech's head snaps up. The Polish officer is addressing them through the megaphone. 'I have serious news for you.' Not a breath of wind stirs the air as every man listens intently. 'The Soviet Army has crossed the border to join in the fight against the Germans. The Polish High Command and the Polish Government have ceased to exist. Our only option is to join the Soviet forces. We are to surrender our arms which will be returned to us later. Long live Poland and the Soviet Union!'

Silence. No one moves. Lech doesn't dare look into the eyes of his fellow men. He's frightened of what he might see there. Acquiescence or defiance? His own heart, thumping madly in his chest, is telling him to resist, but his head is telling him that it's all over.

A cry of despair from the front of the crowd rends the silence and then the crack of a single revolver shot splits the air. Lech's stomach turns over. Dear God, what just happened?

There's a commotion at the front and then the news spreads like lightning through the crowd. A non-commissioned officer has shot himself rather than surrender to the Russians. This is what it has come to, thinks Lech, in fury. Poland has lost its honour and one man has done what he can to salvage his.

All hell breaks out. Polish officers run from group to group, urging the men to comply with the request to lay down their arms. No one else needs to die. And then a Russian starts shouting explicit orders through the megaphone.

'Pile your arms in front of the white hut. All weapons must be handed over. That includes machine guns, rifles, revolvers and bayonets. Concealing weapons will be a treasonable offence.'

No one moves. No one wants to go first, to be the first to surrender to the Soviets. Then two colonels step forward and lay their revolvers down in front of the hut. After that the captains follow their example and lay down their weapons. There's no other option but for every officer and soldier to comply with the order.

Lech unsheathes his revolver and cradles it momentarily in his hands. He's kept it well-oiled and polished, ready for use. He never did get to shoot a German. He feels as if he's parting with a close friend, one that could have saved his life. He lays it down on the ever-growing pile of weapons and walks away feeling unmanned and vulnerable, like a small child facing bullies in the school playground.

As soon as the last man is disarmed, Soviet soldiers jump down from the trucks and run along both sides of the road, aiming their light machine guns at the Poles. The order is given to line up in the direction of Tarnopol. Soviet tanks move into position at the rear, their guns pointing the way. Those in front swivel their guns so they too are pointing at the hapless Poles.

The convoy of tanks, Soviet foot soldiers and Polish

prisoners sets off towards the centre of Tarnopol.

Lech can't believe his misfortune. Not three weeks into the war and he's a captive of the Red Army. He still hasn't fought the Germans.

CHAPTER TEN

The Kowalski baby is sick. He's been running a fever all night and Pani Kowalska comes to Maria for help this morning because she doesn't know where else to turn. Ever since they've been spending so much time in the basement, Maria has become a friend and confidante to the younger woman, helping to keep the three older children entertained whilst Pani Kowalska nurses the baby.

Maria tells her not to worry. She will fetch some medicine from the doctor, and whilst she is at it, she'll bring back some food. Pani Kowalska is looking thinner day by day. She can't be eating enough, with such a large family to feed.

Maria sympathises with her neighbour's plight. No mother can bear to watch her children go hungry. But it's increasingly difficult to find food in the shops. They've been under siege for weeks now and supplies are just not getting through. At the start of the war the mayor said there was no need to hoard food, but Maria thought it prudent to put aside extra sausages and a few jars. She's sure most women will have done the same. It's all very well for the mayor to say not to hoard food, but men don't understand these things. They're not the ones who do the shopping and the cooking. And events have proved her right. The Germans have bombed the flour mills and bread is running out. Farmers can't get fresh produce into the city because of the Panzer columns on the outskirts. They're being starved into submission. It's all very well digging trenches and erecting barricades, but at this rate they'll be dead of hunger before the Germans get here.

She manages to get some medicine from the doctor by claiming that the poor little mite is almost at death's door, but she won't go home until she's found some food to put into her shopping basket. And she wants to make sure Pani Kowalska is eating properly too. Maria has always taken great pride in her cooking, providing her family with hearty stews and broths and thick winter soups. She has always ensured they consume a variety of fruit and vegetables. She normally buys fresh bread from the bakery, and makes a cake for special occasions.

Now she trudges along the bomb-damaged street, praying she won't come back empty-handed. At the junction with the main road she navigates a barricade constructed out of tram rails ripped from the ground and positioned at a forty-five-degree angle to prevent tanks passing through. In a neighbouring street the residents have improvised another blockage out of an old wardrobe, a rickety chest of drawers, and a sofa with the springs bursting through the stuffing. The city has become an obstacle course. She squeezes through the narrow gap at the side, all the while breathing in the smoke from still smouldering buildings.

When she arrives at the baker's she finds him pulling down the shutters.

'Sorry,' he says. 'No more bread today.'

She might have been in time if she hadn't been to the doctor's first.

She presses on, determined not to give up. Rounding a corner, she sees people running along the street. Someone shouts, 'There's a dead horse.' And then she too is running, although she hasn't run for nigh on thirty years and the effort might just finish her off. When she reaches the crowd, she's gasping for breath and sweating like a pig.

The fallen animal lies in the middle of the road, its flank cut open, the ribs exposed, the inedible bits piled in a bloody mess to one side. Men and women with sharp knives are hacking into the flesh, cutting off what they can. She wishes now that she'd brought a knife of her own, but it's not what she normally carries in her basket when she's out shopping. She'll have to bargain with one of these people, see if they'll cut her a slice in return for money. She approaches a man who clearly has some skill with a knife. Maybe he's a butcher by trade.

'Excuse me,' she says. 'I can give you money if you'll cut me a piece.'

He appears not to have heard her, so intent is he on getting every last piece of flesh off the bone.

'Please,' she says, then adds, 'my son and daughter are digging trenches. They'll be hungry when they get home.'

He looks at her then, his face haggard, but there's understanding in his eyes. He hacks off a thick slab of meat and passes it to her with bloodied hands. She takes out her purse but he waves it away.

'Take it,' he says. 'And thank your son and daughter from me.'

'Thank you,' she says. She wraps the meat in the tea towel that she brought for the bread and hurries home, thinking of the stew she'll cook with her last remaining onion. There'll be enough to share with Pani Kowalska and her children.

*

The townspeople line the streets, watching in grim-faced silence as Lech and the other Poles march into the centre of town, accompanied by their Soviet escort. Old men, mothers with babies in their arms, ragged children. It's impossible to tell from their hard-set faces what they're really thinking. But at least this lot aren't firing on them like the *Volksdeutsche* in Oświęcim. Small mercies.

They're supposed to be marching in rows of ten, at least that's how they set off, but they're too exhausted to care about maintaining strict formation and the rows have become ragged. Roughly every five rows a Soviet soldier walks alongside, armed with a light machine gun. Some of the Soviets stare straight ahead, not bothering to watch their charges. The more diligent ones are practically walking sideways like crabs, keeping their eyes trained on the captives.

Lech keeps his head facing front, but his eyes dart from side to side, looking for any chance to slip away and melt into the crowd of bystanders. He senses that others around him are doing the same. In the row in front, the man at the end of the line steps deftly to one side and merges into the crowd, vanishing as if he was never there. It can be done. The escapee's neighbour casually drifts over to fill the empty space so that the row appears complete. Unless the Soviets take the trouble to stop and count them, they'll never know what's happened. The Soviets are surprisingly slapdash. He can't imagine the Germans would be so careless over numbers.

Dusk starts to fall and the outlines of people and buildings become less distinct. They're nearing the centre of the city now, almost certainly heading for the train station to be carted off God knows where. Lech feels his heart thumping hard and a trembling in the tips of his fingers. A voice inside his head is telling him to make a run for it. He would never have deserted from the army when they still had a chance of fighting the Germans. He's not a coward. But this is different. They're prisoners now, not soldiers. If he wants to have any chance of fighting the Germans, he needs to escape from the Soviets, that much is clear to him. If he doesn't take his chance soon, it will be too late.

He looks left and right, assessing the situation. If he were on the end of the row, he would risk slipping away, but there are two men to his left who show no sign of wanting to escape and he doesn't think he can slip past them without causing a commotion that would attract the attention of the Soviet guard up ahead. He's a young lad, a bit jumpy, probably keen to impress his senior officers. He has his finger permanently positioned on the trigger of his weapon. It wouldn't take much to make him fire.

Lech lowers his head so that he can see the feet of the men in the row behind. They were closer when they set off, but now the gaps between rows have widened as people struggle to keep up. He realises with a rush of excitement that there's a space behind him, to the left. If he drops back into the row behind, he'll be closer to the edge, and further from the trigger-happy young communist. It's his best bet.

As casually as he can, Lech slows his pace and drops out of his row, careful not to cause the man behind him to trip over. With a quick side-step to the left, worthy of any Warsaw dancefloor, he slots himself into place in his new row. The men either side of him don't bat an eyelid. There's only one man on his left now. Surely the fellow must realise what Lech is planning to do. He risks a quick glance at his new companion and the man gives an almost imperceptible nod of his head. It's enough to give Lech the final burst of courage he needs. As if on cue, his neighbour drops back and Lech slips into his place.

Good luck, guys, he thinks. Then he steps into the crowd of bystanders and the column of men marches on without him.

*

Jan sits by the window, staring into space. He never expected war to be so tedious. When Britain and France declared war on Germany, he thought they would come to the rescue. He imagined the British navy sailing their ships into the Bay of Danzig and the RAF blasting the Germans to smithereens with their world-class air force. He pictured the French pouring over the border with tanks and thousands of men at their disposal. But none of that has happened and he finds his disappointment hard to swallow.

When they're not cowering in the basement, sheltering from the endless round of air raids and artillery attacks, or digging trenches, they gather around the radio, eager for news of the fate of their country. In his daily address, the city's mayor does his best to keep spirits up with fighting talk of an 'eternal Poland, a bulwark of humanity and culture.' He urges the citizens to stand firm and resist, and for a few moments listening to the doughty mayor, Jan feels a sense of pride and hope. But then the reports come in of Polish losses and his spirits plummet. Kraków has fallen, not even managing to hold out for a week. The battle on the Westerplatte peninsula in Danzig – such a beacon of hope in the early days of the war – has ended in defeat. The news from the front is one humiliation after another. And now the Soviets have invaded from the east and all talk of the family fleeing to Lwów has been dropped.

'Are the Soviets going to push the Germans out?' Jan asks when he first hears the news. He'd rather have help from the British and the French, but he'll accept it from the Soviets if need be.

His father starts to explain something about a pact between Hitler and Stalin – the Molotov-Ribbentrop pact or whatever it's called – and says something about Poland being partitioned yet again, but Jan is only half listening by now. Politics doesn't interest him. He's only interested in fire-power and who's got the biggest guns. The bottom line, it turns out, is that Hitler and Stalin are in cahoots and they are crushing Poland between them. So no, the Soviets are not going to push the Germans out.

Even the bombing has become tedious. There are fires all over the city, blazing long into the night, lighting up the sky so that it's impossible to sleep. The Stukas don't terrify him anymore. Their shriek has replaced birdsong. Jan can spot the aircraft miles off when they're still high in the sky, like black crows. He can tell when the rumble of the aircraft is about to turn into an ear-splitting whine that sets your teeth on edge and makes you want to put your fingers in your ears. But he no longer shakes with terror.

Only death hasn't yet lost its morbid fascination.

The first time he saw a dead body in the street, he approached with caution, both curious and horrified. He'd never seen a dead body before. He didn't know what he expected to discover, but it drew him and repelled him in equal measure. Confronting it was like a personal challenge that he had to overcome, a rite of passage.

A bomb had exploded on a corner of a building, blowing out all the windows and destroying part of the wall on the upper floors so that the inside was exposed like a doll's house. The bedroom had pink wallpaper.

A woman lay on the ground, her dress torn, her pale limbs cut and bloodied by shrapnel. He reached out a hand to touch her, to see if she was really dead. Was she still warm? Would she feel different to a living person? What was death exactly?

'Come away, child!' Another woman grabbed him by the arm and pulled him roughly away. She had a mole on her chin, that's all he remembers now. He'd thought she was ugly, uglier than the dead woman who was still quite pretty. But the woman with the mole had frightened him and he'd run back to the apartment, ashamed of what he'd done.

'Dinnertime,' calls his mother. With a sigh Jan drags himself away from the window. He used to enjoy his mother's cooking but that's become the most tedious thing of all. For a whole week they lived off the meat she'd scavenged from a dead horse. Now all they've got left are a few potatoes which are turning black and starting to sprout.

CHAPTER ELEVEN

The bodies pile up and no one comes to claim them. Emeryk has given up counting.

The mayor has ordered that unclaimed bodies are to be buried in public parks and gardens, or else they will have an epidemic on their hands on top of everything else. Once again, volunteers have been sought and Emeryk has come forward. It's the least he can do.

When he sees the corpses transported in handcarts, piled on top of one another like lumps of meat, limbs dangling over the edge, Emeryk can't help wondering if he made the right decision keeping the family in Warsaw. But Lwów was never really on the cards, whatever Maria thought. And now that Lwów is in the hands of the Soviets, he's glad they didn't go there. But could they have gone somewhere else? The government has fled to Romania. Could ordinary civilians do the same? What about Hungary?

'Where d'you want this lot?' Two factory workers in filthy overalls arrive with another cartload and Emeryk is jolted out of thoughts of exile into the grim reality of the present.

'Just here will be fine.' What does it matter where they drop them?

'Righto.'

Cigarettes dangling from their bloodless lips, the men start emptying the cart. One at the head and one at the feet, they lay the lifeless bodies down in a row, side by side, their actions automatic and repetitive, as if they're unloading logs. But these are human beings. Until a day or two ago they had lives, families, friends, hopes and dreams. Now they lie broken and burnt. Many are starting to smell.

Emeryk kneels on the muddy ground, indifferent to the state of his trousers, and, with a deep breath, thrusts his hand into the blood-soaked coat pocket of the woman lying in front of him. His job is to try and identify these people so that their names can be added to the overgrowing list of the deceased.

Absurdly, he feels he ought to apologise for this intrusion into the dead woman's privacy. He pulls out a bloody piece of paper that looks like a shopping list, but can find no other form of identification. He peers at her face, something that he generally tries to avoid doing, and sees that she can't be more than thirty, thirty-five at the most. She has shoulder-length brown hair which is now singed to a crisp. Like so many of the women here, she was hit by shrapnel whilst queueing for food. It's a dilemma that so many people, especially women, face every day. Risk being killed, or die of starvation. Maybe she had children to feed and didn't want to go home empty-handed, so she stayed in the queue when she should have taken shelter. It's his historian's brain, looking at the available evidence and formulating a theory. But he's used to looking for evidence in archives and dusty libraries, not in a muddy park, his hands covered in the blood of strangers. He tries her other pocket, but fails to identify the woman with the brown hair. She'll be buried with all the other unclaimed bodies in a mass grave.

'Sorry,' he says to her, before moving on to the next victim.

*

He travels by night and hides by day. Ever since his miraculous escape – and Lech does think of it as little short of a miracle – from the hands of the Red Army, he's been on the run, like a hunted animal.

He shuns human contact and trusts no one. This part of Poland has always had a significant ethnic population whose sympathies are unlikely to lie with a Polish soldier escaped from Russian captivity. He doesn't want a repeat of what happened with the *Volksdeutsche* when they were retreating from Oświęcim. Ethnicity and nationality were never things he gave much thought to before, but now they seem to be all some people care about.

Almost from the moment he slunk into the crowd of bystanders, he was filled with doubts, but by then it was too late to turn back and he was forced to stick with his decision, running haphazardly down side-streets and dark alleyways until he was hopelessly lost but far enough away from the Soviets to breathe a little more easily. When he finally stopped to draw breath, he reminded himself that the Soviets have never been a friend to the Poles and are unlikely to start now. Whatever they have planned for the captured soldiers, he's sure it won't be anything good. He wants to help his country, but he can't do that from a Soviet gulag in the middle of Siberia.

He feels the lack of the revolver he was forced to hand over, but he feels the loss of his companions even more. Thrown together seemingly at random by the mobilisation, nevertheless they stuck together throughout the bombing and the long march east, and he misses them more than he ever thought possible.

He's been on the run for three nights now, going across country as much as possible and avoiding main roads. By day he hides in burnt-out villages, scavenging for food, his rations having run out on the long march east. He catches whatever sleep he can, taking shelter in dilapidated barns and stinking cattle stalls. His only thought is to head to the city of Lwów where his uncle lives with his wife and daughter. It's been a few years since he saw his uncle, but he's the only relative Lech has in this part of Poland. Once he's made it to Lwów, he'll think about what to do next.

As dusk begins to fall, Lech prepares for the next leg of his journey. It can't be much further now. He adjusts his pack on his back and sets off across a muddy field of turnips. It's a clear night and the white light of the moon casts a ghostly glow over the flat landscape. Somewhere in the distance, a fox howls.

*

They're living in hell.

Anna passes a cup of water to old Pani Woźniak who takes it with trembling hands and sips from it before passing it to her husband. He gives the empty cup back to Anna who refills it from the bucket.

The Nowaks and their neighbours huddle in the basement whilst bombs and incendiaries rain down on the city. An explosion nearby shakes the foundations of the building, not to mention Anna's nerves, and some of the precious liquid sloshes over her hand. She mustn't waste it after her father risked his life going out shortly after dawn to fill a bucket from the pump two streets away. They haven't had running water in the building for days now and life has become a constant struggle to survive. Emeryk barely made it back to the apartment with the bucket clasped in both hands before the air raid siren sounded and everyone rushed down to the basement. They don't know how long they'll have to stay down here and the water needs to last. She passes the cup to Pani Kowalska who takes nothing for herself but offers it to her children. Even the boisterous Kowalski children have grown quiet in recent days, worn down by terror and lack of food. They sit on the mattress, barely saying a word. Maria is cradling the baby

77

who has grown weak and listless. The girl from across the courtyard, Weronika, is also handing out cups of water to people. Anna marvels at her calmness. She can't be more than eleven, the same age as Jan. It hasn't escaped Anna's notice how her little brother blushes when Weronika smiles at him.

More thundering overhead and the paraffin lamp in the middle of the floor flickers and threatens to go out. Smoke from raging fires penetrates the cellar, making eyes sting and breathing difficult. Windows shatter, masonry falls. Anna's ears are splitting with the constant howl of the Stukas and the pounding of artillery shells. She refills the cup and passes it to her mother. This simple task of handing out water is the only thing keeping her going at the moment.

Only two days ago the mayor gave one of his most rousing speeches ever. They gathered round the radio and listened with tears in their eyes as he spoke of a Warsaw 'at the height of her grandeur and glory, fighting for the honour of Poland.' If oratory and fighting talk could win a war, then Poland would have won a hundredfold by now. But that afternoon the power station must have been hit because the electricity was cut off in the middle of Rachmaninov's second piano concerto. Anna was preparing potatoes for the evening meal, digging out the black bits with a paring knife, the radio playing quietly in the background. For a moment or two she was able to lose herself in the rich textures of the music. The sudden silence coupled with the lights going off made her jump and the knife slipped in her hand, the blade cutting into the soft flesh of her thumb.

But it's the loss of the radio that is the hardest to bare. The body needs food but the mind needs news. The radio was their lifeline to the outside world, and without it they feel cut off and abandoned. They had come to rely on the mayor's stirring speeches to give them hope. Without hope, what is left?

Stukas shriek and dive overhead and Anna feels the urge to curl into a little ball, to make herself as small as possible.

It's a self-preserving human instinct when faced with the threat of imminent death. She can't begin to contemplate the future, her plans to study art at college. All that has been put on hold. The only thing that matters is surviving this minute, this hour, this day. When she lies down to sleep every night, the thought crosses her mind that she might not wake up again. She never used to think about death, but now it's on her mind all the time.

She dips the cup into the bucket of water and a bomb explodes so close by that everyone jumps and emits a collective scream. Anna drops the cup and flings herself to the ground, hands over her head. The Kowalski baby starts to wail and the three older children cling to each other, whimpering. They no longer squabble, but seek comfort in each other's company.

'Sounded like it landed in the courtyard,' says Pan Woźniak matter-of-factly.

That evening they prepare to spend the night in the basement. Emeryk offers to empty the waste bucket which is stinking and making the air difficult to breathe. When he returns, he reports that a bomb has indeed landed in the courtyard. Pan Woźniak looks gratified that he guessed correctly. Emeryk reports shattered windows and masonry damage, but the building is still standing. He makes it sound as if this is something to celebrate, which in a way it is, Anna supposes. It's a near-miss but they're still alive.

'Now then,' says Emeryk, lowering himself with a little difficulty onto the mattress with the three Kowalski children, 'do you know the story of the Dragon of Kraków?'

The children stare at him wide-eyed and shake their heads.

'Well, once upon a time there was a king and he wanted to build a castle on a hill, but there was a cave under the hill and do you know what was inside the cave?'

The children shake their heads again, but Anna can see her father has their attention. He used to tell her this story at bedtime, before she learnt to read. It was one of her favourites.

'There was a huge, green egg.' Emeryk holds his hands wide apart to demonstrate the size of the egg.

The children's eyes grow wider.

'So the king built his castle and the city grew and everyone who lived there was happy. Until one day, there was a huge crack' – Emeryk claps his hands together, making the children jump – 'and an enormous dragon flew out of the mouth of the cave, and past the king's window, blotting out the sun.'

'Did it fly away?' asks the eldest child.

'Sadly no,' says Emeryk. 'The dragon started to destroy the city. It flattened houses with its huge tail; it set fire to trees and scorched the earth with its breath; the river turned black and all the fish died. It plucked sheep and cattle off the fields with its enormous jaws. It slaughtered horses. The army was defeated and the beautiful city lay in ruins. But the king was determined not to give up.'

Now everyone is listening to the story and barely noticing the explosions outside.

'So the king offered a reward to anyone who could kill the dragon,' continues Emeryk. 'Now lots of people tried to kill it and failed, but a poor shoemaker came up with a plan to outwit the dragon. He took an old sheep's hide to the local quarry and stuffed it full of sulphur crystals. Do you know what sulphur crystals look like?'

'No,' chorus the children.

'Sulphur is a yellow rock and you use it to make explosives. So, he stuffed the sheep's hide with this yellow rock and he sewed it up and brushed the fleece to make it look as if it was a real sheep, and then he took it to the king.'

By now the children are actually laughing.

'That night, some brave knights put the stuffed sheep outside the entrance to the dragon's cave. Then everyone waited. At first nothing happened, but then steam began to rise through the castle floor and the night sky was lit with a fiery glow. The dragon emerged from his cave, swallowed the sheep whole, and flew into the sky. Suddenly the earth began to tremble and there was a great roar followed by the loudest bang anyone had ever heard. The sky exploded in a shower of light. The dragon was dead.'

'Hooray,' shout the children, clapping their hands.

'When the king asked the shoemaker what he would like for his reward, the shoemaker said he would like the dragon's skin so that he could make shoes for all the poor people. The king granted him his wish and gave him a new shop near the castle. And the city was made beautiful again and grew rich and everyone lived happily ever after.'

You can face anything, thinks Anna, if you know how to slay a dragon.

*

He walks all night and the first light of dawn is breaking in the sky when Lech reaches the outskirts of Lwów. This will be the most dangerous part of his journey yet, entering what is now a Soviet-occupied city. He decides to take his chances before it's properly light. Sticking to backstreets, he makes his way towards the centre, trying to remember where his uncle's apartment is.

Everywhere, there are signs of how the city tried to defend itself, and failed. Flagstones have been ripped up to form barricades which now lie in ruins. Chunks of masonry are missing from buildings hit by artillery fire. Shattered windows have been boarded up. The few people out at this time of day keep their heads down and their eyes averted. Is this what it's like in Warsaw?

He turns a corner by a shell-damaged church. This is the right street. Modest but smart nineteenth-century town houses and apartment blocks. Most of the windows have been blown out, but otherwise the buildings appear to be intact. He enters the building fourth from the end and checks the names of the occupants on the postboxes in the hallway. Yes, there it is – Jablonksi – his mother's brother.

Better known as Uncle Henryk. He climbs the stairs to the second floor and knocks.

A door opens inside the apartment. He hears quick footsteps, muffled voices. They must be wondering who is calling at this unearthly hour. Maybe they think it's the Soviets. The door of the opposite apartment opens a fraction and an old woman stares at him with frightened eyes before shutting the door quickly and turning the key in the lock. He must look a fright after days traipsing across country and sleeping rough. He doesn't want to attract any more attention, so he knocks again, gently, and calls out, 'Uncle Henryk! It's Lech Nowak, your nephew.'

The door is flung open and Lech finds himself embraced in the big arms of his uncle.

'Come in! You are most welcome,' says his uncle. He holds Lech at arm's length and takes a proper look at him. 'Good God, man, what has happened to you?' His uniform is filthy and torn, he's unshaven, and probably smells like the cattle stalls he's been sleeping in. 'No, don't worry,' says his uncle. 'There's plenty of time for you to tell us later. What you need now is a hot bath and something to eat and drink. Magdalena, heat up some water for this poor chap, and Halina, fetch him some food.'

Only then does Lech notice his Aunt Magdalena and cousin, Halina, regarding him with disbelief. The two women rush off to do as Henryk has instructed them. His uncle, a big bear of a man, takes Lech's backpack from him and leads him into the apartment.

Half an hour later, when he's clean and fed and wearing a set of his uncle's clothes which are far too big for him, he lies down on the bed in the spare room and falls into a dreamless sleep.

*

The German artillery starts again shortly after dawn. The only difference now, thinks Jan as he listens, is that the

Polish artillery isn't making much effort to fire back.

They've all spent the night in the basement. He even had to give in and take a pee in the bucket, something he vowed he would never do, but it was either that or wet his trousers which would have been infinitely worse. He doesn't want to spend another night in the cellar. He'd rather take his chances in his own bed.

The day drags on with constant explosions and then suddenly, in the middle of the afternoon, silence.

Jan looks up in surprise. The sudden quiet is almost as shocking as the continuous roar of shelling. He waits for the bangs and explosions to start again, but nothing happens. He senses that everyone is holding their breath.

When he can't stand the suspense any longer, he turns to his father. 'What's happening?' he breathes, his voice barely above a whisper.

'It sounds like a ceasefire,' says Emeryk.

Everyone starts talking at once.

'What does this mean?'

'Is it a temporary ceasefire to collect the wounded and bury the dead?'

'Are the Germans and Russians in talks about how to carve up the country?'

'Have the British finally arrived?'

'Will they start fighting again?'

Maria gets to her feet. 'Well, I'm not sitting here waiting for another attack. I'm going to check on the apartment.'

'I'll come with you,' says Anna.

Everyone, it seems, has the same idea so, cautiously, like animals coming out of hibernation, they emerge from the safety of their bunker into the daylight, blinking and coughing in the smoke-filled air.

A dismal sight awaits them. Although their building is still standing, all the windows have been blasted out. Amongst the rubble strewn along the street lie the dead bodies of those who ventured out, perhaps for water, but didn't make it back in time. People start to emerge from other buildings, clinging to each other, walking as if in a daze.

Weronika appears at Jan's side. 'Papa has just returned from the hospital. He says that Warsaw has surrendered.'

Jan turns on her in fury. 'No!' he shouts. 'That can't be right.' He feels an urge to grab hold of her and shake her. Surrender? What is she talking about? Warsaw is supposed to fight on and be victorious. The capital, of all places, is not supposed to go the way of Danzig and Kraków. But he can see the truth of what she's saying for himself. A wave of disappointment floods over him, threatening to drown him.

'But that doesn't mean we stop resisting,' says Weronika.

'What's the point?' He turns away. He'll never get to fight now.

Over the next few days, thousands of Polish soldiers march out of the city into German captivity. They're a sorry sight with their dejected faces and days of stubble on their chins. Jan feels embarrassed for this ragtag bunch of men who've fought so hard but have been out-bombed and out-numbered. Everything is over.

'This is not the end,' says Emeryk that evening. 'It's only the end of the beginning.'

'What do you mean?' Jan hates it when his father speaks in riddles.

'Now begins the occupation.'

PART THREE
OCCUPATION
OCTOBER 1939 – APRIL 1940

CHAPTER TWELVE

The photograph of the family, the one Anna took on the day Lech was mobilised, is propped on the mantelpiece in front of a large ticking clock. She doesn't have a spare frame to put it in, but she doesn't want to stick it in a photograph album. She wants it where she can see it. She glances at the black-and-white image every time she walks past. She's seen Maria pick up the photograph and surreptitiously wipe away a tear, before replacing it in front of the clock and continuing with her chores. They haven't heard from Lech since he went off to fight. They've heard reports that the soldiers on the western border fled eastwards, but what that means exactly, no one is quite sure.

The camera now sits on a shelf at the top of her wardrobe, empty of film. Anna doesn't dare take it with her when she goes out in case the German occupiers suspect her of illegal activity and confiscate it. Or worse. Who knows what's allowed anymore? Photography is unlikely to be on the ever-diminishing list of permitted activities. Every day new posters appear in German and Polish, plastered to the walls of buildings. *No one allowed out in the streets between 9 p.m. and dawn; Listening to foreign broadcasts is prohibited; Posting obituary bills is banned; Such and such is strictly forbidden; Ignore this or that order on the penalty of death*. It's hard to keep up with the latest edicts.

After holding out for nearly one whole month, Warsaw surrendered on the twenty-eighth of September. The last remaining pockets of resistance in Poland gave up the fight a few days later. After all that digging trenches, and erecting barricades, and hiding in the cellar in fear of one's life, and surviving on a diet of horse meat and rotten potatoes, and fetching buckets of water from the pump, and witnessing death and destruction, and burying bodies in the parks, after all that, it was a bitter blow to know that it had been for nothing. The British and the French hadn't come to their rescue after all.

The victors marched into Warsaw on the first of October. On the fifth, the Führer himself deigned to visit the Polish capital and spent two hours on a tree-lined boulevard saluting his goose-stepping minions before scuttling back to Berlin. The western regions of Poland have been annexed to the Reich. The central region of the country, including Warsaw, is now known as the General Government. In overall control of this large area is the Nazi lawyer Hans Frank. He has installed himself and his family in the grandeur of Wawel Castle in the old Polish capital of Kraków like a medieval monarch. Stripped of its status as the capital city, Warsaw itself is administered by one of Frank's underlings, Gruppenführer Ludwig Fischer, a man whose zeal for thinking up restrictive measures seems to know no bounds. The Eastern Borderlands, including the city of Lwów where Maria's brother lives with his wife and daughter, are now under the control of the Soviets. Germany and the Soviet Union have carved Poland up between themselves. The fourth partition of the country, which her father so greatly feared, has happened.

Those are the facts as far as Anna understands them. But what does it mean for her? She's still trying to work that out. One thing is certain though – whatever plans she had before, she can forget about them. Secondary schools, colleges and universities are all closed. She won't be starting her art studies any time soon. When so many people have died or lost their homes, she knows she should feel grateful for what she has. She's still breathing, and she's still got a roof over her head, even if they've had to board up the broken windows and the roof is leaking. But still, she can't help feeling a burning resentment towards the invaders who've wrecked her plans for the future.

With nothing better to do, she takes the tram to visit Wanda, the weather having turned too cold and wet for cycling. She squeezes into the carriage designated for Poles where there is standing room only. The near-empty carriage up front is marked *Nur für Deutsche* - Only for Germans. She has never been more acutely aware of her identity and her place in the social hierarchy. She carries her Certificate of Racial Origin, her identity card and a ration card at all times. Without these documents she might as well not exist. The Certificate of Racial Origin states that she is an 'Aryan' as opposed to a Jew or a *Mischling* – a person of mixed Jewish and Aryan ancestry – but she does not see this as a badge of honour. The Germans regard themselves as Aryans and the Germans are the enemy. Why would she want to align herself with them?

The tram trundles northwards through the shattered streets. The city is slowly being put back together, but it will never be the same again. Some buildings were too badly damaged to be rebuilt and have been torn down. Black, white and red Swastika banners billow from public buildings. Jewish shops display a Star of David in the window and Poles are nervous of being seen entering and leaving them. Many Jewish businesses have closed.

The tram stops to let people on and off and Anna slips into a seat by the window. Outside, people trudge past, their eyes downcast, their expressions defeated. An elderly Jewish man with a long beard and broad brimmed hat comes into view. He walks with the aid of a stick, slightly stooped, his gaze fixed on the ground in front of him. His coat is so long, it reaches down to his ankles. He hasn't noticed the two SS officers in their grey-green uniforms striding towards him from the opposite direction. Anna can hardly bare to watch, knowing what is about to happen, but at the same time she can't tear her eyes away from the window. She lifts a hand to rap on the glass, to warn the old man, but it's too late. The SS officers stop in front of him, blocking his path. He tries to move past them but he's nowhere near quick or agile enough. The taller of the two SS men lashes out with his boot, kicking the Jew's walking stick out of his hand. Knocked off balance, the old man stumbles and falls into the gutter where his assailants beat him with their batons and shout insults at him. Doesn't he know that filthy swine like him are not permitted to walk on the pavements? Hasn't he read the notices?

The tram glides away and the old man is lost to view. Anna finds she's trembling all over and a wave of nausea washes over her. She has witnessed this sort of barbaric cruelty on more than one occasion, and it makes her blood boil. She wants to shout at her fellow passengers, 'How can we stand by and let this happen?' But other people bury their faces in newspapers or deliberately avoid looking out of the window. Of course, it's easier not to look. If she'd been on the street instead of stuck in the tram, she'd have… but what would she have done? What could she have realistically done? Everyone is afraid of the SS and the Gestapo, not just the Jews.

She alights at the next stop and cuts through the Krasiński Gardens, hoping a brisk walk will calm her nerves. But the gardens are a shock to her. How different everything is now to how it was in the summer. The ducks are gone from the lake and uprooted trees are strewn around as if a giant hand has ripped them from the ground and carelessly tossed them aside. Where the flower beds used to be, the freshly dug soil is evidence of a mass grave. Estimates put the number of Varsovians killed during the siege at twenty-thousand. The once elegant baroque palace now bears the ugly scars of shell damage and fire, its windows shattered, its walls blackened and part of the roof caved in.

It's a terrible sight, but damaged buildings, even Baroque palaces, don't upset her as much as the attack on the old Jew. During the siege her only thought was, 'Please God, make it stop'. They were living in hell, not knowing if they were going to survive from one minute to the next. Now the bombing has stopped but they are living in a new kind of hell, where German military personnel and Gestapo officers inhabit public buildings, roam the streets and treat the citizens like vermin. And the Jews are treated worst of all. Did anyone stop to help the old man after those thugs left him lying in the gutter? Would she have had the nerve to offer him a helping hand, or would she have looked away, fearful of being labelled a Jew-lover? She doesn't want to think about it.

At the restaurant she finds Wanda taking the order from a table of SS officers. Wanda indicates with a flick of her eyes that Anna should wait for her in the kitchen.

'We're short-staffed,' says Wanda, after she's passed the order to the chef. 'Two waiters dead in the bombing.' She scrutinises Anna's face. 'What's wrong? You look terrible.'

In a hushed voice, Anna tells her about the old Jew.

'The bastards,' says Wanda, with a glance towards the restaurant.

'I feel so guilty.'

'You didn't do anything. It wasn't your fault.'

'I should have helped him, even if I couldn't stop the attack. I should have got off the tram and helped him to his feet.'

'Weren't there other people around?'

'Most people just walk away. They're too scared.'

'Can you blame them?'

'Waitress! More wine over here!' A German voice shouts from one of the tables.

'Oh, God, I'll have to go,' says Wanda. 'We're rushed off our feet.'

'I can help,' says Anna.

'You don't have to.'

'No, really. I'd like to.' If she wasn't able to help the Jew, she can at least do something useful for her friend. 'Tell me what to do.'

Wanda kits her out with an apron and, after the briefest of instructions, Anna starts carrying plates of food and glasses of wine and beer to the tables which are almost exclusively occupied by Germans. It takes all her self-control not to throw the beer into their self-satisfied faces.

'*Kaffee!*', '*Wein!*', '*Bier!*' Their barked orders are not difficult to understand.

In fact, as she moves from table to table, delivering food and drink, Anna soon finds herself picking up snippets of conversation. She's always had a gift for languages and her German is quite good. She's just never had a use for it before. During the course of the afternoon, she learns that the Poles expelled from the Western Territories annexed to the Reich are being sent to live in the General Government and the *Volksdeutsche* are being given preferential treatment. The Jews are abused in the vilest language. It's on the tip of her tongue to retort that she knows many well-educated Jews, but she catches herself. They are talking openly because they think she doesn't understand them. What she might do with the information she gleans, she has no idea, but she feels like a spy who has infiltrated an enemy organisation. It gives her a sense of power.

'*Du bist schön!*' The words, spoken softly into her ear as she's leaning over a table collecting empty glasses, make her start before she remembers that she's pretending not to understand them. But she understood that all right. *You are beautiful.* She feigns incomprehension and hurries back to the kitchen with the empties.

Her admirer, a perfect Aryan specimen with blond hair and blue eyes, leans back in his chair, the ankle of one jackboot resting on the opposite knee whilst his two companions continue a conversation about the Führer's plans for Poland. All three of them look too young to have invaded another country – they should be at home studying chemistry or literature. She tries to avoid their table, but she feels Aryan Boy's eyes following her around the restaurant, as if someone has pinned a target practice to her back. In the end she has no choice but to take them the bill.

'*Wo wohnst du?*' he asks. Where do you live?

She gives him a blank stare, shrugs her shoulders and curses him sweetly in Polish. He must think she's paid him a compliment because he winks at her.

'How do you put up with them?' she asks Wanda later when they are sitting upstairs, drinking tea.

'It's hard,' admits Wanda. 'A lot of Dad's Polish customers won't eat here anymore because they don't want to mix with the Germans. He's been accused of collaborating with them, but what is he supposed to do? We have to earn a living.'

'I picked up quite a bit of their conversations, whilst I was serving them,' says Anna. 'I pretended to only understand basic words, but they were talking about Poles in the annexed areas being moved to the General Government. I understood that much at least.'

'That's incredible,' says Wanda. 'You were always so much smarter than me.'

'If only there was something useful I could do with this information.'

Wanda gazes at her tea. 'Well, there might be something you could do…'

'What? Tell me!'

Wanda looks up. 'If you worked here and found things out, there are people who would be interested in what you could tell them.'

'Who?' She's desperate to know more.

'Tomorrow afternoon at four, meet me on the corner of Ulica Świętokrzyska and Nowy Świat. But for now, no more questions.'

Anna promises to be there.

CHAPTER THIRTEEN

'How could a country of thirty-five million people, with an army of one million, have collapsed like a house of cards?' Henryk throws his hands into the air and lets them fall into his lap in a gesture of despair.

Now that he's had a chance to recover from his ordeal, Lech has had many conversations with his uncle, a lawyer by profession, who doesn't mince his words when it comes to assessing what went wrong with Poland's defence.

Henryk tops up their vodka glasses and launches into his favourite topic even though Aunt Magdalena constantly reminds him that dwelling on the Polish defeat does his blood pressure no good. 'The generals were all boasting of a Polish victory, but where are they now? Tell me that!' Henryk doesn't wait for Lech to respond, but answers his own rhetorical question. 'I'll tell you where they are, they're either in German or Soviet captivity, or they've fled over the border to Romania!'

'I hear there are plans to form an army in exile,' says Lech, feeling he ought to defend the organisation from which he fled. No, he tells himself, that's not true. What he fled from was Soviet captivity, like any sensible person. But if there's a chance to sign up and fight on behalf of Poland, he'll be first in the queue.

'We don't need an army in exile,' splutters his uncle. 'We need them here! Twenty years ago we fought off the Bolsheviks. Now look at us. Pathetic!' He tosses the vodka down his throat in a single gulp.

'The Germans had better equipment than us,' says Lech, remembering the planes that swooped over their camp on the first day of the war and the tanks that thundered across the border, flattening everything in their path. It pains him to admit it, but Herr Hitler was better prepared than the Poles gave him credit for, and the Germans had a plan of attack that was like nothing anyone in Poland had ever imagined.

'And where are the British and the French?' asks Henryk, jabbing a finger into the air. 'Is everyone in the rest of Europe sitting on their backsides?'

Lech has no answer to that. Where are their allies, indeed? It feels as if they've been abandoned.

Aunt Magdalena, who teaches piano to children in the neighbourhood, intervenes by asking if they would like to hear some Chopin on the gramophone. It's her way of calming things down when her husband works himself into a lather about the fate of the country. She selects a record from the extensive collection and drops it onto the turntable, setting the stylus in position. After a crackly start, a soothing melody fills the room and Henryk falls silent, knowing when he's beaten. Lech sips his vodka and Halina smiles at him from across the room where she's reading. He smiles back, and it seems to Lech that not everything is wrong with the world.

The next day, Halina shows him the cellar where they lived with their neighbours during the worst of the artillery bombardments and tells him how they had to queue at wells with buckets when the city's water supply was cut off.

'We tore up the pavements to build barricades to stop the tanks,' she says in her unassuming way, as if this is a perfectly normal activity for a twenty-one-year-old primary school teacher. 'I helped dig an anti-tank ditch and Dad helped build a huge barricade leading up to the citadel. But in the end, it did no good. The Germans dropped their bombs from the sky and fired their tanks from the suburbs. And then the Russians came and the Germans handed them Lwów on a plate. I think that was Hitler's and Stalin's plan all along.' She looks at him with her soft, grey eyes. 'I think Warsaw had it worse, though.'

Mention of his home pierces Lech's heart.

She must have noticed his pain because she lays a hand on his arm. 'I'm sorry, I didn't mean to upset you. I know you're worried about your family.'

'I just want to know they're safe,' says Lech.

News of Warsaw's heroic stand and eventual capitulation after a month-long siege has spread across Poland. But so has the news of twenty-thousand dead. At night he lies awake thinking about his parents and siblings. He's written to tell them where he is and that he's safe, but as yet he's had no reply. Are they dead or alive? Has his letter even been delivered? Heaven knows what state the postal service is in at the moment. As soon as he was back on his feet, Lech wanted to return to Warsaw, but his uncle persuaded him otherwise. It's a nightmare obtaining the right paperwork to cross the border at Przemyśl. People who have tried it report that you have to queue up day after day to have any hope of your case being dealt with. Both sides, German and Soviet, have to approve your petition, and there's a real risk he could end up in a German prisoner-of-war camp.

'You're safe here,' said Henryk. 'Crossing the border between the Soviet and German zones is no laughing matter, and Maria would never forgive me if I sent you off across German-occupied territory and you were arrested. My life wouldn't be worth living.'

That had made Lech smile. His uncle might be a big man with a thriving law practice and strong opinions, but he fears his sister more than the Germans or the Soviets.

But he can't stay here forever, living off his uncle's charity. He needs to find work, something that will give him a purpose.

As if she's read his mind, Halina says, 'If you're going to be staying with us for a while, I know some people – good people – who would value your assistance.'

'Doing what?'

'Providing people with new identities.'

'You mean, forging ID cards?'

'I know it's not active fighting,' she says quickly as if she's worried he might refuse, 'but it's important work and…'

'I'll do it,' he says, relieved that there's a reason for him to stay. 'When do I start?'

*

'Won't be long,' calls Anna, although in truth, she has no idea how long she'll be.

She slips out before Maria can ask her where she's going. Keeping her head down, she walks the short distance from the apartment to the corner of Nowy Świat and Świętokrzyska, arriving five minutes ahead of schedule. Not wanting to draw attention to herself by hanging around a street corner, she fills the time by walking down Nowy Świat, nervous and excited about what she is getting involved in.

Few of the elegant art nouveau buildings on Nowy Świat have escaped damage from bombs and shells. The inhabitants and shop owners in this exclusive part of the city have made a start clearing the rubble, but it's going to be a long job. Some buildings are past saving. She sees a former bookshop that is little more than a shell, its upper storeys gone, the ground floor nothing more than a jagged ruin. Amongst the rubble are the tattered and burnt pages of books. The sight would make her father weep.

When she returns to the street corner, Wanda is hurrying

towards her, a scarf tied around her head, hands thrust into her pockets.

'You came,' says Wanda.

'Did you think I wouldn't?'

'If you're not sure about this you should go home now. Once you're involved, there's no going back.'

'Look, I said I wanted to be involved, didn't I? And anyway, you haven't told me anything yet!'

Wanda's face breaks into a conciliatory smile. 'Just checking.' She cocks her head. 'This way.'

They stop outside the ruined bookshop.

'Here?' says Anna, surprised.

'Appearances are deceptive,' says Wanda, pushing opened a blackened door. 'Watch where you're going.'

They grope their way along a dark hallway and down a flight of worn steps into the basement. Despite the devastation up top, the cellar has survived intact. It's the perfect hiding place. No one would ever suspect there was something going on down here, given the state of the building up above.

Wanda announces herself in a loud, clear voice, and a door opens, flooding the bottom steps with the yellow light from a kerosene lamp. Wanda pushes Anna through the door and closes it behind them.

They are in a low-ceilinged space with a small grated window at street level. The furnishings are sparse: a camp bed with a pillow and blanket; a small iron stove and a shelf stacked with assorted pots, plates and mugs. But Anna's attention is transfixed by the contraption in the middle of the floor. Standing about four feet high and five feet wide, the machine has a large wheel on one side and a circular metal plate at the top. Although she has never seen one before, she guesses straightaway that this is an antique printing press. A relic from the last century.

A man in shirtsleeves, his fingers blackened with ink, is operating the press, producing a pile of bulletins. He glances in Anna's direction, wiping his forehead with the back of his hand, but doesn't stop what he is doing. Another man sits in a corner, clacking away on a typewriter.

The man who opened the door is short and stocky, probably in his mid-twenties. He looks Anna up and down then turns to Wanda.

'Who's this?'

'A friend,' says Wanda. 'She wants to help.'

'You should have asked first.'

'I can vouch for her. She'll be useful.'

Anna feels less than welcome. Then the man at the typewriter ambles over and holds out his hand.

'Hello,' he says. 'I'm Wanda's cousin, Kazimierz. And this is Tomasz.' He tilts his head at the man who let them in. 'And that's Adam at the printing press.' Adam holds up a blackened hand but doesn't pause in his work. 'So you want to help with the Resistance?'

'Yes,' says Anna. 'I'll do anything to undermine the Germans.'

'Anything?' asks Kazimierz with a grin. 'Do you know what we do here?'

'Not exactly, but I'm guessing the printing press has something to do with it.'

He nods. 'When the bombs started falling, the first thing we did was move the press from the bookshop into the basement. It was a smart move. As you'll have seen, the bookshop didn't survive the bombing, but this little beauty did. It's from the nineteenth century.'

'What do you print on it?'

'These.' He passes her a folded leaflet about twenty centimetres by fifteen, headed with the words *Information Bulletin*. In closely packed typeface, it reports on the German occupation in the west and the Soviet occupation in the east as well as news about the Polish government which has now fled to France. 'We're part of a larger Underground network of presses printing accurate and up-to-date information on the progress of the war. The German newspapers are full of propaganda and lies. We want people to know the truth.'

Anna knows straightaway that she wants to be a part of this network. Her father has told her many times that conquering armies always use lies and propaganda to oppress people. Now that Poles are forbidden on pain of death from listening to foreign radio stations, they are being starved of accurate information. The flimsy leaflet in her hand feels as valuable as a rare edition of an ancient text.

'I can help,' says Anna. She explains how she listened in to conversations in the restaurant yesterday.

'See, I told you she'd be useful,' says Wanda.

Kazimierz looks impressed, but Tomasz hasn't once smiled.

'What else can I do?' asks Anna.

'You can help distribute the bulletins to shopkeepers and café owners who in their turn will pass them on to their customers.'

'I'll do it.'

'Welcome aboard,' says Kazimierz, giving her a broad grin.

'But just remember,' says Tomasz, 'if the Germans catch you carrying a stack of these bulletins, they will shoot you.'

'I understand.'

Then he adds, 'And if you betray us, *we* will shoot you.'

CHAPTER FOURTEEN

Jan gazes out of the second-floor window at the street below. Housewives with shopping baskets hurry past, heads bowed; a couple of old men stop for a chat and light cigarettes, gesticulating wildly in the habit of those who have little to do and much to complain about; a small crowd is building up at the tram stop, hands in pockets, faces despondent. Then, without warning, an armoured truck turns the corner, half a dozen German soldiers sitting in the back. The people in the street suddenly melt into doorways, courtyards, shops. The tram stop is deserted. Where did everyone go? Anywhere. No one wants to be hanging around when a patrol drives past. The truck slows to a crawl, the Germans scanning the now empty street. He has a clear view... if only he had a gun, now would be the perfect...

'Jan Nowak! Perhaps you would care to conjugate the verb *avoir* in the present tense? Or is there something more interesting outside that you wish to share with the rest of us?'

Jan's attention snaps back to the room. He has no idea what's been going on for the last five minutes. Behind Madame's back, Wiktor grins at him. The other six boys are also enjoying the distraction. They're not the ones in trouble. At least Weronika isn't here to witness his humiliation. She attends classes with a group of girls.

This is so unfair, thinks Jan. Whilst Lech is doing whatever he is doing in Lwów – they finally had a letter explaining that he was staying with Uncle Henryk and Aunt Magdalena and hinting, without giving too much away, that he has important work to do – and even Anna is working for the Underground, distributing newsletters, he, Jan, still has to go to school. He doesn't see the point of learning French verbs. He wants to be doing something useful, something that will help Poland win the fight against the German occupiers. But his mother has other ideas.

Not that secondary schools are actually open. Polish children are not, according to the Germans, required to learn anything other than primary level reading, writing and arithmetic, skills that Jan has already acquired. In the expanded German Reich, the Poles are to be given manual jobs which don't require a knowledge of French verbs or advanced algebra. In response, hundreds of Underground classes have sprung up, seemingly overnight, and teachers now deliver lessons in secret from their own homes or those of their students. Maria wasted no time in ensuring that Jan was signed up for a full curriculum. At first the idea of an Underground school sounded exciting – he imagined learning to fire weapons, communicate in secret codes, and spy on enemy operations. When he discovered that Underground school meant French, maths, literature and all the rest of it, he soon lost interest.

'*Eh, bien?*' prompts the teacher. She's a tall, thin woman in late middle age with a pinched look about her and a very pointed nose. She always holds herself erect like a statue and makes them conjugate verbs in every conceivable tense until they are word perfect. She calls herself Madame Vernier, although Jan doesn't think she's really French. Madame Vernier lives in a small apartment in the Old Mokotów district of Warsaw. They sit in her living room every Tuesday afternoon whilst she delivers clandestine French classes, right under the noses of the Germans. So in her way, she's something of a rebel. He has to give her credit for that.

But she's a strict task master and is not going to let him off the hook. He hears running and shouting in the street below, but he doesn't dare look and see what is happening. Madame Vernier fixes him with her unwavering stare. The clock on the wall ticks like a timebomb. But his mind is a blank. He can't remember a word of French. He hates being singled out like this but supposes it's his own fault for not paying more attention.

The crack of gunfire is so loud that all the boys jump out of their seats and run to the window, crowding around Jan for a better look.

'*Asseyez-vous!*' pleads Madame Vernier. 'Sit down. It is not safe to stand by the window!'

No one listens. Jan watches, transfixed, as a Polish man – probably a member of the Underground – runs down the street and swerves round the corner. Four German soldiers jump down from the back of their truck in hot pursuit. The driver is dead, slumped over the steering wheel. A hail of gunfire explodes as the Germans chase the assassin down the street. They'll probably catch him but at least he got one of them first.

There is nothing more to see, so one by one the boys drift back to their seats. Madame Vernier dabs her eyes with a lace-trimmed handkerchief and holds onto the back of a chair for support.

'Today's lesson is over,' she says in a faltering voice. Jan can't help feeling a little sorry for her, but he is still itching to be off before she remembers that she asked him to conjugate *avoir*. 'Please learn the present and future tenses of *avoir* for a test next week.' The boys are already on their feet. '*Au revoir*,' says Madame Vernier, regaining some of her customary sangfroid.

'*Au revoir*,' chorus the class.

Jan is the first out of the door, running down the stairs.

'Wait for me,' shouts Wiktor.

Jan waits in the courtyard for Wiktor to catch up. He's stockier than Jan and not as fast on his feet. Wiktor's family lives a few doors down from Jan's and they usually travel to classes together on the tram.

Jan peers around the corner of the building. 'Have the Germans come back?' asks Wiktor. He has more reason than most to fear them.

'Not yet.' The truck is still there with the dead driver. The glazed, sightless eyes are turned in their direction, and Jan shivers as they hurry past.

'We'll pay for that,' says Wiktor sagely once they've left the macabre scene behind them.

Jan knows his friend is right. For every German shot, they can expect fifty Poles to be rounded up and executed. It's a chilling statistic and one that Jan would rather not dwell on. He still wants to shoot one of the German bastards himself.

*

Anna leads a double life now. Outwardly, she is just an ordinary waitress, but inwardly she's a member of the Underground resistance movement. She lives these lives simultaneously, the knowledge of her clandestine work sustaining her during the hours in the restaurant when she fantasises about throwing a hot stew into the face of one of the SS officers. Or worse. In her darker moments, the sharp kitchen knives beckon and she wonders what she's really capable of. Sometimes she frightens herself with her imaginings.

Whilst pretending to only understand the simplest German words – *Wurst, Bier, Wein, Kaffee* – she listens intently to the conversations taking place around her, picking up as much intelligence as she can. After a glass or two of wine, even senior officers can be careless with what they let slip. Then in the evening, when she goes to the Underground printing press, she reports what she has heard. Talk of building a wall around the Jewish quarter. German plans to invade Belgium. Kazimierz is always grateful for her contribution and even Tomasz is less distrustful of her.

Today, the impudent young German who said she was beautiful and asked where she lived is back in the restaurant with his two pals. They're tucking into large plates of stew and knocking back the beer, becoming louder and more raucous with every mouthful. So far Anna has managed to navigate a wide berth around their table, letting Wanda or one of the other waitresses take their orders. But she senses his eyes following her around the restaurant. It puts her off her stride and she misses the titbits of conversation she's trying to pick up from a table of senior SS men.

'*Kellnerin!*' She recognises the voice behind her – full of the arrogance of youth – and her scalp prickles with revulsion. She's being summoned. *Waitress!* Wanda is busy at another table and the other two waitresses are in the kitchen. If she ignores him, he'll only continue to shout and cause a scene. Keeping her face blank, she turns around. They already have plenty of food and nearly full glasses. They eat more in one meal than Pani Kowalska and her four children have in a week.

'I know you can understand me,' he says in German. She has overheard the others calling him Kurt. Kurt Schneider.

'Do you want a coffee?' she asks. *Stick to 'waitress-talk'* she tells herself. *Don't give yourself away.*

'I'd rather have you.' The corners of his mouth curl in a knowing smile and he winks at her. His pals laugh and nudge each other.

'*Ein Kaffee?*' She writes the order on her notepad. Suddenly the restaurant feels stifling and overcrowded. She longs to go outside for some air.

He reaches out to touch her hand and she jerks away as if she's been burnt. A flare of anger flickers in his eyes, then is quickly extinguished.

'*Ein Kaffee, bitte,*' he says with exaggerated politeness. A coffee, please.

Anna fetches the order. When she places the coffee on the table, her hands are trembling.

That evening when she goes to Nowy Świat, she's still out of sorts.

Kazimierz notices immediately. He draws her aside. 'What's the matter?' Tomasz and Adam are carrying out maintenance work on the printing press and don't pay her any attention.

'Just one of those days in the restaurant, that's all.' She tries to shrug it off, but when she looks into his face, she sees his eyes are full of concern. He has kind eyes.

He lays a hand on her shoulder and she doesn't flinch the way she did when Kurt Schneider touched her. Instead, Kazimierz's touch is comforting and infuses her with a warm glow.

'Take a moment to calm down before you go out again. You're doing a really great job for us.' He removes his hand and turns away as if embarrassed at his intimacy. Anna feels the loss of his hand like an ache.

He picks up a pile of Information Bulletins, hot off the press with all the latest news which the Germans do not want the Polish people to know. 'Can you fit a few more in your bag today?'

'Sure. I'd best be going.' She can't afford to hang around too long although she'd love to stay here, talking to Kazimierz. But there's the curfew to think of. If she's out after hours, that would be reason enough for a German patrol to arrest her and if they looked inside her bag as well, she'd be locked up without a moment's notice.

She loads her bag – a leather satchel – with the bulletins and lifts the strap over her head.

Kazimierz accompanies her to the foot of the cellar steps. He's so close that she can smell him – a mixture of ink that stains his fingers black and the soap he uses to scrub away the evidence of his illegal work. His hand brushes against hers and she feels her heart thumping in her chest.

She wants to turn to him, for him to take her in his arms. But time is pressing. She must deliver the bulletins before the curfew.

'I have to go,' she whispers.

'Take care,' he says.

'I always do.'

*

'If they think I'm going to sign papers agreeing to become a Soviet citizen, then they can think again!' roars Henryk across the dining table.

Aunt Magdalena has prepared a simple but tasty meal of bread and vegetable soup. She pats her husband's hand.

'Please, Henryk, not at the table.'

Halina catches Lech's eye and grimaces. He smiles back. He has become accustomed to his uncle's outbursts and knows they're just part of his passionate character. He rather enjoys these exchanges. There were never conversations like this in Warsaw.

'Those elections were fraudulent,' exclaims Henryk, ignoring his wife. He tears his bread in half and dunks it in the soup, splashing liquid onto the tablecloth.

Henryk is referring, of course, to the October elections to the assemblies of the new provinces of Western Ukraine and Western Belorussia. These lands were Polish territories until the Soviets marched across the border in the middle of September and decided otherwise. The Germans and Soviets had a friendly chat about who would get what, as if Poland was theirs to carve up as they saw fit. They agreed the Bug River would be the demarcation line, leaving the eastern Borderlands, including Lwów, in Soviet hands. Then the Soviets held what passed for elections in their new territories.

'They decided in advance that the turnout would be over ninety-nine percent,' fumes Henryk. 'That's not democracy. It's a land grab by Stalin – no, I'm sorry Magdalena, we must call it what it is.'

'But what will happen to us if we don't accept Soviet citizenship?' asks his wife in her calm voice. 'There are bound to be repercussions.'

'Not if sufficient people stand firm,' reasons Henryk. 'This is a time for Poles to unite, not be bullied into accepting a new nationality based on a pack of lies and rigged election results. What would that say about us? I wouldn't be able to walk down the street and hold my head up.'

'What about the Ukrainian and Belorussian minorities in this region?' asks Lech. 'Didn't they welcome the arrival of the Soviets?'

'They were misguided,' says Henryk, shaking his head. 'They thought Stalin would grant them independence. But they soon realised their mistake. Stalin doesn't want an independent Ukraine or an independent Belorussia. He just wants to expand the borders of the Soviet Union. They might not have liked Polish rule, but this just goes to show you should be careful what you wish for.'

How ironic, thinks Lech, that he should have escaped from Soviet custody and found his way to Lwów, only to end up stateless in a city that is no longer in Poland but has been subsumed, by fair means or foul, into the Soviet Union. All it would take is a signature, and they would become fully fledged Soviet citizens. But it's not that simple. He never realised before, but his nationality is intimately bound up with his identity. He has never felt more Polish, just when his Polish identity is under threat. Anyway, Henryk has refused to sign and forbidden his wife and daughter from doing so. He can't tell Lech what to do, but Lech respects and admires his uncle and is in total agreement with him on this matter. The Soviets know where they can stick their papers.

'What about the Jews?' asks Halina. 'You can see why many of them prefer to be governed by Communists rather than Nazis.'

Lech has noticed that Henryk always calms down when Halina speaks in her gentle, but persuasive, manner.

'That is true,' says Henryk. 'The horrors of *Kristallnacht* made the Jews fear the Germans, and with good reason. But I fear life will not improve under the Communists for anyone, Jewish or otherwise. The NKVD is no friend to ordinary people.'

Mention of the dreaded NKVD, the Soviet agency responsible for running the Gulags and known for its uncompromising stance towards those it regards as political dissidents, brings the conversation to an ominous end. When the Red Army invaded, the NKVD was hot on its heels, its mission to win the war over minds, a battle it is losing in this household. They finish their meal in silence.

After they have finished eating and cleared away the dishes, Lech and Halina go for a walk, something they've got into the habit of doing most evenings. As they meander through the Old Town, they spot changes everywhere. The Polish eagle is fast disappearing from signs and monuments as the Soviets systematically dismantle symbols of the Polish state. But they'll never win over hearts and minds, thinks Lech, whilst people are queuing up for bread and other essentials. If the Soviets understood how to win people over, they'd make sure their citizens were well fed. No one cares about ideologies, only whether their bellies are full.

'Tell me about your day.' He enjoys hearing Halina talk about her work in the school.

'We spent the morning trying to memorise all six verses of the Internationale,' says Halina. 'Since the Soviets took over, the children have to sing it during morning assemblies.'

'Oh God, I can't get that damn tune out of my head,' says Lech. 'It's blasting out of the loudspeakers all day long'

'Tell me about it.'

'I think we've got the message by now, don't you?' says Lech. 'Stand up, renounce God, and unite with your fellow citizens in a socialist utopia where the earth belongs to men and the sun shines forever. Blah, blah, blah.'

'Stop it,' laughs Halina, slapping him playfully on the arm. 'You'll get us arrested if they hear you making fun of the Internationale.'

'Sorry, I can't help it. It's such a joke, though. And I don't see many people renouncing God. That message clearly hasn't sunk in.'

'I know what you mean. When Mama went to High Mass on Sunday, she said the church was packed and there were people standing outside to listen.'

'There you go then.'

They walk on in silence for a few minutes as the light fades from the sky.

When Halina next speaks, her voice is serious and quiet. 'Lech,' she says, 'I'm worried about this question of Soviet citizenship. If we don't sign, what will happen to us?'

'What *can* happen to us?' Lech wants to reassure her, but he too has his doubts. The future feels fragile right now.

'I don't know. But I have a bad feeling about this.'

CHAPTER FIFTEEN

'Thank you, Professor Nowak.' The two students shake Emeryk's hand as he sees them out of the door. They are always grateful for the Underground classes which he holds in the apartment, much to the consternation of Maria who worries that they will attract attention to themselves.

'It's no different to Jan going to Underground school,' he tells her. 'The students come to me, that's all.'

'Still,' says Maria. 'We must be careful.'

But today his wife is out, hunting for food on the black market. Whether teaching, or studying, or buying food, everyone is operating in secret, against the law. What else can they do? It's the only way to survive.

Emeryk returns to his study and closes the door. Whilst the apartment is quiet – Anna is working in the restaurant and Jan is, he hopes, attending a maths class in Mokotów – he plans to spend an hour or two working on his paper about the historical partitions of Poland. Now that the university has closed, he does all his work from home. And his work has taken on vastly more significance, now that they are living through the fourth partition of their country. History is repeating itself as it always does. But this time he doesn't know how it's going to end.

He sits down at his desk, puts his reading glasses on and pulls a sheaf of papers towards him. A copy of the Information Bulletin becomes dislodged and floats to the floor. He bends down to pick it up and re-reads the disturbing news that reached Warsaw a couple of days ago. One hundred and eighty-three professors from the Jagiellonian University in Kraków have been arrested and many of them sent to a concentration camp, although no one knows where. The news came as a terrible shock. The Jagiellonian University is the oldest university in Poland and boasts the astronomer Nikolaus Copernicus amongst its alumni. He knows many of the professors there. He counts them as his friends.

He puts his head in his hands, remembering the conversation he had with his wife when she saw the Bulletin.

'You should leave Warsaw,' said Maria. 'It's not safe here for someone in your position.'

'But where would I go and what would I do?'

Hiding out in the countryside is not a feasible option. If he was younger and fitter, he'd volunteer for the Underground, but he's an academic, not a fighter. His weapon is the word, not the pistol. Besides, the Gestapo have put his name on a register. He's already within their sights. He just hopes that by keeping his head down and getting on with his work he can avoid any trouble.

He scrunches the bulletin into a ball and tosses it into the waste paper basket. Then he forces himself to concentrate on his work.

*

Maria hands over the ration coupon and the money in return for a tiny portion of beef. But she can see even before the butcher wraps it that it's one third gristle and one third fat. How is she supposed to feed a family of four with that? Her own nutritional requirements are not so great, but Jan is a growing boy and would eat more by the day given half a chance. This will never do.

She puts the meagre ration into her basket and continues on her way down the street. The Germans, in their wisdom, have decided that the Poles require only six hundred calories per day. The Jews have it even worse. They are permitted a mere five hundred calories a day. It's nothing short of a scandal.

'They're killing us by starving us to death,' Maria complained to Pani Woźniak the other day. The old lady agreed with her, then let her into a secret.

Maria looks over her shoulder, ducks down a side street, and knocks on an unmarked wooden door. It opens a fraction, and an eye peers out at her. When the person inside has satisfied themselves that it isn't the Gestapo come knocking, the door is opened wide and Maria steps into the dimly lit interior. This was Pani Woźniak's secret, and Maria is eternally grateful to her.

The owner of the property is an old man in his seventies, a carpenter by trade, but the sort of person who has a lot of connections. Maria isn't entirely sure about the chain of connections, but thinks maybe this man knows a man who knows another man whose brother-in-law is a farmer. Or something like that. Anyway, the details aren't important. What matters is that by this circuitous route, food is smuggled into the city and sold, at a price, on the black market. It's the black market that has been keeping Maria and her family from starvation these past couple of months.

Their exchange is quick and to the point. No need to hang around, it would only put both of them in danger if this transaction came to the attention of the authorities. Maria hands over a pile of the new German-issued złoty banknotes – rampant inflation means they're hardly worth the paper they're printed on – and in return receives a pound of bacon and some sausages. Within less than a minute she's back out in the street, her basket over her arm, the food hidden under a checked tea towel. She walks quickly with her head bowed. She must get her purchases home before she's stopped and has to show her papers. If the Germans looked into her basket, they'd know at once that she has more food than she's permitted under their measly rules.

But on her way home she slips into the church to stand for a minute in front of the statue of the Virgin Mary and to pray for each of her three children, and her husband who has refused to listen to her advice and leave Warsaw. She loves him dearly, but sometimes he's an old fool. She looks up at the statue of the Virgin, woman to woman. 'Men, eh?' she thinks. 'They cause us no end of trouble.'

With her outstretched hands, the Virgin seems to be saying, 'What can we do?'

*

After their maths class, Jan and Wiktor catch a tram, riding together on the back platform. Ever since the French lesson, when the German was shot in the street, Jan has been on the alert for more attacks by the Underground, but so far nothing. His mother has impressed on him that he must come straight home after each class, that he shouldn't dawdle in the street, and so far he's obeyed her, more or less. If he's late, he tells her that the tram was held up, which it often is. Whether she believes him or not is another matter. But the fact is, travelling to Underground classes instead of being cooped up in school has given him a taste for freedom, which is ironic really, he supposes, when you think about it.

They're passing through a square when the brakes suddenly squeal, metal on metal, and the tram comes to an unexpected stop.

'What's happening?' asks Wiktor, looking around. He worries more about being late home than Jan does. The incident during the French class has left him jittery and on edge.

'I can't see,' says Jan, trying to peer around the crowd on the street. He wishes he was taller. The tram must have stopped for a reason. Has the Underground struck again? He's desperate to see what's going on.

'*Alle heraus!*' All out! Spoken in a harsh, guttural tone. Jan has learnt quite a few German phrases by now, all of them orders. And now he can see the familiar peaked caps with the silver skull and crossbones of the SS, the tips of rifles and a row of trucks. If this is a roundup, he should take his chances and run, but Wiktor isn't a fast runner and would slow them both down. Whatever happens, he can't leave his friend.

Terrified, the passengers shuffle off the tram, mothers clutching the hands of small children. Jan lends his arm to an old woman who has trouble stepping off. 'Bless you, dear,' she says to him.

'Stand over there!' More orders. 'Face forwards!'

The passengers line up as instructed, forming a ragged line. They join other passers-by in the square who have been rounded up. The reason soon becomes obvious.

The Germans open the doors of the trucks and lead out a dozen men, their mouths sealed with tape. They are a ragtag bunch, dirty and ill-kempt, as if they've been living in a stable. Blinking in the sunlight, then look around the square, before catching sight of the makeshift audience that has been assembled.

'Hostages,' mutters a man next to Jan. 'The poor sods. They're paying the price for the Underground's activities.'

Prodding the men into line with their rifle butts, the SS make the prisoners stand in front of a wall.

'I can't watch,' says Wiktor.

Jan doesn't want to see this either, but is paralysed by an inability to look away. He feels as if he's outside his own body, watching in a dreamworld. Sound and rational thought are temporarily suspended. He holds his breath.

In the blink of an eye, the square explodes with rifle fire. A cry of despair sweeps through the watching crowd, but Jan has no idea if he was a part of it.

The shot men lie crumpled on the ground.

'I'm going to be sick,' says Wiktor.

'Not here,' says Jan, grabbing his friend by the arm and dragging him to a nearby alleyway.

Jan stands guard whilst Wiktor makes retching noises behind him.

'Better now?' asks Jan when Wiktor reappears. He's ashen-faced and looks terrible. He gives a faint nod.

The crowd has dispersed and people are boarding the tram.

'We'll walk,' says Jan. 'The air will do you good.'

They set off in silence. He's going to be very late back, but Jan will tell his mother that Wiktor wasn't feeling well and he had to look after him.

He won't tell her about the shooting. She doesn't need to hear about that.

CHAPTER SIXTEEN

Anna glances surreptitiously at the clock on the wall as she clears away plates and glasses. Her shift for the day is almost over.

As soon as she's finished in the restaurant, she'll head straight to the basement on Nowy Świat and collect a pile of Information Bulletins for distribution to local shops and a launderette. Her double life is second nature to her now. She's become adept at avoiding detection and goes about her business with confidence. She suspects her Aryan appearance helps. Even Tomasz seems to trust her now, he who was so suspicious of her when she first volunteered. As for Kazimierz – her heart beats faster when she thinks of him – she knows he likes her, and she's attracted to him, but they can't risk a relationship at the moment. They must be patient and put the needs of the Underground before their own. Maybe, when all this is over... she pushes thoughts of romance from her mind and concentrates on clearing the plates.

Kurt and his pals were in the restaurant earlier, making their usual loud-mouthed racket. She put up with Kurt's wandering eyes, lascivious looks and crude chat-up lines, all the while secretly listening in to their private conversation.

She picked up a few titbits which she'll pass on to Kazimierz and Tomasz later. But it was a relief when they paid the bill and left earlier than usual. The presence of some senior-ranking SS officers at a nearby table must have scared them off.

Anna takes the plates to the kitchen and scrapes the leftovers into the bin. The food the Germans waste is a scandal. When she thinks of her mother haggling on the black market to buy enough to feed the family…

'Doing your laundry today?' asks Wanda, coming in with more plates.

'Yes.' It's their codeword for distributing the newsletters. They usually go to the basement separately now. It's safer that way.

'I'll do mine tomorrow,' says Wanda nonchalantly. 'When I've got a bit more time.' She really could be talking about washing her stockings and underwear. Anna doesn't like to discuss their Underground work, even using their secret code. The words stick in her throat and sound false to her ears. You don't know who might be listening, the way she listens to the conversations of the Germans.

She goes out the back way so she doesn't have to walk through the restaurant, past the table of senior SS men who are finishing their coffee. One of them has a driver waiting outside the restaurant – that's how high-ranking he is.

Spring is here and the days are getting warmer, the evenings longer. The few trees that weren't destroyed in the bombing are putting out their first bright green leaves. Anna has always enjoyed this time of year, before the heat of summer makes the city intolerable. She's determined to enjoy it, despite the oppressive presence of the Germans in the city. She walks briskly to Nowy Świat, looking forward to seeing Kazimierz.

Before loading her satchel, she picks up a bulletin and scans it for news. If it wasn't for the Information Bulletin, no one would have any idea about the real progress of the war. She learns that in the east the Soviets have deported

Polish policemen and other officials. This is a worrying development. Where have they been taken? No one knows for sure, but somewhere inhospitable most likely. Her thoughts fly to Lech. How is he getting on in Lwów under Soviet control? She wishes he would come home, but reading between the lines of his cryptic letters, she believes he too has found work in the Underground. Although she suspects his willingness to stay in Lwów might have more to do with his beautiful and intelligent cousin Halina.

'Hot off the press.' Kazimierz hands her a pile of freshly printed bulletins, the ink barely dry. His fingers linger on her hand for longer than it takes to hand over a stack of leaflets and a shiver runs down her spine. She fills her satchel with bulletins, then sets out, a spring in her step. There's still an hour to go before the eight o'clock curfew. Her thoughts are filled with Kazimierz as she walks along the street, the satchel bouncing against her hip.

'*Guten Abend.*' The voice makes her jump. She'd recognise that voice anywhere, she's heard it so often. *Good evening.*

Kurt Schneider has crept up on her without her realising. How could she have been so careless? He falls into step beside her, dressed in full SS uniform, hands thrust in his trouser pockets. What in God's name does he think he's doing? She looks around for his friends, but he's alone. That makes her even more uneasy.

'*Wo gehst du?*' Where are you going? His tone is conversational, but she doesn't think he'll be easily fobbed off.

She frowns at him, pretending not to understand, but she suspects that particular game is up by now. How long has he been following her? Did he see her leave the ruined building in Nowy Świat? She clutches the strap of her satchel, acutely aware of the bulletins she's carrying. But if Kurt and his cronies have discovered the printing press, it's not just the Germans she needs to fear. Tomasz, for one, would blame her for leading the Germans to them. *If you betray us, we will shoot you.* Her heart hammers in her chest, her mouth is as dry as sandpaper.

Kurt continues to walk beside her, too close for comfort. How can she shake him off? If a Polish boy she wasn't interested in hassled her as much as Kurt does, she would tell him to 'get lost', only not so politely. But being rude to a German is tantamount to signing your own arrest warrant. Poles walking past give them a wide berth and look at her askance. They probably suspect her of collaborating with the enemy. *Nazi whore*, she imagines them thinking.

'Let me carry your bag for you,' says Kurt. 'It looks heavy.'

'No! It's not heavy,' she protests, even though the strap is weighing down on her shoulder.

'Ah, so you do understand me. I always thought so.' He leans closer and she smells alcohol on his breath. Most likely he's just lurched out of a bar and hasn't followed her from Nowy Świat. She's furious with herself for revealing her knowledge of German, but she mustn't let Kurt get his hands on the satchel, whatever happens.

'I only speak a little German,' she says, trying for a bad accent.

'You speak it very well.'

She ignores him. If Kurt doesn't go away, she won't have time to deliver the bulletins before the curfew, and then she'll have to take them home with her. She usually takes one home for her parents to read. Afterwards they burn it in the stove. But it won't be easy to dispose of so many and she hates wasting them after other people have risked their lives writing and printing them.

She hesitates at a crossroads, unsure which way to go. She mustn't lead Kurt to her drop off points, or her home address. Maybe she should return to the restaurant. Wanda would grasp the situation immediately and know what to do. Yes, that's the only sensible…

His hand grips her arm before she has a chance to react. He pulls her roughly into a narrow passageway between two buildings. She's so shocked that she barely notices when he rips the satchel over her head and tosses it to the ground. Then he's pressing her up against the wall, his hand over her mouth, his beery breath in her face. She struggles to free herself, but he's taller than her and strong as an ox. With his spare hand he squeezes her buttock then fondles her breast.

'Don't play hard to get,' he whispers in her ear. 'I know you like me really.'

He pushes her skirt up, his hand between her thighs. He's panting like a pig now, his wet lips smothering her face. She feels disgust and agonising fear and thinks she's going to vomit right into his ugly face.

The crack of a pistol shot pierces the air.

Kurt staggers backwards and collapses on the ground, crying out in pain and clutching his leg as blood oozes between his fingers. Suddenly she can breathe again, and she gulps down air, her heart beating so hard she thinks her ribcage will explode.

She looks towards her rescuer and, with a shock, recognises one of the senior SS officers who was in the restaurant earlier today. The one who had a driver waiting outside. She served his table. Does he recognise her? He's standing there in his black uniform, holding a pistol in his right hand. A black limousine is parked on the main road, its engine purring gently. He calmly returns his pistol to its holster and addresses Kurt.

'Stop making such a fuss, man. It's only a flesh wound. You'd receive far worse on the battlefield. Stand up.'

Obviously too frightened to ignore this order from his superior officer, Kurt staggers to his feet. His right leg is a bloody mess and he seems unable to put any weight on it. He leans against the wall for support.

'Get in the car,' the officer tells Kurt. 'We'll take you to the hospital.'

Not looking at Anna, Kurt limps away in disgrace.

Now Anna is left alone with this man who has come to her rescue. She should be grateful, but she's afraid of him.

He's the enemy. He might have dealt with Kurt, but she has no idea what he intends to do with her. Does he suspect her of seducing one of his men? Surely he can see from her clothes that she's just an ordinary Polish woman, not a prostitute.

'Is that your bag?' he asks, pointing at the satchel on the ground. Before she has a chance to reply, he steps forwards and picks it up.

It's all over, thinks Anna. He's going to look inside and then arrest me.

He holds the satchel by the strap for a moment, as if surprised by its weight. The moment seems to last forever. Then he hands it back to her.

'Go home,' he says. 'It's nearly curfew.'

'*Danke*,' whispers Anna as she scurries away, clutching the satchel to her chest.

PART FOUR
EXTRAORDINARY OPERATION OF
PACIFICATION
MAY – JUNE 1940

CHAPTER SEVENTEEN

'Open up! Gestapo!'

The hammering on the door startles Anna awake. She's instantly alert, her heart pounding in her chest.

It's still dark outside. But then the Gestapo always come in the early hours of the morning, catching people unawares, when they're too disoriented to resist. She's been waiting for something like this.

Ever since the attack in the alleyway – she still has nightmares about Kurt Schneider, his hands pawing at her body, his stinking breath on her face – she has been living on edge. It's true that Kurt doesn't come to the restaurant any more – small mercies – but the man who rescued her – Gruppenführer Müller she's learnt he's called – is often there with other high-ranking SS men. He's never once referred to the incident in the alleyway, but she's never forgotten the way he held her satchel, stuffed as it was with copies of the Information Bulletin. She's become convinced that he suspects her of involvement in the Underground and is simply biding his time, waiting for the right moment to make his move. But why now? Has someone betrayed her? Or has Kurt discovered where she lives and is exacting revenge for the injury he suffered at the hands of

Gruppenführer Müller? Fear paralyses her and she clutches the bedclothes.

More hammering on the door as if they're trying to break it down. Impossible to ignore. She hears her parents' door opening and the tread of her father's step in the hallway. She imagines her mother watching in terror. She can't let them face this alone. She throws back the bedclothes, pulls on a dressing gown and steps into the hallway.

As soon as her father opens the door, six plainclothes Gestapo agents accompanied by a pair of jackbooted Wehrmacht soldiers barge into the apartment.

'I have a warrant for the arrest of Professor Emeryk Nowak,' says the man in charge. 'Are you Emeryk Nowak?'

'I am.'

'Arrest him!' The Gestapo officer gives the order to the Wehrmacht soldiers who grab Emeryk by the arms.

Maria cries out and Anna puts her arms around her mother's shaking shoulders. Jan runs out of his room, barefoot, and joins them.

Anna is stunned. How can the Gestapo have come for her father? Her kind, studious father who never hurt a fly. She should be the one under arrest, not her father who's never done anything subversive, other than continue to meet once a week with his students, and where's the harm in that? But of course university study is illegal now, like the Underground school that Jan attends. When her father refused to leave Warsaw, she admired his quiet courage, but now he looks stricken, as if his refusal to leave has brought this calamity down upon their heads.

'I'm sorry,' Emeryk mouths to his wife. 'I should have listened to you.'

Maria shakes her head defiantly. 'No, this is not your fault.'

'Enough!' shouts the Gestapo officer in charge. 'Search the apartment!'

Anna, Maria and Jan can only stand by helplessly as the Germans ransack the bookcases and rummage through the kitchen cupboards. The photograph of the family taken on the day that Lech was called up is still propped in front of the clock on the mantelpiece. When one of the Gestapo men picks it up and examines it, Anna has an overwhelming urge to snatch it from his hands. That photograph is precious, a reminder of the last time the family was all together. She wishes now she'd hidden it somewhere safe, out of sight. The Gestapo man turns the photograph over, as if expecting to find something written on the back, but there's nothing. He puts it back carelessly, and it slides off the mantelpiece and lands face down on the floor. When no one is looking, Anna picks it up and tucks it into her pocket for safekeeping.

The Germans move on to her father's study. This is where they will find incriminating evidence, if anywhere. The last time she was in there, his paper about the previous partitions of Poland was lying on his desk. He works on it when he's not teaching. If any of these men can read Polish, they will soon understand his political opposition to the current situation. Her father uses words as a weapon in the way these men use violence. But the men merely gather Emeryk's papers together in a box to be taken away.

The agent in charge barks at Emeryk to get dressed. '*Schnell!*' Quickly!

As her husband stumbles towards the bedroom, Maria follows him.

'Not you!' shouts the agent. 'Stay here!'

Maria collapses helplessly onto a chair, the fight gone out of her.

When Emeryk emerges from the bedroom five minutes later, he's wearing his old suit with a shirt and tie as if he's about to deliver a lecture at the university. Anna almost weeps with pity for her dear, kind father, who looks bewildered by everything that has just happened, as if he can't believe it isn't all a bad dream.

She wants to hug him, but the soldiers have him by the arms. They march him out of the apartment just as the first rays of daylight are lightening the sky to a dull grey. Their heavy boots echo in the stairwell. Behind closed doors, their neighbours will have been listening in silent dread. By now, they will be breathing a sigh of relief that the Gestapo didn't come for them. Not this time.

*

For days there is no news about Emeryk. His absence leaves a hole at the heart of the family. Anna has put the photograph back in front of the clock, but now it's even more painful to look at it. Now two of them are missing.

She detects pity in the faces of her neighbours when she meets them on the stairs or in the street, but there's distrust there as well. Pani Woźniak pretends to be too busy to stop and chat. Anna can only guess what the old woman is thinking. *Why was Pan Nowak arrested? Is the whole apartment block now under suspicion? Maybe I should keep my distance from that family, just to be on the safe side.*

Desperate for information, Maria talks to other wives of university professors and lecturers and learns that Emeryk is far from the only one to have been targeted. And it's not just academics. A whole swathe of Warsaw's elite – writers, priests, political leaders – has been rounded up in night-time raids.

Anna remembers reading about the professors from the Jagiellonian University in Kraków who were arrested and sent to a concentration camp. She has never forgotten that particular edition of the Information Bulletin. A concentration camp would kill her father. He's never done a day's physical labour in his life, apart from when he helped bury bodies in the park during the siege, and that nearly finished him off. He came home every evening not just physically exhausted, but as if a part of his soul had died.

Anna eventually plucks up the courage to confide in Kazimierz and Tomasz when she's next picking up bulletins for delivery.

'They take them first to Szucha Avenue,' says Tomasz. 'Gestapo Headquarters. Then they transfer prisoners to the Pawiak.'

Szucha Avenue has become synonymous with rumours of brutal interrogation techniques. As for the nineteenth-century Pawiak Prison, its impenetrable, fortress-like walls only hint at the horrors within.

She must look stricken because Kazimierz puts his arm around her. 'We have contacts,' he says. 'We'll ask around.'

The next day, Gruppenführer Müller is dining alone in the restaurant, tucking into a bean stew. Müller is not like the other SS men, Anna has decided. For one thing, he is always polite and remembers to say 'please' and 'thank you' as if he's been brought up to appreciate the importance of good manners. And he never wastes food. If it wasn't for his SS uniform, he could be a respectable gentleman, a doctor perhaps, or a lawyer, even a professor. She imagines him teaching a subject like jurisprudence or medicine. She has wondered, from time to time, if he has a family at home in Germany, a daughter maybe, and if that's why he was so angry with Kurt for assaulting her. Is it possible that he is a decent German? An idea starts to formulate itself in her mind.

When she brings his coffee, he thanks her. '*Danke, Fräulein.*' *Thank you, Miss.*

'*Bitte,*' says Anna. *You're welcome.* It's the ordinariness of this exchange that gives her the courage to speak. 'Herr Gruppenführer?'

'*Ja?*' If he's surprised at her addressing him, he doesn't show it.

'My father has been arrested by the Gestapo. But he hasn't done anything wrong.' The heat rises to her face. She has just been totally reckless. But hasn't Müller shown himself to be a man of principles, someone who is prepared to right a wrong?

Gruppenführer Müller's face remains impassive. 'What does your father do?'

'He's a professor of history at the university.'

'What is his name?'

'Professor Emeryk Nowak.'

'I will make enquiries for you,' says Gruppenführer Müller. He picks up his coffee and dismisses her with a nod.

'What was that about?' asks Wanda when Anna returns to the kitchen.

'I asked him about Father.'

'You did *what?*' Wanda looks incredulous, but also impressed. Then she adds in a lower voice, 'You can't trust them, you know, even if they look decent.'

But Anna can't stand back and do nothing whilst her father languishes in prison.

A week later Gruppenführer Müller is back in the restaurant. She's looked out for him every day and has so far been disappointed. But now, she hopes, he'll have news for her.

'Guten Tag, Herr Gruppenführer,' she says as she prepares to take his order. Surely, he can sense her nervousness, the way the pencil trembles in her hand. But he orders steak and a glass of beer without once acknowledging their former exchange. Once he has placed his order, he opens his newspaper and settles back to read.

Only when she brings him his coffee at the end of the meal does he lay aside the paper and look at her properly.

'I have examined the matter of your father's arrest,' he says.

Anna nods at him, her mouth suddenly so dry that she can't find her tongue.

'The arrest was carried out in accordance with Nazi policy.'

In accordance with Nazi policy? Doesn't he understand, she's not questioning whether the procedures were followed, but the fact of the arrest in the first place. But before she can think of a suitable reply, Müller continues.

'However, in this case we might make an exception.'

'Really?' Relief floods through her. She was right to trust

this man.

'In return for information.'

Hope starts to drain from her when she realises that this man's help does not come without a price. 'What sort of information?'

'Useful information.'

'I don't understand.' But she thinks she does.

Gruppenführer Müller fixes her with a stare and suddenly she sees him for what he is. He isn't kind. Or to be trusted. He follows the rules laid down by his Party and he carries them out ruthlessly. Kurt Schneider broke the rules and paid the price. And now she has put herself in this man's hands.

'Information about the Polish Underground. Resistance cells. Planned attacks.' He pauses briefly before casually adding, 'Printing presses. That sort of thing.'

At the mention of 'printing presses' Anna's heart thuds so hard she wonders that Gruppenführer Müller can't hear it. What does he already know or suspect? When he picked up her satchel in the alleyway and handed it back to her, did he guess what was inside? She hears Tomasz's voice in her head. *If you betray us, we will shoot you.* The Underground is far larger than just Kazimierz and Tomasz. It's a vast network of Polish people. She's just a tiny cog in a vast, complex machine which she barely understands. But she does understand that a small cog can cause a large machine to fail. She could be putting hundreds of lives at risk.

'I don't know anything about the Underground,' she says. 'I'm just a waitress.'

'Think it over.' Then he asks for the bill.

CHAPTER EIGHTEEN

It's an impossible situation. Anna would do anything to save her father, but she can't betray her friends in the Underground. There is too much at stake, too many people involved. She lies awake at night, unable to sleep. There's no one she can confide in. If Maria thought there was a way to save her husband, wouldn't she want Anna to take it? And she can't speak to Kazimierz or Tomasz because they would say that she's already endangered them by speaking to Gruppenführer Müller in the first place. She tosses and turns at night, only falling into a troubled sleep in the early hours of the morning.

May turns to June and still there is no news. Gruppenführer Müller doesn't appear in the restaurant and Anna alternates between relief that she hasn't had to betray the Underground and anxiety about her father.

Then one day in the middle of June the restaurant is thronged with jubilant Germans, raising glasses of beer. Anna and the other waitresses are rushed off their feet. The reason for the party atmosphere makes the Poles want to weep bitter tears of disappointment. Paris has fallen.

In a brief moment of respite between serving glasses of beer, Anna and Wanda study the German newspaper in the kitchen.

'It breaks my heart,' says Wanda as they look at a picture of Hitler posing on a bridge across the Seine, the Eiffel Tower standing tall in the background. The Führer has been on quite the tourist trail. The inside pages are full of images of the German leader in front of the Arc de Triomphe, at the Opéra, visiting the Louvre, gloating at Napoleon's tomb. Helmeted and jackbooted Wehrmacht soldiers march four abreast down the Champs Élysées, bayonetted rifles pointing skywards on their shoulders. It's a far cry from the day Britain and France declared war on Germany. Then, the Poles had tossed flowers into the air in celebration, full of hope and expectation. They had sung the British National Anthem and the Marseillaise. But that hope has turned to ash and been scattered on the wind. One of their allies has fallen. The Germans are confidently predicting that Britain will be next.

Anna turns the page and there's a picture of Marshal Pétain, the hero of Verdun, who has collaborated with the Germans and set up a new French government in Vichy.

'At least no one in Poland has sunk that low,' says Wanda, jabbing the picture of the French Marshal with her fingernail. Anna shrinks inside herself and says nothing. Is Pétain a traitor or a pragmatist? How often has she lain awake at night, torn between a desire to help her father and revulsion at the thought of betraying the Underground? Sometimes there are no easy answers.

That evening when she makes her way to Nowy Świat, a fug of gloom seems to hang over the city, despite the sunny weather. She expects to find Kazimierz and Tomasz in a similar mood, and is surprised when they greet her with smiles on their faces.

'Read this,' says Kazimierz, thrusting a copy of the latest bulletin into her hands. 'It will cheer you up.'

Anna scans the flimsy pages quickly, eager for some good news. According to a Polish-language broadcast on the BBC, the Polish government-in-exile has escaped from

France and moved to London. What's more, brave Polish soldiers have managed to join the exiled government in England and Polish pilots are flying British Hurricanes under RAF command.

'You see?' says Kazimierz, when she has finished reading. 'We mustn't give up hope. Not when we have allies still standing.'

Anna so much wants to believe him, but it's hard.

*

'Alle heraus!' Everyone out! The command echoes around the walls of the prison, accompanied by the customary stomping of boots and slamming of doors.

Emeryk rouses himself with difficulty from the plank which has been his bed for the last thirty days or more. The ache in his muscles is worse than ever. There are ten men crammed into the damp, dark cell. He hears their sighs and groans as they stir themselves. They look at each other with a mixture of fear and resignation. Emeryk can read their minds. What now? Why the sudden urgency? They've been languishing here for so long, and now they're being ordered outside as if the survival of the Reich depends on them getting their skates on. Emeryk, who was never disobedient even as a child, feels a perverse urge to dawdle. Who do these Germans think they are? He's always loathed bullies, but they're the ones with the guns.

The cell door swings open and crashes into the wall. The men, who've established a bond of friendship through shared adversity, stagger to their feet. A priest, the oldest amongst them, has trouble getting up off the floor so a writer, a young man in his thirties, puts out a hand to help him up. You can always show kindness.

'Outside!' barks the German standing in the doorway, but not before his nose has wrinkled in disgust.

He might well look disgusted, thinks Emeryk. The stink in the cell must be unbearable. He's still wearing the suit he was arrested in and none of them have had a proper wash for a month. If Maria could see him now, she'd be appalled. The waste bucket in the corner is almost full to the brim.

They file out of the cell and join the large group of prisoners in the courtyard, blinking in the bright June sun. There must be about three hundred of them all told. Emeryk scans the sea of sunken, unshaven faces, looking for anyone he recognises. Isn't that hollow-eyed fellow over there a professor of Polish literature who used to lecture to a packed lecture theatre? You'd hardly recognise him now. And if he's not mistaken, that stooped man with the limp is a mathematics professor. And, wait, isn't that man with the swollen black eye the Speaker of Parliament? Well-educated men, all of them. Good people, as far as Emeryk knows. What has become of them?

During his time in the Pawiak he's been subjected to interrogations relating to his work. But it was clear from the start that his interrogators had no interest in Poland's history, his area of expertise. They accused him of fomenting insurrection, an absurd charge in his eyes. It was only in whispered conversations at night with his cellmates that they concluded the Germans had arrested anyone with any level of education and intelligence who might be in a position to influence other people.

'They're wiping out the intelligentsia,' said the priest. 'They want to reduce the Poles to a nation of slave labourers.'

Intelligentsia. Such a pompous word. Emeryk would never have had the hubris to call himself a member of the *intelligentsia*, with its implication of creative greatness. The word suggests writers, thinkers, philosophers, composers. He's not in their lofty ranks. He's merely an academic, teaching students and writing occasional papers. But has he been naïve? The Germans certainly seem to regard him as a threat.

The men are ordered to line up. It seems their personal belongings are being returned to them. When it's Emeryk's turn, a bundle is thrust unceremoniously into his hands with a piece of hard, black bread. A good sign, surely? He overhears others saying they're being sent to a camp, otherwise why bother returning their stuff? It's certainly the logical explanation, but Emeryk no longer trusts German logic.

He stays close to the men he's come to regard as friends as they're herded towards a line of canvas-covered trucks. He's jabbed in the back with a rifle butt, even though he's made no attempt to step out of line. What would they do if he did? Shoot him dead on the spot, most likely. He stumbles forwards, bumping into the man in front. 'Sorry,' he mumbles, as he climbs into the truck to take his place in the cramped space. Such a large number of rifle-toting soldiers. Practically one for every prisoner. Escape from the trucks is clearly out of the question.

The convoy sets off in a choking cloud of exhaust fumes. The canvas sides flap in the breeze and Emeryk snatches glimpses of the city through the gaps. They appear to be heading north.

The most likely explanation is that they're being taken to a work camp. Dear God, thinks Emeryk, what use would I be in a work camp? He's never swung an axe in his life and he doesn't have a clue how to build anything. He's not a practical man. None of them are, he suspects. They're all teachers and professors and politicians and priests, not manual labourers. And with one or two exceptions they're mostly middle-aged or older, not young and strong.

Before long, the sounds of the city subside and they're out in the countryside. The air is fresher, despite the fumes belching from the exhausts. Snatches of birdsong reach them over the rumble of the engines.

The Kampinos Forest. He and Maria used to bring the children here when they were younger. Maria would pack a picnic and they would tramp through the forest, picking up pine cones and seeing who could spot the most squirrels or woodpigeons. Lech liked to climb the trees, much to Maria's anxiety; Anna would draw in her sketchbook; and Jan would chatter non-stop. His dear children! How his heart aches for them now. He fears that as they grew older, they grew apart from him. He should have been a better father, should have spent less time in his study and more time playing board games and football. If he survives the concentration camp, he vows to spend more time with his family.

They turn a corner and he glimpses a cluster of village houses, their windows shuttered. Against the glare of the sun? Or against things the Germans don't want the inhabitants to see? He tries to remember the name of the village. It's Palmiry, isn't it? Yes, that's it. Palmiry.

The trucks turn off the road and bump along uneven ground. The quality of the light changes as they head into the shade of the forest. They come to a stop and the guards order the men out of the trucks.

They're in a clearing in the forest. As he clambers down from the truck, he looks up and sees a skylark fluttering overhead. After a month confined in a prison cell, it's a wondrous sight to behold as it swoops and soars. But he only has a couple of seconds to enjoy it before rough hands grab him from behind and secure a black cloth over his face, completely covering his eyes, nose and mouth, obscuring his vision and making it difficult to breathe.

He struggles against the unexpected constraint and receives a sharp kick in the shin.

'Stand still!' shouts a German voice in his ear. All the prisoners, it seems, are being blindfolded. Now Emeryk feels real fear, flooding his gut and turning his legs to jelly. He knows where this is leading. There is no labour camp. Returning their possessions to them was just a ploy to get them to cooperate without a fuss. The Germans don't want the likes of him and his fellow prisoners chopping logs for them. His thoughts fly to Maria and the children. *Forgive me. We should have left Warsaw when there was still a chance.*

His captor holds him firmly by the upper arm. Although he can't see them, he imagines all the other prisoners being held in a similar fashion. No wonder they needed so many soldiers for this operation.

'Walk!' bellows the German holding him and he hears the same command being shouted down the line. Stumbling, he allows himself to be led by the arm. His hearing, which has suddenly become extra-sensitive, picks up every little sound. The snap of twigs underfoot. The crunch of dry leaves. The song of the skylark overhead.

He has an overwhelming urge to break free and run. But he wouldn't get very far. They'd shoot him on the spot. Besides, he's too unfit. A lifetime reading and writing hasn't done him much good in that respect. The column of men starts to slow. He senses they are nearing their destination. They're a long way from the road, a long way from the village houses with their shuttered windows. A long way from help of any kind.

'Stop here!'

His captor abruptly turns Emeryk ninety degrees and orders him not to move. In his mind's eye he sees the wretched truckload of prisoners strung out in a row. This is it then. He never thought his life would end like this. He feels a sudden surge of love for his country and for his fellow prisoners. Through the suffocating cloth tied around his face he takes a deep breath and stands a couple of inches taller. He's proud to be Polish.

Everything happens very quickly.

The tramp of boots. The click of safety catches being released. The order to fire.

Then darkness and silence.

*

Anna senses the tension as soon she enters the basement. The printing press is standing still. Kazimierz and Tomasz have their heads bowed over a piece of paper. When they look up, she sees pity in their eyes.

Kazimierz walks towards her. 'Come and sit down.'

'What is it?'

'We have news.'

'For God's sake, just tell me.' There is only one piece of news she has been waiting for. She drops her satchel to the floor but refuses the offer of a chair.

Tomasz holds up the piece of paper. 'This is a copy of a secret list which was smuggled out of the Pawiak Prison by a Polish female guard called Janina Gruskowa.'

The name means nothing to her but Janina has done something very brave by smuggling a list out of the Pawiak.

'Show me.' She reaches out her hand and Tomasz gives her the list without a word.

Kazimierz's voice comes to her as though through a long tunnel. 'It's a list of the names of Polish political prisoners who were executed in Palmiry on the twentieth and twenty-first of June. I'm sorry.'

Political prisoners. Executed. The words echo in her head until she can't hear anything else. Frantically she scans the alphabetical list of names until she comes to 'Nowak, Emeryk 20.1.88.'

She's only vaguely aware of Kazimierz guiding her to a chair and sitting her down, his hand on her shoulder.

The list shakes in her hands. There are hundreds of names on the list – three hundred and fifty-eight in total, but she only has eyes for one. The name she shares. That of her dear father, born the twentieth of January 1888. On a list of those executed in the forest.

The list falls from her hand and she's on her feet, tears streaming down her face. Kazimierz encircles her in his strong arms as she sobs against his chest, feeling as if the foundation of her world has been ripped from beneath her.

She imagines the scene of the mass shooting, and her entire body convulses with revulsion. Where is her father now? Thrown into a pit with all the other unfortunate victims. She feels a burning rage within her.

'Drink this.' Tomasz hands her a large glass of vodka. She drinks it in one gulp.

As the spirit infuses her veins, she feels a quiet resolve take root deep inside her. This atrocity at Palmiry will not go unpunished. She will avenge her father's death.

PART FIVE
DEPORTATION AND REVENGE
JULY 1940

CHAPTER NINETEEN

Hammering on the door in the middle of the night. Lech wakes instantly and blinks in the darkness. What time is it? They still have to abide by the rules of the blackout so the small room is pitch black, hot and airless. He fumbles for the bedside light, knocking over a glass of water. The sudden light blinds him and it's a moment or two before he can see the hands on his watch. Three o'clock in the morning. No one calls at that hour, except...

More hammering and then a voice shouts in Russian, 'Open up!'

... except the People's Commissariat for Internal Affairs. The NKVD. In other words, the secret police. Except their visits are anything but 'secret'. They make enough noise to wake the dead, never mind the whole apartment block.

He pushes back the bedclothes and stumbles into a pair of trousers and yesterday's shirt. He was sleeping in his underpants because of the heat. He recalls the morning in Warsaw ten months ago when he was called up. Anna had to wake him because he was dead to the world, sleeping off the night before. He hopes he's learned to be more responsible since then. He would hate Halina to find him in that state.

Only the previous evening the four of them had enjoyed a simple meal of bread and soup and cheese, and then his aunt had played the piano for them – some Chopin nocturnes – and just for an hour or two Lech had been able to forget about the war, about the fact that he was separated from the rest of his family, and that he was living under Soviet occupation. He went to bed feeling more contented than he had in a long time, and that was why he was sleeping so soundly when the knock came.

Of course, they've heard the stories. Who hasn't? Night-time raids; people disappearing, no one knows where. Apartments lying empty, their owners never coming back. Senior policemen, university professors, anyone the NKVD judges to be an enemy of the people. Lech knows that his resistance work puts him in danger, but he's never been more careful about anything in his life. They'll find no evidence of his forgery here in the apartment. He does his work elsewhere and never brings it home with him. He wouldn't put his relatives at risk, even though his uncle approves heartily of his work for the Underground.

When Lech emerges from his room, his uncle is already stomping to the front door, muttering to himself as he pulls on a dressing gown. Halina has her arm around her mother who looks terrified. Lech joins them, but feels awkward. A cuckoo in the nest. Have the NKVD somehow discovered his escape from the convoy of prisoners last year? He'll never forgive himself if his aunt and uncle are arrested for harbouring a deserter.

Henryk opens the door and is shoved out of the way as a gang of armed officers swarm into the apartment. Lech counts them quickly. Ten. Why so many? They brandish their weapons as if they're expecting the family to be lying in armed wait behind the sofa. If only he hadn't been forced to hand over his revolver when the Polish soldiers were taken into custody. His trigger finger twitches in frustration. How he'd love to take a pot shot at these villains and hang the consequences.

Henryk shrinks in size next to these gun-toting maniacs and moves to stand beside his wife and daughter.

A stout, red-faced man with a bulbous nose, who looks as if he's spent too much time in the company of a vodka bottle, steps forward.

'Henryk Jablonski?' He squints at a piece of paper.

'Yes,' says Henryk. 'What do you want?'

The Russian waves the paper in front of Henryk's face, not giving him a chance to read it. 'I have a search warrant for these premises.'

'On what grounds?'

Lech is pleased that his uncle is not cowed by this jumped-up toady of the Soviet state.

But the officer has already stuffed the paper back into his breast pocket and ignores the question. Instead, he orders his men to begin their search. They fan out through the apartment, kicking open doors, rummaging in drawers and cupboards, not caring about the mess or if anything gets broken. In fact, they seem to be deliberately going out of their way to cause havoc. A porcelain vase topples and crashes to the floor, smashing into a thousand pieces. Aunt Magdalena looks close to tears. When one of the brutes opens the piano lid and then lets it bang shut with a crash, she cries out and buries her face in her hands.

'Be careful with that, you great oaf,' hisses Lech.

The Soviet looks at him with incomprehension and gives a smirk. His Polish is clearly not up to much.

Halina lays a restraining hand on Lech's arm. 'Don't provoke them.'

'Sorry,' mumbles Lech. 'It's just so infuriating to see them rampage through your home. What are they looking for?'

'They're just trying to intimidate us,' says Henryk. 'Ignore them.'

That's easier said than done, though.

Half an hour later, when the apartment has been turned

upside down, the men return to the hallway, weapons in hand. They form a protective barrier around the family in case any of them have thoughts of escape. The officer in charge steps forward and points at Henryk.

'You, come with us!'

'What for?'

'To answer some questions.' He makes it sound as if it's no big deal. But it is. It's an interrogation, thinks Lech. Then suddenly the man swivels on the balls of his feet and points at Lech. 'And you too!'

'I'm coming with my husband,' says Aunt Magdalena unexpectedly.

'No, dear,' says Henryk, 'I don't think that's a good…'

His wife cuts him off. Lech has never seen her so determined. 'We stay together.'

'Yes,' says Halina. 'That's what families do.'

Lech wants to protest. Halina at least should stay here. It's crazy for them all to be taken for interrogation. But one look at his cousin's face silences him. And deep down, he's glad they're staying together. He doesn't want to be separated from those he loves ever again.

'We have to get dressed,' says Magdalena.

'Two minutes,' says the officer.

Lech puts on a clean shirt, socks and shoes. Then, on impulse, he stuffs some essentials into a canvas bag – underwear, three pairs of socks, a couple of spare shirts, a comb, his wallet. Who knows when, or if, they'll be back?

'Hurry up!' barks the officer in charge.

When Lech reappears in the hallway, the others have obviously had the same thoughts as him because everyone is clutching a bag or small suitcase. Aunt Magdalena has thought to bring the remains of the bread and a few apples from the kitchen. Then, surrounded by the armed escort, the family is marched out of the apartment and down the stairs. Waiting cars drive them off at high speed.

Fifteen minutes later, Lech is sitting opposite another officer behind a wooden desk. He stares fixedly at the five-pointed star on the maroon band of the officer's blue peaked cap. A symbol of oppression. A portrait of Stalin gloats at him from the wall. The officer consults his notes.

'Lech Nowak?'

'Yes.'

'You are Polish?'

'Yes.' *And proud of it,* thinks Lech. He sits a little straighter, taking a lesson from his uncle's book.

'Where were you born?'

'In Warsaw.'

'Why are you in Lwów?'

Because I managed to escape from you lot eight months back, he thinks. *Otherwise I'd be somewhere deep in the heart of darkest Russia.* Instead he says, 'Henryk Jablonski is my uncle. I work with him.' It's not a lie. Officially he carries out administrative tasks in his uncle's law firm. It provides a cover for his real work, producing false identity papers for people who want to disappear. And then, of course, there's Halina. How much does she have to do with his reasons for staying?

'What work do you do?'

'I'm training to be a lawyer.' The lie comes easily enough and has the ring of plausibility.

'Lwów is now in the Soviet Union, you understand?'

As if a city can be plucked out of one country and deposited in another. *It's nonsense,* thinks Lech. The Germans and Soviets have redrawn the borders of Poland between them but you don't have to be a lawyer to understand that there's no validity in international law for their actions. Nationality isn't about lines drawn on a map. It's something you feel deep inside you. He's not sure he understood that before, but he's learnt a lot in the past few months.

'Lwów is a Polish city,' counters Lech. He's treading on thin ice, but he can't seem to help himself.

The officer slams the palm of his hand down on the table, making Lech jump. 'How can it be Polish when Poland no longer exists?'

But I exist, thinks Lech. *I and millions like me. I'm just as Polish as I've always been.* More so, in fact. All his life he's taken his nationality for granted. Now it's being denied him, he feels the urge to shout his Polishness from the rooftops.

'You did not accept Soviet citizenship when it was offered to you,' says the officer, shaking his head. 'That was a big mistake.'

He bellows for back-up and two of the ruffians who searched the apartment appear. They escort Lech out to a waiting van where Henryk, Magdalena and Halina are already huddled in one corner. The van soon fills with other bewildered-looking prisoners, the doors slam shut and they drive away.

CHAPTER TWENTY

'Heil Hitler!' Kurt Schneider clicks his heels together with exaggerated emphasis and shoots his right arm out at a forty-five-degree angle as if it were spring-loaded at the shoulder. As a teenager he spent many hours in his bedroom perfecting the manoeuvre in front of a mirror until he could perform it better than Hitler's closest circle. Not that Müller pays any attention. The Gruppenführer hands him a stack of records to process without so much as looking him in the eye.

'Get that lot done by the end of the day.'

Jawohl mein Herr!' More heel clicking and thrusting out his chest like a rooster trying to attract a mate. Müller dismisses him with a brief nod. Kurt returns to his desk, doing his best to hide the limp from his superior officer. He doesn't want to give Müller the satisfaction.

As soon as he's alone, he puts his head in his hands and groans inwardly to himself. Paperwork. Always so much paperwork. At this rate they'll have to cut down every tree in Poland to keep up with the demand for meticulous record keeping. Everything has to be documented in precise detail. Columns with name, date of birth, occupation, crime, method of execution. The lists run to hundreds, thousands even. Kurt Schneider can't see the point. These people are dead, or soon will be. Why bother?

Sitting behind a desk was not what Kurt envisioned when he joined the elevated ranks of the *Schutzstaffel.* With his political idealism fanned by the sporting accolades awarded to him by the Hitler Youth, he rose through the ranks and easily gained a place at one of the elite Adolf Hitler boarding schools where racial purity and physical fitness counted for more than aptitude with pen and paper. In fact, academic ability had been somewhat sneered at. And yet now, thanks to the leg injury inflicted on him by Gruppenführer Müller, Kurt finds himself stuck behind a desk, shuffling stacks of paper, documenting the highly successful Extraordinary Operation of Pacification. The campaign to eliminate Poland's intelligentsia is going well – it's essential if the Nazis are to have control of this country that they eradicate all subversive elements, especially those in positions of authority and leadership – but it has created unbelievable mountains of paperwork. Meanwhile, Kurt fears his leg will never be the same again.

He lights a cigarette and, not for the first time, contemplates the chain of events that forced him into a desk job.

First and foremost, he blames Anna for his misfortune. And after he tried to be nice to her! He'd been missing the girls from his native Bavaria – lithe Lieselotte in her Dirndl, buxom Belinda from the Bierkeller. Even Olga, a stalwart of the *Bund Deutscher Mädel,* wasn't without feminine charms once you got her out of her neckerchief and hiking boots. German girls had practically thrown themselves at his feet when he appeared in uniform. Anna had seemed like the same sort of girl, maybe not quite as pretty as Lieselotte, or as curvaceous as Belinda, but certainly softer than Olga. Of course, she pretended she didn't understand German, but he saw through that ruse pretty early on. The way she would slow down when passing a table of Germans who were talking too loudly, the slight incline of her head towards the speaker. She probably didn't even realise she was doing it. Once he understood her game, he suspected she was a spy, planted in the restaurant to eavesdrop on his fellow officers. He took care to never talk business if she was in the vicinity. He could have arrested her there and then – he often regrets not having done so – but it would be more rewarding to bring down the whole cell. She can't be working alone. Who does she report to? He was hoping to find that out when Müller discovered him having a bit of fun and shot him in the leg. Another five minutes and she'd have coughed up the names of her co-conspirators if only to save her virtue. Müller is someone else Kurt blames for his current predicament.

He takes a long drag on his cigarette and scans the list of names, most of them unpronounceable. Reading and writing were never his strongest suits and the Polish language is completely alien to him with its clusters of consonants and strange accents. A language fit for *Untermenschen*. Subhumans. Only when he sees the name *Pan Professor Emeryk Nowak* does he pause a moment and sit back in his chair, frowning.

Pan Professor Emeryk Nowak, Professor of History.

Anna Nowak, isn't that what she's called? Could this professor be her father? Shot a couple of weeks ago in one of the largest executions of the Extraordinary Operation of Pacification. He runs his finger along the row and checks the man's date of birth. January the twentieth, 1888. He does a quick calculation on a scrap of paper. Fifty-two. The right sort of age. On an impulse, he jots down the Nowak family address. Królewska 32. Then he gets back to work with a new-found appreciation for the value of paperwork.

CHAPTER TWENTY-ONE

The train jolts over a set of points and Lech's head bangs against the wooden slats of the cattle truck. Halina, slumped against him, barely stirs, her breath on his arm shallow and rapid. Uncle Henryk and Aunt Magdalena are sitting a short distance away, their arms around each other. It's hot and dark, the air thick with the stench of unwashed bodies and human waste. Lech's mouth is dry from the lack of water, his lips cracked, his scalp itching with lice. Even in the days retreating from the Germans in September and October '39, things were never as bad as this. The train clears the points and continues on its relentless journey to God knows where.

It's a week since the NKVD barged into his uncle's apartment and carted them off for questioning. Lech was right when he thought they might not be going home afterwards. Following the interrogations, the Soviets escorted them, with many others, directly to the train station. They've been in this rattling, stinking cattle truck ever since.

At the time of his arrest Lech thought he was being sensible packing a few essentials into a canvas bag, but now he sees how inadequate his handful of belongings are. He remembers with fondness the huge kitbag he had with him the day he was called up and how his mother and Anna had stuffed it full of food. His heart yearns for his mother in a way it hasn't since he was a little boy. How will he ever get word to his family now?

When they first embarked on this journey into the unknown, Uncle Henryk, gregarious by nature, went out of his way to engage people in conversation. He talked to everyone, no matter who they were. Young, old, male, female, Catholic, Jewish, it didn't matter. Everyone was worthy of respect and everyone had a story to tell. The oldest was a woman in her nineties, the youngest, a baby in its mother's arms. What united them was their shared Polishness and their shared misfortune – how the NKVD came for them in the middle of the night, hammered on their doors until they opened up, ransacked their possessions, and then took them away. And their crime? Wanting to remain Polish.

The train grinds to a halt at some godforsaken station in the middle of nowhere. Lech squints through a crack in the slats but all he can see is the endless steppe, flat and monotonous, stretching to the horizon. He holds his breath as the metal latch is lifted from the outside and the heavy door creaks open. Is this their destination? There's nothing here as far as he can see. The sunlight that streams into the dingy carriage is so bright he blinks his eyes in pain. Halina lifts her gaze, shielding her eyes with her hand.

'Now what?' she whispers.

A guard climbs aboard, unable to keep the disgust off his face. The stench must be unbearable for someone who's just come from outside. It's bad enough for those who have to put up with it all the time. The guard steps between the legs and bodies sprawled on the filthy floor. Two dozen pairs of eyes follow him, except for one old woman in the corner who hasn't stirred from her slumber. It's the woman in her nineties. The guard pauses in front of her, prods her with his rifle butt. She doesn't respond.

Halina clutches Lech's arm and whispers exactly what

he's thinking. 'We should have noticed. The poor old thing.'

The guard calls for his comrade who is outside smoking a cigarette. 'Hey, Ivan. Need a hand here.'

Ivan climbs aboard muttering curses under his breath. Between them the two guards haul the old woman off the train and toss her shrivelled body onto the waste ground at the side of the tracks.

'Bastards,' whispers Lech.

He has no words to describe the horror he feels. That old lady was someone's wife, mother, grandmother. And now she's been discarded like a piece of old junk, left on the side of the track where wild animals will feed on her wasted remains.

The guards return with a bucket of water and small, hard loaves of bread which they hand out. It revolts Lech that he accepts the bread from the same hands that just threw the old woman off the train. It is almost inedible, hard as a rock, but it's all they get each day to keep them going. The water is tepid and stinking. Lech takes a sip, his parched body crying out for more. But the water is for sharing and he passes the container to Halina.

Lech knows his uncle blames himself for encouraging his family not to sign the papers agreeing to Soviet citizenship. Lech has tried to persuade him that he wouldn't have signed them anyway, but it makes no difference. Henryk is a broken man.

Half an hour after they stopped, the door clangs shut and the bolt is fastened into position. The train lurches forward and they are off again, more endless miles with no end in sight.

Lech could weep at the irony of it. When he was captured by the Red Army in Tarnopol, he thought he was doing a brave thing in running away. But it seems you can't escape your fate because here he is being deported to the Soviet Union anyway. The difference this time is that he's with people he loves so there won't be any solo heroics on his part. He sees it as his job – his destiny if you like – to look after his uncle, aunt and cousin. They're in this together. He intends to keep it that way.

CHAPTER TWENTY-TWO

When Gruppenführer Müller appears in the restaurant – after an absence of some weeks – Anna can hardly bear to look at him. A coldness creeps over her as he strides in and takes his seat with his customary calmness, giving no outward sign that anything is different. But he must know what has happened to her father and all the other men. Over three hundred prisoners can't just disappear overnight without men like Müller knowing all about it. Was he involved in the killings? How could he not have been?

Another unwelcome thought nags at the back of her mind. Could she have saved her father by giving Müller what he asked for? Information about the Underground. But he put her in an impossible situation. She could never have lived with herself if she'd betrayed Kazimierz and Tomasz and everything they stand for.

'Do you want me to take his order?' asks Wanda.

'No, I'll do it,' says Anna. 'I want to see if he can look me in the eye.'

The last couple of months have been worse than anything she has ever known. It was she who had to break the news to her mother and brother that Emeryk would never be coming home. She had to tell them that she'd seen his name on a list of executed men. Men shot in a forest and thrown into a mass grave. They didn't even have a body to bury.

After all they'd been through – surviving the siege, adapting to life under the occupation – the senseless killing of so many good men, their beloved father and husband amongst them, was almost too much for Maria to bear. For days she took to her bed and Anna had to coax her to eat small quantities of soup which she spooned into her mother's mouth the way she remembered Maria feeding Jan when he was a baby. She feared for her mother's life, feared that she and Jan would be left orphaned.

She wrote to Lech, the hardest letter of her life, explaining what had happened. But she's heard nothing back. She's heard reports, via the Underground, that educated people in the East are being deported to the Soviet Union and she fears the worst.

Then one day Pani Kowalska came knocking. Anna opened the door. Pani Kowalska explained that she had to go out, just for a short time, and could Anna or Maria look after the children? Anna was on her way to the restaurant and was about to say that her mother was in no fit state to babysit, but then to her astonishment, Maria appeared and said of course she'd watch the children. She'd love to see them again. And that was just the catalyst she needed to pick herself up. Her mother has always loved to be needed. She clings to the belief that Lech is still alive, saying that she would feel it in her bones if he wasn't. They're living on hope.

Taking a deep breath, Anna approaches Müller's table. 'Herr Gruppenführer. Are you ready to order?'

He orders beef stew and a glass of beer. There is not so much as a flicker of remorse or recognition for what Anna, and others like her, have suffered. She writes down his order and delivers it to the kitchen.

Then she removes her apron and prepares to follow through the plan she has agreed with another Underground cell that Tomasz introduced her to. All Müller had to do to save himself, thinks Anna, is show some remorse. But the man clearly has no human feelings, in which case Anna refuses to show any herself.

*

The man hasn't moved from the street corner for the last twenty minutes. Jan has been watching him all that time from his bedroom window. He's wearing a plain raincoat, but there is something about his bearing that gives him away. Way too confident and self-assured to be a Pole. *Gestapo?* Jan thinks not. SS in disguise? Could be. But why is he watching the apartment block?

Jan has no lessons today so he remains where he is, watching by the window, taking care to stay just out of view. He's quite enjoying this game of spying on a spy.

His father's death has shaken his world more than he likes to admit. For weeks he didn't go to classes, too scared that he would break down in front of his friends. When he saw Weronika in the courtyard, she threw her arms around him in a show of sympathy that he found deeply awkward. She said it was important not to bottle up feelings of grief, but let them out into the open so that the healing process could begin. She really does talk rot sometimes. Jan prefers to bury his grief, somewhere deep inside himself where it can't catch him unawares. Only Wiktor – solid, slow, sensitive Wiktor – understands that he doesn't want to talk about it.

The man in the raincoat lights a cigarette and looks at his watch. Is he waiting for someone? If so, then they're late. He smokes his cigarette then throws the stub on the ground and grinds it out with the toe of his shoe. Then he looks at his watch once more, turns on his heel and starts to walk down the street.

Jan doesn't hesitate. He's out of the apartment, down the stairs and out of the front door, just in time to see the man turning right at the corner of the Saxon Gardens. It's not difficult to keep up with him because he's walking with a limp.

Almost as soon as they've rounded the corner, a tram appears, heading north. With an air of entitlement, the man boards the carriage marked *Nur für Deutsche*. Only for Germans. *I knew it,* thinks Jan. *He's got German stamped all over him.* In hot pursuit, Jan jumps on board the crowded Polish carriage seconds before the doors shut, apologising for treading on a man's toes. Squeezing past an old woman clutching a loaf of bread under her arm, he positions himself at the front of the carriage. He can just see the back of the German's blond head in the carriage up ahead.

When the German alights near the Krasiński Garden, Jan also leaves the tram, once again apologising for treading on other people's feet. The German starts to cross the park, his limp becoming more pronounced the further he walks. *How did he get that injury?* Jan wonders. A war wound? Serves him damn well right.

In the open space of the garden, Jan feels exposed. He mustn't make it obvious that he's following this man. He lingers beside the lake, allowing the German to get ahead, then walks quickly to catch up when the German reaches the bomb-damaged Krasiński Palace.

Jan tails the man through the narrow streets of Stare Miasto, slipping into doorways now and again to avoid being spotted.

In Freta Street, the man stops about twenty yards from the restaurant where Anna works. Jan is now convinced that the German's behaviour – hanging around outside their apartment and then coming here – has something to do with his sister. He needs to warn her that she's being spied upon. If he can slip into the restaurant and get a message to her…

And then Anna appears at the restaurant door. She glances up and down the street, then sets off, walking with a purpose. The German has slipped into a doorway and Anna hasn't spotted him.

Anna walks purposefully to the corner of the street, looking neither to right nor left. She has thought about this day for so long, and now it's finally arrived. If this goes according to plan, a man will soon be dead, and she, Anna, will have played her part in fighting back against the enemy.

Surprisingly, it's Tomasz who has made this possible. When she saw her father's name on the list of prisoners executed at Palmiry, she thought she would go crazy. Her grief knew no bounds. Kazimierz embraced her with his love – and she was grateful – but she yearned for something more tangible than sympathy. It was Tomasz – Tomasz who had appeared not to trust her when she first started working for them – who provided her with an opportunity of avenging her father's death. He understood that delivering Information Bulletins was no longer enough. She had a thirst for real, direct action. He understood that for her, the war was now personal.

Gruppenführer Müller is just one of a number of high-ranking German officers in Warsaw targeted by the Polish Underground for crimes against Polish citizens. Anna's role in the plan to assassinate Müller is to pass a message to one of the organisers whenever Müller appears in the restaurant. For weeks there was no sign of him and Anna wondered if he was still in Warsaw. And then today he finally appeared, as if nothing had changed. But for Anna, everything has changed. Her father is dead, and she is not the same person she was a month ago.

At the door of an old house, she gives the agreed knock – two slow knocks and three short taps. The door is opened from the inside. Anna slips inside.

*

What is she up to? She never used to leave the restaurant in the middle of the lunchtime shift. She was always so conscientious. Kurt notes the door through which Anna disappeared a moment ago. Is she meeting a lover? Or members of the Underground?

There's a kid – a boy of about eleven or twelve – banging on the same door now. But this time no one opens up. This tells Kurt that the boy, whoever he is, doesn't know the right signal to use. So this must be a secret house, a place for illegal Underground activities. The upstairs windows are closed and shuttered, making it look as if no one lives there. The boy moves away from the door, looking disappointed. There's something familiar about him, although Kurt doesn't think he's seen him before. He dismisses him without a second thought.

Whilst Kurt is contemplating his next move, he hears a car coming down the street. It's Müller's limo. It pulls up outside the restaurant and Müller himself appears, looking as if he's just enjoyed a hearty meal. Kurt misses eating in the restaurant – the food really was very good – but hasn't been able to face going back after the incident in the alleyway. Müller is just about to get into the vehicle, when a blue car coming from the opposite direction slows down outside the restaurant and there's a hail of gunfire.

Kurt dives into a doorway and watches the scene play out before him as if in slow motion. Müller's driver is dead, slumped over the steering wheel, and Müller – who tried to run back into the restaurant – is lying in a bloody mess on the pavement.

Kurt knows that he should respond by shooting at the rebels in the blue car, but it's already accelerating away from the scene. The assassination lasted no more than a few seconds. It was a planned operation if ever he saw one. If asked about the incident, he decides, he'll claim that he couldn't give chase because of his dodgy leg.

If it was anyone other than Müller who was assassinated, Kurt would be outraged in the name of the Führer and the Fatherland. But the man who shot him – and ruined his career – is now lying dead on the pavement, and Kurt feels nothing except satisfaction.

*

Jan is already at the corner of the street, on his way home, when he hears the gunshots. After he failed to gain admittance to the shuttered house – a house obviously used by the Underground – he knew there was no point in hanging around. He would only draw attention to himself, and the German with the dodgy leg was watching him.

Now he turns and sees a blue car speeding away from the restaurant in a cloud of exhaust fumes. There's a body lying on the pavement, next to a black limo.

People are running and screaming. Any second now the Waffen-SS will be on the scene. If there's one thing Jan knows, it's that you don't want to be anywhere in the vicinity when there's been an assassination of a German.

He turns on his heel and runs away as fast as he can.

CHAPTER TWENTY-THREE

Hammering on the door. Again. It's two o'clock in the morning. Anna knows that this time they've come for her.

She hasn't slept a wink anyway. Not after what happened.

She thought that taking revenge on her enemy – and she saw Müller as her enemy – would ease the pain she's felt since her father was murdered. But it's only added to her misery. This is not who she wants to be. She might not have pulled the trigger – she doesn't think she could ever have done that – but Müller was killed as a result of her actions. She gave the signal. She informed her contact – someone whose name she doesn't even know – that he was dining in the restaurant that day. The team assigned to carry out the assassination was ready and waiting. She doesn't know who fired the fatal shots or even if they managed to get away successfully. She was just a small cog in a much larger machine. She played her part and then she went home.

Maria begs her not to answer the door. 'Pretend we're not here.' The terror in her mother's eyes pains her as much as the death of her father.

'They'll break the door down if we don't open it,' says Anna. She's heard the stories from Kazimierz. Hiding and resisting never does you any good.

As soon as she opens the door, half a dozen *Gestapo* swarm into the apartment. But the last man through the door walks with a limp and is wearing SS uniform.

'Anna Nowak,' says Kurt Schneider, 'you are under arrest. You must come with us now. Get dressed.'

She shrinks from his lecherous gaze, berating herself for not putting a dressing gown on over her nightdress.

'She hasn't done anything,' says Maria boldly. 'Leave her alone.'

It's a mistake. Kurt slaps her across the face. 'Shut up, woman. Or I'll arrest you too.' He looks at Jan, frowns as if in recognition, and turns back to Anna. 'Get dressed.'

Anna hurries away to her room, but she's not allowed to close the door. She has to dress under the watchful eyes of the *Gestapo*. She turns her back on them, trying to preserve what little modesty she has left but she's shaking so much she can hardly do up the buttons on her blouse. They're brutes, all of them.

When she reappears, Maria thrusts her leather satchel at her. 'I've packed some essentials,' she says. 'You know.' Anna can imagine. Bread, sausage, toiletries. For a second, she holds her mother's gaze, that face that she knows and loves so well – the hazel eyes, the tracery of veins on the cheeks, the brown hair now greying at the temples. She sees sorrow in her eyes, but also fierce love and defiance. There's so much she wants to say to her, she feels as if her heart is bursting. All she can manage is, 'I'm sorry.' And then rough hands pull her away, propelling her towards the door. The last thing she sees before they march her down the stairs is her mother and Jan standing together in front of the mantelpiece, the family photograph propped against the clock behind them.

*

The words just won't come. Maria is unable to pray. She

can't get the words past the wall of anger, resentment and grief that has her in its vice-like grip. All she wants to do is scream.

She doesn't even bother to light a candle because a candle is a symbol of hope and she has none. She looks at the statue of the Virgin Mary and sees nothing but resignation in the saint's outstretched hands. *Everything is hopeless. There is nothing we can do.* Why has she bothered to come here?

Family has always been the most important thing in Maria's life, and it is being systematically dismantled. Scattered to the four winds. Her beloved Emeryk is lying in a mass grave in the forest having been brutally murdered. Her eldest son is almost certainly somewhere in the depths of the Soviet Union, God only knows where. And now her daughter is in Nazi custody, a thought too terrifying to contemplate.

Only Jan is left to her now. Her baby. But for how much longer? He's growing up fast – too fast – and she senses in him a desire to get involved in the fight. What does he get up to when her back is turned? She saw him react when that SS officer walked into the apartment. Jan recognised him, she's sure of it. Anna too for that matter. What are her children involved in? She longs for the time when they were small and would come to her for comfort. Now she is the one who needs comforting, and there is no one to give it to her.

*

'Who else is involved?'
    'No one.'
    'You're lying. Who do you report to?'
    'No one.'
    'What are their names?'
    'I don't know what you're talking about.'
    Her head is yanked backwards and she barely has time

to grab a lungful of air before her face is plunged once more into the tub of freezing water. She screws her eyes tight shut and holds her breath for as long as she can, but this time they hold her down for even longer and the pressure builds until her lungs are burning and she can't stand it a moment longer. The air explodes from her mouth in a burst of bubbles and she's going to swallow a lungful of water. There's nothing she can do to stop herself. Death would be a welcome release.

This has been going on for what feels like hours. They want the names of everyone in the Underground she's ever worked with. But she would rather drown than give them the names of Wanda, Kazimierz and Tomasz. As for the people who shot Müller, she genuinely has no idea who they are. The Underground works on a need-to-know basis. Cells are tightly knit. People use codenames anyway.

Last night they brought her to Gestapo Headquarters in Aleja Szucha, an imposing building in the heart of what has become an exclusively German district. The building is so well guarded, they had to pass through a number of checkpoints to get here. She might as well be in the heart of Berlin.

They took her straight down to the basement and threw her into a room on her own with nothing but an iron bed and a bucket in the corner. She sat on the bed, hugging herself and crying with the shock. The interrogation started a few hours later.

Just as she starts to draw the water into her mouth, the hands holding her yank her head backwards and she comes up gasping for air, a rasping sound in her throat as she sucks in much-needed oxygen. Water runs down her face, into her eyes, blurring her vision.

The ordeal goes on. The same questions over and over; head forced down, head yanked back. She gives them nothing.

In the end they give up. Even Germans have to eat, drink and piss, she thinks.

She expects to be taken back to the cell in the basement, but instead she's loaded into a truck with a dozen other women who all look as if they've had similar treatment or worse. One of them has a bruised face, her right eye swollen shut. Another has a bleeding lip and a tooth missing. No one speaks. Anna closes her eyes and lets her body give way to the motion of the truck.

When they arrive at their destination, she knows exactly where they are. It's the women's wing of the Pawiak, known locally by the nickname Serbia. Her father spent his last days in the Pawiak. Is this the end for her too?

PART SIX
EXILE
AUGUST – DECEMBER 1940

CHAPTER TWENTY-FOUR

The clanking of a steel rail signals the start of the day's work. This is how they do things in Siberia. Novolyalinsky Region, Sverdlovsk Oblast to be precise, not that Lech expects to be receiving post any time soon.

'Go,' says Halina. 'I'll look after her.'

'She needs a doctor,' says Lech, looking at his aunt who is lying in bed, sick with fever.

'I'll see what I can do.'

Lech knows Halina will do her best, but medicine is like gold dust in the camp. The nearest town – as Igor, the NKVD overseer, gleefully told them when they arrived after a two-day trek in the unbearable heat – is fifteen kilometres away. 'The people there don't want anything to do with Polish bourgeois pigs.' Igor spat on the ground to emphasise his point.

The single room Lech shares with his cousin, aunt and uncle is hot and airless, infested with insects. The barracks are crudely constructed out of logs and poorly insulated with moss. Lech believes they date from the time of Stalin's purges in the thirties. Needless to say, there is no electricity or running water in these primitive dwellings. Water is pumped by hand from a well, a tiring business after a day felling trees. When the Poles moved in, they did what they could to make the buildings a little more habitable. The women swept the earth floors and the men tried to mend the holes in the walls where the wood had rotted and the moss had fallen out. But this only landed them in trouble. Igor reported them for 'bourgeois behaviour' and their work quotas were increased to teach them a lesson. Now they carry out minor improvements more surreptitiously, hoping that Igor won't notice.

Uncle Henryk kneels by his wife's bed, clutching her hand. Magdalena's illness has hit him hard. He blames himself for his family's predicament.

'We should have signed the damn forms,' he says. 'We could have feigned allegiance to the Soviets. We'd still have been Polish in our hearts.'

Lech tries to reassure his uncle that they will get through this, but deep down he's not so sure.

The clanking of the steel rail continues, harsh and insistent. Lech puts a hand on his uncle's shoulder. If they don't work, they don't eat, it's as simple as that. With Halina staying back to look after her mother, Lech and Henryk will have to work extra hard to achieve their impossible quotas. Henryk nods and struggles to his feet. Always a big man, now his clothes hang off him and he keeps his trousers up with a length of string.

Lech and Henryk shoulder their axes and join the long line of men setting off for the four-kilometre trek into the forest. They'll do eleven hours of hard physical labour before they return exhausted. It's only seven in the morning but already it's getting hot. By midday they'll be drenched in sweat, their skin blistering in the sun. Lech scratches his arms and torso where the bed bugs got him in the night, the little critters.

They've been here almost a month already, but it feels like much longer. The train journey from Lwów lasted nearly four weeks. Four weeks of utter hell that Lech will never be able to erase from his mind. He still has nightmares, dreaming that he's trapped in that stinking cattle truck, the only man alive amid a pile of corpses. He wakes gasping for air, his heart thumping in his chest, and it takes him a moment or two before he remembers that he's no longer on the train. By the time they reached their destination, eighteen people from their truck alone had died. There would have been a similar number from each of the other carriages. Tossed out of the train by the guards like so much discarded waste. The tragedy was that it became routine. After a while you barely noticed, you just had more room to stretch your legs. Except when the baby died and was tossed from the train like a piece of rotten meat. The mother's anguished cries of despair still ring in Lech's ears in his darkest moments.

They arrive at their workplace and split into teams. The air is heavy with the scent of resin. Spruce as straight as altar candles, golden-trunked pines and snowy white birches as far as the eye can see. Dense and impenetrable, the forest is so vast it's mind-boggling. Wolves lurk within its primeval interior.

After all he's been through, Lech isn't afraid of wolves, at least not the four-legged kind. The only living things you need to fear around here are the NKVD overseers. Igor, a leathery-skinned old communist die-hard, teeth yellowed from the Russian cigarettes he chain-smokes, made his opinion of the Poles known from day one.

'You are bourgeois oppressors of the working class. Here in the Soviet Union you will pay for your crimes. You will learn how to work. No work means no food. Understand?'

Whatever you say, comrade, thought Lech, too exhausted from the horrendous journey to protest that he had never oppressed anyone to his knowledge.

It turned out that when Igor said 'No work means no food', he wasn't kidding. Only those who work are allocated rations, the size of the ration determined by how much of your daily quota you manage to achieve. Hit your target and you can get two and a half pounds of bread per day. Miss your target, and the ration is lowered proportionally. But everyone misses their targets because they're set absurdly high.

Lech grasps the axe in his blistered hands and prepares to take the first swing of the day. There'll be hundreds more before the day is over. They have to fell trees, saw branches and haul timber. It's physically exhausting and mentally mind-numbing, the worst possible combination. It would be easier if they had better tools, but the axe blades are blunt, the rough wooden handles give you splinters, and the saws have as many teeth as a toothless old crone.

When the bosses come to inspect, Igor is always keen to show them how hard his men are working. And it's true, as they sweat and toil with blunt tools, they're working themselves to the bone. Lech has realised that the appearance of hard work is more important than the actual result. As long as they are seen to be working, Igor can claim that the quotas are being met. Lech wonders what lies Igor tells his superiors just to save his own skin. The system works because it's based on fear.

The tree that Lech has been hacking at for the last forty minutes finally starts to creak and sway. He leans his weight against the spindly trunk and gives it a shove. The muscles in his arms and shoulders are already sore. By the end of the day he'll barely be able to pick up the axe.

In its death throes, the tree gives one last groan and crashes to the forest floor, releasing a powerful scent of resin. Another man helps Lech haul it over to the team that saws off the branches. This is where Uncle Henryk is working.

Seeing his uncle struggling with a saw that would have trouble cutting through jelly, Lech's mind turns, not for the first time, to thoughts of escape. It's not as if they're enclosed in barbed wire. They could get away. But where to? No, at the moment it's impossible. Aunt Magdalena can't even get out of bed, let alone walk fifteen kilometres to the nearest town. And if Igor is to be believed, the townspeople would hand them straight back to the authorities rather than risk being sent to the gulag themselves. It's a hopeless situation. But Lech would do anything to save his relatives after they took him in without question when he was on the run.

At midday the guards wheel in a large thermos of watery soup. Lech and Henryk join the queue of listless men. A few measly vegetables float in the liquid. There's never any meat. Finding a patch of bilberries, Lech picks as many as he can and puts them in his pockets to take back for Halina and Aunt Magdalena. He has learned, from those who know about such things, which mushrooms and berries are safe to eat. It's the only way to ensure they get any vitamins. But what will they do when the winter comes?

At six o'clock in the evening, they begin the long, slow trudge back to the camp. Henryk is silent all the way and Lech knows he's worrying about his wife. There's nothing Lech can say that would help so he stays silent, dreading what they will find when they arrive.

Henryk goes in first, and Lech follows close behind.

Halina is perched on a stool by her mother's bed, bathing her forehead with a damp cloth. Lech lets out a sigh of relief. At least Magdalena is no worse. At least she's still breathing.

Henryk rushes over to his wife's side and takes her hand. 'How is she?'

'The same,' says Halina. 'I spoke to the doctor but there aren't any medicines. They won't be delivered for another week.'

'That's not good enough!' roars Henryk, showing something of his old spirit. 'What's wrong with these people?' Then he collapses onto the stool which Halina has vacated. 'I'm sorry,' he says, his head in his hands. 'This is all my fault.' He dips the cloth in the bowl of tepid water, wrings it out and lays it on his wife's forehead. 'I'll sit with her a while.'

Lech and Halina go outside, giving her parents some privacy. They sit side by side on a log and watch a couple of small children playing with sticks in the dirt.

'I brought you something,' says Lech, suddenly remembering. He reaches into his pocket and scoops out the bilberries, half of them squashed, their purple juice staining his fingers. He offers them to Halina. 'Have you eaten today?'

She shakes her head, a tear running down her cheek.

'Take them,' he urges her. 'They'll do you good.'

She picks up a single bilberry and puts it in her mouth. The smile that spreads across her face is like a ray of sunshine to his heart. 'You too,' she says. 'They're so sweet.'

They eat the bilberries one at a time, savouring their sweetness, making each one last as long as possible. Lech knows he will remember this moment forever, no matter how long or short the rest of his life is.

That night Magdalena's condition worsens. She becomes delirious, she cries out, and then, in the early hours of the morning, sometime around three o'clock, she dies.

When the clanking of the steel rail starts up at seven the next morning, Lech and Henryk ignore it.

CHAPTER TWENTY-FIVE

Dogs barking. Angry, vicious barks that rend the air and make you want to turn and run in the opposite direction. That's the sound that greets them as the women stagger off the cattle cart, dazed and disoriented after two days in unspeakable conditions with nothing but stale bread and tepid water to sustain them and a hole in the middle of the floor through which to relieve themselves. Anna shrinks inside herself at the sound of the barking. She's terrified of dogs, at least big ones that sound like hellhounds.

Large blonde women in capes and black boots scream at them to get off the train. Each one brandishes a baton or a whip in one hand and a taut leash in the other at the end of which a brute of a dog snaps its jaws and bares its teeth. There must be a dozen of these women and their dogs all told. Some of them are armed with pistols.

The Nazi women come as a shock. In Warsaw you saw plenty of well-dressed German wives who rode in the *Nur für Deutsche* carriages on the trams and looked with disdain on their Polish sisters, but there were no women to compare with these screeching Furies who are engaged in a decibel war with their canine counterparts. The louder they scream, the more the barking intensifies, and vice versa. And they're so young, these Nazi women. Most of them look no more than early or mid-twenties. Is this really the life they've chosen to lead?

A hand clutches Anna's arm. 'Are we in Germany?' Krysia is only sixteen but was arrested with her older brother for Underground activities. She doesn't know where he's been taken.

'I think so.' Anna sees a sign on the tiny platform. Fürstenberg. She's never heard of it. They left the women's wing of the Pawiak in canvas-covered lorries that took them to the train station where they were herded onto cattle trucks. After that, time and distance became meaningless. Sometimes the train rattled on at great speed, sometimes they were held up for what felt like hours. It's anyone's guess how far they've actually travelled and in which direction, although there was a general consensus they were heading west.

'Try and stay together,' says Krysia.

'Of course.' During their time in the Pawiak the two women discovered a shared love of art. Krysia is like a younger sister to Anna.

But it's hard to stick together when they're being jostled on all sides by more and more women tumbling from the train with their bags and suitcases, bewildered and scared, blinking in the morning sun after the dark, windowless cattle trucks. There must be hundreds of them crowding onto the platform.

More screaming from the women with the dogs. 'What are they saying?' asks Krysia.

Anna shakes her head. She can't make out the orders amid the screeching and barking. The guards start to move amongst them, pushing and shoving them into lines of five. A baton comes down on their joined hands and they are forced apart. Krysia cries out and tears spring into her eyes.

It takes an age before they're all lined up to the satisfaction of the guards. Then the march begins. They walk, five abreast, through the silent, shuttered town, past a glistening lake, and along a cobbled path through a pine forest. In other circumstances it would be a beautiful place to go for a walk.

The woman in front of Anna stumbles and falls. Her suitcase is clearly too heavy for her.

'Let me help you,' says Anna, reaching for the case. A leather whip cracks through the air like a pistol shot. Anna rears back in shock, the back of her hand stinging in pain.

'No helping!' screams the guard.

Anna is too stunned to reply. For a moment she stares into the eyes of the woman who struck her. She is a similar age to Anna, and actually quite pretty with her blonde hair curled into a bob and her little, upturned nose. But there's a hardness in her, like steel. Her eyes narrow as she takes a good look at Anna, and Anna knows she is being marked as a troublemaker.

'Walk!' shouts the guard, giving Anna a shove. Her dog, a snarling Alsatian, barks to reinforce the message. Anna continues on her way, blinking back the tears that threaten to blur her vision.

All around her, she hears muttered prayers, barely audible. *Hail Mary, full of grace... Lord Jesus, have mercy on us...* She finds herself mouthing the words of the Lord's Prayer. It's something familiar to hold on to.

They arrive at a massive grey wall and pass through a gateway. The urge to turn and run is so strong, Anna wonders if the others can feel it too. And yet, they put one foot in front of the other, coerced by the female guards with their batons and whips, and the snarling dogs who haven't let up their incessant barking the whole time.

Rigid rows of single-storey barracks stretch before them. It's a depressing sight, not improved by the red flower beds and spindly saplings that must be some official's idea of homeliness. The effect is jarring, mocking even.

They stop at a large sandy square where the guards order them to wait.

Lines of thin women in shapeless, blue-and-white

striped dresses and matching headscarves file past. Each one carries a tool over her shoulder – a pickaxe, a shovel, a spade. They regard the newcomers with mild curiosity, but offer no smiles of encouragement. Anna catches Krysia's eye and sees alarm in her friend's face. Are they going to become like these women, grey and worn down?

Time passes and nothing happens. It's exhausting just standing around. One by one they collapse onto their bags, heads in their hands. But the guards are on them in seconds, brandishing whips, shouting obscenities. It seems they are to stand outside until their legs ache and their backs are stiff. Anna's throat is parched and her stomach contracts in hunger.

The women who passed by earlier with pickaxes, shovels and spades now return, bedraggled and filthy, some of them so worn out they can barely put one foot in front of the other. They don't seem at all surprised that the new arrivals are still waiting on the square, but walk past with hardly a sideways glance.

Eventually the guards shout at them to line up again. 'Ranks of five. Eyes ahead.'

The women are marched into a building near the gate where tables are piled high with blue-and-white striped garments. Male guards stand around watching.

'Clothes off,' orders a female guard.

Are they kidding? Apparently not. It seems they're expected to take everything off. Underwear, the lot.

'I can't,' whispers Krysia. 'Not here, like this.' Her hands are trembling.

Anna looks aghast at the leering male officers standing around with hungry looks on their faces as if they've come to a striptease club. Some of them have bayonets and prod the women when they are slow to respond to the order to undress.

'Don't look at them,' says Anna, turning her back on them. She tries to detach her mind from what is happening as she fumbles with the buttons on her blouse. She steps out of her skirt. Now she's standing in her underwear. She sees other women hesitating over this last step as the male guards catcall and wolf whistle, calling them sluts.

'Let's just get this over with,' says a middle-aged woman with stretch marks across her sagging belly and pendulous breasts that have probably fed a whole brood of children. She whips off her greying undies, a look of defiance on her face. After that, others follow suit, and soon they're all standing there stark naked, one arm across their chests, the other hand covering the space between their legs. The guards whoop and cheer and make obscene gestures with their hands.

Their clothes go into large brown paper bags. The female guards are ruthless when it comes to tearing watches off wrists and ripping rings from fingers.

'That won't come off,' says the woman with the stretch marks, looking at the wedding ring on her puffy, nail-bitten finger. But after much tugging and swearing on the part of the guards, it does.

'Nearly took my bloody finger off,' mutters the woman, rubbing her swollen knuckles.

Anna is glad she doesn't wear any rings for these bitches to get their hands on. But they take her watch away, the one her parents gave her for her seventeenth birthday.

Naked and robbed, they shuffle en masse into the showers and emerge dripping and shivering. The female guards are waiting for them in a long line, shavers at the ready. They shave the women's hair from their heads. Blonde, brunette, auburn and ginger locks fall to the floor and are trampled underfoot. Anna finds herself standing face to face with the pretty blonde guard who wielded her whip with such relish on the walk to the camp. Recognition sparks in the guard's blue eyes and the corners of her mouth curl in a cruel smile. *How long does it take you to do your hair each morning?* Anna wonders. *At least I won't have that problem now.* The blonde woman shaves Anna's hair, then shoves her out of the way and moves on to her next victim.

By the time another guard comes down the line and shouts at them all to stand with their legs apart – apparently all body hair is to be removed – Anna is numb to the humility of it all.

The blue and white striped dresses are handed out, with no thought as to whether they will fit. Anna pulls hers over her head, relieved to be no longer naked. The dress is a baggy, shapeless thing that hangs just below her knees. Not such a bad fit. On others the dresses are way too small or too big. Krysia's drowns her small frame and reaches almost to her ankles. They also receive a jacket in the same striped material, worn underwear, rough knitted socks and a pair of ill-fitting wooden clogs. It's difficult to walk without dragging them over the ground.

Finally, each prisoner is issued with a number on a small piece of white cloth and a red felt triangle with a black letter P. They have to sew these identifiers onto the left shoulder of their jackets. Anna is now prisoner number 7549.

CHAPTER TWENTY-SIX

If they pile any more furniture on the cart, Jan worries it's going to topple over. The emaciated horse waiting patiently in harness makes a whinnying noise, its breath misting in the cold November air. Jan pats the animal's flank, feeling the ribs beneath the skin. He just hopes the creature doesn't drop dead before they've reached their destination.

Wiktor and his family are moving into the Jewish quarter of the city, by order of the Gestapo. They've been given a deadline to vacate their nice apartment by the twelfth of the month. When Jan heard about the move, he immediately offered to lend a hand. He wants to know where his friend is going so that he can continue to visit him.

'Dad tried to get a van,' says Wiktor, coming to stand beside him, 'but no one would lend him one. This was the best he could find.' He keeps his voice low so as not to offend the old man whose horse this is. The old man is sitting some distance away on the side of the kerb, chewing tobacco and spitting into the gutter.

The cart has been packed and repacked as the Zielińskis try to fit in as much as possible. So far, they've managed a dining table and chairs, a writing bureau, four lamps, kitchen utensils, mattresses and bedding. The sofa was too large and the piano was out of the question. Pani Zielińska was particularly upset about the piano because it belonged to her grandmother, but her husband said they would buy another one for their new apartment. Jan could see that wasn't really the point.

Eventually they're ready to go. Pan Zieliński and Pani Zielińska are both carrying heavy suitcases, and Wiktor and his little sister, Antonina, have bundles on their backs tied with string. Jan wishes they would give him something to carry. However, as soon as they try to move, it becomes apparent that the horse isn't up to the job. Jan can't say he's surprised.

'Give her a shove from behind,' shouts the old man. Jan puts his hands on the back of the cart and leans into it, the muscles in his shoulders straining, his feet slipping on the cobbles. With a sudden jolt, the cart lurches forwards and the furniture load shifts. Jan looks up, worried that the dining table is going to come crashing down on his head, but nothing falls off and he breathes a little easier. However, as soon as he stops pushing, the horse grinds to a halt so he's obliged to keep up the effort. Wiktor joins him and together they just about manage to keep the cartwheels turning.

They haven't reached the end of the road before Antonina starts to complain. Her backpack is too heavy. She sits down on the curb and refuses to get up. She's only seven, so what can you expect?

'I'll carry your backpack,' offers Jan, glad to be of more use.

Once they've sorted out the backpack, they have to get the horse moving again.

'I want to ride in the cart,' wails Antonina, before they've gone another twenty yards.

'There isn't room,' says Wiktor. 'Can't you see how full it is?' He rolls his eyes at Jan as if to say, *Little sisters, honestly!*

It takes them an age to cover the distance on foot, what with the slow plodding of the horse, the heavy suitcases that the parents are struggling with, and Antonina who drags her feet and cries intermittently. Twice they have to stop to adjust the load which has a tendency to lean to the right, threatening to unbalance the cart.

It's during one of these enforced breaks that Jan sees a large group on foot – men, women and children – being herded by armed guards in the same direction as the Zielińskis. The women wear headscarves knotted under their chins and blankets around their shoulders. The children are bundled up in winter coats and hats. The men's clothes are dirty, as if they've just come from working in the fields. The expressions on their pinched faces are grim. They shuffle forwards one step at a time as if they have already come a long way and don't want to take another step. The horse and cart suddenly seem like a luxury. These people don't even have suitcases, but carry their possessions wrapped in bundles, strapped to their backs.

Once the Zielińskis' furniture has been secured, they set off for what Jan hopes is the last time.

'Here we are,' says Pan Zieliński with forced jollity when they eventually arrive outside a tall apartment block in Sienna Street. 'We're on the top floor.'

Pani Zielińska looks up at the five-storey building in dismay. 'How are we going to get this lot up the stairs?' She waves a hand at the furniture piled on the cart. 'We shouldn't have brought so much stuff.' But Jan knows how hard it was for them to leave so much behind – comfortable chairs, paintings. The piano.

'I'll help,' says Jan.

'You've done more than enough already,' says Pan Zieliński.

'It's no trouble.'

So for the next two hours they trudge up and down the stairs, lugging the heavy furniture between them.

'Which room is mine?' asks Antonina, running around the new apartment. 'There are only two bedrooms.' It's much smaller than the apartment they've left behind. There wouldn't have been room for the piano, even if they could have fitted it on the cart.

'You'll have to share with Wiktor,' says Pani Zieliński. This produces yet more tears from the little girl. Wiktor doesn't look too happy with the arrangement either.

Once everything has been brought upstairs and dumped in the living room, Pan Zieliński shakes Jan's hand.

'Thank you for your help, young man. It's much appreciated. You'd best be off now, before it gets late.'

'I'll come and see Wiktor soon,' says Jan. Now he knows where his friend lives, he'll be able to pop round after Underground school.

Pan Zieliński nods his head but says nothing. There's a deep sadness in his eyes.

As Jan retraces his steps along the cobbled street, he experiences an unfamiliar and unpleasant feeling in his chest. No doubt Weronika would be able to diagnose whatever is ailing him and advise on a course of action, but he doesn't want to ask her so he tries to analyse it himself. Of course, he's angry that Wiktor and his family have had to leave their comfortable home and move into that tiny, dilapidated apartment. They didn't deserve any of this. And neither did those people who had walked from the countryside. But what he's feeling is more than a sense of injustice on their behalf. It's almost as if he's done something wrong himself… And then it comes to him. He feels guilty. Guilty because he's going home and doesn't have to move into an unfamiliar building with strangers. Guilty that he has 'Aryan' stamped on his identity card and Wiktor doesn't. Guilty for not being Jewish. There is only one way he can make amends. He will return to Sienna Street as soon as he can. Wiktor is his best friend, and he won't let the Germans keep them apart. Just let them try.

*

Three days later, after French class, Jan is back in Sienna

Street.

Even in the short time since Wiktor's family moved in, the area has changed. Jewish bricklayers, under the supervision of Nazi guards, are building a wall around the quarter. Jan watches as they lay brick upon brick, sealing themselves into the ghetto. The guards pace up and down, cracking their whips and lashing out at anyone who doesn't work fast enough. Jan hurries on to the end of the street where the traffic has not been stopped completely, fearful of attracting attention to himself.

A German sentry demands to see his identity card. Whilst the guard scrutinises his papers, Jan reads a wooden sign painted with black gothic script warning against entering this part of the city because of the risk of typhus. He isn't entirely sure what typhus is, but it doesn't sound good. He'll have to ask Weronika and hope that she doesn't think him stupid.

'What have you got there?' The guard points to a bulge in Jan's jacket pocket.

'Just a bit of sausage.' He wrapped it up and stuffed it in his pocket at the last minute before setting off, thinking that he and Wiktor could share it.

'It is not permitted to take parcels into the ghetto.' The guard holds out his hand.

'But…' Jan wants to protest that it's only a bit of sausage wrapped in paper, hardly a parcel. The guard moves to block his path and fingers the rifle slung over his shoulder. Reluctantly, Jan hands over the sausage and proceeds empty-handed. What a waste of a good sausage.

The streets of the ghetto are bustling. Everyone who is out and about wears a white armband with a blue Star of David. He passes a street market where people are selling bread and dried fish from wicker baskets. A woman with a steaming metal urn is selling hot drinks and an old man with a long beard is peddling armbands from a rickety wooden table. Jan is so distracted by everything going on around him that he doesn't see the rickshaw coming down the street. He jumps back just in time as the young man swerves around him.

At the Zielińskis' building, the smell of boiled cabbage hangs in the stairwell. Jan has always hated boiled cabbage and tries not to breathe in through his nose. When he knocks, the door is opened by a woman he doesn't recognise. Her hair is wrapped in a scarf tied like a turban and she wears a dirty apron over her dress. A toddler perched on her hip regards Jan with baleful eyes, then turns its head away, sucking its thumb. Jan is confused. Isn't this the right apartment? He was here only three days ago. He asks for his friend.

The woman nods and moves aside for him to enter, but Wiktor must have heard him because he suddenly appears from one of the rooms. 'Let's go for a walk.'

'Who was that?' asks Jan as they go down the stairs.

'A family from Poznań have moved in with us.'

'What, permanently?'

Wiktor nods.

'But why?'

'They haven't got anywhere else to go. The *Judenrat*, the Jewish Council, are trying to accommodate all the refugees.'

'But you've only got two bedrooms in that apartment. Where do they sleep?'

'We have one bedroom, and they have the other.'

Jan doesn't know what to say to that. It's bad enough that Wiktor had to move house, but how can they all live in the same room? No wonder Wiktor suggested going for a walk.

Jan tells him about the sausage. He's still angry with the guard who took it off him. Surely, he just made up that stupid rule about no parcels. But Wiktor nods his head sagely.

'You should have eaten it yourself before coming here,' he says. It seems to Jan that Wiktor has suddenly grown up in the space of three days. In that time he's experienced a different life, and Jan senses a need to be tactful, and not remind Wiktor of everything he's left behind.

After that, they fall silent, walking at random. What strikes Jan are the huge contrasts in the ghetto. Live music streams from packed cafés, street sellers tout their wares, beggars hold out bowls, people pass by dressed in fine clothes or rags. But wherever they go, sooner or later they find their way blocked by the wall and they have to retrace their steps. It's like living in a prison. Later, when he exits through the gate with the sign warning about typhus, he can't help feeling an exhilarating sense of freedom. He too is living under German oppression, but now he sees there are degrees. Some are more oppressed than others.

CHAPTER TWENTY-SEVEN

Wolves in the dead of night. Lech lies awake, peering into the impenetrable blackness, listening to the howls from the forest. Is it his imagination or are they getting closer day by day? They must be as desperate for food as the people in the camp.

Beside him, Halina lies so still she could have turned to stone. Only the faint whisper of her breath on his cheek reassures him that she's still alive. In these temperatures, you can go to sleep and not wake up again. Every day another body is added to the pile of corpses outside. They can't bury them because the ground is too frozen to dig. They'll have to wait until the spring. But that's months away. The cold has slowed time.

Lech and Halina are both fully clothed, including hats and gloves. You don't want to wake up and find a finger or a toe has turned black and needs amputating. You can't hold an axe with half your fingers. They've also piled all their blankets and coats on the bed, but even so Lech is too cold to sleep.

The sweltering heat of the summer, with its mosquitoes, scorpions and snakes, has turned into the severest cold he's ever known. A cold so savage it grips you with its teeth, drills into your bones and freezes your muscles. If they have to spend much longer here, he dreads to think what will become of them. It's just the two of them now.

After Aunt Magdalena died in August, Uncle Henryk lost the will to live. He couldn't keep up with his quotas so his rations were cut and he refused to share Lech's and Halina's food, saying they'd earned it so they should eat it. Halina was beside herself with worry, but there was nothing they could do. Lech tried talking to his uncle but it did no good.

'I'm an old man,' said Henryk.

'Nonsense,' protested Lech. He couldn't be, what, much more than late fifties?

But Henryk shook his head. 'Magdalena was my life and soul. In her quiet way, she was the bedrock of my life. I'll never forgive myself for being the cause of her death.'

'Halina needs you,' said Lech, trying a different tack.

Henryk placed his hand on Lech's. 'She needs *you*,' he said. 'She can do without me.'

When there was an outbreak of typhus, Henryk devoted himself to caring for the sick, refusing to work another day in the forest. He eventually succumbed to the illness himself at the start of October. They buried him beside his wife in a clearing where lots of other Poles were buried.

Those were the darkest days. Halina was wrapped in a grief so profound, Lech couldn't reach her. To have lost both her parents in such a short space of time, he couldn't even begin to imagine what she must be going through. But he had to carry on working in the forest otherwise neither of them would have had anything to eat. He prayed for a miracle.

And then one day he came back from work to find ten children crammed into their single room. Halina was telling them a story, the youngest – aged about three – sitting on her lap.

Afterwards, when the children went back to their parents, laughing and happy, he asked her what she'd been doing.

'I'm a teacher,' she said. 'It's what I do. The children need looking after and teaching when their parents are working all day. They need me.'

And you need them, thought Lech. He was delighted to see her smiling for the first time in weeks.

That night, the first snow fell. And the temperature plummeted. Halina suggested they share a bed to keep warm.

Lech, who would have jumped at such a suggestion from an attractive young woman in the days before the war, felt shy and awkward. He was in no doubt that he loved his cousin very much, but did she feel the same way about him? What if she simply meant they should share a bed, fully clothed, just for the warmth?

'Don't be shy,' she said. 'It's just the two of us now.' Not long after that, they became lovers. It was just the most natural thing in the world.

But the cold in October was only the start, a hint of things to come. The temperature dropped faster than a lead weight and now it's regularly twenty or thirty degrees below freezing. The tiny wood-burning stove in the corner of the room is totally inadequate, as is their daily allowance of two small logs. But Igor punishes anyone who tries to take more wood from the store. It's a choice between food and warmth. There are no more berries in the forest.

The thought of the forest fills him with terror. He trudges to work each day in snow that comes up to his knees. The landscape is so piercingly white, his eyes ache from snow blindness. His hands are almost too stiff to hold the axe.

Halina stirs in her sleep, burrowing into him, seeking a modicum of warmth. Lech takes her hand in his and closes his eyes. Outside, the wolves howl.

PART SEVEN
DARK DAYS
1941

CHAPTER TWENTY-EIGHT

Wiktor has always loved the first snow of winter. That moment when you open the curtains and gaze out into a world so white it hurts your eyes. Bright, clean, crunching underfoot, the snow transforms grey streets into something magical. Jan and he would go to the Saxon Garden and build the largest snowman they could manage. Then they would have a snowball fight with other kids from the neighbourhood. It didn't matter that they went home soaking wet and freezing cold because they could thaw out in front of the fire with a nice hot cup of cocoa. The cold was exhilarating and gave them rosy cheeks.

But now the snow covering the ghetto is like a death shroud. There is no heating in the apartment and they wear their coats inside. Wiktor doesn't think he'll ever be warm again. His fingers and toes are blue with the cold. When he gets into bed at night, the sheets feel damp from the chill. The whole family sleeps in one room now, ever since the family from Poznań moved into the apartment. Antonina has developed a cough that won't go away and keeps them awake half the night.

Wiktor usually volunteers to go and buy bread just to escape from the overcrowded apartment. But nowadays when he ventures out in the early morning, he sees naked corpses in the street covered in newspaper. People have stripped them of their clothes. The dead don't need trousers and shirts, but the living do. Two men with a handcart trudge around the streets every morning, collecting the bodies. When Wiktor hears the now familiar clatter of iron-rimmed wheels on the cobbles, he averts his gaze. The sight of lifeless limbs dangling from the sides of the cart is more than he can stomach.

Today the queue at the baker's is longer than ever. Despite the numbers dying, there are more people than ever in the ghetto. As demand outstrips supply, so prices are soaring. Bread is now ten złotys on the black market. Those who have been fortunate enough to secure a loaf scurry home with it tucked inside their coats, fearful of being robbed. The queue has barely moved since Wiktor joined it and he stamps his feet to keep the circulation going. There are raised voices up ahead and people in the queue lean sideways to see what's going on. No one steps out of line for fear of losing their place, but people look at each other with anxious faces. And then the news travels down the line. *Sold out! No more bread today!* And it's not yet eight o'clock.

Disgruntled housewives fall into a debate about what to do, but Wiktor slips away. There's no point hanging around any longer. It's time to do something that he's thought about for a while but hasn't yet plucked up the courage for.

He has got to know other children in the ghetto and they have shared their secrets with him. Secrets that seemed way too daring for a slowcoach like him. But he's asked himself what Jan would do in the same situation and the answer is obvious. Jan wouldn't think twice about the danger. So Wiktor makes up his mind. Tonight he will cross over to the Aryan side in search of food.

He waits for dusk to fall, then he slips out of the apartment and hurries along the street, keeping close to the buildings in case he encounters a German patrol. The streets along the border are filled with small figures flitting between the shadows.

This is the place he's heard so much about – a bombed-out house on the edge of the ghetto. The jagged outline of the walls is topped by a layer of crisp, white snow that glitters in the moonlight. He hangs back in the doorway of the building opposite and observes what happens. After a minute he sees the small figure of a boy – he can't be more than eight or nine years old – clambering over a pile of rubble and disappearing underneath the ruined remains. Wiktor follows him through the hole, stumbles in the dark, and slips down a short flight of steps, landing on his bottom.

'Who's there?' calls a small voice from down below.

'A friend,' calls Wiktor. 'I won't harm you. I want you to show me the way.'

'You want to go to the other side?'

'I need to get bread for my family.'

As his eyes adjust to the gloom, Wiktor makes out a scrawny kid who barely comes up to his shoulder.

'You'll have to crawl,' says the boy. 'It'll be a tight squeeze for someone like you.'

'Please, just show me the way.'

The boy nods.

The cellar leads into a tunnel no more than four feet high. The boy bends his knees and hunches his shoulders, moving with the agility of a sewer rat. Wiktor, struggling to keep up, has more difficulty. He's at least a foot taller than the boy and has to bend almost double, which makes it tricky to see where he's going.

The tunnel extends for what feels like the length of three or four houses. The last bit of the tunnel is the lowest. Here the roof is only three feet high and the tunnel looks as if it has been recently dug out of the ground. The boy drops to his hands and knees and Wiktor follows suit. If the knees of his trousers rip, he doesn't know where he'll get another pair from. He baulks at the idea of stripping clothes off a corpse.

Not before time they emerge in the ruins of a house on the Aryan side. Wiktor dusts himself off and is about to thank his young guide, but the boy has already disappeared.

Wiktor walks with care. He has the presence of mind to remove his armband and hide it in his pocket. Even so, he feels like a stranger in this part of the city and worries that someone will spot he's from the ghetto and report him to the Germans. Most of all he fears a German patrol. On more than one occasion when he hears the sound of a vehicle in the distance, he darts into a doorway or down a side street. He doesn't really have a plan, he realises. The shops are shut and he doesn't know where he's going to find food at this late hour. The only place he can think to go is Jan's apartment.

He creeps into the building like a fugitive and hurries up the stairs. At the door he hesitates, but then knocks softly. If there's no answer, he'll return home and try again another day. But the door opens, cautiously at first, then suddenly wider.

Pani Nowak takes one look at him, says nothing, but grabs him by the arm and pulls him inside. She hugs him to her bosom so tight that Wiktor thinks he might suffocate.

'Mum, let him breathe,' says Jan. 'Wiktor, mate! What are you doing here?'

Pani Nowak releases him from her embrace but holds him at arm's length. 'However did you get here?' She looks him up and down. Wiktor is aware that he's none too clean after crawling through the tunnel.

'I'm sorry to bother you,' he says. 'A boy showed me the way through a tunnel and I…'

His words sound distant to his own ears and his vision starts to blur as he sinks to the ground. He's only vaguely aware of Pani Nowak crying for Jan to catch him before he falls.

When he comes round, he's lying on the sofa wrapped in a blanket. Pani Nowak is rubbing his frozen feet to bring them back to life. Wiktor has never seen Jan looking so worried. He tries to sit up.

'I'm sorry…' he starts to say.

'Don't worry,' says Pani Nowak in her kindest voice. 'You fainted that's all. You were frozen to the bone when you got here and from the look of you, you're not getting enough to eat.' She turns to Jan. 'Go and fetch a bowl of that soup that's on the stove.'

Jan returns with a bowl of hot vegetable soup and a spoon. Wiktor spoons the hot broth into his mouth and thinks it's the best thing he's ever tasted. Once he's finished, he tells them how he crawled through the tunnel hoping to find bread on the Aryan side.

'And Antonina has had a cough for weeks,' he says. He doesn't mention the corpses in the street. They probably wouldn't believe him.

Pani Nowak bustles into the kitchen and returns with a loaf of bread wrapped in newspaper. 'Take this.' She thrusts the package into his hands.

'But what will you eat in the morning?' he asks. Everyone is on rations. He hates the thought of depriving Jan's family.

'We will manage,' says Pani Nowak. 'I know how to get more.'

'Thank you.' Wiktor stuffs the loaf inside his jacket where it bulges. He stands up. 'I'd best be heading back.' He's sorry to have to leave, but his parents are probably worried sick about him.

Jan accompanies him down the stairs. 'I didn't realise things were so bad over there.'

Wiktor shrugs.

'Tell me where the house is,' says Jan suddenly. 'Next time I'll meet you there. Then you won't have to come all the way over here.'

'Are you sure?' asks Wiktor doubtfully. 'You'd be taking a huge risk.'

'I want to help.'

'All right then.' Wiktor gives him the directions and they arrange to meet in two days' time.

He returns to the ghetto with his precious bread.

CHAPTER TWENTY-NINE

Two days later, Jan is waiting opposite the bombed-out house with a bag of potatoes that his mother acquired on one of her black-market shopping expeditions. Beside him stands Weronika with a loaf of bread and a portion of cheese. As soon as Jan told her about Wiktor's plight and his daring excursion to the Aryan side, there was no holding her back. She insisted on coming too.

'It'll mean being out after curfew,' he said, not at all sure he wanted her company and wondering why he'd told her about it in the first place. Was he just trying to impress her?

But Weronika isn't the sort of girl who takes no for an answer, and now she's here he's glad. It's cold and dark, and not a little spooky by this ruined building. Every time he hears footsteps or a vehicle, he tenses in case it's a German patrol but Weronika retains her cool. To pass the time, he asks her about typhus. She's bound to know all about it.

'It's a bacterial infection spread by infected lice,' she says. 'The main symptoms are fever, headache and a rash. Untreated, it's often fatal.' This is not at all reassuring.

'There are signs at the ghetto gates warning of the risk of typhus,' says Jan.

Weronika scoffs. 'The Germans want everyone to think

that the Jews spread disease. But that's nonsense. Unhygienic living conditions cause disease.'

'There are a lot of people in overcrowded houses in the ghetto.'

'There you go,' says Weronika matter-of-factly. 'Listen, do you hear something?'

Jan peers into the gloom of the ruined house but can make out nothing. But then he hears a scuffling sound and a figure emerges from the shadows of the house and darts across the road. It's Wiktor. He's already looking better than he did the other night. When he fainted in the apartment, Jan got the fright of his life thinking that his friend had dropped dead.

Wiktor holds open a canvas backpack and they quickly fill it with the food. Then Wiktor heads back into the bowels of the house for the return journey.

Half an hour later he is back with a pile of coins, having sold most of the food for twice what it would fetch on the Aryan side. With this money Jan and Weronika will be able to buy more food which Wiktor will sell on at an inflated price, keeping back just enough for his own family.

By the end of the week, Wiktor has recruited two more ghetto children to help with the enterprise. Antoni and Agata, fraternal twins aged eight, are two of the scrawniest human beings Jan has ever seen. The first time he saw them emerge from the bombed-out house, he thought they must have been no more than five or six years old. But they are quick and scurry in and out of the house like rats down a sewer. Between the three of them they can sell more food in the ghetto and make more money. In return, Jan and Weronika – ably assisted by Maria – are able to buy more on the black market. It's a thriving business and what's more, they're doing it right under the noses of the Germans.

Jan discovers a newfound confidence that he never knew he possessed. He's becoming a shrewd negotiator, picking up better bargains every day. Today he has half a pound of beef in his bag, a rare treat. Weronika has proven to be a real stalwart and has negotiated some good deals herself, acquiring much-needed antibiotics from her father.

'When this is all over,' she tells him, 'I'm going to go to university and then I'm going to travel and see the world.'

'Where will you go?' asks Jan. He hasn't thought that far ahead. Getting through each day is enough of a challenge.

'Italy, obviously. Florence and Rome in particular. I want to see the great works of art by Michelangelo.'

'Uh huh,' says Jan, losing interest. Paintings and sculpture bore him.

'But I also want to see America and go to the top of the Empire State Building.'

'Me too!' blurts out Jan.

'Let's go together. How about it?'

'I, er… oh look, here they are!' He's saved from having to give Weronika an answer by the arrival of Wiktor and his two young pals. Was she serious about going to America together? He's not sure what he thinks of the idea.

Agata makes straight for Weronika with whom she seems to have developed a special bond. Whilst Weronika explains to her about the antibiotics and what they're good for, Jan puts the food into Antoni's backpack.

'Can you manage all that?' asks Jan.

'Course I can,' says the younger boy. 'I'm strong.'

Jan wants to laugh at that. Antoni reminds him of a stick insect. But he admires the kid's courage. He wonders if Antoni would like his old football. He'll bring it next time.

'We should get going,' says Wiktor. 'There's a bright moon tonight.'

It's true, the moon is especially large and white, casting a cold light on their illicit activities. Wiktor seems more nervous than usual. He keeps glancing up and down the deserted street as if he expects a patrol to appear any second. He shoulders his own backpack and sets off after Antoni and Agata, who are already disappearing from view in the ruins of the bombed-out house.

Jan and Weronika wait for Wiktor to return with the

money which will enable them to buy more food tomorrow. Weronika doesn't mention her travel plans again and Jan thinks it best not to resume that particular conversation.

Time drags. It's so cold Jan can no longer feel his toes. He wishes Wiktor would get a move on. What's keeping him? He's usually much quicker than this. He's about to ask Weronika if she thinks they should stick around or go home, when the crack of a rifle shot splits the silence. A volley of shots follows, then silence.

'Where was that?' Weronika stares at him, the whites of her eyes bright in the moonlight.

'In the ghetto.' He sets off across the road.

'Wait, where are you going?'

Jan ignores her. He's already clambering over the ruined house, looking for the way in.

Weronika grabs his arm. 'What do you think you're doing?' she hisses in his ear. 'You can't go over there.'

'But what if Wiktor has been hurt? I have to help him. He should have been back by now.' His voice cracks but he doesn't care. His heart is beating so hard he thinks it will explode. They stand still a moment and listen. Silence. The shooting has stopped. But there's still no sign of Wiktor. Jan can't stand not knowing what has happened to his friend. He shakes Weronika off and stumbles over fallen masonry until he finds the entrance to the tunnel. To his surprise, Weronika is right behind him.

'I'm coming with you,' she whispers. 'If someone has been hurt, I'll be more use.' He can't argue with that. He's always hated the sight of blood.

Without a light, they have to feel their way through the tunnel, bent double, even crawling on the ground. Progress is painstakingly slow. More than once Weronika bumps into him. 'Keep going,' she whispers. By the time they emerge on the other side, bruised and dirty, Jan has a newfound respect for Wiktor, Antoni and Agata.

An eerie silence greets them on this side of the wall. The street is deserted, like a ghost town. No one dares leave their apartment after curfew.

At least they haven't run straight into a dead body which was what Jan feared. But where is Wiktor? Where are Antoni and Agata? Did they decide it was too dangerous to be outside and just go home? The obvious place to look for Wiktor is his apartment, but what if he's not there? Pan and Pani Zieliński would naturally assume the worst.

'Patrol,' whispers Weronika.

They duck into the shadows of the bombed-out building as a vehicle turns the corner. It's a small open-topped truck with four armed guards in the back. They drive past, brandishing their weapons and roaring with laughter. Whatever they've been doing tonight, it's all a big joke to them.

They wait until the truck is safely out of sight, then Jan and Weronika set off in the direction it came from. The painful cries of a young girl carry on the still night air. They follow the sound.

In a side street, they find Wiktor kneeling on the cobbles, hunched over a skinny figure. Jan would recognise those scrawny legs anywhere.

Antoni.

Beside him, Agata is clutching her brother's hand, her tears falling freely onto his face.

'What happened?' Jan sinks to the ground beside his friend. He can see straightaway that it's too late for Antoni. He's been shot in the chest. His thin cotton jacket is soaked with blood. Weronika's nursing skills will be of no use here. Instead she puts her arms around Agata and draws her into a tight embrace. 'We heard the shots.'

'They just appeared out of nowhere and started shooting at us,' says Wiktor bitterly. 'Agata and I ran for cover. We thought Antoni was with us… The bastards! It was just a game for them.'

'We saw them,' says Jan. He'd like to line every one of those Germans up against a wall and shoot them himself. He holds Antoni's hand which lies cold and lifeless within his own. 'I was going to give him my old football,' he adds.

'He'd have liked that,' says Wiktor, which just makes Jan feel even worse.

Agata's tears have subsided for now and she's clinging to Weronika. Jan turns to Wiktor. 'What now?' They can't leave Antoni lying here. Wiktor has told him how people steal the clothes off dead bodies.

But Wiktor isn't listening to him. Instead, he hits himself on the side of his head with the heel of his palm. 'This is all my fault. I shouldn't have got the twins involved in smuggling. If it wasn't for me, he'd still be alive.'

'No!' shouts a high-pitched voice. It's Agata. 'We knew it was dangerous. Without your help we would have died of hunger a long time ago.'

'She's right,' says Weronika. 'You were only doing what you had to do to survive. The Germans are to blame for Antoni's death, no one else.' She turns to Agata. 'Where do you live? We'll take Antoni home.'

Agata hangs her head and says in a very small voice, 'Our parents are dead. It was just Antoni and me. We've been living in an abandoned basement.'

The enormity of this pronouncement strikes them all dumb.

'I had no idea,' says Wiktor, visibly stunned. 'I met them in the street, you know how it is. I should have realised.' He looks close to despair. 'She could come back with me, but…' He trails off.

Jan understands his dilemma. His family already live in one room of an apartment that they share with the family from Poznań. Jan comes to a decision. 'She can come home with me.'

'Don't be stupid,' says Wiktor. 'It's illegal for Jews to live on the Aryan side.'

'And what she's been doing smuggling food wasn't illegal?'

'That's different,' says Wiktor. 'Besides, what if the Gestapo discover you're hiding a Jew? You and your mother would be shot!'

But Jan has made up his mind, and Weronika is looking at him with undisguised admiration which only spurs him on. 'We'll hide her in our apartment.' It's not like they haven't got the space, what with Lech and Anna and his father all gone. His mother won't turn away an orphaned girl.

Wiktor looks like he wants to raise another objection, but Weronika interrupts. 'What about Antoni? We can't leave him here.'

'We'll take him to the *Judenrat*,' says Wiktor.

Jan takes Antoni's feet and Wiktor lifts his shoulders. Between them, the boy weighs next to nothing. They deposit his broken body outside the administrative building of the Jewish council.

'Now go,' says Wiktor. 'And stay safe.'

Leading Agata by the hand, Jan and Weronika hurry back through the deserted streets and through the tunnel under the bombed-out house to the Aryan side.

Only then, darting through the streets with this filthy, ragged girl, does Jan sense the enormity of what he's just done.

CHAPTER THIRTY

'Get up, lazy bitches!'

The groans of a hundred and fifty-odd women fill the block as they begin to stir themselves. At least those that are still breathing. There's always someone who doesn't wake up.

Anna clutches the edge of her blanket, missing the oblivion of sleep. It's still dark and it's freezing cold. But the siren is sounding, loud and insistent, as it does every morning at five o'clock sharp. That's the way they do things here. Ravensbrück is the name of this place. Hell is another word for it.

Irmgard, the German prisoner in charge of their block, is on the move. Every morning, as soon as the siren goes off, she lumbers up and down the rows of tightly packed bunks, shouting at the women to get a move on. *Filthy Polish whores! Lazy Polish swine!* It's the most work she does all day.

It was a shock, at first, to find other prisoners – *Blockova* is their official title – ruling the roost in the accommodation blocks. But Anna has come to realise it's a deliberate ploy on the part of the SS to control them. Divide and rule. The Blockovas do the bidding of the SS in return for an extra sausage and their own bed. Obedience is cheaply bought.

'Out of bed, lazy swine!' Irmgard is getting closer. Her wooden clogs rap on the concrete floor.

With a huge effort, Anna climbs down from the third tier of the bunk she shares with Krysia and Jadwiga, a young woman who came with the January transport from Lublin. Jadwiga is already up, trying to rouse Krysia who has been coughing for days now.

'She's in a bad way,' whispers Jadwiga. Krysia's thin shoulders poke through the blue and white checked blanket.

Irmgard has now arrived at their bunk. 'Still asleep, lazy bitch?' She pokes Krysia with her finger. 'Polish swine!' She shakes Krysia's shoulder, inducing a coughing fit, precisely what Anna and Jadwiga were hoping to avoid.

Irmgard's vocabulary is limited. The Polish women are either bitches, whores or swine, lazy or filthy. Once Anna realised this about Irmgard, the words ceased to have any effect on her. *Water off a duck's back,* she thinks. Still, you don't want to get on the wrong side of your Blockova. They can be almost as dangerous as the SS. In her former life – according to a Polish countess Anna has befriended – Irmgard was a *Puffmutter.* A brothel madam. Apparently, she ran a thriving establishment in a side street off Hamburg's Reeperbahn. The black triangle on her sleeve marks her out as one of the *asocials,* someone who didn't fit the Führer's definition of a good German *Hausfrau* devoted to *Kinder, Küche, Kirche.* Children, kitchen, church. A big, fleshy woman who might have been considered voluptuous in her prime, now her jowls sag and two of her front teeth are missing. Even so, Irmgard still carries herself as if she's got what it takes to seduce half the Wehrmacht.

'Krysia's not well,' says Anna. 'She needs to go to the Revier.' The camp has a hospital of sorts, although Anna has not heard anything good about it.

Irmgard turns on her. 'Who put you in charge, Polish whore?'

'No one.' Out of the corner of her eye she sees women on their way to the latrines slowing down to watch. But not stopping to intervene. Krysia is not their problem.

'Get her up!' shouts Irmgard. 'Or you'll be late for *Appell*.' She continues down the rows of bunks.

Between them Anna and Jadwiga hoist Krysia out of bed.

'Sorry I caused a row,' says Krysia, rubbing her eyes. 'Just a bit tired, that's all.'

Who isn't tired in this place? They sleep on lumpy mattresses filled with wood shavings, with one sheet and one thin blanket. The night is a constant racket of coughs, cries, sighs, weeping and snoring.

They visit the latrines which are blocked, as usual, then hurry outside to join the thousands of women streaming from their blocks onto the *Appellplatz*, the huge, sandy square where they waited for hours when they first arrived at the camp.

The daily ritual of *Appell* is the first torture of the day. Line up in rows of five. Hands by your sides. Noses to the front. And wait to be counted. Anna and Jadwiga position Krysia between them so they can catch her if she falls.

As usual, it takes an age for everyone to assemble. The black and green triangles are the worst – the asocials and the hardened criminals. They're always late and can't seem to line up in fives without a great deal of pushing, shoving and swearing. In contrast, the Jews (yellow triangles) and Jehovah's Witnesses (lilac triangles) line up quietly with no fuss. The Lilacs keep themselves to themselves and refuse point blank to do so-called war-work for the Nazis. As a result, they receive the worst punishments, but nothing breaks them. You've got to hand it to them, they're a tough bunch. The red triangles worn by the Polish women mark them out as political prisoners, putting them in the same category as the German Communists. The Reds are reviled by the Blacks and Greens whilst the Blacks and Greens are feared and detested by everyone. Divide and rule.

A bitter wind blows across the *Appellplatz* as the women stand shivering in their cotton dresses and jackets. Anna resists the urge to hug herself and stamp her feet to keep warm. They have to stand straight, hands by their sides, facing forwards at all times. The punishment for not doing so is a slap or a crack of the whip, depending on the whim of the guard doing the counting.

In the months she's been here, Anna has learnt the names of the guards most to be feared. The pretty, blonde guard who whipped her on the hand the day they arrived is called Dorothea Binz, a local girl with next to no education and a sadistic pleasure in petty acts of cruelty. Then there's Emma Zimmer, deputy to the female superintendent Johanna Langefeld, who usually takes charge of the counting at the morning *Appell*. Today is no exception.

A thin-faced, thin-lipped woman in her fifties, Zimmer is marching up and down the rows, slapping anyone who moves. The jackboots are getting nearer, stomping on the sandy ground. Anna repeats a mantra inside her head. *Stand still. Eyes forward. Neutral face. No fear.* But don't appear too confident either because that can get you into trouble. Next to her, Krysia sways and Anna wills her to stand still. Just a minute longer. Surely, she can manage that, can't she?

Zimmer is coming down their line. Footsteps approaching, black cloak flapping in the wind. Anna holds her breath as Zimmer's sharp face appears in front of her. *Don't look her in the eye.* She stares past Zimmer at the badly shaved head of a woman in the row in front. There's a tuft of hair that the shaver missed. The black cloaked figure is slowly moving on. Too slowly. *Go away,* thinks Anna. *Leave us alone.*

The slap is like a pistol shot in the silence. Krysia stumbles forwards. Anna turns and puts her hands out to prevent her friend falling to the ground. If she falls, Zimmer will kick her with her jackboots.

'Stand still!' barks Zimmer into Anna's face, spittle flying.

Krysia regains her balance and Anna drops her arms and faces forwards. She only did what any normal person would have done, but these guards are not normal people. Simple decency is an alien concept to them. Anna would like to see Emma Zimmer standing in the freezing cold in nothing but a thin cotton dress on an empty stomach after weeks and months of hard labour, and see if she manages not to flinch a muscle. But Zimmer has moved on, looking for the next victim.

The counting finally over, they return to the block where Irmgard is doling out the black liquid that passes for coffee and a piece of bread. This is the first dilemma of the day – how much of the bread to eat now and how much to save for later. Newcomers always make the mistake of eating all the bread in one go. But you soon learn. Eat half now and save half until the evening. Other things you learn are never to drink the water, and pick out your lice.

Anna has barely eaten half her bread and drunk the disgusting black liquid before the siren sounds for the second time. Selection for the work gangs is about to begin.

This is the moment of truth. This will determine how many of them are still standing at the end of the day.

CHAPTER THIRTY-ONE

Let the little children come to me, and do not hinder them, for the Kingdom of Heaven belongs to such as these.

Maria has taken these words of her Saviour very much to heart and for the first time since the outbreak of war she feels that she has found her true purpose. When Lech went off to fight, she knew the anguish of all mothers and worried constantly for his safety. When Emeryk was arrested and killed, her world fell apart. For days she was prostrate with grief, unable even to get out of bed. She had only just picked herself up from that tragedy when Anna was arrested and sent to the concentration camp. That was the final straw. Maria railed against her God who seemed intent on punishing her for she knew not what.

Jan was all she had left and he was impossible to control, sneaking out after curfew to take food to the ghetto, coming home at all hours. She was proud of him, but that didn't stop her worrying every time he set foot outside the apartment. If she were to lose him too, she would have no reason to go on living.

And then one night he was out even later than usual. She remembers how she sat in the living room with her sewing, listening to the ticking of the clock on the mantelpiece. Her imagination ran away with her – he'd been rounded up, he'd been arrested. He'd been shot! What if he was lying somewhere hurt? She should go and look for him! But what would happen if she was arrested for being out after curfew and he came home to an empty apartment? Her nerves were in such a state of tension that when she finally heard footsteps on the stairs, she ran to the door and yanked it open, ready to give her youngest an earful about causing her so much stress and anxiety.

But the words died on her lips.

Jan wasn't alone. Clinging to him was a young girl, thin and dirty, with a tear-streaked face.

'This is Agata,' said Jan by way of explanation. 'I've brought her to come and live with us.'

That was four weeks ago.

Now, when Maria stands before the statue of the Virgin Mary, she no longer sees a gesture of helplessness in the Saint's outstretched hands, but rather an invitation to those in need. *Come*, the Holy Mother seems to say, *and I will look after you.*

How could Maria turn Agata away? Especially after Jan had risked life and limb to bring her to the apartment. Her relief at having Jan home safe and sound outweighed all other considerations. That first evening, she bathed Agata, dressed her in a clean nightdress, fed her, and put her to bed in Anna's room. The poor little mite was so overcome with exhaustion that she was asleep before the door closed.

Only then did Maria insist that Jan tell her what was going on. And Jan – who was soon to turn thirteen – broke down and cried on her bosom as he told her what had happened to Antoni and how they'd left his body outside the *Judenrat*. Maria's heart nearly burst with pity. She agreed that Agata would stay with them until she was stronger, and then they would decide what to do.

For the first couple of weeks, Agata barely said a word. She retreated inside herself, overwhelmed by grief for her brother. Maria understood that feeling only too well and tried to give the little girl the time and space she needed to grieve. Then one day, when Maria was reading her a bedtime story, Agata kissed her and said, 'Are you my mummy now?' Maria's heart flooded with love for the orphaned girl and she said, 'Yes, if you'd like that.' She knew then that she would never send Agata back to the ghetto. From everything that Jan had told her, the ghetto was no place for children, let alone orphaned children with no one in the world to care for them.

Now there are practical matters to sort out. You can't hide a Jewish child in your apartment without one of the neighbours noticing. Sooner or later someone is going to get suspicious, and you never know who you can trust these days. They've got away with it until now because Agata is such a quiet little thing, hardly making a sound, and understanding instinctively that she has to stay out of the way when Pani Woźniak calls around or Pani Kowalska comes knocking with one of her noisy children in tow.

But with the right paperwork, maybe Maria can say that Agata is the orphaned child of a friend from the country. Her goddaughter perhaps. How does one obtain such papers? Who to ask? It occurs to her to speak to Father Piotr. When Lech was called up, the elderly priest told her that everyone would have a role to play, even if they couldn't then see what it was. Now that Maria has found her role, she needs help in making it a reality. When she requests a meeting, the good man is happy to oblige.

Father Piotr invites her to sit down. His book-lined study reminds her of Emeryk's study which she never enters now, afraid of the memories it would stir.

'I need your help, Father,' she begins, unsure where to start.

Father Piotr regards her sympathetically and invites her to continue with a nod of his head.

'My son, Jan, is very brave and he–' No, the priest doesn't need to hear all that. She should get to the point, she's sure Father Piotr is a very busy man. She starts again.

'There is a little girl staying with me. She doesn't have any papers. I was wondering if you knew where I might obtain some for her?' There, she's said it. For a second, she fears that the priest will turn her over to the authorities there and then. But then the old man's face breaks into a smile.

'God bless you,' he says. 'You are doing a very brave thing. I wish there were more people like you in Warsaw. Heaven knows, the need is great enough.'

'But without the right papers…' Does she have to spell it out?

The priest holds up a hand to silence her. 'Have no fear, Pani Nowak. What you are asking for is nothing new. I have contacts who deal with this sort of thing all the time.'

'You do?'

'Of course.' He pulls a pen and piece of paper towards him, suddenly becoming brisk and business-like. The years seem to fall off him, and Maria catches a glimpse of the young, fervent man he must once have been. 'How old is she?'

'Eight. But she's small for her age. She could pass for six or seven.'

'All the better.' Father Piotr makes a note. 'When a Christian child dies in one of the orphanages, my colleagues don't report the death. Instead we give the name and registry number to another child in need of a new identity.' He is careful to avoid saying 'a Jewish child.' Caution is a way of life now.

'I had no idea,' says Maria.

'We just do what we can,' says the priest modestly. 'It's never enough, but we do what we can. Leave it with me.'

Maria returns home feeling that there's a chink of light in all this darkness. You must never give up hope.

CHAPTER THIRTY-TWO

Shovelling sand. Of all the pointless, meaningless tasks in the world, this has to be right at the top of the list. The *Sandgrube*. The sandpit. Anna has no doubt that this is her and Krysia's punishment for causing a disturbance at *Appell* that morning. Emma Zimmer made sure of it.

Under the watchful eyes of two female guards, the women in this work gang shovel sand from one pile to another. And then shovel it back again. The sand is wet and densely packed, like cement. It's impossibly heavy to move. Men twice their size would find it tough. And the sand works its insidious way into their clogs, rubbing the soles of their frozen feet until they bleed.

Anna keeps one eye on Krysia. She barely has the strength to lift her spade when it's empty, never mind when it's loaded with sand. And she's coughing again. A dry, raucous bark that sounds as if her lungs are being ripped to shreds.

An icy wind blows off the lake, numbing their hands and freezing their emaciated bodies. On the far shore, the town of Fürstenberg might as well be on another planet. What do the inhabitants know of what goes on here? They must hear rumours, but do they pay attention? It's probably easier not to know.

A thud behind her makes her turn round. Krysia has collapsed. It was bound to happen sooner or later. She's sprawled on the sand, a limp figure in her oversized dress. Anna and Jadwiga both drop their spades and rush over to their friend, anxious to get to her before the guards do. The guards are standing a little way off, keeping their shiny boots clean.

'Grab her ankles,' says Anna. 'I'll take her shoulders.' Together they heave Krysia out of the sandpit so that the pointless work of shovelling sand can continue, otherwise the whole work gang will be punished for slacking.

Krysia's eyes flutter open. She just fainted for a moment. Another coughing fit wracks her tiny frame, and this time when she takes her hand away from her mouth, Anna sees spots of blood.

'What is going on here?' One of the guards has marched over, her whip at the ready. It isn't anyone Anna recognises. Not Dorothea Binz, thank goodness, otherwise they would all have received a lashing by now.

'She's sick,' says Anna. 'She needs to go to the Revier.'

'Take her then,' says the guard to Anna and Jadwiga. 'Then come straight back here.'

Anna can't believe their luck. The two friends don't need telling twice. They take an arm each and drape Krysia between them. Unbelievably, despite the freezing temperature, Krysia feels warm to the touch. Her thin face is flushed, her eyes glazed.

'Can you walk?' asks Anna.

Krysia nods. Even so, they make painfully slow progress. Every few seconds, Krysia doubles over with another coughing fit.

They're about to cross the now deserted *Appellplatz* when two men emerge from the Revier, deep in conversation. One is tall with an aquiline nose and sticking out ears: Dr Walter Sonntag. Anna has heard about him on the camp grapevine. Dressed in the black uniform of the SS with the *Totenkopf* on his cap, Sonntag is never without his bamboo cane tucked into one leather boot. The rumour is that he prods patients with his cane when examining them, hitting them when the fancy takes him. His companion is shorter, with a pudgy face, wispy moustache and round wire-framed spectacles. As he speaks, he makes emphatic gestures with his hands. Sonntag, hanging on every word, nods his head enthusiastically.

'That's Heinrich Himmler,' whispers Jadwiga. 'What's he doing here?'

The head of the SS and the Gestapo, Himmler is one of Hitler's closest associates. His presence in the camp cannot be a good sign. The three friends stay out of sight whilst the two men stride off in the direction of the SS Headquarters outside the camp gates. When they judge that the way is clear, they cross the *Appellplatz*, and enter the block designated as a sick bay.

The stench hits them first. A stomach-churning cocktail of rotting flesh, stale sweat and excrement. Anna's first instinct is to turn around and walk straight back out again. They can't leave Krysia in this miserable excuse for a hospital. It's like nothing Anna could have imagined in her worst nightmares. Women with sores oozing pus, soiled clothes, and faces running with sweat are lined up, or collapsed against the wall, waiting to be admitted. But it's too late to make their escape. A female doctor in a white coat has spotted the new arrivals and swoops down on them like a vulture sighting her prey. A name badge identifies her as Dr Gerda Weyand.

'What's wrong with her?' demands Weyand, barely glancing at Krysia.

The ensuing coughing fit should be explanation enough but Anna explains as calmly as she can that Krysia has been sick for weeks and now she's coughing up blood.

'She collapsed in the sandpit,' adds Jadwiga.

What's the point? The doctor isn't paying attention, isn't even looking at Krysia, and certainly isn't writing any of this down.

'Shut up,' screams Weyand at a woman who is moaning softly to herself. She turns back to Anna and Jadwiga. 'Leave her there.' She indicates the end of the row of sick women. Anna and Jadwiga exchange a wide-eyed look, but what can they do? They can't take Krysia back to the sandpit and if they return her to the block Irmgard will continue to throw her out of bed at five every morning for *Appell* in the freezing cold. Maybe things will be better once Krysia has been examined and is given a bed on the ward.

'You're going to be all right,' says Anna to Krysia. 'You just need to rest and then you'll recover.' She wills it to be true.

Krysia nods her head weakly. 'Thank you.'

'Go back to your work gangs,' Weyand tells Anna and Jadwiga. 'You're in the way here.'

They return to the sandpit too shocked by what they've seen to speak.

*

Sunday. The only day in the week when they don't have *Appell* at five o'clock in the morning. Only the Jews have to work on Sundays.

But Anna can't sleep. She keeps thinking of Krysia in the Revier. She wishes they'd never taken her there, but what choice did they have? Krysia couldn't go on as she was, the work would have killed her. She needs to rest and build up her strength. Anna will try to take her some extra food. They get a blob of jam on Sundays, a square of margarine and a sausage. Practically a feast.

After breakfast, Irmgard is in her element, ordering the women to make their beds in the Prussian style. Strutting up and down the rows of bunks like the brothel madam she once was, she finds fault with everyone. That mattress isn't as flat as a millpond; puff that pillow out so the corners are at right angles; that blanket isn't straight; do it again!

Anna and Jadwiga make their own beds – three times before Irmgard is satisfied – and Krysia's empty bunk.

'Where is she?' demands Irmgard, pointing at the bottom bunk. She's only just noticed Krysia's absence. You could die here, thinks Anna, and Irmgard's only concern would be that you didn't make *Appell* in time.

'She's in the Revier,' says Anna. 'She collapsed yesterday in the *Sandgrube*.' *You should never have forced her to go to Appell*, she wants to add. Instead she gives Irmgard a hard stare. If the brothel madam doesn't understand Anna's meaning, then she must be stupid as well as heartless.

But Irmgard shrugs her shoulders as if to say, well she was a bother that one; no longer my problem. 'That blanket's not straight,' she says as her parting shot. 'Do it again.'

Appell is at midday on Sundays. Emma Zimmer must be in a hurry to get back to the comfort of her guards' accommodation – well-appointed villas surrounded by trees – and a tasty lunch in the SS canteen because the counting is done in record time with only a handful of slaps.

Back in their blocks, the women receive their monthly letter from home. They are also permitted to write back. It's always a moment of anxiety for Anna, wondering if she'll receive a letter this time. What if something has happened to her mother and Jan and there's no letter for her?

Irmgard hands out the letters like a queen distributing favours. Anna receives hers with a mixture of relief and trepidation. She opens it with trembling fingers, eager for news but praying that nothing bad has happened. She scans the letter quickly to reassure herself, then she settles down to read it more carefully. Her mother and brother are all right, that's the most important thing. But the situation in Warsaw is not good. The Jews are living in a ghetto now, walled in, and separate from everyone else. Reading between the lines, Anna understands that Jan is doing what he can to help. Her heart swells with admiration for her little brother. Just as long as he doesn't take unnecessary risks. Look what happened to her when she stuck her neck out.

Ribald chatter and laughter emanate from Irmgard's curtained off quarters. A coterie of black triangles has joined her for a natter about old times. Anna sits on her bunk with a single piece of thin paper and a stub of pencil and tries to block out the coarse voices. What to write in reply? Prisoners' letters are censored by the SS so there's no point saying that the Blockova is a bitch, the deputy *Lagerführerin* beats people at the morning *Appell*, and Dorothea Binz is a sadist. No point trying to describe the hunger, the disease, the exhaustion, the appalling living conditions. Besides, Maria would only worry herself sick if she knew the half of it. And who would believe them anyway? Unless you've been here, you can't imagine it. So Anna does what she always does and writes a simple letter reassuring her mother that she's all right. After all, things could be worse. Look at Krysia.

In the late afternoon there's the obligatory walk along the *Lagerstrasse*, marching music blaring from the loudspeakers. At least the music enables the women to talk without being overheard by a Blockova, guard or prisoner spy.

'We have to check on Krysia,' says Anna to Jadwiga once they are some distance away from their block.

'I agree.'

'I saved her some bread and sausage.'

'Me too.'

'Can we slip away without anyone noticing?'

They scan the Lagerstrasse, looking out for Emma Zimmer or Dorothea Binz or any of the other mean guards. Thousands of women in identical blue-and-white striped dresses are trudging up and down, heads bowed against the wind, their feet dragging in their wooden clogs. No one will miss them for ten minutes.

On their next lap of the Lagerstrasse, Anna and Jadwiga inch their way to the edge of the line so they can slip into the Revier. As soon as they are level with the sick bay block, they dart inside.

It's quieter than yesterday. A handful of women are being processed by prisoner nurses with yellow armbands. The atmosphere is brisk and efficient, but not unkind. There are no German doctors anywhere in sight. Anna asks one of the nurses about Krysia and they are directed to a ward crammed with dozens of beds. It takes them a while to find Krysia amongst the feverish, groaning, coughing women. She's curled on her side, her eyes closed. Her skin is waxy pale, but she looks more restful than they've seen her in ages. At least she isn't coughing.

'I don't want to wake her,' says Jadwiga.

'No,' agrees Anna. They did the right thing, bringing her here after all.

'Hang on.' Jadwiga moves closer to the bed and holds the back of her hand in front of Krysia's nose and mouth. She frowns. Then she lays two fingers on Krysia's neck. 'She's not breathing. I can't feel a pulse.'

What?! No, Jadwiga must be mistaken. Krysia was alive when they left her yesterday. She can't be dead in the space of twenty-four hours!

But now she looks more closely, Anna can see for herself. Krysia is lying as if carved out of marble. Her thin shoulder pokes up under the blanket but there is no rise and fall. The rattle in her chest has ceased forever. She lays a hand on Krysia's forehead. Yesterday it burned with fever. Now it's cold as stone.

Anna sways on her feet. Her vision darkens and the sounds in the ward seem to come from a very long way away.

'I've got you.' Jadwiga's arms are around her, guiding her to the floor. 'Sit down. Put your head between your knees.'

They sit on the floor, hugging each other in their shared grief. There is no need to say anything.

But they can't stay here forever. The walk on the Lagerstrasse will be finished soon and if they're not back in their block, Irmgard will raise the alarm.

'I'll find one of the nurses,' says Anna.

She staggers from the ward. How can this have happened? The Revier was supposed to make Krysia better. They should never have brought her here. She wanders down the corridor, looking for one of the prisoner nurses.

She finds what looks like an office. It could be a doctor's surgery. She knocks on the door and when she hears a woman's voice say *Ja* she opens the door and walks in.

In her shock and grief, it takes her a moment to understand what she's seeing.

Dr Walter Sonntag – he has his back to her but she recognises him from the cane poking out of his boot – is leaning over the desk grunting like a pig. Gerda Weyand, the female doctor on duty yesterday when they brought Krysia in, has her arms around his neck, and her startlingly white legs wrapped around his bottom. *'Ja,'* says Weyand into her lover's ear, begging him for more. *'Ach, ja!'*

Too late, Anna starts to back out of the room. Sonntag is oblivious to anything except his own animal instincts, but Weyand sees her and gives Anna a look of utter loathing. Anna turns and flees back to the ward where two prisoner nurses have covered Krysia's body and are comforting Jadwiga.

'We have to go,' says Anna, grabbing Jadwiga's hand.

'But...'

'I can't explain now.'

Anna drags Jadwiga out of the Revier. She doesn't want to tell her what she saw in Sonntag's office. Did Weyand recognise her? They make it back to the block just as the last women are returning from the Lagerstrasse.

'For God's sake, tell me what the matter is,' whispers Jadwiga when they are sitting on Krysia's empty bunk. 'You're shaking like a leaf.'

'Sonntag and Gerda Weyand,' says Anna, trying to catch her breath.

'What about them?'

'They're having an affair.'

'How do you know?'

'I found them. In Sonntag's office. They were... you know.'

'What? In the Revier?'

Anna nods. Of all the things she has witnessed in this place, she never expected to see anything like that. She screws her eyes shut and shakes her head, trying to erase the memory from her mind. But she can't get Gerda Weyand's fleshy thighs or Sonntag's grunts out of her head.

'Did they see you?' asks Jadwiga.

Anna nods. '*She* did.'

'Oh God!'

And then Anna's tears start to fall. She cries for Krysia. She cries for all the helpless women in this place. She cries for herself. She cries for the senselessness of it all.

A shadow falls over her. Irmgard.

Anna lifts her head to see the former brothel madam looking at her with an expression that she has never seen before.

'Stand up,' says Irmgard. 'They want you outside.' She doesn't say who. Anna can guess well enough. And she suddenly realises that Irmgard hasn't called her a *lazy Polish whore* or *a filthy Polish swine*. Is that pity in her eyes? The Blockova is uncharacteristically subdued. Jadwiga, on the other hand, looks terrified.

Anna stands up. There's no point resisting.

'Follow me,' says Irmgard.

When Jadwiga comes too, Irmgard pushes her back. 'Not you, you Polish bitch.'

Irmgard takes Anna outside. 'I'm sorry,' she whispers, before pushing Anna towards two female guards. Dorothea Binz with her blonde hair immaculately curled, and Maria Mandl who has acquired the nickname *the beast*.

Anna is seized with a terror she has never known before. She looks around for the familiar figure of Irmgard – despite her coarse ways, Anna realises that the brothel madam was just trying to keep order in her block in the only way she knew how – but Irmgard has vanished back inside and Anna is on her own with two of the most feared guards in the entire camp.

They grab her arms, one on either side, and drag her towards the *Strafblock* – the punishment block.

'No, please,' says Anna. 'I haven't…'

Binz punches her in the mouth. Anna tastes blood and a tooth wobbles loose. 'You were snooping in the Revier where you shouldn't have been' – so Weyand did recognise her after all – 'and we're going to show you what happens to bitches like you who sneak around where you're not wanted.'

Emma Zimmer is waiting for them at the entrance to the *Strafblock*. 'Take her to the *Bock*.'

Dear God, thinks Anna, please no. She's heard about the *Bock*. Everyone has. Her legs go weak as Binz and Mandl take her to a cell with a wooden block in the middle of the floor. A grim-faced Johanna Langefeld, the *Lagerführerin*, is present, as is the arrogant Dr Walter Sonntag.

Resistance is useless. She's weak from months of overwork and underfeeding. She's also grieving the loss of Krysia. Binz forces her, stomach down, over the wooden block whilst Mandl secures the leather straps to hold her in place. Then one of them – Anna can't see who it is – lifts up her dress and pulls down her underwear to expose her buttocks. She knows what's coming, yet even so the first lash of the whip stings so much that she cries out in shock, and tears spring into her eyes.

'*Ein, zwei, drei…*' It's Binz's voice doing the counting. Is she the one wielding the whip?

After five lashes, Anna is in so much pain she's gasping for breath. Tears and snot run down her face.

'*Acht, neun, zehn…*' Eight, nine, ten. The lashes go on and on.

Anna drifts in and out of consciousness. Binz's voice is coming from a long way away. Nothing exists except the pain in her buttocks. Something warm trickles down her leg but she's only vaguely aware that she's wet herself. She's past caring about such things.

'*Fünfundzwanzig!*' Twenty-five. The final lash of the whip is the most violent of all. Her buttocks are on fire. She is consumed with pain like nothing she has ever known.

She's only vaguely aware of hands unstrapping her and hoisting her to her feet. She can't stand up straight, can't walk.

On Zimmer's orders, Binz and Mandl drag her to another cell and throw her inside, like a piece of discarded rubbish. The door clangs shut. She's in the dark.

CHAPTER THIRTY-THREE

Fever rages. In the sweltering days of summer, typhus spreads through the Warsaw ghetto like fire in a tinder-dry forest, leaving death and grief in its wake. The tumultuous news that Germany has invaded the Soviet Union – thus tearing up the Molotov-Ribbentrop pact – has gone almost unremarked in the Zieliński household as they fight their own battle with disease.

Wiktor kneels by his sister's mattress, dips the rag into a bowl of water, wrings it out and lays it across her burning forehead. She moans and turns her head away, but he presses the cloth down firmer until she lies still once more. It's up to him to look after her during the day. Their father works on the team maintaining the ghetto walls. From dawn till dusk he collects bricks from ruined buildings and wheels them to the wall. It's all part of the Germans' efforts to prevent the spread of typhus beyond the ghetto. But at the same time they do nothing to cure the disease. The Soviets left a large supply of anti-typhus serum in Lwów when they were driven out by the Germans in June. Some of this precious medicine has found its way to Warsaw via smugglers, but it's difficult to get hold of and the price is exorbitantly high. Thousands of złotys for a course of treatment. Meanwhile, their mother works long hours in the Többens and Schultz textile factory in Nowolipie Street making uniforms for the Germans. She comes home each evening exhausted but at least she can buy food with her earnings. Wiktor's smuggling activities have had to be put on hold for the time being.

Antonina moans something unintelligible, her eyelids fluttering, hovering between consciousness and unconsciousness. Wiktor puts a hand under her bony shoulders, lifts her into a sitting position – she weighs next to nothing these days – and holds a cup of water to her lips. He tips the cup gently, trying to get some of the liquid inside her, but most of it runs down her chin and drips onto her chest which is covered in a flaming red rash. He lays her back down, feeling so helpless. If only Weronika was here now, she'd know what to do. But he doesn't want Jan and Weronika to come into the ghetto at the moment, it's far too risky. You only have to brush against someone in the overcrowded streets to pick up the infection.

Wiktor goes to stand by the open window. In the winter they all froze, but now in the summer they're wilting like flowers without water. He sticks his head outside but there is no breeze, nothing to take away the cloying odour of sickness and death.

Yesterday, more than two hundred people died of typhus, apparently. Wiktor and his father have tried to get Antonina into a hospital but it's hopeless. The hospital on the corner of Leszno Street and Rymarska Street has a sign saying "No vacancies" as if it were a hotel. The hospital on Zelazna Street has also closed its doors. One woman laid her sick child down in front of the hospital and walked away, utterly broken.

'We will keep Antonina at home and care for her here,' says Pan Zieliński. 'We are not going to leave her on the hospital steps.'

Wiktor agrees it's the only thing to do. But her condition is worsening and he feels utterly helpless. Sometimes he weeps, something he hasn't done for years.

That evening, Antonina takes another turn for the worse. She becomes delirious, crying out and muttering gibberish. She thrashes on the mattress and it's impossible to get her to drink anything. Wiktor watches helplessly as his mother and father take it in turns to nurse their daughter. He even prays, just in case it helps. But it doesn't.

In the early hours of the morning Antonina stops thrashing around and grows quiet. Her emaciated body can't take any more. Her head flops back as she lies in her mother's arms. Her spirit flies free of its ravaged body and the prison of the ghetto.

For a moment no one makes a sound. Then his mother lets out a howl of grief and his father bursts into choking sobs. Wiktor curls into a ball on his mattress and cries until the mattress under his face is soaking wet. He's seen some terrible things in the ghetto. When Antoni was murdered, he thought things couldn't get any worse. But the death of Antonina pierces him with a pain so great he thinks he will never recover. She was only eight years old.

The next day they take her to the cemetery and arrange for her to be buried. But there's a backlog of burials to deal with. She'll have to wait her turn.

That evening Wiktor is overcome with dizziness. It must be the heat and the fact that he hasn't eaten properly for days. He's also exhausted from lack of sleep. If he can just lie down for a little while, then he'll be all right, or as right as he's ever going to be. It's time he restarted his smuggling activities. The last coherent thought he has before closing his eyes is that Jan must be wondering what has happened to him.

*

Time no longer has any meaning. Hours and days are indistinguishable. How long has he been lying here? He has no idea. The only sensation he recognises is heat.

Sometimes it's so hot he feels as if he's been thrown into the fires of hell. This is his punishment for having failed to save his sister. In his dreams he sees the faces of the dead and the dying. They crowd around him, reaching out their skeletal hands, demanding bread. But he has nothing to give them.

At other times, he feels a hand on his forehead. A cool, damp cloth. But it only stays cool for a few seconds and then the water sizzles and steams.

Hands – he doesn't know whose – raise him into a sitting position and a cup of water is pressed to his lips. He remembers that he's supposed to drink, but his muscles don't respond and the liquid runs down his chin.

He hears voices but they sound far away as if they're coming from another world. His limbs are so heavy, he just wants to lie here forever.

And then one day he wakes up from a deep sleep and opens his eyes.

A fly is crawling across the cracked ceiling and he knows where he is. He turns his head and sees his father standing by the window with his back to him.

'Dad?'

His father turns around and Wiktor sees the face of an old man. Gaunt and hollow-eyed. But then the face lights up and a smile of wonder spreads across the cracked features. 'Wiktor? You're awake!' He falls onto his knees by the mattress and takes him in his arms.

'Was I very sick?' asks Wiktor.

His father nods, brushing away a tear. 'You've had typhus. But it looks as if you've recovered. You're going to be all right.'

Wiktor has so many questions, but the one he asks is, 'Is Mum at work?'

His father's face crumples. And Wiktor knows. He wishes then that he hadn't woken up. This new agony is too much to bear.

'She fell sick,' says his father. 'But she wasn't as strong

as you. It's just the two of us now.'

Father and son hug each other and cry until there are no more tears left.

CHAPTER THIRTY-FOUR

They're leaving. The trucks rumble over the dusty earth and Lech waves goodbye to the forest. They're finally getting out of this backwater in the middle of nowhere. Lech is almost dizzy with relief. Halina looks happier than he's seen her in ages. They and the other survivors from their year in hell are being transported, courtesy of the NKVD, to the nearest train station. After that, they'll have to fend for themselves. But Lech isn't bothered. If they've survived this far, he has every hope for the future.

Back in June, when Hitler tore up his pact with Stalin and invaded the Soviet Union, life in the camp went on just as before. They still had to work every day, chop down trees, saw off the branches and pile up logs. No work, no food, as Igor was fond of reminding them. But you could tell that something was afoot. The NKVD overseers were less sure of themselves. You could see it in their eyes, the way they held huddled conferences, the furrowed brows, the shrugs of bewilderment. Igor developed a nervous twitch and smoked even more cigarettes than usual.

And then, at the start of August, came the news they'd all been waiting for. A Soviet-Polish amnesty had been signed. How many hours and days of negotiation had that entailed? Who cared? It was done, that was all that mattered. A party atmosphere erupted in the camp. Jubilation. After all the death, disease, gruelling work, sweltering heat and freezing cold, things were changing at last. There was talk of a Polish Army being formed, under the control of the Red Army. 'Are they serious?' asked Halina, unable to keep the incredulity out of her voice. The irony of it was not lost on Lech – the idea that he could find himself fighting alongside the Soviets, the very people who had expelled him from his country and sent him into exile, was laughable. And yet, if it meant they could defeat the Nazis… Best to keep an open mind and not bear too many grudges.

The NKVD called everyone to a formal meeting. Lech, in his happiness, even found it in his heart to feel sorry for Igor who looked like he'd had the stuffing knocked out of him. The Russians handed out release documents, food rations and said they would take the Poles to the nearest railway station as a gesture of goodwill. No hard feelings, eh comrade?

Now, as they clamber down from the trucks, the full reality of their situation hits them.

'This is a nightmare,' says Halina as they pick their way through the mass of starving Polish families, many of them huddled in rags. So many people. It's chaos, there's no other word for it. Lech makes enquiries, tries to find out what is happening. Bottom line is, everyone wants to board a train, any train, so long as it's going south. When is the next train? Anyone's guess.

They sit on the crowded platform in the heat of the day and watch helplessly as packed trains pass through the station without stopping. Where have they come from? The Poles, it seems, have been dispersed throughout Siberia and it's going to be a Herculean effort to move them all out again. If it's going to be anything like the train journey they had getting here… But no, Lech refuses to contemplate the idea. For one thing, the NKVD can't lock them in the carriages this time. They're all friends now, apparently.

Eventually, in the early evening a goods train pulls into the station and there's a mad scramble to climb on board.

Lech and Halina sit on their single suitcase, holding hands.

'Do you know where we're going?' she asks.

Lech shakes his head. Anywhere has to be better than where they've been for the last fourteen months.

'Will we ever return to Poland?'

Now there's a question he really can't answer.

CHAPTER THIRTY-FIVE

It's December and winter has returned with a vengeance. Once again frozen corpses litter the streets of the ghetto. The daily rations would barely keep a chicken alive. If it wasn't for the smuggling, there'd be even more bodies on the streets. The typhus epidemic shows no sign of abating. And now to cap it all the sewage pipes are frozen and human excrement is dumped in the street along with the rubbish. When he ventures outside, Wiktor keeps his eyes on the ground and watches where he's walking.

Back in October, Wiktor and his father were evicted from their apartment in the small ghetto and forced to move to the large ghetto. Big white placards went up announcing that those living in Sienna Street and other streets near the border would have to leave and find alternative accommodation. As if there was anywhere for them to go. The vacated streets would be disinfected and returned to the Aryan side of the city. Pan Zieliński complained to the *Judenrat*, but they said their hands were tied. 'Puppets of the regime!' said Pan Zieliński in a rare outburst of anger. Wiktor helped his father pack their few remaining belongings into suitcases. This time there was no horse and cart. They could only take with them what they could carry themselves. Most of the furniture had to stay behind. Wiktor took a photograph of his mother and sister.

A wooden bridge over Chłodna Street now links the small and large ghettos. It's so high you can peer into the third-storey windows of nearby houses. The road beneath is an Aryan thoroughfare busy with trams, cars and well-heeled pedestrians. The top of the bridge affords a tantalising glimpse of the world beyond the ghetto walls. Whenever he crosses from one side to the other, Wiktor gazes at the tops of towers and churches, and even catches a glimpse of the Saxon Garden where he used to play with Jan. From the top of the bridge you can dream of freedom. No wonder the bridge has been nicknamed the Bridge of Sighs. But you mustn't linger. The policemen move you on if you dawdle.

Their new accommodation is a single room at the top of a house on Chłodna Street, right up against the wall. They share a kitchen and a bathroom with six other families. The only ray of light is that America has entered the war and given people a glimmer of hope. Surely the Americans can manage to achieve what the British failed to do!

Today is Wiktor's day for helping out at the community kitchen on Grzybowska Street. It's the largest soup kitchen in the ghetto and the place is always awash with beggars. But Wiktor doesn't mind because he'll be with Julia Rubenstein, the one person who has been able to make him smile since his sister and mother died. The day he first met her was one he'll never forget.

He was trudging up the stairs, unable to think of anything except the gnawing hunger in his belly, wondering if it wouldn't have been better for him to die of typhus. What was the point of surviving just to eke out such a meagre existence? As he turned the corner, he bumped into someone coming down the other way. He expected to be snapped at for not looking where he was going. People are so short-tempered these days. But instead he heard a laugh, and a girl's voice said, 'Whoops! My fault. Sorry.'

He looked up into a smiling face with intense brown eyes and a dimple in each cheek, framed by glossy black hair that fell in waves to her shoulders.

'I'm Julia,' she said. 'I live on the floor below with my mother. She makes dresses.'

'Wiktor,' said Wiktor, feeling inexplicably tongue-tied. 'I live with my father on the top floor,' he added.

'I know.' She didn't ask him about his mother. She just seemed to understand that wasn't a topic to be broached on a first meeting.

'I went upstairs to ask if you and your father would like some extra potatoes,' she continued. 'We've... acquired some.' She dropped her voice. 'But keep it quiet, or we'll have the whole apartment block knocking on our door.'

Wiktor couldn't believe his ears. Extra potatoes? Who was this creature sent from Heaven?

Since then, he's got to know Julia better. She's like an angel administering to those in need. As well as the soup kitchen, she has introduced him to Dr Janusz Korczak's orphanage where they go to help the younger children with their reading and arithmetic. Inspired by the gentle and wise Dr Korczak, Wiktor has decided he would like to be a teacher when he grows up.

He dawdles at the turn on the stairs, where he first bumped into her, waiting for her door to open. As soon as he hears the handle turning, he hurries down the stairs to arrive on her floor just as she appears, looking as radiant as ever.

'Hello, Julia! Ready for the soup kitchen?'

She smiles at him and her dimples appear. 'Absolutely.' How he loves those dimples! 'But first I have a job to do.' She indicates the bag on her arm. Inside is a parcel wrapped in brown paper. Wiktor knows just what is in that parcel.

Before they were sealed in the ghetto, Julia's widowed mother ran a thriving dress-making business and boasted many well-to-do Polish women among her clients. And it seems that even in these straitened times, Aryan women of means simply can't do without her services. The law court, of all places, has become a trading place for the illicit exchange of goods between enterprising Jews and Poles.

When Julia explained the process to him, Wiktor marvelled at her audacity. It's one of the things he loves best about her. It also explained where the potatoes had come from.

'It works like this,' she confided in him one evening shortly after they'd first got to know one another. 'The law court has two entrances. The entrance on Leszno Street is in the ghetto, but the entrance on Ogrodowa Street is on the Aryan side. So people arrange to meet inside. Brilliant, isn't it?'

Of course, it's not as simple as she made it sound. Nothing ever is. Otherwise, why wouldn't you just leave the ghetto via the law court and never come back? No, the gates are guarded and any Jew attempting to exit by the wrong door would be shot on the spot.

'I'll come with you,' says Wiktor now. He's only too happy to tag along wherever Julia goes.

They wait until there's a bit of coming and going, and then slip past the Jewish policeman on the door. Their feet echo on the polished floor. Red and white banners bearing black swastikas hang from pillars. The corridors are bustling with smartly dressed employees – clerks and secretaries carrying files from room to room, ensuring the smooth running of the justice system for those fortunate enough to live on the right side of the law. But if you keep your eyes open, you notice other things going on. Hushed exchanges taking place. Parcels and bundles changing hands. A handmade leather belt for a loaf of bread. An altered suit for a bag of flour.

Wiktor follows Julia along a corridor, alert for any sign of danger. She walks with such confidence for a thirteen-year-old girl. He likes to imagine himself as her self-appointed protector, but who's he kidding? If the Gestapo stop them, they're done for.

'That's her,' whispers Julia. She approaches an elegantly dressed woman in a fur coat standing beside a pillar.

Wiktor stays back, trying to make himself look inconspicuous, whilst Julia and the woman make the exchange. The dress for a bag of sugar, four onions, a jar of marmalade and a pile of złotys. It's all over in the blink of an eye. Then Wiktor and Julia are heading back towards the Leszno Street entrance.

They step back into the ghetto and Wiktor breathes a sigh of relief. They got away with it, and in broad daylight too. He much prefers to carry out his smuggling activities under the cover of darkness. Now he can relax and enjoy Julia's company on the way to the soup kitchen.

'Hey, you two!'

Wiktor and Julia stop and turn at the sound of the voice behind them. Wiktor sees the dark blue police cap with a metal badge bearing the Star of David. That's all they need.

'What were you doing in there?' The policeman cocks his head towards the law court. He's not that old, mid-twenties maybe. His skin is pockmarked and the moustache on his upper lip is wispy and unconvincing.

None of your business, thinks Wiktor, but he knows the policeman would disagree. In addition to protecting community buildings, directing traffic, and guarding the ghetto gates with the German gendarmes, the Jewish police have the job of detecting and suppressing smugglers. Whose side do they think they're on? But Wiktor knows the answer. Their own side. They do the bidding of the Germans and in return they're well looked after, they and their families. They know which side their bread is buttered.

'Nothing important,' says Julia, coolly. 'Just dropping off some papers.' She gives the policeman one of her smiles, but it doesn't reach her eyes. The dimples are barely pronounced.

'What's in the bag?' This is obviously what he's been itching to ask all along.

'Just some rations,' says Julia. Wiktor can tell she's losing

239

her sangfroid.

'Show me.' The policeman's fingers hover over the rubber truncheon attached to the military belt around his middle. On his arm he wears a white armband with a blue Star of David, just like everyone else in the ghetto, but also a yellow armband with the inscription *Jüdischer Ordnungsdienst*. Jewish Police. How he must love the power conferred by that strip of yellow cloth.

Julia is about to open the bag, but Wiktor steps in. 'Actually, if you don't mind, we're just on our way to the soup kitchen in Grzybowska Street. So many starving people. They're waiting for us and if we don't get there soon, some of them will die.'

Has he overdone it? Maybe he shouldn't have laid it on so thick. Five minutes here or there isn't going to make any difference to the mortality rate. The policeman gives him a sceptical look, but Wiktor's intervention seems to have done the trick because the policeman waves them off. Perhaps he does have a heart after all.

'Get a move on, then. And don't let me catch you around here again.'

PART EIGHT
TRANSPORTS AND EXPERIMENTS
1942

CHAPTER THIRTY-SIX

'Another list from Teege and Mauer.' Countess Helena Korewina gives Anna the latest list to process. Bertha Teege and Luise Mauer, a pair of dyed-in-the-wool German Communists, share the title of Chief Kapo and are the most powerful and feared prisoners in the camp. Anna steers well clear of them whenever she sees them strutting around as if they own the place.

Thanks to the influence of the countess, Anna has acquired a job in the *Schreibstube*, the camp office. Although a prisoner herself, the charming Polish aristocrat has won the trust of the *Lagerführerin*, Johanna Langefeld, and has used her influence to help other Polish women gain better positions within the camp hierarchy. Thanks to her, Jadwiga now works in the *Effektenkammer* where prisoners' clothes are sorted and stored in large brown paper bags. Anna, with her knowledge of German and good level of education, has been sent to the *Schreibstube*. The office is always in need of anyone who can spell. There are no black or green triangles in the *Schreibstube*.

Anna scans the new list of names. A random selection of Jews, Jehovah's Witnesses, asocials and those imprisoned in the *Strafblock* due to some minor misdemeanour, or because their Blockova took a dislike to them and found an excuse to denounce them to the camp authorities.

The *Strafblock*. Anna can't suppress an involuntary shiver and a sick feeling in the pit of her stomach. She'll never forget the horror of that place as long as she lives.

When she was released after two months in confinement, she was a different person. Locked in a cold, dark cell, the walls covered with black mould, and no mattress to lie on, she thought she was going to die. There were days when she wished she was dead. She survived on coffee and bread once a day with a bowl of soup once every four days. Time lost all meaning. She longed for unconsciousness, but the cold prevented her from sleeping for more than minutes at a time. The tooth that had come loose when Dorothea Binz punched her in the face fell out.

Then one day Emma Zimmer let her go. Ordered her back to her block. Probably they wanted her cell for some other poor woman. The *Strafblock* was always full – Anna would lie awake listening to the cries and groans. Often it was she doing the crying and groaning.

So it was that on a mild spring day, she limped back to her block on wasted muscles and sore feet. It was one of the longest walks of her life. When she arrived, she hesitated before going inside. What was the point? Maybe she should just throw herself at the electric fence that surrounded the camp and put an end to all the pain and misery. Krysia was dead, and in that moment, Anna envied her.

Then Irmgard appeared in the doorway and said, 'Well, I never! Look who's here.' The Blockova threw her big arm around Anna's shoulder, almost knocking her over, and marched her inside. Jadwiga ran to greet her, and Anna collapsed onto her straw mattress as if it was filled with the softest feathers in the world.

It was not long afterwards that the countess found Anna and Jadwiga new jobs. Now they don't have to shovel sand for hours every day, or work in the dreaded sewing workshop where the air is thick with dust, and the supervisors beat the women if they don't make their quotas. Slowly Anna is regaining some of her strength. She is going to get through this. She has to.

She feeds a new sheet of paper into the typewriter and starts to type up the handwritten list, struggling to read the unfamiliar names. There's been talk in the *Schreibstube* of a *Sondertransport*, a special transport, but no one knows what that means. If the rumours are to be believed, the sick and those who can't work are being sent to a sanatorium. It sounds almost too good to be true. Anna types up the list, trying to ignore the feeling of unease that has been growing over the past week. *I'm just doing my job,* she tells herself.

But not all jobs are equal. She always feels a sense of guilt when she sees the work gangs trudging off to their hard labours, knowing that she'll be spending the day in a heated office, sitting at a typewriter. But you don't turn down a job in the *Schreibstube* when it's offered to you, not if you want to have a chance of surviving.

She types the final name, pulls the sheet of paper from the typewriter, and adds it to the growing pile. Lists, lists and more lists. The Nazis are obsessed with documentation. It's a wonder there are any trees still standing in northern Europe.

That evening in the block, Jadwiga tells her about her day in the *Effektenkammer*. 'We're rushed off our feet,' she says. 'We're having to return loads of clothes. What's going on?'

Anna decides to tell her about the lists and share her secret fears, but just as she's about to speak, Irmgard strides down the block, shouting orders. 'Everyone to stay inside! No one to leave the block! And no looking outside!' At this, a hundred heads turn instinctively to the windows. Outside dusk is falling. 'I said, no looking outside, Polish whores!'

Cold fear clutches at Anna's heart. A picture is emerging but she doesn't yet understand what she is seeing. She thinks about the list she typed up today, and others like it during the week; the clothes that Jadwiga and her *Effektenkammer* co-workers were told to return; the Jews, Jehovah's Witnesses and asocials who are too sick, weak or old to work. Are they really going to a sanatorium to recover? Why would the Nazis bother when these women already receive the worst treatment in the camp? Nothing makes sense.

Next day in the *Schreibstube*, whispered rumours are rife. Sitting at her desk, Anna eavesdrops on conversations.

'Lorries at the gates yesterday, you say?'

'Yes, my friend who works in the Revier saw them. They took away loads of women, and...'

'What? Tell me!'

The speaker drops her voice and Anna has to strain to hear. 'Paralysed women from the Revier. They *threw* them onto the lorry, like chunks of meat!'

Anna's fingers freeze on the typewriter keys. *Like chunks of meat!* She feels physically sick. There's no way those women are going to a sanatorium. She doesn't know how the Nazis will dispose of them, but she knows that those women are going to their deaths. They'll never be coming back. She looks at the remaining names on the handwritten list she's typing up, feeling like a despicable collaborator. Six more names left. It's not right that she should have the power over who lives and who dies, but she can't bring herself to type up those last few names. She'll pretend she hasn't seen them. She pulls the sheet of paper from the typewriter and puts it on the pile. She scrunches up the handwritten list and throws it into the bin.

Two days later, she finds Jadwiga sitting on her bunk, sunk in gloom. Anna sits down beside her and takes her hand. 'Tell me what's wrong.'

'The lorries came back today,' says Jadwiga, blinking back tears. 'They parked outside the *Effektenkammer*, and when they opened the backs of the lorries, clothes tumbled out. And not just clothes. There were crutches, dentures, spectacles, walking sticks. We had to sort through them all. I recognised a dress that I'd handed out two days ago.' She looks at Anna with an agonised expression. 'What has happened to the women who went away?'

'They don't need clothes anymore,' says Anna.

The next day, she's given a different job to do in the *Schreibstube*. There are stacks of pre-prepared death certificates to be completed. Each certificate gives the place of death as Ravensbrück, but as for the cause of death, that's up to Anna to decide. She has a number of options to choose from. Heart weakness, infected lungs, circulation problems, to name a few. With each certificate, she types a brief letter explaining that, for a fee, the ashes of the deceased can be returned in an urn if the relatives wish. All very polite and considerate.

But lies, all of it lies.

When she sees Bertha Teege and Luise Mauer that evening on her way back to her block, she doesn't shun them like she normally would. Who is she to judge them? She, who has spent her day filling out false death certificates and writing lies.

*

With the arrival of spring, Lech joins the other men in the village as they go out in search of agricultural equipment that has been left out over the long, hard winter. In this featureless landscape, no one dared leave the village when it snowed, for fear of becoming lost in the wilderness. Now, with the thaw starting, it feels as if they're emerging from months of hibernation. He hopes this means they'll soon be able to finally leave the Soviet Union, although the prospect of another arduous train journey doesn't fill him with joy. They barely survived the last one.

It took them weeks to get here, trundling through the deserted wastes of Kazakhstan. They survived, but only just. Many didn't. The journey was even worse than the one they had endured from Poland to Siberia. The only difference this time was that they weren't locked in and were able to get out and stretch their legs whenever the train stopped at some poky village in the middle of nowhere. It was a chance to buy food from the locals, but as soon as you heard the hiss of the engine you had to get back on board, food or no food, for fear of missing the train and being left behind. Two of the carriages were designated as sick bays due to outbreaks of typhus on board. The dead were disposed of each time the train stopped.

Still, they made it to Tashkent by the end of September '41. Lech went straight to the army camp and enrolled in what everyone was calling Anders' Army, after General Władysław Anders, the man at the top. Lech was keen to fight. But that was six months ago and he's still stranded in the Soviet Union, along with thousands of other Poles. He's swapped the forest of Siberia for the steppe of Uzbekistan. Not much of an improvement in Lech's opinion.

Someone points out a tractor on the horizon, and Lech follows a group of men heading in that direction. They'll probably have to push the damn thing back to the village. He and Halina have survived by living and working on a kolkhoz, a collective farm, in one of the most inhospitable landscapes on Earth. Miles and miles of flat, windswept nothingness. In the autumn he helped bring in the harvest. And then the snow came and obliterated everything. They didn't leave their hut for months. There are times when he finds himself actually missing the forest – the shelter of the trees and the refreshing scent of pine resin. He wonders what Igor is doing these days now that the old Russian NKVD overseer doesn't have his Polish labourers to bully.

The tractor is in a poor state, the body rusted and the engine dead. If it was up to Lech, he'd write it off as scrap. But the hardened locals aren't fazed by a spot of rust. One old farmer pats the machine as if it's a prized cow. Lech now understands enough of the local dialect to know that they fully expect to be ploughing the fields with it once it's had a quick overhaul. Lech is directed to the back of the tractor where, as he thought, he's expected to help push it back to the village. After much shoving and grunting, they finally get the thing moving. It's a real slog pushing the tractor over the rutted earth. By the time they get it back to the farmer's workshop, Lech is bathed in sweat.

Halina brings him a drink of water. She's the only thing keeping him going these days. He gulps the water down and wipes his mouth with the back of his hand. 'Thank you,' he says. 'I needed that.' The other men are ready to set off again in search of more broken-down equipment. 'I'd better get going.'

Halina grasps his hand. 'Take it easy,' she says. 'You've hardly done any exercise all winter.'

Doesn't he know it. His shoulders are already stiff from pushing the tractor. The enforced period of hibernation has left him even more enfeebled than when they first arrived. But it's the same old story – you have to work to eat. And if they don't eat, how is he ever going to be strong enough to fight, when the time comes for them to leave? For surely the Anders' Army will leave one day soon, won't it?

CHAPTER THIRTY-SEVEN

The news spreads like wildfire. Wiktor can't believe it. An official poster has gone up at the *Judenrat* offices announcing that all Jews will be sent to work in the East. With typical German pedantry, there are a number of specific exceptions, namely anyone working for German institutions or companies, members of the *Judenrat*, hospital staff, members of the Jewish Order Service, wives and children of the aforementioned, and patients in hospital. Each person will be permitted 15kg of luggage, valuables, gold and money. They should pack enough food for three days. The resettlement is to start on the twenty-second of July at eleven o'clock sharp.

'Six thousand people a day!' exclaims Julia. 'What can they possibly want with that many people?' They're crossing the bridge over Chłodna Street, on their way back to the large ghetto after spending the morning at the soup kitchen on Grzybowska Street. One of Wiktor's favourite times of the day, when he has Julia all to himself and doesn't have to share her with the beggars. The *Judenrat* is just down the road from the soup kitchen, so Wiktor and Julia were amongst the first to hear the news.

'It'll be to help with the war effort on the eastern front,' says Wiktor despondently. 'Probably in ammunition factories. But I don't want to go.' Despite the obvious hardships of living in the ghetto, he doesn't believe life in the East would be a picnic. On the contrary, they'd probably be stuck in some awful village full of peasants resentful towards the newcomers. They'd be starting from scratch all over again, whereas at least here they've got systems going for welfare and smuggling. You can survive here – just – if you're smart about it.

'Me neither,' says Julia. 'It sounds horrendous.' She slips her hand into his and gives him one of her dimpled smiles. Wiktor's heart flips over as it always does when she smiles at him. It never ceases to amaze him that someone as beautiful as Julia can exist in this cesspit. She's like a rare flower that grows in the ruins. He makes a silent vow that whatever happens, they'll stay together. He's not going to lose her.

Ever since their encounter with the Jewish policeman outside the law court, they've become inseparable. If anything, the policeman did him a favour. Julia was so grateful to him for getting them out of the fix they were in, that she let him kiss her.

When he's with Julia, Wiktor can forget about the grinding poverty all around him and the difficulties of his own life. One day, when all this is over… But this is no time for dreaming. The priority now is to obtain work permits so they can claim exemption from deportation.

The morning after the announcement, Wiktor and Julia, Pan Zieliński and Pani Rubenstein join the long line outside one of the many workshops. Half the ghetto population seems to have had the same idea. Suddenly, a work permit is more prized than a loaf of bread. *This is hopeless,* thinks Wiktor, *we won't stand a chance.* But for once, luck is on their side and by midday all four of them are the proud owners of permits stating that they are employed by Többens and Schultz, the clothing manufacturing company. The company has taken on so many employees that they won't all have to work all the time. The important thing is the work permit. They will sleep better tonight with this precious document tucked under their pillows.

And then just when they're rejoicing in their good fortune, another shocking piece of news flies around the ghetto. Adam Czerniaków, the rotund, bespectacled, bow-tie-wearing head of the *Judenrat* has committed suicide. *How? A cyanide pill, they say. Where did he get a cyanide pill from? Goodness knows! But why? It must be to do with the deportations!*

That evening, Wiktor's father invites Pani Rubenstein and Julia upstairs to discuss the current situation. Wiktor is glad that he and Julia are to be included in the conversation. After all, they're both fourteen now. Old enough to have an opinion. Kids grow up quickly in the ghetto, at least the ones that don't die of hunger, disease or bullets.

Julia smiles at Wiktor from across the room. They've kept their relationship secret from their parents, but Wiktor thinks his father has guessed how he feels about Julia. He's not sure what he thinks of Pani Rubenstein. She's quite a formidable woman, tall and thin, with a superior air, but he supposes that's why she got along so well with her wealthy Aryan clients.

'I'm sorry I can't offer you a glass of something,' Pan Zieliński says to his guests. 'But you know how it is.' Wiktor's father has grown even thinner since his wife and daughter died. His cheekbones are quite pronounced now, his eyes sunk deeper in their sockets.

'Think nothing of it,' says Pani Rubenstein. She always knows how to be gracious. 'We must be thankful that we got our work permits this morning. At least now we won't have to go to the East.'

An awkward silence falls on the little group. Wiktor knows everyone is thinking, why did Pan Czerniaków kill himself if it was just a matter of sending people to work in camps? Are the conditions there really so horrendous?

'They say,' begins Pan Zieliński, 'that Czerniaków killed himself because he was told the expulsion order applies to children as well. He left a note saying he would not hand over helpless children for destruction.'

'Who's talking about destruction?' says Pani Rubenstein fiercely. 'We're talking about resettlement. I'm not saying it would be easy, I certainly don't want to go as I've already said. But we're not talking about... about mass murder!'

Wiktor flinches. Mass murder! Is that what this is all about? When he catches Julia's eye, he sees that this is precisely what she fears. But the adults seem determined to put a brave face on things.

'Of course,' says Pan Zieliński, 'we must trust that the nation that produced Beethoven and Goethe is not capable of such atrocities.'

It sounds to Wiktor as if his father is trying to convince himself as much as them.

CHAPTER THIRTY-EIGHT

The midday sun beats mercilessly on the *Appellplatz* where Anna, Jadwiga and about seventy other young Polish women have been called to line up in the usual rows of five. But this isn't the normal morning *Appell*. This is something else entirely. Not even Irmgard could tell them what it was about.

'What's going on?' whispers Jadwiga.

'I don't know,' says Anna, 'But I don't like it.' Ever since the transports in February, she's grown suspicious of anything out of the ordinary.

The camp Kommandant, Koegel, is there with a fat, red-haired SS man in round spectacles that Anna has never seen before. There are also three doctors from the camp Revier, one of them a tall, blonde woman whom Anna has heard called Herta Oberheuser. The cane-wielding Dr Walter Sonntag whom Anna caught 'in the act' with Gerda Weyand is, thankfully, not present, having left the camp some months ago. Small mercies. However, the way this present lot are conferring is giving Anna the creeps. They've clearly got something in mind, although she can't imagine what.

She doesn't have to wait long to find out.

Kommandant Koegel orders the women to lift their

dresses and expose their legs. Anna and Jadwiga exchange bewildered glances, ignoring the strict rule about 'noses to the front' at all times. This is the most bizarre inspection ever. Seventy women stand there with their striped dresses bunched up around their thighs whilst Koegel, the doctors and the red-haired SS man walk up and down the rows, peering at and prodding their legs, treating them like cattle at a market. As they progress down her row, Anna hears their comments. *A bit on the short side; way too long; ankles like drainpipes; calf muscles not bad; wasted thighs.* The only thing all the women have in common is that none of them are fat. Not on the camp diet. Herta Oberheuser makes notes on a clipboard.

It's Anna's turn to be inspected. Her legs tremble and she can hardly breathe. She braces herself for criticism, but the doctors are surprisingly complimentary – she has good muscle tone apparently. It must be all the cycling she used to do around Warsaw. Herta Oberheuser makes a note and the doctors move on to Jadwiga who also receives a favourable assessment.

'What was that all about?' asks Jadwiga afterwards. They've been given no explanation, just told to return to their blocks.

'Goodness knows,' says Anna. 'But nothing good ever comes of being on a list.' She's still tormented by the lists she typed up at the start of the year. She has no doubt those women who were taken away in the lorries, their clothes returned a couple of days later, were killed. Is she to suffer the same fate?

A few days later, an order goes out for the same seventy women to report to the Revier.

Anna's stomach is in knots. She hasn't set foot in that hateful place since the day she and Jadwiga found Krysia dead in her bed. The day she caught Sonntag and Weyand going at it like animals, and her subsequent beating and banishment to the *Strafblock*.

Dr Herta Oberheuser meets them at the entrance,

clipboard in hand. When everyone has gathered, she reads aloud the names of those who are to stay behind.

'Agnieszka Wójcik, Krystyna Wilkowa…'

Anna holds her breath. What does it mean if your name is called? Equally, what does it mean if your name isn't called?

'Jadwiga Biała.'

Anna hears a gasp as her friend's name is read out. Jadwiga's fingers reach for Anna's hand.

Oberheuser reads out six more names and then pauses. She consults with one of the doctors, pointing at her list. He shakes his head and taps one of the names with his pen. Oberheuser nods her head in understanding.

'Anna Nowak.'

Anna grips Jadwiga's hand tightly. At least they're together. But what for?

Ten names have been chosen out of the original group of seventy. Those not selected are sent back to the block, relief on their faces.

'Come this way.' Herta Oberheuser is brisk and business-like. She ushers the ten women into a clean, white-tiled room and tells them to lift their skirts. The doctors, including the red-headed SS man, prod and poke, pinch and pull, until their legs are covered in bruises. But there's still no explanation of what is going on.

More conferring amongst the doctors, and then Oberheuser reads out the names of six who are to stay behind overnight. Anna, Jadwiga, Agnieszka, Krystyna, Adela and Bronisława. The four not chosen return to the block.

Anna's instinct is to run after them, but she wouldn't get very far. The Germans would catch her and punish her. As it is, the six who have been chosen are treated with a surprising degree of hospitality. A warm soapy bath, and beds made up with clean sheets. But none of this does anything to allay Anna's fear. None of the doctors will look her in the eye. She'd rather have Irmgard calling her a Polish whore. At least the Blockova manages eye contact. She doesn't trust these Nazi doctors, in their white lab coats, with their clipboards and their hushed consultations.

When the nurses arrive, bearing syringes, terror engulfs her. They're going to kill her by lethal injection. She tries to get out of the bed, but firm hands hold her down. 'This won't hurt if you stay still.'

'Get your hands off me!'

The nurse plunges the syringe into Anna's arm. It's like a wasp sting – sharp and painful. Her breath catches in her throat. Then her body goes limp and the room starts to swim. She's only vaguely aware of being wheeled down the corridor before darkness engulfs her.

*

Anna is in a long, dark tunnel, not sure which way to go. Familiar voices call to her, distant and faint. Her mother is intoning the *Ave Maria*, her father is reciting the story of the Dragon of Kraków. Jan's voice interrupts to ask if she's killed any Germans. Lech tells her to be brave. But she can't see any of them. Everything is black.

'I'm here,' she calls, but no one seems to hear her. She tries to go towards the voices, but her legs won't move. Her ankle is encased in an iron band attached to the tunnel wall with a heavy chain. She pulls at the chain, and the band cuts into her flesh. The voices are fading now. She mustn't lose them. If they disappear, she'll never get out of here. Why does no one come and find her? She yanks at the chain with both hands and…wakes up.

The bright light dazzles her and she blinks her eyes until she can see properly. Memory dawns. The last thing she remembers is being given an injection.

She's lying in a hospital bed in the camp Revier, tucked in tightly with a crisp, white sheet. The tunnel was just a dream. A nightmare. She is relieved to find she isn't really chained to a wall, but also sad that her family were just figments of her imagination.

She turns her head to the side. Jadwiga is in the bed on her right, still sleeping. She looks so peaceful, Anna hopes her dreams are less terrifying than her own. On her other side Krystyna is muttering something in her sleep. Anna tries to raise herself on her elbows to see the three women on the other side of the room, but her right leg is heavy and doesn't want to move. Fighting a rising sense of panic, she reaches under the bedclothes and feels something hard. What the hell? Her right leg is encased in plaster. It's impossible to bend her knee or move her ankle. Only her toes move, and even that's an effort. What have they done to her? She lifts the sheet and blanket and peers in horror at the thick, white plaster cast that runs from the top of her thigh to the ankle. She falls back onto the pillow, letting out a sob of despair.

The other women are stirring now.

'Where am I?' murmurs Jadwiga. 'Anna, is that you?'

'My leg!' moans Krystyna. 'I can't move my leg.'

And then a wail of anguish from Agnieszka silences them all. 'I used to be a dancer,' she cries. 'What have they done to me?'

They each have a leg in plaster.

This is an outrage, thinks Anna. And then she remembers the lists of names she typed up, the women who were sent away on the lorries, whose clothes were returned two days later. Is this some kind of divine retribution for the part she played in those women's deaths?

The door opens and Dr Herta Oberheuser enters in her starched uniform, her clipboard as ever at the ready. 'Good, you're all awake at last!' As if they've been having a lie in because they're too lazy to work. Even the *Sandgrube* would be welcome instead of this horror.

Oberheuser inspects each of the casts, making notes on her clipboard. Anna notices there are numbers and letters written on her cast. What does that mean? It looks like some sort of secret code.

'What has happened to our legs?' ventures Anna.

Oberheuser looks at her with contempt. 'That is no business of yours.'

They spend the day lying in bed. Anna's leg starts to itch and grow hot. The other women complain of the same problem. When the nurses bring bowls of watery soup and lumps of hard, dry bread, Anna has to force herself to eat. The others are struggling too. No one has any appetite. Visiting the bathroom on crutches is a huge effort that leaves them all exhausted.

As evening approaches, Agnieszka is the first to start writhing in pain. A petite, dark-haired girl from Lublin who once had dreams of becoming a professional ballet dancer, she shrieks in agony.

The itching in Anna's leg has grown steadily worse throughout the day, and then shooting pains dart up her leg into her pelvis. She twists from side to side, trying to find relief, but nothing helps. In the next bed, Jadwiga is moaning incoherently. On the other side, Krystyna is gasping for breath, tears streaming down her face. No one has any strength left for conversation.

The nurses monitor them, but do nothing to relieve the agony.

Swimming in and out of consciousness, Anna loses track of time. Hours turn into days. The top of her thigh, the only bit of her leg not encased in plaster, swells and turns black. The plaster cuts into her flesh.

Every day Herta Oberheuser carries out her inspections, leaning over the casts to sniff their legs, and making notes on her clipboard.

And then one day Anna wakes from a disturbed dream to find herself being wheeled along the corridor once again. She sees the bright lights of the operating theatre, but only for a moment because someone ties a cloth over her eyes. She's too weak to protest at this latest violation.

She hears footsteps. A man's voice, barking instructions. 'Remove the plaster.' The whine of an electric saw sets her teeth on edge. The vibrations of the saw on the plaster send shock waves up her spine and down into her fingers. Suddenly the plaster is gone and her leg throbs so violently she thinks it's going to explode.

And then she gags at the stink of rotting flesh filling her nostrils. Is that her leg that smells like a lump of meat left out in the sun? She writhes on the trolley as cold metal scrapes against her skin, burrowing deep into the flesh. It feels as if something is being removed from her leg. She hears pus dripping into a bowl. She blacks out.

When she wakes, she's back on the ward, a fresh plaster cast on her leg. But the stink of rotting flesh hangs in the air. Flies buzz around the beds, crawling over their legs. Anna cries out for water. Oberheuser gives her a foul mixture of water and vinegar that leaves her throat burning.

One by one the women are wheeled down to the operating theatre. They all return with fresh casts, having suffered unspeakable agonies.

That evening Agnieszka cries that she can't move her neck. She calls for help, but no one comes. None of the other woman are in any state to do anything for her.

Anna slides in and out of consciousness. She's back in the tunnel, chained to the wall, then she's in the ward, hearing the moans and cries of the others. She moans and cries herself.

When she next opens her eyes, daylight is flooding the room and there's a strangled cry coming from Agnieszka's bed.

'What's happening to her?' asks Jadwiga.

Anna hoists herself up, ignoring the pain in her leg. Whatever is happening to Agnieszka is obviously much worse than anything the rest of them are suffering.

Agnieszka's pretty face is contorted into a mad grimace. Her head is twisted at an uncomfortable angle, incoherent sounds emerging from between pursed lips. Two nurses come in and try to prise her lips apart. They pour water into her mouth. Most of it dribbles down her face, over the sheets. Only her eyes have any animation in them and they are wide with terror. Anna and the others can only watch in horrified silence, their own agonies paled into insignificance beside those of their friend.

Eventually Dr Herta Oberheuser comes into the room. She takes one look at Agnieszka's deformed body, makes a tutting sound with her tongue and gives one of the nurses an instruction that Anna can't hear.

The nurse walks out and returns a minute later with a syringe. Agnieszka's throat rattles, she manages an agonised scream that chills the blood in Anna's veins. The nurse jabs the needle into Agnieszka's stiff arm. And then silence.

Agnieszka lies still, her dreams of dancing gone forever.

CHAPTER THIRTY-NINE

Halina feels as if she's about to throw up. She's been feeling like this for days and has put it down to the unbearable heat. When Lech offers her a piece of bread, she shakes her head. The air is fetid with the stench of oil from the Baku oilfields and it's making her stomach roil. They're in Krasnovodsk in Turkmenistan with hundreds of other Polish soldiers and civilians, waiting to board a ship to take them to Persia.

If they, and the tens of thousands who had joined the Anders' Army, had stayed much longer on the kolkhoz they would have risked starvation. The Soviets had seemed incapable of – or more likely unwilling to – provide sufficient rations for so many men and civilian dependants. The news that General Anders had negotiated their evacuation to Persia, where the British would take care of them, was greeted amongst the exiled Poles with jubilation. Anything has to be better than Soviet hospitality.

At last it's time to board the ship. Lech helps her to her feet and her vision momentarily darkens – a sign of low blood pressure. She hopes it will be cooler on the sea. Maybe then she won't feel so queasy. It must be the smell from the oilfields making her want to vomit.

The vessel, a rusty old oil tanker, is not a reassuring sight.

It doesn't look sea-worthy, but she keeps her thoughts to herself. She wants to leave the Soviet Union as much as Lech does.

Before departure, they stand at the railing and look back at the country they are leaving behind. 'I am never, ever, setting foot in the Soviet Union again as long as I live,' says Lech.

The ship sets sail and Halina immediately throws up over the side. 'I guess I don't have sea legs,' she says weakly, leaning against Lech for support.

'We'll get through this,' says Lech, hugging her to him.

Halina isn't so sure.

*

There follow two days of absolute hell. The hot, salty breezes of the Caspian Sea do nothing to calm Halina's queasiness. She is sick over the side of the ship more times than she can remember. But somehow, she manages to survive. Many don't. Those who die from disease or dehydration are unceremoniously tossed overboard.

When the ship finally docks in Pahlevi, Halina disembarks with legs barely strong enough to support her. She drops onto her knees on the golden sands and offers up a prayer of thanks for their safe passage.

They spend the next three days in a camp overlooking the sparkling blue Caspian Sea with the snowy peaks of the Elburz mountains rising behind them. Compared to where they've come from, it looks and feels like paradise. Halina's queasiness starts to settle down at last. Showered, powdered with insecticide and dressed in new khaki clothes, they start to feel human again. And then it's time to leave for Tehran.

A convoy of hired lorries and buses arrive. Halina hopes the journey isn't going to be too long and tiring, but they can't stay by the sea forever, more's the pity. Halina and Lech are directed to one of the buses whose driver, a wiry young man, introduces himself as Babak.

'Welcome to my bus,' he says to each of them as they board the old wreck. Halina does her best to smile in return, but the state of the vehicle is not reassuring.

To begin with, the journey is surprisingly pleasant. The bus chugs along the shore of the Caspian Sea, with wide fields to either side, crops swaying gently in the breeze. But then they start to climb through mountain gorges and dense forests and the bus starts to show its age. The engine coughs and splutters like an old man, and the passengers lurch backwards and forwards with every change of gear. Halina is thrown against Lech as the bus sways around a sharp bend in the road. When she looks out of the window, she sees they are travelling along the edge of a precipice, high up in the mountains. The view is breath-taking and hair-raising in equal measure. Snowy peaks and plummeting gorges make her gasp in awe and terror. She wishes Babak would slow down.

'Oh my God, look at that!' Halina clutches Lech's arm. There's an overturned lorry in a ravine by the side of the road, its burst tyres sticking into the air. That could be us, she thinks. The next second, they plunge into a tunnel and the dizzying view is lost to sight. Halina breathes a sigh of relief. They can't topple off the edge of the mountain so long as they're in a tunnel.

A few minutes later they emerge from the tunnel into dazzling light. Halina hopes Babak can see the road ahead properly and isn't blinded by the sudden brightness. She reaches for Lech's hand and gives it a gentle squeeze. He's actually nodded off in the tunnel. She doesn't know how he can sleep on this bus. She's too terrified they're going to nosedive into a ravine. But Lech is exhausted from months of back-breaking work and inadequate rations. His bony knees stick out beneath the end of his khaki shorts; his arms are grown thin, his cheeks hollowed out. And he's not the only one. All the men who've signed up to fight are in the same condition. How are they ever going to fight the Germans in this state?

Her other hand goes to her stomach. She wasn't sure before they set sail, but now she thinks she is. She just needs to find the right time to tell Lech that he's going to be a father.

CHAPTER FORTY

The deportations are impossible to ignore. They're happening every day, organised by the Jewish police, those blasted collaborators who think they can save their own skins by carrying out the orders of the Nazis. Wiktor doesn't know who he despises more, the Jewish police or the SS. Each policeman is under orders to deliver five Jews every day, on pain of death. That might not sound like a lot, but when you consider that there are two thousand Jewish policemen in the ghetto, then you get some idea of the scale of the operation.

The first people to be rounded up are the prisoners, the beggars, the homeless and the old. Now, if they were really going to work in the East, why would the Germans choose such sorry specimens of humanity? Wouldn't they prefer those who've managed to maintain some semblance of vitality? Doubts begin to grow. These people are not going to work. Another fate awaits them, one that Wiktor doesn't want to think too hard about. Having deported the flotsam and jetsam, they then move on to clearing whole apartment blocks, whole streets. When will it end? Wiktor never leaves the apartment without his precious work permit, even when he's not going to the factory, and takes care to avoid streets where round-ups are underway for fear of being caught up with a bunch of strangers. He doubts his work permit would do him much good then.

Julia and her mother, with their sewing skills, spend more time in the factory these days making uniforms for the Wehrmacht, so Wiktor often finds himself crossing the bridge over Chłodna Street alone. He wants to shout at the Poles walking below, 'Do you know what's going on in here?' But that would be the surest and quickest way to get himself deported. So he stays quiet, and keeps his head down. Sometimes he despises himself almost as much as he despises the Jewish police.

It's a couple of weeks since the deportations began, and Wiktor is slowly making his way back to Chłodna Street in the heat of the afternoon sun when Julia runs to meet him in tears. It's not like her to cry, and already he fears the worst. Have they taken her mother? His father?

'What's happened?' He clutches her hand.

'It's the children,' she sobs. 'They've taken the children!'

She means the children from Dr Janusz Korczak's orphanage. 'What, all of them?' There are two hundred children there.

'Come on,' she says, 'we have to try and save some of them!'

'But…' This is a crazy idea. What can they possibly do? But Julia has taken his hand and is pulling him along the street. He can see she's determined and he can't let her go alone. Didn't he make a vow to always stay with her?

'Look!' She bends down to pick up a small toy rabbit with floppy ears that is lying in the gutter. 'One of the children must have dropped it.'

Wiktor takes the opportunity to voice his concerns. 'What can we do to help them? Aren't we just putting ourselves in danger?'

Julia fixes him with her intense gaze. She's not smiling now. 'Didn't you tell me once that you helped a little girl to escape the ghetto? That she's now living with your friend

Jan on the other side?'

'Yes, but... Agata was just a one-off. Besides, I felt partly responsible for getting her brother killed. Pani Nowak won't be able to take any more Jewish children.'

A look of intense sadness washes over Julia's face. 'I had a little sister,' she whispers. 'And she died because I failed to look after her properly.'

This is the first Wiktor has heard of a sister. He's told Julia about Antonina and is a little hurt that she never confided in him about her own family.

'I'm sure it wasn't your fault,' he says.

'It was,' she shouts. Then in a calmer voice, 'She was shot by the SS for making fun of them. She didn't understand, you see. She had... learning difficulties.'

This is obviously painful for Julia to talk about. 'I understand,' says Wiktor. 'And I'm truly sorry. But we can't save everyone.'

'I know we can't save everyone,' says Julia. 'But that doesn't mean we shouldn't try to save at least one.'

Wiktor can't argue with that, so they set off again, Julia clutching the toy rabbit in one hand and holding onto Wiktor with the other.

'Do you have your work permit with you?' she asks as they approach the *Umschlagplatz*.

'Always,' says Wiktor. 'And you?'

Julia nods. 'Listen, this is what we'll do.' The resourceful Julia is back, confident and full of ideas. 'We'll pretend to be brother and sister, and when we find one of the smaller children, we'll say there's been a mistake and that he or she is our sibling and needs to come with us.'

If Wiktor has any doubts, he pushes them aside. He loves Julia, even though he's never told her so, and if he walks away now, he'll never be able to look her in the face again. They tag onto the end of a group being herded into the *Umschlagplatz*, and straightaway Wiktor knows he's just made the biggest mistake of his life.

The *Umschlagplatz* is huge. There must be thousands of

people crammed into it. It's bordered by railway buildings and fences, and guarded by hundreds of Jewish policemen, SS troops and rough-looking foreign conscripts. There's no sign of Dr Korczak and his orphans.

'They must be here somewhere,' says Julia, pushing her way through the mass of bodies. It's as much as Wiktor can do to keep up with her. 'There they are!'

In the distance, Wiktor can see the tall, gentlemanly figure of Dr Korczak, surrounded by a group of children who all look as if they've been washed and dressed in their best clothes. With them are the assistants and childminders in their white aprons.

Julia kneels down by a small boy and shows him the rabbit. 'Is this yours?' The child shakes his head and points to a little girl of about four years of age with her hair in pigtails. Julia shows her the rabbit. At once the child's face lights up in an expression of pure joy. Julia gives her the rabbit and the child hugs it to her chest. Then Julia takes the little girl's hand and starts to lead her away from the group.

'Stop! Where do you think you're going?'

Wiktor is dismayed to see the Jewish policeman who accosted them outside the law court in December last year.

'This is our sister,' says Julia. 'She shouldn't be here. She was picked up by accident.'

Fortunately the little girl is too absorbed with her rabbit to contradict Julia's lie.

'We're not part of the deportation,' says Wiktor. 'We have work permits. Look.' He reaches into his pocket and pulls out the precious piece of paper that exempts him from deportation. Julia shows him hers too.

The policeman peers at the documents as if he's never seen such a thing before. Then he looks suspiciously at Wiktor and Julia. 'Don't I know you two from somewhere?'

'I don't think so,' says Julia brazenly.

But the policeman is not so easily convinced. 'I remember now. You were smuggling food out of the law court.'

'We were doing no such thing!' protests Julia.

'Let me take a closer look at those permits.' The policeman snatches them out of their hands, and then, to Wiktor's horror, proceeds to tear them to pieces. The scraps of paper blow away on the breeze and are lost forever. 'That's what I think of your precious work permits,' scoffs the policeman. 'That will teach you to lie to an officer of the law. Now get back over there.' He brandishes his truncheon at them, forcing them to re-join the group of children.

Wiktor knows this is the end. Escape is impossible now. His only regret is for his father who is alone in the world. He always thought he would fear death, that it would overwhelm him, but when he sees Julia's stricken face, he finds renewed strength. His job now is to comfort and support her. They will face whatever comes together.

'You did the right thing,' he says, taking her in his arms. 'You stood up for justice, and no one can do more than that.' Then he adds, 'I love you, Julia Rubenstein. I've loved you since the first day I met you, and I love you now more than ever.'

'I love you too, Wiktor Zieliński.'

'I'll always stay with you.'

And then the German guards start herding everyone towards the cattle wagons. Dr Korczak walks with his head held high, reassuring the children that everything is going to be all right. Wiktor tries to follow his noble example.

He never once lets go of Julia's hand, even when they are shunted inside a dark, stinking wagon, even when other bodies are pressed in against theirs, even when the doors slam shut and are bolted on the outside, plunging them into darkness. Even when the wheels of the train start to move, transporting them to their final destination.

CHAPTER FORTY-ONE

'Got you! You're it!' The shouts of children's voices fill the air as they run around, laughing. Halina smiles to herself. If only Lech were here with her now. But he has gone with the army to Iraq where he'll be trained to fight. Her heart contracts at the thought of him going into battle. But it's what he wants – the honour of fighting for his country. She had to let him go, even though it broke her heart. When she told him she was going to have a baby, he was at first delighted and then fraught with worry for her. She had to assure him that she would be safe in Persia, teaching at the Polish orphanage which has been set up in the mountains near Isfahan. Here, in the shade of apple and pomegranate trees, watching the children playing a game of tag, she can almost forget the war that has torn her country apart, displaced so many people, killed her parents.

A little black-haired boy – no more than three or four – trips and falls over. Halina starts to go to him, but a girl a year or two older helps him up and he's back on his feet and running around with the other children in no time. Two muddy knees, but otherwise unscathed. What's a bit of mud after what they've been through? How quickly they bounce back, she thinks. With an adequate diet, proper beds to sleep in, free from the strain of hard labour and extremes of temperature, most of the children are thriving. That's how it should be. There's a shortage of teachers, but they do what they can, running classes on a rota system. The only thing these children are missing are their parents.

'Pani Jablonska?' Halina turns at the sound of her name being called. The director of the orphanage – a harried but competent woman in her forties whose husband died of typhus in Siberia – is walking across the lawn with a woman that Anna has never seen before. But she recognises the type. A mother who has lost her child.

There have been a distressing number of such women calling at the orphanage recently. *We got separated at the camp. I couldn't find him. I've looked everywhere. You have to help me!* Weakened by months of hard labour and malnutrition, sick with grief for their lost children, these women are always desperate. Sympathetic to their plight, nevertheless Halina has learnt to be wary of them. Are the children they claim really theirs? Sometimes, especially with the younger children, it's impossible to be sure.

The director introduces the woman as Pani Czarna and explains that she's looking for her young son. The director, Halina knows, will have gone through the records in the office, but these are often incomplete and patchy. It's difficult to get accurate information out of a traumatised child. Impossible from the youngest.

'What's his name?' asks Halina.

The woman's sunken eyes dart about frantically, scanning the garden. She clutches her bony hands in front of her. 'Borys. He's called Borys. Is he here?'

Halina doesn't recognise the name, but then she hasn't been able to learn the name of every child. There are over two and a half thousand children in the orphanage. Some of them – scarred by what they've been through – haven't been able to tell anyone their name. Some of the younger ones just don't know.

'How old is he?'

'Four. But he's small for his age.'

'What colour hair?'

'There he is!' Before Halina or the director can stop her, the woman charges into the middle of the game of tag, causing the children to scatter in all directions. They stand and stare at her as she swoops down on the little boy with the black hair who fell over during the game. She scoops him up into her arms and holds him tight against her chest. The expression on his face, once she's put him down, is one of bewilderment. The woman has him by the hand as if she will never let go.

'Just one moment,' says the director. She crouches down in front of the boy. 'What's your name, child?'

The boy stares at her, open-mouthed, as if he doesn't understand why she is asking him this simple question.

'He's always been shy,' says Pani Czarna. 'He doesn't like talking to adults.' She bends down to his level. 'It's all right Borys, I'm here now. I've looked all over for you.' She takes out a handkerchief, licks a corner, and rubs at a smudge of dirt on his face. It's an intimate gesture, one that Halina remembers her own mother doing when she was a little girl. No mother wants her child to look dirty.

The director tries again. 'Can you tell me your name, child?'

Pani Czarna starts to sound desperate. 'His name is Borys.' Tears spring to her eyes. 'He is named after his grandfather.'

'Pani Jablonska?' Halina feels someone tugging her hand. It's the girl who helped the boy to his feet when he tripped. 'That's my brother Emil. Where is that woman taking him?' Halina scrutinises the girl's face and sees only sincerity and concern for her brother.

'Is that your mother?' asks Halina, pointing at Pani Czarna.

The girl shakes her head. 'I've never seen her before. Please don't let her take Emil away, will you?'

With a heavy heart, Halina approaches the director and

Pani Czarna. 'I'm sorry, but there may have been a misunderstanding here.' She repeats what the girl just told her. 'We need to establish the truth.' Although in her heart, Halina already knows how this is going to play out. It's not the first time something like this has happened.

'No, that can't be right,' says Pani Czarna. She grips the boy's hand tighter than ever. But the girl takes his other hand, and for a moment the child is strung helplessly between the woman claiming to be his mother and the girl claiming to be his sister. It doesn't take long for him to make his choice. He wrenches his hand free of Pani Czarna's and turns to his sister who embraces him in her arms.

Pani Czarna lets out an animal cry, full of grief and pain, and falls to her knees. Halina and the director help the woman to her feet and lead her away from the children. Her visceral reaction has frightened some of the younger ones.

'What happened to Borys?' asks the director.

Pani Czarna is sobbing hysterically now. 'He died,' she cries between sobs. 'He had a weak chest. He couldn't survive the cold in Siberia.' An all-too-common event.

'I'm so sorry to hear that,' says Halina.

'I just want a child,' sobs the woman as they lead her back to the building. 'I just want my child back.'

Halina has no words of comfort to offer her.

PART NINE
FIGHTING BACK
JANUARY 1943 – OCTOBER 1944

CHAPTER FORTY-TWO

Anna, Jadwiga and Krystyna sit on the bunk that used to be Krysia's, sewing buttons onto shirts for the Wehrmacht.

After two long and terrible months in the Revier, they have finally been released, their wounds only partially healed. Anna has a scar running from the middle of her right thigh all the way down to the calf muscle. Where the skin has grown back, it is puckered and tight. Her leg aches in the cold and she will always walk with a limp. The others have similar injuries, their legs a patchwork of scar tissue, wasted muscle and angry, red skin.

They now understand the full horror of what happened to them. The doctors in the Revier inserted alien objects into their legs: shards of glass and metal shrapnel. They were injected with bacteria, simulating the types of infection found on the battlefield. They have been used as human guinea-pigs so that the Germans can learn how to treat battle wounds. They've acquired the nickname *Polish Rabbits*.

Unable to go out to work, they have been given sewing and knitting to do in the block. The other prisoners treat them with respect. Even Irmgard proudly protects her *Polish Rabbits*, as if it's an honour to have such women in her block. They are no longer lazy Polish bitches. She leaves them in peace and doesn't fuss if their blankets are not one hundred per cent straight. It's little consolation for the suffering they've endured.

In fact, Anna can't get the suffering out of her mind. And the thought that other women could still be enduring the same fate makes her seethe with anger. Agnieszka's agonising death will haunt her forever. Distributing the Information Bulletin in Warsaw showed her the importance of sharing the truth. If only there was a way that they could get the truth out into the world. But the SS read their letters before they are posted. Could they devise a secret code? It seems far-fetched, but now that she's thought of it, she can't get the idea out of her head. Speaking in a whisper, she tells her friends what is on her mind and is gratified when Jadwiga and Krystyna don't tell her it's a crazy idea.

'Do we really want our families to know the truth?' asks Jadwiga.

It's a fair question. Until now, Anna has deliberately kept her letters bland and uneventful. Apart from the obvious problem of SS censorship, she hasn't wanted to worry her mother. But things are different now. The Germans have crossed a line that can't be ignored. What further atrocities might they commit if allowed to get away with these experiments?

'We've kept quiet for too long,' says Anna.

'I agree,' says Krystyna.

'All right,' says Jadwiga. 'But how do you get something like that past the guards?'

'Invisible ink,' says Krystyna. This is what Anna feared – that they wouldn't take her suggestion seriously. But, it seems, Krystyna isn't joking. 'I read once that urine can be used as invisible ink. The recipient has to apply heat for the writing to become visible.'

'Urine?' asks Anna. She never imagined it could it that simple. Pee into a bowl, and you've got invisible ink at your disposal. Excused the obligatory Sunday walk around the *Lagerstrasse*, they could use that time when everyone else is outside to write their secret messages.

That Sunday, whilst all the other inmates of their block are trudging around in the freezing cold, Anna and the others sit down to write. They haven't got long. Irmgard could appear at any moment and Anna doesn't want to risk their Blockova's anger.

Anna writes her letter in pencil, the usual platitudes about how everything is fine. But the first letter of each paragraph spells out *list moczem*, Polish for "letter in urine". Then she writes a line which she hopes Jan will understand.

Do you remember the stories we used to enjoy? They were such fun! My favourite was by Kornel Makuszyński. I think it was yours too.

Will Jan get the hint? The story was about a man who sent coded messages. He'll certainly wonder why she's referring to stories that they haven't read in years.

Then she dips a sharpened stick into a small bowl of urine and writes in the margin: *I want to tell you the truth.*

There isn't much space so she just writes a few sentences about the medical experiments.

'Should I tell them about Agnieszka?'

'Yes,' says Krystyna. 'Agnieszka deserves that.'

A woman was murdered by lethal injection, writes Anna. *We saw her die.* A lump catches in her throat and she has to blink away the tears.

'Look,' says Krystyna. 'It's working.'

It's true. As the urine dries, it becomes invisible. The SS will never know it's there.

'We need a code word,' says Anna. 'Something they can use when they write back to show they've received the message.'

They all think for a moment.

'It needs to be something innocuous,' says Jadwiga. 'Something the SS will never suspect.' They have no doubt that all letters into the camp, as well as those going out, are read and censored. The SS and Gestapo are ever on the lookout for Underground activity.

'How about "The cat has kittens",' suggests Krystyna.

Anna nods her approval of this anodyne statement which could mean exactly what it says or could, they hope, indicate that their message has been understood and received.

Writing in urine, Anna adds the instruction to the bottom of the letter. Then they sneak back to their bunks. The letter goes off with all the other letters. It will be another month before they receive a reply.

*

Why does Anna always have to write in German? Jan supposes it's because the letters are censored by the SS, otherwise why not write in good old Polish?

It's his job to decipher these letters, which he does with the aid of a heavy Polish-German dictionary from his father's study. He fetches the dictionary now and takes it to the dining room table. He doesn't like to hang around the study where the memories of his father threaten to overwhelm him. Maybe he should just keep the dictionary in his own room.

Agata watches him with her wide, dark eyes. Since coming to live with them, she's become as devoted to Jan as a puppy. Unfortunately her German isn't up to anything. Wiktor was always better at languages than Jan, but he hasn't heard from his friend for months now. He fears that Wiktor was a victim of the transports to Treblinka which he read about in the Information Bulletin. A handful of Jews who managed to escape came back with stories of unbelievable horror. Local residents complained about the stench of death. That's why it's always a relief to hear from Anna, to know that she's still alive, even if her letters take some effort to translate.

He scrutinises the first sentence. It begins with *Letzte Woche*, easily translated as *last week*. But it still takes him another fifteen minutes before he's worked out that last week Anna worked on sewing tasks. He moves on to the next paragraph.

Ich bin gesund. He's seen that phrase many times before and recognises *I am healthy*. She always says that, though. He's not sure he believes her. He suspects she's just saying it so that their mother won't worry. But Maria worries all the time, anyway.

Sag mir… More riffling through the dictionary until he's deciphered *Tell me, have you heard from Lech?* Short answer, no.

Täglich denke ich… God, this is hard work. He was hoping to get this finished before Maria returns from haggling on the black market. He eventually comes up with *Daily I think of you all.*

He frowns. There's something odd about this letter. Anna isn't normally so sentimental. What's got into her?

There are four paragraphs in which she talks about her friends in the camp, or asks about people in Warsaw.

And then the second to last paragraph begins *Erinnerst du…*

After much effort and swearing – with Maria out he can say what he likes even though Agata is listening – he comes up with:

Do you remember the stories we used to enjoy? They were such fun! My favourite was by Kornel Makuszyński. I think it was yours too.

Now he's truly baffled. Why on earth is Anna referring to books from his childhood? And why that author in particular? *Kornel Makuszyński.* Jan can't even remember what the story was about. He asks Agata if she knows.

'It's about a secret message,' says Agata, as if it's the most obvious thing in the world.

'Of course,' says Jan, remembering. Does this letter contain a secret message?

The last paragraph, beginning *Meine Wünsche* – my wishes – is just a sign off.

'I think there might be a secret message in this letter,' he tells Agata. 'Come and help me find it.'

She runs around the other side of the table and together they pore over the document.

If there is a message, Jan can't for the life of him see it. He tries reading it backwards. He looks at the first letter of each word to see if it spells something. Then Agata suggests they take the first letter of each paragraph.

It's worth a shot. Anna usually only writes three or four paragraphs, but here there are – he counts them quickly – ten!

He jots down the first letter of each paragraph and comes up with *listmoczem*. A nonsense word. And then he has it. *List moczem*. Two words. *Letter in urine*.

Urgh! He drops the letter in disgust. Agata giggles at him. He sniffs his fingers. He can't smell anything, but he'll make sure to wash his hands thoroughly later.

Letter in urine. But where? Now he notices that the paper is a bit crinkled around the edges as if it got wet at some point. Has Anna written a secret message in the margins? He's desperate to find out. But how do you reveal an invisible message? He asks Agata, who shakes her head and shrugs. Who would know something like this?

Weronika, that's who.

'Back in a minute,' he tells Agata. He runs across the courtyard and climbs the stairs to Weronika's apartment.

She's clearly surprised to see him standing there, but as soon as he's explained the problem her face brightens.

'You need to apply heat,' she says.

'But how will we do that?'

'With a hot iron.'

'Are you sure?'

'Absolutely. Why don't I show you?'

She's already out of the apartment and on her way to his. Jan hurries to catch up.

He still has his doubts. 'Won't the letter just burn?' he asks her once they've got the ironing board set up and the iron plugged in.

'Only if you're incompetent,' says Weronika. 'If you know how to iron shirts without burning a hole in them then you can iron a letter without setting fire to the apartment.'

Jan bows to her superior knowledge on such matters. He's never used an iron in his life. Now he regrets this gap in his knowledge.

Weronika tests the iron by licking her finger and tapping the iron's hot surface. Jan's admiration grows by the second.

He gives her the letter and watches anxiously as she presses the hot iron over the surface of the paper using firm, quick strokes.

'The trick,' she says, 'is to keep the iron moving, not hold it still.'

'Of course,' he says. He would have done exactly the opposite.

At first nothing seems to be happening, but after about fifteen seconds of pressing, Weronika puts the iron to one side, and they peer at the sheet of paper, which is now super smooth and slightly browned. Jan can't believe his eyes. There, in the margin, is yellowy brown writing and, what's more, it's in Polish.

'You're a genius,' he says.

They read in silence. *I want to tell you the truth.*

This is what Anna has been hiding from them all these long months.

They read about the medical experiments. *A woman was murdered by lethal injection. We saw her die.*

Jan doesn't know what to say. What Anna has written is far worse than anything he ever imagined.

'I'm sorry,' says Weronika. She reaches for his hand and he lets her take it.

They are still staring at the letter when Maria returns with the food.

CHAPTER FORTY-THREE

Not much work is being done in Pan Piotrowski's algebra class today. The third-floor apartment, with its neatly arranged bookcases and paintings of landscapes, is close enough to the ghetto wall to afford Jan and his fellow students a ringside view of the violent scenes being enacted over there. Like a horror show, it's terrifying and compelling in equal measure. Jan finds it impossible to concentrate on calculus when a short distance away orange flames are leaping into the sky and columns of thick black smoke are billowing into the air, blotting out the sun and carpeting everything in sight in a blanket of grey ash.

'Whoa!' exclaims the class in unison as a giant flame whooshes into the air and wraps its hungry tendrils around a nearby building, reaching inside the smashed windows, seeking out its victims. Pan Piotrowski abandons any attempt to continue with the lesson and joins the boys by the window.

The uprising in the ghetto started in April and has been raging for three weeks now. Surely, it can't go on for much longer. Most of the ghetto is already a smouldering ruin. By all accounts, it started when the remaining Jews decided enough was enough. They armed themselves with the help of the Polish Underground and started fighting back. No one expected them to hold out for so long, least of all, it would seem, the Germans. Now the SS have resorted to using flamethrowers in the streets in a last-ditch attempt to smoke out those hiding in basements. It was always going to be an unequal struggle, but you've got to hand it to the Jews. They've given the Germans a good kicking.

Jan senses that the war is finally starting to turn. The Germans are no longer having everything their own way. Back in February, everyone welcomed the news of the German defeat at Stalingrad. And then Russian night bombers targeted the military installations around Warsaw, inflicting heavy losses on German supplies. April brought less welcome news with the discovery of some twenty-thousand Polish officers in a mass grave in the Katyń forest near Smolensk in the Soviet Union. They had been shot. The Germans and the Soviets both blamed each other in a juvenile game of finger-pointing. But for once, it turned out that the Germans were right. Identification on some of the bodies proved that the officers were shot before the German invasion of the Soviet Union, so the Soviets were the guilty party.

Now fifteen, Jan would like nothing more than to join the Underground and fight back. Seeing the ghetto burning, he yearns to do it for his friend Wiktor, and to avenge his father's death.

But how does one join an organisation which, by its very nature, is clandestine? He's an avid reader of the Information Bulletin whenever he can get his hands on a copy. In March, he read about Operation Arsenal, which took place here in Warsaw. Some prisoners from the Underground scouting organisation, the Grey Ranks, had been captured and were being transported by truck from the Pawiak prison to Gestapo headquarters in Szucha Avenue, no doubt for a round of torture and interrogation. But the Underground ambushed the vehicle close to the Barbican, a sixteenth-century fortification in Stare Miasto, and in the ensuing firefight all twenty-five prisoners were freed. The downside was that one hundred and sixty inmates of Pawiak were executed in retaliation. But to Jan, the Grey Ranks are the epitome of bravery and active resistance. What wouldn't he give to be able to join them!

Their hour is up and Pan Piotrowski dismisses them with a promise that next time they'll do more algebra. Jan can hardly bear to tear himself away from the window. He gathers his things together, says goodbye to the teacher, and follows the others down the stairs and out into the street.

There are six of them in the class. Because Jan has always been quite good at maths – certainly better than languages – he's with boys a year or two older than himself. But he's still small for his age and this makes him feel even younger in the presence of these boys who are practically men. He listens with awe when they talk about girls they're seeing.

He sets off alone, but a boy called Stefan falls into step beside him and asks if they can walk together.

'Sure,' says Jan, flattered that Stefan has even noticed him.

Stefan is seventeen years old and already shaves. He's a full head taller than Jan and always has lots of adoring girls following him around, at least if his stories are to be believed. Stefan takes a packet of cigarettes from his breast pocket and offers one to Jan. Jan shakes his head, sorry that he doesn't smoke. He doesn't want to give it a go in front of Stefan and make an idiot of himself. He's heard that the first time you try it, you cough your guts up. He would need to practise in secret, although his mother would have a fit if she smelled cigarette smoke on his clothes. And Weronika probably wouldn't approve either. But why does he care what Weronika thinks?

Stefan lights his cigarette and blows a plume of smoke skywards. 'I've had my eye on you,' he says.

'You have?' Now Jan's worried that he's done something wrong.

'Yeah,' says Stefan. 'You could be just the sort of person

we're looking for.'

'What do you mean?'

Stefan stops, turns to face him and smiles with his head cocked to one side. 'I've seen the way you watch what's going on in the ghetto.'

'It's hard to ignore,' says Jan. He wonders if it's safe to say he had a Jewish friend. He decides to trust Stefan. 'I had a friend in the ghetto once, but I'm sure he's dead now.' He swallows hard, not wanting to shed tears in front of Stefan of all people.

Stefan nods sympathetically. 'I know how you feel. And you want to do something about it. Am I right?'

'Absolutely,' says Jan, delighted that Stefan understands.

Stefan studies his face a moment longer, assessing him. 'All right, here's the deal. Tomorrow evening, meet me by the lake in the Krasiński Garden at six o'clock and I'll introduce you to some interesting people.'

'I'll be there,' he says. 'Thank you,' he adds, but Stefan is already walking away, giving a casual wave of his hand.

Jan is so elated that he walks the rest of the way home feeling as if he's grown two inches taller. He's long suspected that Stefan plays a role in the Underground because he often comes to classes late and Pan Piotrowski never admonishes him for his tardiness, as if there's an understanding between them. It occurs to Jan then that the mild-mannered Pan Piotrowski might be more than just a maths teacher.

When he arrives home, his mother is reading to Agata, so he's spared having to answer any questions about his maths class. And he definitely isn't going to say a word about Stefan's invitation. If his mother thought he was about to go and join the Underground, she'd never let him out of her sight again.

The next day, Jan looks at the clock every ten minutes, willing it to move faster. He picks up the family photograph taken the day Lech was called up and wishes he could tell his brother and sister what he's about to do. He was just a kid when this photograph was taken, but he's older and wiser now. War has taught him a lot in the last four years.

At five thirty he can't bear waiting any longer. He makes an excuse about having an extra maths class and slips out of the apartment. Hopping on a tram, he rides a couple of stops to the Krasiński Garden, nervous that Stefan may have had second thoughts. He's relieved when a familiar figure detaches itself from behind a tree trunk accompanied by a plume of cigarette smoke. Stefan tosses the half-smoked cigarette into the lake and greets Jan with a brief smile and an approving nod of the head. He's passed the first test just by showing up.

'This way,' says Stefan, setting off with a loping stride.

They leave the Garden and enter the maze of streets in Stare Miasto, arriving at a tall, narrow house in a cobbled street just off the market square. Stefan knocks twice slowly, then three times in quick succession. A minute later, the door opens and they enter a dark, unlit hallway. A woman invites them to come upstairs.

Jan follows Stefan and the mysterious woman up the creaking stairs to the top floor. The ceiling is low and sloping, right under the eaves. They enter a small room at the back of the house overlooking the courtyard below. An oil lamp on a table in the centre of the room is the only illumination. In its orange glow, Jan sees the faces of three other teenage boys, all about his age or slightly older. They stare at him with undisguised curiosity.

The woman turns to face him and he is startled to recognise Anna's friend Wanda. Jan hasn't seen her in nearly four years, not since they spent a day digging anti-tank trenches together on the outskirts of the city. She'd had her hair hidden under a scarf that day and her face had been covered in streaks of mud, but he remembers her energy and enthusiasm for the task. Now there's a steeliness about her, as if the war has hardened her. It's hardened them all.

'Here's our new recruit,' says Stefan, clapping Jan on the shoulder. 'He's keen to help.'

Wanda shows no sign of recognising Jan and Jan doesn't want to remind her of the skinny, little kid he used to be. 'Why do you want to join the Underground?' she asks.

That's not a difficult question to answer. 'My older brother was called up before the outbreak of war and was deported to the Soviet Union. My father was killed because he was an academic. My sister was arrested by the Gestapo and sent to a concentration camp in Germany.' Wanda nods in understanding as if she's suddenly realised who he is. 'My best friend was in the ghetto. I think he was deported to Treblinka. I can't continue to sit back and do nothing. I want to fight.'

He must have made quite an impression because when he's finished, he sees the other boys staring at him wide-eyed.

Wanda nods her head grimly. 'You might be wondering why we haven't asked you your name and haven't told you ours. The fact is, for security it's best if we know as little as possible about each other. And so we each adopt a *nom de guerre*.'

Nom de guerre. He must have learnt something from his French lessons with Madame Vernier because he immediately translates this as *war name*. He finds the idea thrilling. 'I'm sorry if I said too much about myself. I just wanted you to understand how much this means to me.'

'We understand,' says Wanda. 'But if you want to join us you have to take an oath of allegiance.'

Jan nods enthusiastically. He'll agree to anything if it grants him access to this clandestine world.

Wanda passes him a piece of paper. 'Read this to yourself, and if you agree with it, please read it aloud to the rest of us.'

Jan glances at the words on the piece of paper and immediately starts to read them in a loud, clear voice. 'I swear to serve with the Grey Ranks, safeguard its secrets, obey orders and, if need be, sacrifice my life.'

'Welcome to our cell,' says Wanda.

The other boys all jump up and shake his hand. He can hardly believe he's done it! He's joined the Underground and now he's going to do his bit to fight the Germans. He's never felt prouder in his whole life. He can't wait to tell Weronika.

CHAPTER FORTY-FOUR

The Commander-in-Chief of the Underground has been arrested by the Germans.

It's a terrible blow to Jan, coming just a couple of months after he joined the organisation. The commander who went by the codename Grot, but who was really General Rowecki, was betrayed and captured. The *Nowy Kurier Warszawski*, the Nazi Polish language newspaper, is full of the story, accusing Grot of being paid by the British and of being responsible for terrorist outrages against the Reich. You have to turn to the Information Bulletin to find out what a brave man and fine leader he was. Even though Jan never met him, and wouldn't expect to encounter such a high-ranking figure, he feels the loss keenly.

Then, a mere four days later, he hears that General Sikorski, Prime Minister of the Polish government-in-exile and Commander-in-Chief of the Polish Armed Forces, has been killed in a plane crash in Gibraltar. Once again, the *Nowy Kurier Warszawski* can't get enough of the story. Sikorski, claims the paper, was shot down by the RAF because his insistence on blaming the Soviets for the Katyń massacre was damaging Churchill's relationship with Stalin.

Jan doesn't believe a word of it. Either Sikorski's death

was a tragic accident, or the Germans sabotaged the aircraft. The British would never sink to such depths. But there's no doubt that losing two such high-profile figures in less than a week has had a serious impact on morale within Jan's cell and throughout the wider Underground.

The cell is like a new family to him. After he read his oath of allegiance and was formally accepted into the group, they told him their codenames. Wanda goes by the name Hanka. The others are all named after animals. There's Lew (lion) so named on account of his shaggy red hair and the fact that he's big and strong. Then there's Królik (rabbit) who has very prominent front teeth, and Sowa (owl) who wears round, wire-rimmed glasses that give him a studious appearance. When it came to choosing a codename for himself it was Lew who suggested, not unkindly, that he should be Mysz (mouse) because he was small and fast on his feet and would be good at hiding. Jan took that as a compliment and has become rather fond of his new name.

His initial tasks have not been too onerous. His first job was to distribute copies of the Information Bulletin. He has quickly become adept at dropping the newsletter into random postboxes in the hallways of apartment buildings. This task has also given him an opportunity to devour the bulletin from cover to cover, a necessary antidote to the Nazi propaganda in the *Nowy Kurier Warszawski*.

One edition of the bulletin has an account of the German retreat at Kursk. Gleaning their details from illegally listening to the BBC, the writers conclude that Hitler has been forced to divert his troops to Italy where the Allies have now landed. We've got them on the run at last, thinks Jan with glee. It's also thanks to the bulletin that he learns that General Grot has been replaced by General Bór-Komorowski who has promised to continue the struggle until Poland has won. That's the sort of fighting talk he likes to hear.

Having proved himself reliable with delivering the Information Bulletins, Wanda/Hanka has now given him a new job. He delivers messages to people who are at risk of being sent to work in Germany. The Underground has infiltrated the Employment Office with undercover agents who leak the names of those destined for deportation. But with an *Arbeitskarte*, an Employment Card, stating that you work in a factory doing something useful, you can avoid being sent away. Jan himself now carries a forged *Arbeitskarte*, courtesy of the Underground, that claims he is gainfully employed in a furniture factory, even though he's never held a chisel and wouldn't be able to carve a dovetail joint if his life depended on it.

He also passes on Anna's letters after revealing the secret writing using a hot iron, the way Weronika demonstrated. When he showed Wanda the letter about the medical experiments, she broke down in tears. 'Poor Anna. She didn't deserve this.' It's the only time Wanda has admitted that she knows who Jan really is. Since that first letter, Anna has revealed more horrors at Ravensbrück: the *Idiotenstübchen* in the Revier, a special room where those considered mad are incarcerated; the lethal injections given to those unable to work – the so-called *useless mouths*; the lorries that take women away, never to return; and, most recently, the new crematorium which belches smoke into the air every hour of the day. Wanda has promised to pass the news on to people who will get it out into the world.

But today Jan is doing what he most enjoys – painting the *Kotwica*. The anchor. This symbol of Polish resistance is formed from the letters W and P, the P rising out of the centre of the W. There's some confusion about what the letters actually stand for. Some claim the original meaning was *Pomścimy Waver* – we will avenge the massacre in Waver that took place in December '39. But most people take it to mean *Polska Walcza*, Fighting Poland, or *Wojsko Polskie*, Polish Army. Whatever. The important thing, Jan has realised, is that it boosts morale, and this is what people need in these days of increasing German brutality, when public executions are on the rise and bodies are left hanging from the balcony of the courthouse as a warning to others not to resist the German occupation. The anchor tells people that the Underground is still there, and it's still resisting. It's a beacon of hope, and without hope, what is left? So he roams the streets, pot of white paint and brush in hand, looking for any blank wall on which to leave his mark. He's got it down to a fine art now. All it takes is a couple of strokes with the brush and he completes his handiwork in a matter of seconds before moving on to the next site. He's completed nine today already.

He dips his brush into the pot of paint and touches the brush to the wall of his old school, smiling at the thought that four years ago painting graffiti would have got him expelled. Nowadays, old ladies who would have been outraged by such vandalism tell him what a fine job he's doing. He's just completed the 'W' when he hears running footsteps and a shout.

'German patrol! German patrol!' A young boy hurtles down the street, warning everyone to take cover.

A truck turns the corner and Jan drops the paintbrush. Abandoning the tools of his trade, he legs it down the road, diving into the first turning he finds.

When he peers back round the corner, he sees the truck screech to a brief halt next to his unfinished artwork, before the engine roars back to life. They can see the paint is still wet, so they'll know he can't be far away.

Jan doesn't hang around. The Germans have the advantage of firepower, but he's small and fast and knows how to hide. *Mysz* is his codename and he intends to live up to it.

The truck rounds the corner. He doesn't stop to look back but he can hear the wheels bouncing over the cobbles. It's still fifty yards behind him, but closing quickly. He can't outrun it, but maybe he can slow its progress.

He sees what he needs. A metal bin has been left out in the street. Jan tips it over onto its side and rolls it into the path of the oncoming truck. A squeal of brakes, a crunch of metal, and a tyre explodes as the truck runs over the makeshift obstacle. There's another bang, as a shot is fired.

He turns into an alleyway and runs for his life but bullets whizz through the air, narrowly missing him. He keeps going, pushing as fast and hard as he can until his lungs are burning. If only Weronika could see him now.

He doesn't stop until he's sure the Germans are not following him. They must have given up, more concerned with their mangled truck than with one lone resistance fighter. But they nearly had him back there!

A paint brush is all well and good, but what he really needs is a gun. It's time for some real action.

CHAPTER FORTY-FIVE

Reconnoitre. Advance. Attack. Defend. Withdraw. The five basic tasks of an infantryman. Jan repeats them to himself until he's got them off by heart. After months delivering the Information Bulletin, warning potential deportees of their impending fate, and decorating the city with anchors, in the spring of '44 he has at last graduated to Battle School. When Wanda recommended him and the other boys in his cell for this next stage in his Underground career, he couldn't have been happier. He reads the pre-war manual *Combat* in bed every night, committing to memory all the theory of the battlefield. He dreams of the organisation of a column and the duties of a sentry.

The training meeting is the highlight of his week and today's session is one he's been especially looking forward to.

'This,' says the instructor, pointing at the weapon on the table in front of them, 'is an MP40 Schmeisser submachine gun.' They all crowd around, eager to see a real weapon in the flesh. 'We captured it from the Germans in a raid. I'm going to show you how to strip and reassemble it. Then you can have a go.'

'Awesome,' says Lew.

'Brilliant,' says Królik.

Sowa says nothing but stares at the gun through his spectacles as if he's afraid it will explode.

Jan looks at the weapon with a mixture of awe and respect. Before it fell into the hands of the Polish resistance, this gun was used by the enemy. How many Polish men and women has it killed? It's a sobering thought but one that strengthens Jan's resolve. The weapon belongs to the Underground now, and Germany is going to regret ever setting so much as a toe on Polish soil. Only last month the Nazi Chief of Police, Franz Kutschera, was assassinated in a highly organised attack by the Underground.

The instructor, a young man in his twenties calling himself Zych, picks up the submachine gun and begins the demonstration.

'Remove the magazine by pressing this button here.' The magazine drops into Zych's hand. 'It holds thirty-two rounds of 9mm Parabellum cartridges.'

Jan nods. He already knows this from his reading.

'Next, rotate this disk, then pull the trigger whilst rotating the upper and lower halves of the gun away from each other.' The weapon comes apart in the instructor's hands. 'Finally, remove the telescopic firing pin and the bolt, like this.' Zych makes it look easy.

He shows them how to reassemble the firearm, then says, 'Okay, now it's your turn.'

Lew goes first and does a reasonable job, although he has to be reminded to rotate the disk before separating the two halves of the gun. Królik and Sowa both take it apart well enough, but have a bit of trouble putting it back together. By the time Jan has a go he's memorised the whole routine from start to finish and strips and reassembles the weapon in record time.

'Well done,' says Zych. 'You're a natural!'

Inside, Jan glows with pride, but he tries not to let it show on his face. He doesn't want the others to think that he's gloating. They're a team and they have to stick together.

That's something that has been drilled into them all from the beginning.

When he goes to bed that night, he can't get thoughts of the Schmeisser out of his head. He's wanted to handle a real weapon for such a long time, imagining an object of immense power. But stripping and reassembling the gun was really very simple, almost mundane. If anything, the weapon lost some of its mystique in the process. And perhaps that's for the best. He needs to think of it as a tool, not an object to be fearful of. The real question is, will he ever get the chance to fire it at a German? And will he be up to the job? He falls asleep plagued by doubts.

*

'What do they think they're going to teach you?' Maria stands in the kitchen doorway with her hands on her hips, her shoulders squared, ready for battle.

Jan has only just told her about the training course in the countryside this weekend. He knew she'd be like this – obdurate and sceptical. But he can't disappear for the whole day without telling her where he's going. Above all, he wants her to be proud of him. How can he make her see how important this is? 'It's a training day in the forest. We're going to practise column formation and shooting with a pistol.'

Her hands fly to her face. He's obviously said the wrong thing. 'You're going to learn to shoot?'

'We'll be firing blanks. We don't have any live ammunition.'

'That is not the point! They're teaching you to kill. Who do these people think they are? What are they going to do with you? Send you into battle against the Germans? This is ridiculous. You're just children, for goodness' sake.'

'I'm nearly sixteen, Mama, and I'm not a child anymore.' Jan hates being called a child. He might be the youngest in his cell, but he's one of the fastest learners and has proved himself to be every bit as brave as Lew or Królik. His nickname of Mysz now seems ironical and the others know it.

'You're a child as far as I'm concerned,' says his mother, 'and children have no place fighting in a war. You could be killed. Have you thought of that?'

'I could have been killed when the Germans were dropping bombs on Warsaw,' he counters. 'This way I'll be fighting back, not hiding in the basement.'

'Hiding in the basement kept you safe!'

'But we're not really safe, are we? The Germans have occupied our country and we won't be safe again until we've regained our freedom!'

'What sort of talk is that? You're not a soldier. You should be concentrating on your studies, not wasting time playing battle games.'

'It's not a game! We're learning useful skills that will win us back our country.' Jan can feel himself getting hot under the collar. Why does his mother always refuse to see his point of view? He knows she hates the Germans, but as soon as he does anything in the fight against them, she treats him like a little child who can't tie his own shoelaces. It infuriates him. He goes into his bedroom and slams the door. He won't miss this training day for the world.

The next morning he braces himself for another argument. He's prepared to apologise for his temper last night, but he's going on the training day, whatever his mother says. He finds her in the kitchen, cutting slices of bread and cheese. She's bent over her task and he notices how grey her hair has become. Suddenly he feels a pang of pity for her. She's lost so much in this war. He can understand why she's so afraid of losing him too.

'Mama…' he begins.

She looks up and gives him a faint smile. There are dark smudges under her eyes as if she hasn't slept well. 'If you're going to be out all day,' she says, 'you'll need some sandwiches to keep you going.'

'Thank you,' he says, giving her a hug. 'And I promise to be careful.'

She presses him tight to her chest then lets him go. 'Get yourself ready then.'

Seeing her preparing food reminds him of the morning Lech was called up. He goes to the mantelpiece and picks up Anna's photo. How small and young he looks. Only eleven. He cringes when he remembers how innocent and naïve he was then, how much confidence he had in a swift Polish victory. But Lech shared that confidence and fully expected to be back in a matter of weeks, and now Jan hasn't seen his brother in four and a half years. And Anna has been gone three years. There's still hope that Lech and Anna will return one day, but his father will never come back. Although he can understand why his mother is so reluctant to let him go, it's because of Lech and Anna and his father that he has to do what he's doing. When he sees Lech and Anna again, he wants to be able to say that he did his bit.

The sandwiches bounce in his backpack as he runs to the train station, worried he's going to be late. At the station, he meets Lew, Królik and Sowa in the crowds, doing his best to avoid attracting the attention of the Gestapo who regularly monitor the station. The Polish Blue Police are no better, always on the lookout for smugglers and black marketeers. His backpack might look suspicious to an over-zealous officer, so he slips it off and carries it by the straps.

They board the train without incident and soon they're heading out of the city, past dilapidated suburbs and the occasional abandoned tank. Jan keeps one eye peeled for German spies, and doesn't start to relax until they're out in the countryside, miles from Warsaw.

Zych meets them at their destination, a small town northeast of Warsaw, where they join forces with another cell. They walk to a wooded area on the outskirts of the town where Zych organises them into column formation with flankers and rearguards. It's good to be finally putting theory into practice. If anyone challenges them, they'll claim they're just out for a ramble in the woods.

After a couple of hours practising column formation, Zych tells them to collect as many large stones as they can find. Once they've assembled a sizeable collection, he takes them to a clearing and instructs them on the basic principles of throwing a hand grenade.

'Twist and pull the pin,' he shouts – they have to mime this part of the action – 'and then immediately adopt a stance with your left leg forwards and your right leg back. Bend your right elbow and launch the grenade from shoulder height. Then drop down on one knee and take cover. Off you go.'

Jan throws stone after stone until the skin on his hands is raw and his right shoulder is aching. Being shorter than the others, he can't throw as far as them. It's frustrating and he pushes himself harder and harder, grunting with the effort. With his final throw, he hits one of Lew's stones and punches the air with glee. Next, they practise throwing from a prone position, lying on their backs and rolling over onto their sides to throw the stones. By the time they stop for something to eat, they're all covered in mud and grime and have bits of dead leaves sticking in their hair. But Jan has never felt so alive. He wants to take part in a real battle as soon as possible.

After they've eaten their sandwiches – his mother made so many for him that Jan is able to share them around the group – Zych announces with a grin that he has something a bit different planned for the afternoon session. Jan hopes they're going to learn how to shoot. Unlike throwing, shooting shouldn't require you to be tall and strong, just to have a good eye and a steady hand, and Jan thinks he might be quite good at it. But then a group of girl scouts appears out of the forest. Their leader, a young woman in her twenties, greets Zych as if they're old friends. She has eight teenage girls with her. Jan and his friends look at each other in confusion.

'And now,' says Zych, 'The guides are going to give us a

lesson in basic first aid.'

A nervous laugh runs through the group of boys. Lew and Królik nudge each other. But Jan isn't laughing. Because one of the girls is Weronika.

Clapping her hands together and giving Lew and Królik a stern stare which sobers them up, the Girl Guide leader takes charge of proceedings. 'Okay everyone, find a partner.' She makes it sound as if they're about to have a dancing lesson. She turns to the boys. 'My girls are going to start by showing you how to dress a wound and prepare a basic arm sling.'

'You've got to be joking,' mumbles Lew under his breath.

But the Girl Guide leader is clearly in earnest, and so is Zych. 'Get a move on, fellas,' he says. 'They're only girls. They don't bite.'

Weronika, of course, is the first to step forward. Singling Jan out, she goes straight up to him and says in her clear, ringing voice, loud enough for all to hear, 'Fancy seeing you here!'

'No need to sound so surprised,' mutters Jan.

After that, everyone else finds a partner, some with more enthusiasm than others.

'Sit on the ground,' says Weronika, bossy as ever. Jan does as he's told. He could do with some remedial work on his shoulder which is aching after all that stone throwing, but it seems that Weronika has other ideas. 'We'll start with a basic dressing on your leg. Roll up your trouser leg.'

'Which one?'

She gives him a withering look. 'It doesn't matter, does it?' Jan rolls up his right trouser leg.

Weronika kneels on the ground beside him and produces a roll of white gauze bandage from her satchel. 'Of course,' she says in her matter-of-fact way, 'if you'd injured your leg in a real fire-fight I'd have to cut your trousers off for you. But for now we'll just pretend, all right?'

Jan can only nod mutely. He hasn't seen Weronika in

months, he's been so busy working for the Underground and attending Battle School. He's astonished at how much she's changed. She's transformed from a gawky girl into a young woman. As she leans over his exposed thigh, he becomes acutely aware of the outline of her breasts through her shirt. The top button is undone and in the open neckline he catches a glimpse of soft, round flesh. He has to look away and pretend to cough. He can feel himself getting aroused and prays that Weronika won't notice. When she touches his leg with her fingers a tingling sensation shoots up his spine. He can feel himself beginning to sweat, even though the air is cool. She starts to wrap the bandage around his leg with quick, deft movements. But after a couple of loops, the bandage is so tight that he fears she's going to cut off his circulation. His arousal soon fades. Now all he can think about is the discomfort of his leg.

'Bandages have to be tight,' explains Weronika, 'to help staunch any bleeding.'

'Right,' says Jan. 'That's certainly very tight.' The muscle above the bandage is throbbing with restricted blood vessels.

She finishes wrapping the bandage and secures it in place with a safety pin. Then she sits back on her haunches and admires her handiwork. 'How does that feel?'

'Great,' says Jan through gritted teeth. There's no way he would get far with this thing on his leg. He looks across at his companions and sees that they are also suffering at the hands of their trainee nurses.

'Okay,' says Weronika, hitching up her skirt. 'Now it's time for you to practise on me.'

CHAPTER FORTY-SIX

The top of the mountain is lost in the early morning haze. Lech draws in a deep breath, savouring the cool, fresh air. If this is going to be his last day on earth, he wants to fully experience every single heartbeat. When the order is given, they'll begin their ascent, not knowing if they'll still be alive by sunset. If previous attempts to capture the monastery at Monte Cassino are anything to go by, this could be a suicide mission. He feels as if every moment of the last five years has converged on this point in time. Fate, call it what you will, has brought him here. But it's been a long road to get to this point.

In the end, he didn't stay long in Tehran. The city was in the Soviet zone of occupation and since the Poles didn't have a good word to say about their recent sojourn in the Motherland, it was deemed politically expedient to move them to the British zone as quickly as possible.

It was hard leaving Halina behind at the orphanage in Isfahan but she assured him she would be safe there.

'I know how much you want to fight for your country,' she told him.

'I'm doing this for us,' he said, clasping her to him.

Lech travelled with the army to Qizil Ribat in Iraq and

then on to a training centre near Mosul. By then, they were part of the British 10th Army and were named the Polish Second Corps. If it hadn't been for the roasting temperatures during the day, the freezing temperatures at night, and the danger from scorpions and black-widow spiders, he would have said he was better off than he had been since the start of the war. Fed and trained by the British, the Poles grew stronger. They regained some self-respect.

The news in February '43 that the Germans had been defeated at the Battle of Stalingrad gave everyone a big morale boost. Finally, the war was turning. The faint whiff of victory was in the air.

In June '43 they transferred to Palestine. Their joy at the surrender of 275,000 Axis troops to the British and Americans in Tunisia was tempered by the news, when it finally reached them, of the mass graves discovered at Katyń. Twenty thousand Polish officers shot by the Soviets. Those who understood these things concluded it was nothing short of revenge for the Polish victory over the Bolshevik Army in 1920. So much for not bearing grudges, eh, comrade?

By the time they transferred, yet again, to Egypt in August '43, most Poles, Lech included, were itching to get back to Poland and fight for their country. But they were as far away as ever. Warsaw was rapidly becoming a distant memory.

And then, finally, a move in the right direction. The vanguard of the Second Corps sailed to Italy in December '43. Lech's division followed in the early months of '44. They were back on European soil at last.

But home is still a long way away. First, they have to capture the monastery of Monte Cassino, high on the top of Monastery Hill. This strategic stronghold is key if the Allies are to have any hope of breaking through the Gustav line and advancing north to Rome. It won't be easy, but the Poles are older and wiser now than they were five years ago.

And after all they've been through – defeat at the hands of the Germans, exile to the Soviet Union, evacuation to the Middle East, the annihilation of their country – they are ready for a fight.

Lech cringes when he thinks how naïve they were back in the summer of '39. As if a mere Polish mobilisation would deter the Germans from invading. When the attack came, they'd been no more able to defend themselves than a child's sandcastle is able to withstand the incoming tide. And then to be invaded on their eastern borders by the Soviet Union, just when they were still reeling from the shock of the Nazi Blitzkrieg. Was it any wonder that Poland collapsed like a house of cards?

The mist is starting to clear, revealing the rocky mountain ahead. Scarily high and inaccessible. How will they ever reach the top? Are they on a fool's errand?

In February, an American assault on the mountain ended in abject failure amid snow and freezing rain. Not ones to give up easily, the Yanks then tried bombing the monastery from the air, but the Germans only responded by fortifying the ruins. Further attacks by multi-national forces resulted in the capture of Castle Hill and Hangman's Hill, but Monastery Hill remains stubbornly in German hands. And now General Anders has been given the opportunity of letting his troops have a go where others have failed. A lesser man might have baulked at the idea, but not Anders.

The first Polish assault on the mountain five days ago resulted in a shocking number of casualties and a tactical retreat. But now they're preparing for round two and Lech knows they'll give it their all because what have they got to lose? This is what they've been waiting for ever since their humiliation in September '39.

Are you going to fight the Germans? An image of his kid brother comes unbidden into Lech's mind. He supposes Jan isn't such a little kid anymore. Still, Lech can't go home and look his brother in the eye unless he can say, 'Yes, I fought the Germans.'

They sit in neat ranks, waiting for the order to move. Reports estimate there are fewer than a thousand Germans still on the top of the mountain, so the Poles have the numerical advantage. But their enemy is out of sight, and they literally have an uphill challenge before they can meet the Germans face to face. If they even get that far. Don't think like that, Lech tells himself. Think of your family, think of Halina, think of–

And then it comes. The order to advance. Lech stops thinking. He scrambles to his feet like everyone else and begins the ascent of the mountain.

At first, he can't see much except the back of the men in front. He follows blindly, his feet slipping and sliding on rubble loosened by previous bouts of shelling. He grits his teeth and leans into the climb, willing himself on and upwards, a combination of mental and physical effort. But his kit weighs a ton. Apart from the usual ammunition, he's loaded up with forty pounds of grenades. It's hot and his throat is already parched and dry. God, they've only just started. How is he going to last the day?

The formations soon start to break up on the steep hillside. Not everyone can keep up the pace. Lech presses on doggedly, not sure if he's somewhere near the front or falling behind. Don't look back, keep going. One step at a time.

There's a hail of machine-gun fire from a neighbouring height and the man in front of Lech is hit. He tumbles down the mountainside like a rag doll. Lech throws himself to the ground. Sharp stones pierce his knees and palms. Coughing and blinded by dust, he crawls into a hollow only to find it full of decomposing bodies left over from previous attempts to capture the monastery. He gags at the stench but buries himself amongst the dead until the current barrage has died down.

When he crawls out of the hole, the Poles are in chaos. Whole sections have scattered. Lech doesn't recognise any of the men nearby. Never mind. He joins a group who are hurling hand grenades at a German position up ahead.

His first attempt falls short. He tries harder and this time he thinks he's hit someone. But there's no time to celebrate.

Mortar shells fly overhead. Artillery explodes nearby. Clouds of dust and debris choke him. Another hail of machine-gun fire. He drops to his bloodied knees, heedless of the pain.

Dead bodies lie beside him. Torsos without limbs. Limbs without torsos. An unrecognisable face. A hand still clutching a grenade. A patchwork of horrific images imprints itself on Lech's mind.

Are they winning or are they being slaughtered? He always thought you'd be able to tell the difference, but in the heat of battle it's impossible to see the bigger picture. The world shrinks to your little bit of hell – the man next to you who's there one minute and blown to pieces the next, the weight of the grenade in your hand, the shell that whistles past your ear and explodes, breaking apart the rock you're standing on so that you suddenly sink five feet. But so long as your heart keeps beating and your lungs draw in the dusty air, you crawl out of the pit and keep fighting.

Watch out, there's a mine! Bloody hell, could have been blown to smithereens there. A thunderous explosion nearby. Get down! The dust settles and you do a quick body check. Is your hand still attached to your arm and your arm to your body? Good. Then you can throw another grenade. What are you waiting for?

Unbelievably, by the end of the day, they've broken the northern defence ring and captured the Colle Sant' Angelo.

But the dead and injured are too many to count, and they've almost run out of ammunition. Lech has used up all his grenades. How many Germans has he killed? God knows. Will it make a difference to the war? He's too tired to care. As they lie down to sleep on the mountainside, none of them knows what the morning will bring.

The next morning, a thick mist rolls up from the valley. All is quiet. Unnaturally calm after the noise and chaos of yesterday.

Word on the ground is that the French Expeditionary Corps in the Liri Valley have caused the Germans to withdraw from Monte Cassino to a new defensive position. There's only one way to find out.

Lech and twelve other men are ordered to move towards the monastery. No longer weighed down by grenades, the going is easier, but it's unnerving to be approaching the summit not knowing what they're going to find there. The stink of decay wafts on the breeze.

As they approach the ruins, it becomes clear that the last remaining Germans have indeed withdrawn. They must have slipped away in the night, too few in number to hold the fort. As Lech moves through rooms once inhabited by monks, he sees evidence of a hasty retreat – spent ammunition, discarded uniform, a photograph of two blond, blue-eyed children trampled into the dirt.

Back outside, they hoist an improvised Polish flag over the ruins. And then one of the lancers lifts a bugle to his lips and plays the Kraków Hejnał, the St Mary's Trumpet Call, familiar to all Polish people.

Lech can't help himself. At the sound of the Polish anthem, tears stream down his face. When he looks at his fellow countrymen, they're all sobbing like children. The voice of Poland rings out loud and clear from the previously impregnable German fortress. He will treasure this moment forever.

CHAPTER FORTY-SEVEN

MONTE CASSINO!

Jan stands back to admire his handiwork. Now whenever he paints the anchor, the symbol of Polish resistance, he adds underneath in capital letters the name of the battle that was won with the help of Polish troops fighting under General Anders.

The victory in Italy is only one of a string of 'good news' stories that the Information Bulletin has reported recently, lifting the national mood to match the hot, sunny days of summer. The Allied offensive in the west is progressing apace, and by all accounts the Red Army is making headway in the east. Any day now Lwów will be in Russian hands again. The citizens of Lwów won't know if they're coming or going.

Only the other day there was the thrilling news that a group of senior Wehrmacht officers had made an assassination attempt on Hitler's life, exploding a bomb at the Wolf's Lair in the middle of a strategy meeting. It was too bad that Hitler walked away with nothing more than a few scratches. But it shows that support for the Führer is cracking if German officers are prepared to go to such lengths to remove him. Anyone with half a brain can see that Germany is losing the war and German civilians are leaving Warsaw in droves. You can't move at the train station for panicked *Volksdeutsche* making a hasty exit back to the Reich. Good riddance to the lot of them, thinks Jan, picking up his pot of white paint and moving on to his next location.

The big question is, what is going to happen next? Radio Moscow has started broadcasting appeals for an uprising in Warsaw. It's heady stuff. Poles who are 'thirsting for a fight' are called on to 'smash the foe'. There are promises of assistance from the so-called Polish People's Army, the Polish Corps within the Red Army under the leadership of General Berling. Zych warns against putting their trust in Berling's Army, who, he says, will have been indoctrinated with Communism. But Jan prefers to be optimistic. These men are Polish first and foremost, whichever flag they're fighting under. Surely their allegiance to Poland will be stronger than their allegiance to Stalin? And with the Red Army on their side, how can they lose?

Jan is just waiting for the call to take up arms. If there's an uprising in Warsaw, he sure as hell wants to be a part of it. Only the memory of the ghetto uprising the previous year gives him pause for thought. The ghetto was razed to the ground in a firestorm, the last remaining Jews smoked out of their ruined homes like rats. The ghetto is now an empty wasteland. That simply cannot be allowed to happen to the whole city. But, Jan tells himself, the Jews who put up such a brave stand in April '43 were already half dead through starvation and didn't have sufficient weapons or training. They must have known theirs was a hopeless battle. They just preferred to die fighting than be transported to the death camps. All credit to them.

He paints a further five anchors accompanied with the words MONTE CASSINO, before heading back to the cell HQ in Stare Miasto where he finds Lew and Królik laughing.

'What is it?' he asks.

'Look at this.' Lew thrusts a poster under his nose.

Jan reads it quickly. Ludwig Fischer, the Nazi Governor of Warsaw, is calling on men and boys between the ages of sixteen and sixty-five to help dig anti-tank ditches around the city. Just like those early days when he and Anna dug trenches to defend against the German invasion. And that old man gave him a swig of vodka that had him coughing his guts up. Now Fischer's poster is exhorting the citizens of Warsaw to *defend themselves against the Bolshevik enemy!* The irony of it! Doesn't Fischer understand that for the people of Warsaw, the enemy is already here, within the city?

'Utterly ridiculous,' he says. 'Who's going to volunteer for that?'

'No one,' says Królik, 'because the Underground is going to cover these up wherever we find them. General Bór-Komorowski has given orders that people shouldn't comply.'

'Good,' says Jan. 'So what's the plan?'

'We cover up Fischer's posters with these,' says Lew, showing Jan a pile of Home Army posters telling people to ignore the governor's request for assistance.

'Give me a stack of those,' says Jan, 'and I'll get started straight away.'

He heads back outside, having swapped his paint pot for a pile of posters and a pot of glue. As he gets to work, he has the feeling that something big is about to happen. The city is poised on the brink. Any day now, the people will rise up against the German occupiers. And Jan will be ready.

*

Jan is on his way home from Pan Piotrowski's maths class when he hears running footsteps behind him. Very little maths gets done these days in lessons. Instead Pan Piotrowski tells them stories about his days fighting the Bolsheviks in 1920. It's hard to imagine this softly spoken man taking up arms against an aggressor, but that's what Jan finds so inspiring. If his maths teacher can stand and fight, anyone can.

'Mysz.' Jan turns at the sound of his codename. It's Zych and he's out of breath, his face gleaming with sweat in the late July sun.

'What is it?' asks Jan. 'Has something happened?' Or, he thinks, is something about to happen?

'Tonight,' says Zych, gulping down lungfuls of air. 'Report to Dąbrowski Square by half past seven. The password is *Wilno*.'

'Tonight?' Is this it? Is this the call to arms? Somehow, he'd expected a bigger fanfare for such an announcement, not just Zych catching him in the street.

Zych nods. 'Those are the orders. And bring your rucksack. You'll be away from home for a few days.'

'I'll be there,' says Jan. He has more questions, but Zych pats him on the shoulder and says he has to go and speak to the others. He runs off and disappears round the corner.

Jan stops dawdling and picks up his pace. It's starting, he thinks. The uprising that Radio Moscow has been calling for is finally starting.

He mentally runs through the contents of his rucksack which is already packed and hidden under his bed. Clean shirts, underwear, soap, a small towel, a torch and tinned food supplied to him by the Underground. Is there anything he's forgotten? He doesn't think so. And he has his story prepared. The mobilisation has to be secret so he's concocted a story about going on a training course in the countryside. He just hopes his mother buys it. Otherwise all his training and planning will have been for nothing.

She's busy cooking when he arrives home. He would like to check the contents of his rucksack one last time before telling her about the 'training course', but she intercepts him as he's passing the kitchen door. 'How was your maths lesson?'

'Fine.'

'What is Pan Piotrowski teaching you?'

How to stay calm under fire, he thinks. 'Algebra.'

'You don't sound too sure.' She's always been able to see through him.

He might as well bite the bullet. 'I have to go on a training course this evening. I'll be away a few days, so…' He trails off under his mother's scrutiny.

'A training course? At such short notice?' It's obvious she doesn't believe him.

He stares at the carpet. She's never going to let him go.

She gives a heavy sigh. 'Training course, my foot! You must think I was born yesterday. They want you to go and fight.'

He looks at her then and sees a whole sea of emotions pass across her face – love, fear, pride, anger, sorrow. He's been so selfish, thinking only about wanting to do his bit, he hasn't given a moment's thought to how she must be feeling. But he has to persuade her to let him go.

'Please,' he says. 'I've trained for this. I can't just sit at home. General Bór-Komorowski has called the uprising now because the Red Army is ready to support us. It's the best hope we have of defeating the Germans.'

She cups his face in her hands. 'My darling boy, how you've grown up these last five years. The war has stolen your childhood but it has turned you into a brave young man.' He can feel a lump starting to form in his throat and tears well up in his eyes. She draws him into a tight hug, then pats him on the back. 'If you're going to fight, we'll have to make sure you've got everything you need.'

He can't believe what he's just heard. He pulls away and looks at her through eyes blurry with tears. 'I'm sorry to do this to you.'

She wipes her own eyes with the back of her hand. 'I will pray for you every day, until you're back home, safe.' She takes a deep breath. 'Now then, where's this rucksack of yours? You won't have packed enough clean underwear. And I have some spare food I can give you. They might have taught you how to fire a pistol, but do these people know how to feed a growing boy?'

Jan feels a burst of love for his mother so fierce that he has to turn away in case he breaks down completely.

They sit down to a simple meal of bread and soup. Jan tries to fill the silence by repeating everything he's heard: the Russians are just across the Vistula in Praga and will cross the river any day; the British and Americans are sending supplies of arms; the Germans are already a spent force – it won't take much to finish them off. Agata stares at him wide-eyed as if he's already some sort of hero. This only makes him feel awkward. After a while his mother pats him on the hand and says, 'Let's enjoy this meal without talk of fighting, shall we?'

And then it's time to leave. Jan thought he was ready, but suddenly he's rushing around at the last minute. Has he got everything he needs? Has he packed enough socks? What about toothpaste? He nearly forgets his toothbrush. He takes one last look at his bedroom – the single bed, the bookshelves, the chest of drawers, the bedside rug. All so familiar and comforting. Part of him wants to stay here, in his childhood home, the only home he's ever known, and where he's always felt safe. And part of him can't get away fast enough. He belongs with his comrades in the Underground. He checks his pocket for the umpteenth time and makes sure he has the white-and-red armband which will identify him as a legitimate member of the Home Army. Then it's time to say goodbye.

His mother hugs him to her so tightly he can hardly breathe. Then she releases him and says, 'Just make sure you come back.'

'I will.'

Agata tugs at his arm. 'Stay safe,' she whispers.

'I'll do my best,' he promises her. He grabs his rucksack and heads out of the door, unable to bear seeing his mother and Agata in tears.

At the corner of the street he looks back one last time. He thinks he sees two figures in the window – one small, one large – but he's not sure. It might just be a trick of the light.

*

At Dąbrowski Square, elegant eighteenth-century town houses encircle an open green space. In the centre is a small circular pond and fountain, currently out of action. The square is in the heart of Warsaw, just south of the Saxon Gardens.

'Hey, Mysz!' It's Lew, carrying a rucksack big enough for a month-long campaign. 'Know where we're going?'

Jan looks at the grand façades facing the square. 'I think it's over there.' He points to a building with a massive entrance gate through which people are coming and going.

His guess is proved correct when they're met in the courtyard by a man wearing one of the obligatory white-and-red armbands and carrying a Russian light machine gun. They both don their armbands and give the password.

'Welcome,' says the man. He directs them upstairs where they run into Zych, Królik and Sowa.

'About time you two showed up,' says Zych. 'Dump your stuff in there' – he points to a room with about thirty camp beds – 'then give us a hand bringing up the ammunition.'

For the next half hour or so they run up and down the stairs, carrying sacks of ammunition. A man in a black beret, Lieutenant Jankowski, is in charge of the arsenal of weaponry. They have at their disposal a collection of pistols, two submachine guns and boxes of British grenades. It doesn't seem like a lot but there will be groups just like theirs gathering all over the city and they all need to be supplied with weapons. Jan's heard that the Home Army has been digging up weapons buried back in '39 when the Polish Army was in retreat from the Germans. Heaven knows what state these weapons will be in after five years buried underground.

Later that evening Lieutenant Jankowski calls everyone together for a briefing. Jan guesses the lieutenant is in his twenties and from the way he talks, he sounds as if he's had some military experience. Jankowski commands two platoons, both around thirty strong. The fighting platoon consists of adult men. Jan's platoon, on the other hand, consists entirely of teenagers. Zych has been appointed the leader of Jan's squad – including himself, Lew, Królik and Sowa.

'Your jobs,' Jankowski tells the boys, 'will be auxiliary roles, for example, carrying messages. But don't think for one minute that it isn't important. Or dangerous. In a war, timely and accurate communication between fighting units and command HQ is vital.'

General Bór-Komorowski, the commander-in-chief of the Home Army, Jan learns, will be based at Home Army headquarters in Wola, in the west of the city. Jan's group, on the other hand, is bang in the city centre. Does that mean this is where all the action will be? He's not sure how he feels about that.

For the next couple of days Jan, Lew, Królik and Sowa hang out with the other teenagers in their platoon, waiting for something – anything – to happen. It's a bit boring just hanging around, playing ping-pong and talking about what they plan to do with their lives once they've seen off the Germans. Lew wants to travel to America but Sowa is going to study medicine and become a doctor. The noise of artillery across the Vistula is getting louder and Soviet bombers leave a pattern of white contrails against the clear, blue sky. But still they're sitting around, waiting for the command to begin.

Talk of future plans reminds Jan of the conversation he had with Weronika whilst they waited for Wiktor outside the ghetto wall. She suggested they should go to New York together. Did she really mean it? At the time he was horrified at the idea, but now he thinks he'd rather like it. He wonders where she is now. No doubt preparing to inflict her nursing skills on some unsuspecting Home Army soldier. He smiles to himself.

'What are you grinning about?' Lew tosses a pillow at him. 'Dreaming about a girl?'

'What? No, I just…' Jan feels himself blushing. 'It's nothing. I wasn't thinking about anything.' He wishes the uprising would just start. What is General Bór-Komorowski waiting for?

CHAPTER FORTY-EIGHT

The day and time of the start of the uprising has finally been decided. W-Hour – the codename for the start of Operation Tempest – has been set for five o'clock this evening, Tuesday the first of August. The torpor of the last few days suddenly lifts and now there's a sense of urgency as Jankowski's two platoons rush to put their final preparations in place.

The bright, sunny days of July have given way to clouds and a persistent drizzle, but Jan barely notices the rain when he is sent out to collect supplies of tinned food. The streets are swarming with young people hurrying to their appointed destinations, tell-tale rucksacks on their backs. *Really*, thinks Jan, *if the Germans haven't noticed that something is afoot then they must be blind as well as evil.*

Jan returns to Dąbrowski Square with his supplies and finds Lieutenant Jankowski supervising the distribution of weapons. There aren't enough guns for everyone so priority is given to the platoon of adult men. No one, it seems, is expecting the teenagers to do any actual fighting. *Just one bullet*, thinks Jan, *that's all I need.*

As the clock ticks through the final hours and minutes, the tension in the house becomes unbearable. Jan can't sit still, there's so much nervous energy coursing through his veins. Every thirty seconds or so he jumps up to look out of the window at the square below. The employment office opposite is one of the group's prime targets, the strategy being to seize as many public buildings across the city in as short a time as possible.

'Sit down and rest,' advises Zych. 'Save your energy for when it's going to be needed.'

Jan slumps onto his camp bed, but within seconds he's back on his feet.

'What was that?' Lew jumps to his feet. 'Has it started already?'

It's only mid-afternoon, but the crack and pop of gunfire can already be heard across the city.

'Damn it!' shouts Jankowski, storming up the stairs. 'We'll lose the advantage of surprise. W-Hour was supposed to coincide with rush hour to cause maximum inconvenience.'

Jan goes to the window and looks out. A truck of SS men has driven into the square.

'Prepare to attack!' shouts Jankowski. It's only four o'clock but they can't afford to wait another second. The Germans must already realise that an uprising is underway. Suddenly shots are heard in Dąbrowski Square. The armed men go into action, firing from the windows. It seems to Jan as if all hell has broken loose. Everything is much more chaotic than he imagined it would be.

The SS men in the square immediately fire back. The cacophony is deafening. Glass shatters, plaster falls from the ceiling.

'Here!' A man crouching by one of the open windows slides a hand grenade across the floor in Jan's direction. It rolls awkwardly on the wooden floor, coming to rest by his foot. He picks it up. It's the real thing, not one of the dummy grenades and stones they practised with in the forest. He's surprised at how heavy it is. He clutches the pineapple casing in his right hand whilst the middle finger of his left hand fumbles with the ring of the safety pin. He closes his eyes and tries to remember everything he learned so assiduously. It's crucial to keep the spring-loaded lever pressed against the case until the grenade is thrown. But he's never thrown a real grenade before. What if he messes up and the thing explodes in his face, killing him and those around him?

'Throw the bloody grenade!' The voice in his ear is so loud it makes him jump. He presses the grenade against his chest, pulls the cotter pin… and it's stuck. It won't come out.

His heart is hammering louder than the gunshots. What's wrong? Why can't he do it? Then he remembers.

He's forgotten to twist the pin. What an idiot! He twists it and gives it an almighty yank so that his left hand jerks out to the side. Then his training kicks in and he's suddenly back in the forest throwing stones. He hurls the grenade through the open window and ducks down with his hands over his head.

Time seems to stand still as he waits for the grenade to explode. He counts: one, two, three… Why is nothing happening? And then there's a thunderous boom.

He peers cautiously over the ledge of the windowsill.

At first, he can make out nothing, the air is so full of dust and smoke. As the air clears, he sees the Germans running across the square to the safety of their truck. He doesn't think he actually hit anyone, but then he wasn't looking where he was throwing.

It doesn't matter. He's thrown his first grenade. He's a proper soldier now.

*

'Stand back! Wardrobe coming down!'

Jan, Sowa, Lew and Królik stand to one side as a heavy mahogany wardrobe is shoved through an upper-floor window and lands with a crash on the cobbles below. The doors swing open and splinter in half, but the rest of the wardrobe remains remarkably unscathed. It's a sturdy piece of furniture that must have cost someone a good week's wage when it was brand new. But now the owners have sacrificed it for the greater good. All along the street, people are donating tables, chairs, iron bedsteads, anything that can be used to build barricades.

'Thanks!' shouts Lew to the owners of the wardrobe, a middle-aged man and woman, who are leaning out of their bedroom window.

'You're welcome,' replies the man. 'Good luck to you all!'

'Okay, heave ho!' says Lew. 'This one's going to weigh a ton.'

They each grab a corner of the wardrobe and manhandle it to the end of the street where a huge barricade is under construction. Jan's platoon has been assigned the job of building barricades and digging trenches. Civilians have turned out in droves to lend a hand. An overturned tram carriage forms the centrepiece of the barricade, with furniture and paving stones piled high around it. They've been working all morning and Jan's arms are tired, but he's never felt more exhilarated. There's almost a party atmosphere with the cheering tones of the Polish National Anthem – *Poland is Not Yet Lost* – blaring from the loudspeakers.

It's day two of the uprising and when he woke that morning after a brief night's sleep, it was to general good news about progress. Jankowski's men have succeeded in capturing the employment office and another group have captured the eighteen-storey Prudential Tower near Napoleon Square. Admittedly, there have been one or two losses, but these are not significant when compared with the gains.

At mid-day he and the others sit down by the edge of the completed barricade whilst housewives from the nearby houses bring them tea and slices of bread.

When the news comes through in the afternoon that the Home Army has captured the Powiśle Power Station and most of Stare Miasto, Jan feels sure that victory can't be too far off. Just a few more days, he tells himself, and Warsaw will be ours.

*

'A foot! There's a foot over here!' Jan shouts from the top of a pile of rubble.

Lew, Królik and Sowa scramble up the slope and the four of them start scrabbling at the fallen masonry with their bare hands, tossing aside bricks and splintered wood.

The foot clearly belongs to a woman. It's delicate in shape with a high instep and a slim ankle. Remnants of a torn stocking still cling to the lower leg which is gradually emerging from beneath the rubble. They work silently, no one saying a word. None of them expect to find the owner of the leg still breathing. But they will get her out and bury her properly.

The building was destroyed when it was hit by a two-ton bomb. The powerful weapon crashed through the roof and the floors before exploding and reducing the building to smithereens.

Over the last few days, the Germans have fought back with everything they've got. For the first time since September '39, Stukas have flown over the city, dropping bombs and incendiaries. When Jan heard the all-too familiar, head-splitting whine, his legs turned to jelly and for a moment he was an eleven-year-old boy once again, cowering in the basement with his hands over his head. It was as if he'd learned nothing in the intervening years and all his training was forgotten in an instant. It wasn't until Zych slapped him on the back and told him to pull himself together that Jan overcame his childhood terror of the Stuka dive-bombers.

But it's not just the Stukas they have to watch out for

now. Nebelwerfer rocket launchers are showering the city with high explosives and incendiaries, setting fires to rooftops and upper storeys. They've nicknamed them 'moo cows' because of their distinctive moaning sound. And then the bombs lobbed by the siege mortars are in a category all of their own when it comes to sheer destructive power.

They've cleared the dead woman's leg and can now see her other leg, bent underneath her at an awkward angle. It's all very well digging out legs, but it's the rest of her that Jan doesn't want to face. When it's just a foot, he can almost detach himself from what he's doing, but when he encounters torsos and heads, that's when the awful reality hits home.

The bottom of the woman's dress comes into view. It's cotton and might once have been blue, but it's almost impossible to tell in the dirt. Who was she? What was her name? What was she doing in the moments before the bomb hit? If she'd popped out, to fetch a loaf of bread, say, instead of staying in, she could be alive now. It strikes him how precarious life is. How much survival is a matter of chance.

The early successes of the uprising are a distant memory, although it was only a few days ago. Since then, there have been reports of a massacre in the western suburb of Wola. Ten thousand dead, according to some accounts. Men, women and children, scorched out of their homes with flame throwers and gunned down in the streets. Horrific tales from those who managed to flee. It's the ghetto uprising all over again, but on a bigger scale. The Germans think nothing of tying Polish women to the front of their tanks to act as human shields. But these despicable tactics only strengthen Jan's resolve to fight on.

General Bór-Komorowski and his staff have reportedly decamped from Wola to Stare Miasto where the Home Army is still holding out. Jan's group in the city centre is also holding its own, but for how much longer is anyone's guess. If only the Soviets would hurry up and get a move on but they're still on the wrong side of the Vistula. What's keeping them? Russian artillery east of the river has fallen eerily silent and Radio Moscow doesn't even seem to have noticed the start of the uprising.

'Here she comes,' says Lew. 'Gently now.' They've cleared the last of the rubble from the dead woman's body. Jan looks cautiously at her face and is relieved to find it has suffered only minor damage – a trickle of dried blood runs down one cheek. Her eyes are closed. She wears a silver crucifix around her neck and can't have been much more than twenty years old. A similar age to Anna.

'Ready?' asks Lew as they prepare to lift her.

They all nod in silence. This is the hardest part. Earlier that morning, when they uncovered a man's body with a face that had been ripped apart, Jan threw up his breakfast. That's why he prefers to carry the feet if he can. He and Sowa grab the woman's ankles whilst Lew and Królik take her under the arms. They totter unsteadily down the piles of rubble with their burden and lay her beside the other bodies they unearthed earlier. Six in total so far today. They will bury them later, in a courtyard somewhere, or a patch of garden. A priest, if one can be found, will say a prayer. A makeshift cross will be placed at the head of each grave. But for now they will keep looking. Just one survivor would mean so much to them.

CHAPTER FORTY-NINE

By the light of a carbide lamp, Maria kneels by the stove, trying to heat soup. But it's an unfamiliar stove and she hasn't yet got the hang of keeping the wretched thing lit. She's also in an unfamiliar basement, and half the people here are strangers, although they'll get to know one another soon enough. No one can stay a stranger for long in these conditions. She's just grateful that she's safe and that she's found somewhere to rest her head at night. Her own home is missing half its walls, and the roof has disappeared entirely.

When the bomb landed in the courtyard of the apartment block, destroying half the building, Maria and her neighbours, who were sheltering in the basement at the time, had no choice but to leave. Owning nothing but the clothes they stood up in, Maria and Agata organised Pani Kowalska and her children, and old Pan and Pani Woźniak, to come with them to Stare Miasto, the one place in the city which is strongly defended. Maria knew people there who might be able to help them. She had in mind Pan Lewandowski, the restaurant owner.

They almost didn't make it. It was the middle of the night when they set off under cover of darkness. There was a steady stream of people moving in the same direction. They squeezed past barricades, skirted buildings on fire, and scrambled over mounds of rubble. They had to keep stopping so that Pani Woźniak could catch her breath. On more than one occasion the old woman declared that she couldn't take another step and they might as well leave her there to die.

'No one is leaving anyone anywhere,' said Maria in her strictest voice. 'I have a son who is risking his life in this fight. The least the rest of us can do is try to stay alive.'

'Lean on me,' said Pani Kowalska to the old woman. She was no longer encumbered with a babe-in-arms, her youngest, Feliks, now five years old. The older Kowalski children, all in their early teens, scouted ahead, looking around street corners for dangers and blockages. Maria held on firmly to Feliks in one hand and Agata in the other. None of her neighbours had questioned the fiction that Agata was a relative from the countryside, for which Maria offered up a prayer of thanks.

Feliks reminds Maria of Jan when he was that age, so innocent and trusting. But what a time in which to grow up! Feliks has never known his father, almost certainly one of the twenty thousand Polish officers murdered at Katyń. Pani Kowalska never talks about her husband, but as widowed mothers, the two women share a silent understanding. They will keep going for the sake of their children.

At last the soup starts to bubble. She stirs it a couple of times, then ladles it into bowls and passes it around. People are seated on mattresses and wooden chairs in the cellar under Pan Lewandowski's restaurant. Life is lived almost entirely underground these days, in a subterranean parallel universe. Refugees from Wola, the first suburb to be destroyed in the fighting, have fled to Stare Miasto, hence the overcrowding, but so far morale is holding up. It won't be long, they tell themselves, before the Russians cross the Vistula. Until then, they just have to sit tight and pray.

There's nothing else they can do.

'Pani Nowak, Pani Nowak, guess where we've been!' cries Feliks, running up to her. He has just returned to the cellar with his older siblings and Agata.

'Where have you been?'

Feliks points a skinny arm in the direction they've just come from. 'There's a tunnel and it goes all the way to the next house.'

'Really?' says Maria. 'How exciting.' In fact, a whole network of underground routes has been established beneath the old houses. Corridors, cellars, passageways and vaults all inter-connect, with signposts to indicate which direction you're going in. It's possible to live entirely underground and never see the light of day. Pani Woźniak, for one, has declared that she's not leaving the cellar until the war is over.

Stare Miasto certainly feels like the safest place to be at the moment. The narrow streets are barricaded with concrete slabs, about a third of the way down, so that the Germans find themselves funnelled into a killing zone from where the Home Army can attack from three sides. Incendiaries pose the biggest danger to the civilians – these old timbered houses go up in flames in no time. It's a constant job, putting out the fires.

Pan Lewandowski takes his place in the centre of the cellar and opens his Bible, adjusting his reading glasses on his nose. A hush falls on the assembled group. Maria closes her eyes and tries to pretend that she's in church. She folds her hands in her lap and listens with rapt attention as Pan Lewandowski, selected for the resonance of his rich baritone voice, reads from the Psalms.

'For He shall give His angels charge over thee…'

Bible readings and prayers are now part of the daily routine. Sometimes, they sing a hymn. Something soothing or uplifting. When Pan Lewandowski has finished the Psalm, everyone joins in with the Hail Mary.

'Hail, Mary, full of grace, the Lord be with Thee…'

In her mind's eye Maria sees the statue in the church, the Virgin's palms held out in supplication. She mentally lights a candle and places it at the Virgin's feet.

'…Mother of God, pray for us sinners now, and at the hour of death. Glory be to–'

A Stuka suddenly whines overhead. Everyone freezes, eyes cast to the ceiling. They wait, listening as the Stuka's ear-piercing shriek grows louder. An explosion nearby shakes the building and a shower of plaster dust descends on those praying. When nothing worse happens, they bow their heads and continue.

'– the Father, and to the Son, and to the Holy Ghost. Amen.'

*

On the fifteenth of August, Maria attends a service to celebrate the Assumption of the Blessed Virgin Mary at the Church of the Nuns of Perpetual Adoration. She doesn't leave Pan Lewandowski's cellar often, but today is a special day and she feels safe in the presence of the nuns, who have carried on regardless of the worsening situation.

The nuns opened their doors to insurgents during the first week of the uprising and they continue to feed all who come to them. They have even set up a hospital on their premises, with surgeries performed day and night. Maria is not alone in her admiration for this group of women who, true to the name of their order, steadfastly adhere to their daily prayer schedule, despite the dangers they face. They are an example to us all, thinks Maria, as she takes her place in the vaults beneath the church which, like so many buildings in Stare Miasto, has been raked by fire.

Home Army soldiers join civilians for the celebration of the High Mass and Maria looks for Jan amongst the young men crammed into the crowded space, but she can't see him anywhere. He probably isn't even fighting in Stare Miasto, she tells herself, quelling her disappointment. She realises that her main reason for coming out today was the hope, however faint, that she might catch a glimpse of him. She would give anything just to know that he's all right. That he's still alive. She closes her eyes and lets a tear run down her cheek as the smell of incense pervades the enclosed space.

Today is also the anniversary of the Miracle on the Vistula, a decisive victory of the Polish Army over the Red Army in August 1920. What they need now is another miracle on the Vistula, but still there is no sign of the Soviets crossing the river. As in September '39, there is the feeling that they've been abandoned. Nowadays, when Pan Lewandowski reads from the Bible, there is less conviction in his voice. The hymns are more muted and people seem to take less comfort in them. Maria fears they are losing hope.

CHAPTER FIFTY

'Mysz! Sowa!' Zych appears in the dormitory where Jan and the other boys from his squad are catching some rest. It's become almost routine now, dragging corpses out of collapsed buildings, digging bodies out of rubble and burying them in any spare plot of land. Jan longs for something different to do. He sits up at the sound of his codename being called.

'Jankowski wants a word with you both. He's got a job that will... suit you.'

'What is it?' asks Jan.

'You'll see,' says Zych with a wry smile.

Jan and Sowa exchange bewildered looks. Why haven't Lew and Królik been selected? They're both bigger and stronger than them.

They follow Zych into the room Jankowski uses as his command centre. There are two other boys from a different squad already there.

Jankowski eyes all four of them, then nods his head. 'Perfect, you're all the right size.'

Jan has never considered himself to be the 'right size' before. He's not tall like Królik or broad like Lew. He often feels at a disadvantage when they're shovelling rubble or carrying corpses. Although he grits his teeth and gets on with the job, he doesn't find it easy like Lew, who seems capable of digging all day long.

'We need to send some dispatches to General Bór-Komorowski in Stare Miasto.' Says Jankowski. 'You four will be the couriers.'

At the mention of General Bór-Komorowski, Jan's ears prick up. Bór-Komorowski is a hero. He's the leader of the uprising and the man they all look to for inspiration. Jan never imagined he would come within a hundred yards of the great man. Yet here he is, being specially chosen as a courier to take an important dispatch to the Home Army headquarters. He's so excited at the prospect that he almost misses what Jankowski says next.

'...so you'll be guided through the sewers by an experienced guide who's done the journey many times herself.'

Sewers? Did Jan hear that correctly? He glances across at Sowa who has visibly paled at the news. The other two boys don't look all that keen either. Jan realises that they've all been chosen because they're small. Being small is good for some things after all.

'It's a responsible job with significant dangers,' says Jankowski. 'If you don't think you'll be up to it, say so now.' He looks at each of them in turn.

Suddenly Jan knows this is the job for him. He's not going to win a medal for his grenade throwing. He's not built for hours of digging. He's too young to fly a plane. But a secret mission through the sewers carrying important messages is something he can do, he's sure of it.

'It would be an honour,' he says.

Jankowski nods his head approvingly. 'That's what I like to hear.'

The others also agree to take part, although with less enthusiasm.

Zych takes them off to prepare them for the mission. The dispatches are wrapped in waterproof cloth and strapped to their chests and stomachs.

'You'll need your hands free for this,' says Zych, passing each of them a short, sturdy stick.

Jan and Sowa look to the other two, Borys and Donat – almost certainly not their real names – for an explanation, but as none of them has ever gone down a sewer before, they shrug their shoulders.

Daria, their guide, is a diminutive, nineteen-year-old girl. She has thick rubber boots on her feet and is dressed in a camouflage jacket with the sleeves rolled up because it's too big for her. She wears her hair plaited and pinned on top of her head in two loops. In one hand she carries a stick, in the other a torch. Despite her petite stature and ridiculous outfit, she addresses them with the voice of authority.

'Listen up,' she says. 'One simple rule. You do everything I tell you. Is that clear?'

They nod their heads in silence.

'There are two types of sewers. The storm sewers are big but we won't be using those because General Bór-Komorowski has decreed that they have to be kept clear in case of the need to evacuate from Stare Miasto. So instead, we'll be moving through one of the waste sewers. They're oval in shape and between three and five feet tall.'

We might be small, thinks Jan, but we're taller than that!

'We will pass under German positions,' continues Daria, 'so it's essential we keep as quiet as possible at all times. We must take extra care whenever we pass underneath a manhole because the Germans sometimes watch through the hole and drop grenades down if they suspect any movement. Is everyone still up for this? Because there's no turning back once we're down there.'

'I'm in,' says Jan. He would rather be blown up by the Germans than pull out now.

'Me too,' says Sowa.

The others murmur their consent.

'Good,' says Daria. 'Follow me and wait for my instructions.'

They wait in a doorway for the mortar fire to stop. Daria points out the nearest manhole, but it's so far away they can hardly see it.

'Now!' says Daria as soon as there's a break in the shelling. She sets off across the open ground at a sprint, Jan and the others following in hot pursuit.

One minute Daria is there in front of them, the next she disappears from view. When Jan peers over the edge of the manhole, he can just see the top of her head descending into the pitch black below. He crouches down and lowers himself into the hole, feeling for the iron rungs of the ladder with the soles of his feet.

The ladder is so narrow, he has to keep his hands and feet close together. The iron is rusted and cold against his palms. Once or twice he misses the next rung and his feet flail in the air. The packages tied to his front don't help matters. They get in the way and make it difficult to cling tightly to the ladder. The next person to descend – Sowa he thinks it is – treads on the fingers of his right hand.

'Ouch,' says Jan.

'Hurry up,' hisses Sowa. 'They've started firing again.'

Jan does his best to speed up so that everyone can get down safely. He's just starting to get the hang of moving rung by rung like a monkey when he hits the bottom of the shaft. He staggers back from the ladder, overcome by the awful stench and the deadening silence. His stomach heaves and he tries to breathe through his mouth in a futile effort to lessen the smell.

By the time everyone has made it down the ladder, the five of them are crammed into a tiny space, with hardly any room to turn around.

Daria passes her torch to Jan and tells them to follow her. 'Remember,' she whispers, 'no talking from now on. This way.' She indicates a small black hole. 'Lean on your sticks, and copy what I do.'

Daria enters the small tunnel, reaching forwards with her stick until it touches the bottom of the sewer. Then she leans on it and moves towards it, her back rubbing against the top of the sewer. Jan follows her, holding the torch. He can't afford to lose sight of Daria. Without her to guide them, they could get lost down here and die.

As soon as he enters the tunnel, Jan almost loses his balance. He'd forgotten that Daria said the tunnel is oval-shaped. Just in time he catches his hand on the filth-covered wall and stops himself falling into the slime which comes up around his ankles. Then he leans forwards on his stick and tries to copy Daria's movements. After about five minutes, they must have gone ten yards. This is unbelievably slow. Jan's back and shoulders are aching with the effort of walking hunched over. But already, he notices, the smell is not so overpowering. Behind him he can hear the squelch of footsteps as the others follow. He can't help smiling to himself when he thinks what his mother would say if she could see him now.

He's so lost in thought that he doesn't notice Daria has stopped ahead of him until he bumps into the back of her.

'Sorry,' he whispers under his breath.

'Manhole coming up,' breathes Daria. 'Be careful.' Jan passes the message back down the line, then they set off again.

Up ahead, light penetrates the blackness. A vertical shaft leads up to ground level. As he moves into the shaft, Jan straightens up with relief. Suddenly he starts and nearly drops his stick. In the corner there's a dead body, pallid and bloated, its face half-submerged in the sludge. It's a young man, probably not much older than himself. He feels the bile rising in his throat, but Daria seems unconcerned. She's probably passed the same body numerous times on her trips through the sewer. She could have warned them. As soon as they've all had a chance to stretch, she hurries them on, into the next tunnel. Jan gives the dead body one final glance. Poor sod. What a place to end up.

Time ceases to have any meaning in this stinking, subterranean world. It feels as if they've been trudging through these tunnels forever. He has a sudden moment of panic. What if they're lost? Will they ever get out of here? He's so tired, sometimes he thinks he could just lie down and die in the filth. Maybe that's what happened to the poor bugger back there.

They come to another stop and Daria signals to warn them that they are under a German-controlled zone. A manhole cover up ahead clatters as a heavy vehicle rumbles over it. If they're discovered now, they'll fall into enemy hands and be shot on the spot. They inch forward, one step at a time. Jan can feel his heart thudding in his chest. He hardly dares breathe. As they pass beneath the manhole, he can actually hear a voice shouting orders in German. There's a grating sound. The manhole is being lifted. Daria speeds up and Jan stumbles after her. He can sense Sowa behind him, close on his heels. He has no idea how far back the other two are.

Suddenly light floods the tunnel behind him. Jan looks back and sees Borys's outline silhouetted against the tunnel wall. Borys tries to run forward, stumbles, and falls face first into the sludge. Donat hoists him back up.

'I've lost my stick,' splutters Borys, spitting filth out of his mouth. He plunges his hands into the sludge. It hardly matters now that he's caked from head to foot in shit. 'Found it!'

'Come on,' hisses Daria. 'We have to go!'

No sooner are they on the move again, when there's an ear-splitting explosion behind them and the sound of falling debris. The tunnel quakes under their feet and hot air rushes into the confined space. Jan gasps for air, sure he's going to expire any second. He imagines a fireball chasing them down the tunnel. But somehow his legs keep moving in the rhythm they've grown used to and he's surprised to find after a few minutes that he's still alive and still breathing, albeit in short, panting gasps.

At the next junction, Daria stops and does a headcount. All still present and correct, although Borys is unrecognisable. Jan and the others keep their distance from him.

'Nearly there,' says Daria. 'Just another quarter of a mile to go.'

Dear God, thinks Jan. A quarter of a mile? At this pace, that'll take another hour, at least.

Jan's mind is a blank as he trudges after Daria, doggedly putting one foot in front of the other.

Eventually Daria announces, 'Stare Miasto!'

They emerge from the tunnel into a shaft with light streaming down it.

'After you,' says Daria, pointing to the ladder.

Jan is so weary, he doesn't think he'll be able to climb all the way up. His feet are caked in so much excrement that they slip on the rungs of the ladder. He pities the other guys behind him, having to put their hands where his feet have just trod.

As he reaches the top of the ladder he emerges into open air. The sunlight is dazzlingly bright after hours in the darkness. A pair of strong hands grab him under the armpits and he feels himself being hoisted out of the manhole. He rolls onto his back and for a few seconds enjoys the feeling of the sun on his face. The air is fresher and sweeter than he's ever tasted it.

Last to climb out of the hole is Daria, looking only marginally more dishevelled than when they set off.

'Well done,' she says to them. 'You did well for your first time.'

The welcoming committee consists of two young men carrying submachine guns. They can't keep the amusement out of their faces when they see Borys who looks thoroughly hacked off with the whole experience. They lead the way through the narrow streets, past gutted buildings and graves marked with crosses.

At Home Army headquarters they hand over their packages which are taken away to be disinfected before being opened. Then they collapse in a corner of the courtyard – no one seems inclined to invite them inside the building – and munch gratefully on chunks of bread which are handed out.

Jan leans back against the wall and closes his eyes for a moment. He's so tired and the sun is so warm. He starts to drift off, thinking of summer days, before the war…

Suddenly a shadow falls over him and someone nudges him in the ribs. He wakes with a start. A very tall man is standing over them, his hands clasped behind his back. He's dressed in military uniform with a black beret on his head. His features are thin, gaunt even, but he sports a neatly trimmed moustache above his upper lip.

Jan and the others scramble to their feet. Jan is horrified to have been caught napping in the presence of the leader of the uprising.

'Well done, boys,' says General Bór-Komorowski. 'I wanted to pass on my thanks personally.'

'Thank you, sir,' they all croak in unison.

Bór-Komorowski smiles at them and nods. 'Get some rest,' he says. 'Before the return journey.' Then he turns and strides back into the building.

The return journey? Jan had never really thought about the fact that they would have to do the whole thing in reverse. But he doesn't care. He's just been personally thanked by the man charged with securing Poland's freedom. He'll treasure this moment until his dying day.

CHAPTER FIFTY-ONE

The tent stands on a piece of waste ground. In winter this area is a swamp and in summer a dumping ground for rubbish. Now, in the middle of August, it's buzzing with flies.

Anna has observed the erection of the tent with a growing sense of unease. It's a huge, old army tent of brown canvas, designed to house soldiers out in the field. And from the state of it – worn and patched with a sagging roof – it looks like it's seen hard service in a war zone. Are they going to put women in there? There's no sanitation for one thing.

'They can't expect people to live in that,' says Jadwiga. 'I mean, you wouldn't keep a herd of cattle in there.'

Anna isn't so sure. The camp has become more and more overcrowded recently with new arrivals from the east – desperate women from Auschwitz and the Polish ghettos. Romanians, Hungarians, Serbians. Children too, and babies born in the camp. The babies don't last long. In some of the worst blocks, she's heard reports of up to seven women sharing two mattresses. The lines of sick outside the Revier grow ever longer. A pall of acrid smoke hangs over the camp. The mortuary now operates round the clock to cope with the backlog of bodies. The dead are piled up in the washrooms until the corpse cart takes them away.

Anna watches closely, gathering facts to include in her secret letters. In May she received confirmation from Jan that a Polish-language radio station based in England had broadcast a report about vivisection experiments in Ravensbrück. The report named as responsible, amongst others, Kommandant Suhren and the chief guard Dorothea Binz. This small victory has made her even more determined to carry on smuggling information to the outside world.

Even more frightening than the overcrowding and squalor is the increasingly erratic behaviour of the guards. Wild drunken orgies can be heard from the canteen. The Germans are losing control, not only of the war, but of themselves.

Anna has heard rumours about an uprising in Warsaw. It fills her with hope and fear at the same time. She worries about her mother and younger brother. How will they survive? Knowing Jan, he'll want to take part in the fighting. He'll be sixteen now, but she can't imagine him in a battle. Some good news at least – Paris has been liberated. A convoy of women from France brought the news with them. The Western Allies came to the aid of France, but who will come to the aid of Warsaw? The Red Army? If they don't, then what chance does Warsaw have?

And then within days of the tent being erected, women from Warsaw start to arrive in the camp. Thousands of them – young, old, children, pregnant women, nuns. Anna can hardly believe her eyes. So many women. Are they evacuating the whole city? Taking every woman prisoner? Is her own mother one of these bewildered creatures? She wants to talk to them, find out what is happening, look for her mother. But the new arrivals are herded inside the tent and not allowed to mix with the rest of the camp.

No, you wouldn't keep cattle in there, thinks Anna, but it's good enough for the women of Warsaw.

They're running out of food and nerves are wearing thin. Maria tries to calm a squabble that has broken out between two of the women from the district of Wola over the stove, but they won't listen to her and in the end, she leaves them to sort it out between themselves.

No one gets any proper sleep these days and tempers are frayed. German planes fly over day and night, nosediving and dropping their bombs and incendiaries. The endless crashing, smashing and shattering is enough to try the patience of a saint. Everyone just wants it to stop.

More planes drop leaflets inviting the civilians to leave Stare Miasto and go to a transit camp at Pruszków. But nobody knows what this means. In between the bangs and crashes, they debate their options.

'You can't trust them,' says one of the women from Wola. 'They massacred whole streets of people in our district. I only escaped because I was lying under a pile of dead bodies. I pretended to be dead, then crawled away whilst no one was looking.' She starts to tremble as she recounts the horror of what she went through in the first week of the uprising. Maria takes her hand.

'What is a transit camp anyway?' asks Pan Woźniak. 'It's somewhere you pass through on your way to somewhere else. But where? That's the question.'

'They told the Jews they were sending them to work in the east,' says Pani Kowalska. 'And they disappeared.' Rumours of the massacres at Treblinka have spread fear and terror.

'I vote we stay put until we're forced to move,' says Pani Woźniak. 'They can carry me out in a coffin.'

'Let's hope it doesn't come to that,' says Maria.

On the last day of August, news reaches them that the vault of the church of the Nuns of Perpetual Adoration has been hit during the celebration of the Blessed Sacrament. The ceiling of the vault collapsed, killing hundreds of people, including many nuns and some priests.

For Maria, this dreadful news affects her even more than the bombing of her own home. The nuns were such good people, sharing God's love with those around them. They provided sanctuary in a world that was falling apart. And now, they too are gone. The world is devoid of hope.

The next day, Pan Lewandowski returns from a visit to the makeshift hospital for wounded soldiers with shocking news. The Home Army has evacuated Stare Miasto through the storm sewers, leaving behind a couple of thousand of their wounded comrades.

'But what about us?' cries Pani Woźniak. 'They can't just leave us here to perish. Who is going to defend us now?' As if to illustrate her point, a shell explodes in a nearby street.

'There's nothing we can do except surrender,' says Pan Lewandowski. 'The Germans have said they will send civilians to the transit camp at Pruszków. We don't have any other choice.'

Maria weeps silently. They've suffered so much, endured for so long, and for it to end like this. If she goes to the transit camp, where will the Germans send her after that? Pani Kowalska is hugging her children, comforting them. Agata, noticing Maria's tears, climbs onto her lap and puts her little arms around her neck. 'Don't cry,' she says. 'I'll look after you.'

It's almost too much for Maria to bear. Children are so brave, she thinks, but it's because they don't really understand what's going on. And what about Jan? She hasn't heard anything of him for a month now. She has no idea if he's still alive, but she knows she would feel it in her bones if he wasn't. But if she leaves Warsaw now, how will they ever find each other again?

Pan Lewandowski leaves the cellar then returns with a pile of white sheets in his arms. 'It's time,' he says, handing them out to all the adults present.

They venture outside, waving the white sheets above their heads. Within minutes the firing stops, and German soldiers appear in the streets, pointing guns. It's over, thinks Maria. We fought, and we lost.

CHAPTER FIFTY-TWO

Jan's platoon is being redeployed to the Zośka Battalion. They are to leave the city centre and go to Czerniaków, on the west bank of the Vistula. The loss of Stare Miasto dealt a severe blow to Home Army morale. Now their best hope is to strengthen Polish defences at the bridgehead so that the Soviets can cross over from Praga, if they ever feel like getting round to it. No one wants to admit what Jan increasingly believes – that the Soviets have been stringing them along all this time. The news of the liberation of Paris has brought both hope and resentment. If the British and Americans can drive the Germans out of the French capital, why can't the Soviets drive them out of Warsaw? Isn't my enemy's enemy supposed to be my friend? Jan is starting to have doubts about this maxim.

After a month of fighting, Jan's platoon is a motley bunch, to say the least. Dressed in an assortment of camouflage smocks and grey-green Wehrmacht trousers which the Home Army has pilfered from German stockpiles, they prepare to make the hazardous journey to Czerniaków on foot.

As soon as the order is given to depart, they run across a broad avenue, then descend into a maze of underground cellars. At least they're not using the sewers this time. The return journey from Stare Miasto, carrying more dispatches from General Bór-Komorowski, was hardly less eventful than the outward journey. They narrowly missed being hit by grenades again when passing underneath a manhole in German territory. When they returned to their base in the city centre, they stripped off and their clothes were burnt. Jan was issued with a pair of Wehrmacht trousers too big for him. He cut two inches off the legs and improvised a belt with a length of string. He has also acquired a pair of German boots to replace his ruined shoes.

They walk single-file through the dark cellars, holding onto each other's clothing so as not to get lost. Speaking is prohibited because there are Germans on some of the upper floors. Jan reflects that he has spent so much of this war underground. When he joined the Grey Ranks, he thought he would get an opportunity to do some actual fighting, but it hasn't been like that. Instead, Jan's war has been unpredictable and messy. It has involved digging dead bodies out of collapsed buildings and wading through shit to pass messages between different groups.

They emerge into an area of Warsaw almost entirely unscathed from the uprising. Jan can hardly believe his eyes, he's become so used to the sight of destruction. Here in Czerniaków, houses are still standing, people are going about their everyday activities, and there are orchards and vegetable plots growing fresh produce. He hasn't eaten an apple in weeks. But he sees at once that this leafy suburb with its parks and open spaces will be much harder to defend than the streets of the city centre and Stare Miasto.

They are assigned to an apartment building overlooking the river. From the top floors they have a good view of Praga on the opposite bank where the Red Army is kicking its heels.

Jan is sorting out his kit in the room designated as a dormitory, when a familiar voice surprises him. 'Hello.'

He turns round and sees Weronika standing in the

doorway. She's wearing a nurse's uniform with a big red cross on the apron. He's so delighted to see her, he rushes over and almost gives her a hug before remembering that Lew, Królik and Sowa are all watching him. Jan and Weronika go out into the corridor.

'What are you doing here?' he asks.

'I've been assigned to your platoon as a medic,' she says with a smile. 'I'll look after you if you're injured.'

Jan remembers how tightly she bound his leg during the training exercises in the forest. 'I'm sure we couldn't be in better hands,' he says. He has so many questions he wants to ask her. What has she been doing all this time? Has she been involved in any fighting? But above all, Weronika might know what has happened to his mother.

'Is there any news from home?' he asks, fearful of what she might tell him.

She takes his hand in hers and for a dreadful moment he fears the worst. 'Our building was hit,' she says. 'But as far as I know, everyone got out safely. They went to Stare Miasto. But I don't know what happened to them after that. We have to hope that they survived. The civilians in Stare Miasto surrendered after the Home Army pulled out. Your mother is probably at the transit camp in Pruszków.' She doesn't add 'if she's still alive' but the unspoken words hang in the air between them.

'Pruszków,' says Jan, repeating the name to himself. 'Yes, I'm sure that's where she'll be.' He wants to convince himself. 'Thank you. I'll know where to look for her after…' He doesn't know what to say. After we've won? Or, after we've lost?

'She won't stay in the transit camp,' says Weronika. 'They'll send her someplace else, but there will be records.'

He wants to tell Weronika that now they've found each other again, they should try and stick together, he's had enough of losing contact with people in this war, but just then the other boys emerge from the dormitory, and he drops her hand.

'Hey, Mysz,' says Lew, slapping him on the back and giving him a wink. 'We've got a briefing now.'

'Right,' he says. He turns back to Weronika. 'I have to go.'

'I have to get back too. I'll see you around, then?'

'I hope so.'

*

The early days in Czerniaków are quiet. Too quiet, thinks Jan, as they spend their time digging communication trenches between different positions and foraging for potatoes and onions in the allotments. This will never last, he thinks. And he's right. On the tenth of September they hear the sound of Red Army artillery for the first time in five weeks. About bloody time, thinks Jan. What have the Soviets been doing all this while? Taking a holiday?

The air-fight over Praga is exactly the sort of scene that Jan has been hoping to witness ever since the German invasion five years ago. Soviet fighter aircraft go into action and shoot down five Stukas in a fierce battle that lights up the night sky. But he's no longer an eleven-year-old boy who thinks that knocking German planes out of the sky is all it's going to take to win the war. It's the fighting on the ground that matters. The battle in the sky is only the prelude to what's to come.

He doesn't have long to wait.

The very next day, the fight is brought to Czerniaków and this previously quiet suburb explodes in a hail of artillery and air bombardment. The Nebelwerfer rockets make their infernal mooing sound overhead, and all the civilians run for cover.

Jan's platoon is ordered out to help reinforce a front-line position in the middle of the night. He's been issued with an MP40 Schmeisser submachine gun, just like the one he stripped and reassembled when he was training. Those days seem like a distant memory now. Crouched down behind the barricade, he tries to remember everything Zych taught them. Now that he has a loaded weapon in his hands, it feels much heavier. Or maybe it's just the weight of responsibility he's carrying. Was this how Lech felt? He wishes his brother were here with him now and he could ask him.

His leg starts to cramp and as he shifts position, a hail of bullets suddenly flies overhead, so close they miss him by inches. He throws himself flat on the ground. Flashes of orange light in the distance reveal the direction of the enemy attack.

'Fire!' shouts the lieutenant in charge of their group.

Jan raises his weapon over the top of the barricade and pulls the trigger. He's firing blind and has no idea if he's hit anyone. But he doesn't stop until he's run out of ammunition.

As is often the way with these things, the battle peters out in a haze of confusion. Probably both sides are counting their wounded and running low on supplies. Jan helps carry the dead and wounded to the makeshift hospital. Lew has taken a bullet to the leg and is bleeding profusely. Jan and Królik hoist him between them and the three of them shuffle awkwardly towards the hospital.

In all the chaos, Jan looks for the one person he knows he can trust. Weronika is dressing a head wound. As soon as she's finished, she comes over to them.

'Bring him over here and lay him down,' she instructs. Brandishing a huge pair of scissors she proceeds to cut away Lew's trouser leg. Lew looks alarmed.

'Don't worry,' says Jan, patting him on the shoulder. 'You're in good hands. Trust me.'

CHAPTER FIFTY-THREE

The boy holds out his tin can and Maria ladles as much soup as she can into it, careful not to spill any down the side. He's a skinny lad, about eleven, and he reminds her of Jan at that age. She wishes she could take him home with her and feed him up. A good stew, that's what he needs. Jan always enjoyed a hearty stew, with plenty of meat and flavoured with paprika.

At the thought of Jan her heart contracts. She doesn't know where he is or if he's still alive. But she would know, wouldn't she, if he wasn't alive? She would feel it in her heart. She has to believe that her youngest child is still out there, fighting for his country, otherwise her world would fall apart completely and irrevocably. How could she go on?

'Thank you,' says the boy.

'Enjoy it,' says Maria. She wishes she could give him more, but the queue for soup is snaking around the yard. There'll only be just enough to go round.

A young woman steps forward and holds out a vase. There aren't enough dishes in the camp and people have to be creative with whatever they can find. Maria volunteered to lend a hand in the field kitchen run by the Polish-run Central Welfare Council. It's best to keep busy, she finds.

Otherwise she dwells on the unthinkable.

When Stare Miasto fell at the end of August, the Germans kept their word and transported the civilian population to the transit camp at Pruszków, a few miles southwest of Warsaw. Durchgangslager 121, or Dulag 121 for short. Even though it's such a large site, the former railway repair workshops are inadequate for the thousands of refugees flooding in every day.

Upon arrival, they were herded into the largest building in the camp and sorted by the *Arbeitsamt*, the German employment office, assisted by the military police. It was a brutal process, the Germans not caring about splitting up families. Anyone young or fit enough to work was sent to workshop three or four, to be deported to labour camps in the Third Reich. Those suspected of having participated in the uprising got the harshest treatment and were kept under armed guard in workshop number six. They would almost certainly end up in a concentration camp.

Maria found herself left with the largest group – the elderly, the sick and women with children. She held tight to Agata's hand throughout, terrified that the Germans would pick the girl out as a Jew.

'Who do we have here?' said a German soldier, tapping Agata under the chin. 'You're a dark-haired little thing.'

'She's my niece,' said Maria defiantly. 'Her parents died. She lives with me.'

'Does she now?' said the German. 'And does she know the Lord's Prayer?'

'Of course she does.'

'I'd like to hear her say it.'

Agata stared at him with her huge, dark eyes. Then she launched into a faultless rendition of the Lord's Prayer, beginning with 'Our Father,' and ending with a resounding, 'Amen.'

Maria breathed a sigh of relief. 'You see?' she said. 'A good little Christian.'

'Humph,' said the German.

They were taken to workshop number one where they've been languishing for days now, unsure what the future holds for them.

But they can't stay here. New people arrive every day. There's talk of them being sent to the countryside. But to do what? And how will Maria find her family again? The future is unknown. All she can do is focus on the present. Ladling soup.

*

In the middle of September an advance party of soldiers from the Polish First Army – otherwise known as Berling's Army – finally makes it across the Vistula. Subordinated to the Red Army, there are about three hundred of them and they bring with them heavy machine guns, anti-tank rifles and mortars. They're a welcome sight. And yet, Jan starts to have doubts as soon as he meets some of them.

For one thing, they seem to be speaking a different language. Their Polish is peppered with words like 'brother' and 'citizen' and 'comrade'. And they are accompanied by a so-called 'political education officer', whatever that means. And as for their clothes! On their heads they wear big, Soviet helmets with a Polish eagle stencilled on the front. Other parts of their attire are positively primitive. Instead of socks, they wrap their feet in flannel cloths and stuff their kit into hessian sacks instead of rucksacks.

Talking to a couple of the younger lads, Jan learns that they're mostly peasants from the eastern plains who've been forcibly enlisted, which doesn't bode well for their commitment to the cause. Many of them have never set foot in a city before and seem rather overawed by the prospect of defending the Polish capital. When Jan asks one of them if he thinks the Red Army will soon send reinforcements – he means 'real soldiers' not just unwilling conscripts – the lad, a pig farmer from Kresy, shrugs his shoulders. He neither knows nor cares.

And then the fight for the bridgehead is on. All day and night, they come under attack. Machine-gun fire, mortar bombs, parachute flares. They're in a living hell, fighting for their lives. Jan is so sleep-deprived, he doesn't know if he's coming or going. He follows orders like a robot – Take up your positions! Fire! Retreat! Regroup! Fire again! Leave him he's dead!

They're defending the upper storey of a house, trying to prevent two Germans climbing the stairs, when Królik receives a direct hit in the chest. One minute he's standing beside Jan, firing his Schmeisser sub-machine gun for all he's worth, and the next he topples down the stairs, like a rag doll, banging his head on the treads, his eyes staring in surprise. Jan fires at the Germans in fury and manages to hit one of them in the thigh. The wounded man drops his weapon and falls back with an anguished cry. His companion throws up his hands in defeat. Jan stops firing. The rule is that ordinary Wehrmacht soldiers are taken prisoner if they surrender. General Bór-Komorowski has been quite clear on that point. If they want the Germans to treat the Home Army as legitimate combatants, then they must play by the rules of warfare themselves.

As soon as the Germans have been led away, Jan runs to Królik who is lying at the bottom of the stairs in a crumpled heap, the front of his smock stained bright red. His eyes are still open and his jaw hangs slack. Jan presses his eyelids closed with his thumb and forefinger. He's dead. The poor sod, thinks Jan. He didn't deserve this. None of them do. He eases the strap of the sub-machine gun over the top of Królik's head and wipes the blood on his trousers. A weapon like this is too valuable to leave behind. They'll come back and collect the body later, but the weapon he takes now. Somewhere, deep down, he understands that he should be more upset about Królik's death, but tiredness, he's discovered, is like an anaesthetic, numbing the senses, making him indifferent to all the bloodshed. If he ever gets the chance to sleep properly, he'll sleep for a week.

That evening he's given the job of keeping watch on a vacant plot of land from a cellar window. Earlier he ate a plate of pickled herring prepared by the female nurses. He picked at his food, until Weronika sat down beside him and told him that he had to eat to keep his strength up. Really, she is worse than his mother at times. He forced the food down, but with every mouthful all he could see was Królik lying on the ground, covered in blood. In the end it was all too much for him, and he rushed outside to be sick. After that Weronika was kinder to him and brought him some plain biscuits which was all he could stomach.

Now, as he sits on the large window sill, his legs drawn up, gazing out at the patch of ground in the gathering darkness, his limbs feel like straw and his head is so heavy it keeps lolling forward onto his chest. It looks as if it's going to be a quieter night tonight. In a room next door, Home Army soldiers are drinking vodka with the latest batch of Berling soldiers to arrive from Praga. They won't notice if he grabs five minutes' shut-eye.

He doesn't know how long he's been asleep, but something causes him to wake with a start. From the raucous singing coming through the wall, it sounds as if the party is still going on next door. He peers through the cellar window. It's quite dark out there now, but in the faint glow of the moonlight he can just make out something moving across the open ground. Although he's never seen one of these objects before, he knows precisely what it is. A Goliath. For a moment he watches in stunned fascination as what looks like a scale model of a First World War tank trundles across the cobbles, zigzagging from side to side. It might resemble an outsized toy, but in actual fact it's a deadly weapon, loaded with high explosive and operated at a distance by control wires attached to the mother tank. The only way to stop its progress is to get behind it and cut the wires. But it's a hugely risky thing to do. There's no telling when the operator will choose to detonate the explosive.

Jan jumps off the window sill and runs next door. Empty

vodka bottles are lying around, as are most of the men. Some have fallen asleep, for heaven's sake. The Berling Army soldiers are nothing but a bad influence.

'Goliath approaching!' shouts Jan. No one stirs. What's he supposed to do? They're all older and more senior than him.

Giving them up as a bad lot, he runs up the stairs, hoping to find someone who will listen to him. If they can't stop the Goliath then they'll need to evacuate the building. He's half way to the second floor when the explosion comes. It throws him off his feet and rips part of the façade off the front of the building. When he opens his eyes, he's lying on the landing, covered in a pile of debris and plaster dust. He spits dust from his mouth and does a quick mental check. Fingers. Toes. Arms. Legs. He's still in one piece, with no obvious injuries that he can identify. He scrambles to his feet, shakes bits of plaster out of his hair, and staggers up the remaining stairs. There's machine-gun fire coming from the top floor.

Someone thrusts a rifle into Jan's hands and orders him to fire. When he looks over the remains of the wall, he sees Germans running towards the building, shooting wildly. Jan pulls the trigger and to his astonishment, one of the Germans falls to the ground. Was that him? Did he do that?

The next hour is a confusion of explosions, shooting, grenades, and contradictory reports. One minute the Germans have invaded the cellar. The next minute it turns out they've been seen off. Jan keeps firing his rifle until he runs out of ammunition.

Finally, the shooting dies down. The Germans, it seems, have withdrawn. The building, or what's left of it, is still in the hands of the Home Army. But their losses are devastating. In the morning they'll have the job of pulling the dead bodies out of the rubble of the cellar. The idiots, thinks Jan. If only they'd listened to him.

CHAPTER FIFTY-FOUR

The uprising is falling apart. Jan doesn't want to admit it – he'll never give up the fight – but anyone with half a brain can see that it isn't going their way. The Red Army still hasn't materialised on the west bank, just these half-trained, half-hearted lads from Berling's Army who are next to useless. As soon as they see a German tank approaching, they're likely to flee in the opposite direction. They might as well not have bothered crossing the Vistula for all the use they've been.

In the kitchen of the half-ruined house which now constitutes the Zośka Battalion's headquarters, Jankowski sends daily requests to the Soviets for food, ammunition and, above all, troops. The Soviets send none of these things. If it wasn't for the Soviet artillery fire aimed at the German positions, the game would have been up long ago. But it's impossible to ignore the obvious – the Soviets are using the Poles as cannon fodder.

It's not just tanks and infantry that they're dealing with. The Germans are trying to smoke them out of their last remaining buildings. Jan is on constant fire duty, stamping out the blazes as they occur. It's exhausting work. And their food supplies are running low.

Towards the end of September, Jankowski calls together what's left of his battalion and informs them that they will be evacuating Czerniaków through a storm sewer to Mokotów, in the south of the city. *They've got us on the run*, thinks Jan. The positions held by the Home Army are shrinking by the day.

The evacuation is set for one in the morning. Beleaguered civilians and combatants gather in a house near the river, prior to the departure. Weronika is there, tending to the walking wounded. Jan goes over and asks if there's anything he can do to help her.

'Yes,' she says. 'We need people to help carry the wounded.' She indicates men lying on stretchers, some of them barely conscious.

'I'll help,' he says. He can hardly refuse such a request. Still, he has his doubts about the sanity of the operation. Are they really going to transport people on stretchers through a sewer? Sowa also offers to lend a hand, and together they are assigned a young man called Karol whose right leg is bandaged from the thigh to the calf.

'Shrapnel got me,' says Karol, in a remarkably cheerful voice considering his situation. 'Lacerated half my leg. Weronika did a good job of patching me up though.'

Jan can't help feeling a surge of pride at this praise of Weronika. 'She's always wanted to be a nurse,' he tells Karol. 'Ever since she was a young girl.'

'Friend of yours, is she?' asks Karol.

'Yes,' says Jan. 'She's a good friend.'

Jan and Sowa lift the stretcher – Jan at the front and Sowa at the back – and then join the line of people preparing to descend into the sewer. Suddenly, shells start exploding along the river bank and the orderly queue becomes a desperate mass of people, pushing and shoving their way to the manhole.

When the rush has died down, they lower the stretcher and then the injured man into the shaft using ropes. Jan and Sowa wait at the bottom of the shaft as Karol swings precariously at the end of the rope, bumping into the sides of the shaft.

'Nearly there!' calls Jan in encouragement.

When his feet are just above their heads, Jan and Sowa each grab an ankle and, as gently as they can, guide the injured man the last few feet. He lands on the bottom with a grunt.

'Sorry for being such a nuisance,' says Karol.

'Not your fault, mate,' says Jan.

In the confined space it's quite a job to manhandle their patient onto the stretcher without causing him more agony. They try lifting him but soon put him down when Karol cries out in agony. After some debate, they roll him onto the stretcher.

'Okay,' says Jan, lifting the foot end. 'Off we go.'

Thankfully they're using a storm sewer this time, not a waste sewer, so it is at least possible to walk upright and the smell less offensive. Even so, carrying a man on a stretcher for hours through a tunnel with the water sometimes up to your thighs isn't the easiest thing in the world. To keep Karol dry, they often have to lift him higher than is comfortable.

Female guides are posted along the route at each junction where the main sewer connects with smaller ones. Just as well, thinks Jan. You wouldn't want to get lost down here. At one of the junctions he recognises the diminutive figure of Daria, the guide who led them through the waste sewer from the city centre to Stare Miasto on that memorable first trip. Jan is overjoyed to see her. When so many have died, every familiar face feels like a small victory. If he wasn't carrying the stretcher, he'd give her a hug. She shines her torch in his face and gives him a nod of recognition. We've made it this far, is the unspoken understanding between them. Keep going.

'Careful at the next bit,' she says. 'The Germans have dammed some sections with sandbags and the water is high.'

'Thanks,' says Jan through gritted teeth.

As they wade on through the water, Karol passes in and out of consciousness. After four exhausting hours during which Jan seems to have lost the ability to think straight, they hoist Karol up to ground level and emerge into a bright, sunny day.

It's like when they first arrived in Czerniaków. The uprising doesn't seem to have reached this part of the city yet. But the respite doesn't last for long. Within days of securing a victory in Czerniaków, the Germans turn their attention on Mokotów.

By now the Home Army is so depleted, their food and ammunition rations so low, that after only two days of fighting the order is given to retreat through the sewers yet again, to the city centre. The difference this time is that the status of all Home Army soldiers has been upgraded. They are now part of the Warsaw Army Corps which means they can expect to be treated as prisoners of war if captured. As a result, there is no need to evacuate the injured, much to Jan's relief.

When he emerges in the city centre after six hours wading through a storm sewer, he finds himself back in the part of the city where he grew up. But it doesn't feel like a homecoming. When he looks around at the once familiar streets, he sees nothing but destruction.

*

Jankowski tasks Jan with delivering a message to Home Army headquarters, detailing the number and condition of fighters who have made it safely from Mokotów. Jan is hoping for a second encounter with General Bór-Komorowski, but when he arrives at the building in Jasna Street, he's told that the great man is busy in meetings. What had he expected? That the man charged with delivering Poland's freedom would spare a minute to take a message delivered by a teenage foot soldier? Disappointed nevertheless, Jan passes the message to one of Bór-

Komorowski's lieutenants and turns to leave.

He really ought to return to his squad straightaway, but he's made good time and he doesn't think he'll be missed for half an hour if he makes a small detour. His old home is only round the corner, and he can't resist paying a visit, just to see for himself. He might not get another opportunity.

He's seen so much death and destruction in this uprising, he doesn't think that anything can shock him anymore. But the sight of the street where he grew up – now empty and bomb-damaged – is especially painful. How many people died here? How many are still buried under the collapsed apartment blocks?

His own building is still just about standing, but the roof has been blown off and the inner courtyard where he once talked to Weronika is piled high with rubble. He clambers over fallen masonry and piles of debris and makes his way up the stairs to the apartment he used to call home.

The door is unlocked, as if his mother left in a hurry. He almost expects to see her emerging from the kitchen in her apron demanding to know where he's been all this time, but of course there's no one there. The kitchen, once so spick and span, is now a mess of rubble. There's a gaping hole in the wall. The windows have been blown out and shards of glass crunch underfoot. It would break his mother's heart to see her home in this state.

He presses on through to the living room, once so full of well-loved things – the mahogany writing desk, the upright piano, the dining table. He didn't appreciate beautiful furniture when he was an eleven-year-old boy – what child does? – but he feels their ruin now. He runs his hand over the top of the piano lid, thick with dirt and chunks of plaster. Can anything be salvaged from here? It's unlikely. He looks at the mantelpiece where the clock used to stand – an ugly piece in his humble opinion – and sees that the clock has fallen onto the floor and shattered on the hearth. Suddenly experiencing a perverse affection for the old thing, he stoops to pick it up. Buried under the remains of the clock – like discovering a body in a collapsed building – he finds the photograph of them all that Anna took on the day Lech was called up. It's creased and is stained with water damage, but it feels like a miracle that it has survived at all. He straightens it out and stares at the faces of his family. His mother putting a brave face on things, his father looking solemn, Lech with a hint of impatience at the enforced delay, Anna looking as lovely as he remembers her, and himself just a scrap of a kid with no idea about the horrors of war. Where are they all now? Overcome with emotion, he sits amidst the rubble of his old home and weeps for the family he's lost.

The sound of artillery in the distance brings him back to his senses. He's stayed away from his platoon far longer than he intended. They'll be wondering what has happened to him, might even take him for dead. Carefully, he places the photograph inside his leather wallet. Then he puts the wallet back in his breast pocket and stands up. He retraces his steps over the debris-strewn floor and back down the stairs with a renewed sense of purpose. From now on he will carry his family close to his heart, and as soon as this war is over, he will make it his mission to find them and re-unite them all. Nothing else matters.

Back at the warehouse where it's his job to help distribute wheat and barley to the civilian population, things are not looking good. These two grains are the only source of food left in the city centre now, the warehouse having been saved from destruction by nothing short of a miracle. A long line of hungry people snakes its way around the building. They'll each be given a cupful of grain which they will have to take home and mill in a coffee-grinder before it can be used to make a soup of sorts. The soup is always full of husks which you have to spit out. Jan longs for the pickled herring they had in Czerniaków. You can't even get horsemeat these days. The only option is to hunt down stray cats and dogs, even pigeons if you can catch them. And as for water, you run the risk of being used as target practice by German grenade throwers when queuing at the handful of functioning wells. No wonder General Bór-Komorowski is busy in meetings, thinks Jan. They must be close to giving up.

When he's finished in the warehouse, Jan goes in search of Weronika at the makeshift hospital which has been set up in a series of cellars. He'd like to show her the photograph he found. As ever, he is appalled by the squalid conditions. Sick and wounded soldiers and civilians are crammed into the basements, the air thick and suffocating. Weronika has told him how operations are performed by candlelight, without the use of anaesthetics. It doesn't bear thinking about. Whenever he ventures into one of these hospitals, he hears gut-wrenching cries of pain that make his legs feel weak. He doesn't know how Weronika can stand working here all day long.

He finds her dressing a suppurating leg wound on a man who is delirious with fever. He looks as if he won't last the night. Even Weronika, normally so fastidious in her appearance, looks tired and dishevelled, loose strands of hair sticking to her face and neck, her uniform covered in stains that Jan would rather not think about. Even so, she manages a smile when she sees him.

'How are you?' he asks.

'Managing. Just about.' She gathers the old dressings into a bucket. 'Come with me.'

He follows her into the courtyard where they burn their waste. 'Look what I found today,' says Jan when she has finished disposing of the soiled dressings. He retrieves the photograph from the wallet and hands it to her. 'Anna took it the day Lech was called up.'

'I remember that day,' says Weronika, nodding.

'You do?'

'Yes, of course. You were kicking a stone around the courtyard of our old building. We talked about what we would do in the war. Don't you remember?'

'Yes, I do,' says Jan. He's never forgotten it. 'You were

quite scary back then.'

'Was I?' She sounds surprised.

'You were so certain about what you wanted to do, whereas I had no idea.'

She laughs. 'Well, you've made up for it.' She hands the photograph back. 'You're lucky.'

'I am?'

'To have found this photograph. I have nothing like that of my family.'

'But we're scattered all over the place. How are we going to find each other again?'

'By looking and never giving up.' She takes his hand in hers, then she leans forwards and kisses him on the cheek. 'I have to get back to work now.'

Jan is so surprised by the kiss, Weronika is gone before he has a chance to respond. He returns the photograph to the wallet and puts it back in his breast pocket for safe keeping. Then he leaves the hospital as if walking on air, touching the spot on his cheek where she kissed him with the tips of his fingers.

CHAPTER FIFTY-FIVE

The news that Mokotów has fallen on 27 September is just another nail in the coffin of the uprising. But there are still an astonishing three hundred thousand people in the city centre and someone has to defend them. Soviet planes drop a few bags of ammunition now and then but it feels like a token gesture. They also drop sacks of grain which split on impact with the ground, the precious contents spreading far and wide. People rush out and collect every last grain, despite the danger of being hit by a German shell. Anyone who still thinks that the Soviets are ever going to cross the Vistula is, in Jan's opinion, a deluded fool.

That night Jan and Sowa are part of a team manning the barricades close to their billet. They've been issued with Schmeisser sub-machine guns, but they're woefully low on ammunition, so shooting is reserved for emergencies only.

Jan has come to appreciate the quiet steadfastness of Sowa, whose real name, it turns out, is Albin. Not so long ago, Jan discovered that Sowa – he'll always think of him by his codename – is Jewish. His parents and two sisters were sent to the *Umschlagplatz* and put on one of the trains for Treblinka. Sowa survived because he was smuggling food from the Aryan sector at the time. When he learned what had happened to his family, he fled from the ghetto under cover of darkness and never went back. He has been living incognito as part of the Underground ever since.

'I've always felt guilty for surviving,' he confided to Jan one night in the darkness of their dormitory. Their mattresses were so close together they could talk in whispers without being overheard.

'You've got nothing to feel guilty about,' Jan replied. 'Your parents would want you to survive. They would be proud of you if they could see you now.'

'But I couldn't save them,' said Sowa. 'I feel such a failure.'

Jan heard his friend sobbing quietly into his pillow. There was nothing he could say. He thought then of Wiktor and all those lives lost. He too, should have done more to save his friends.

Now, as they crouch side by side at the barricade, Jan knows he can't bear to lose another friend in the fighting. Sowa, Weronika, these are the people he has now. He joined the Underground with grand ideas about doing his bit to help liberate his country, but in the end what matters are those closest to you. If you free your country but lose your friends and family, what have you achieved?

An explosion nearby shocks him out of his philosophical musings. Suddenly he's on high alert, his finger reaching for the Schmeisser's trigger. It's too dark to see properly what's happening. He hears running footsteps. Are they Germans or Poles? A burst of machine-gun fire. Bullets skim over his head, so close it feels as if his hair is singed. Next to him, Sowa responds with a volley of shots, and Jan knows that he has to fire too. But what will happen when they run out of ammunition? He doesn't want to waste precious bullets firing into thin air. There's a brief lull in the shooting from the opposite side and Jan risks a quick look over the top of the barricade. If he can see where the enemy is, he'll have a better chance of hitting his target. He sees two figures approaching. He's surprised there aren't more of them. He raises his Schmeisser to shoulder height and prepares to take a shot. In that moment, something slams into his chest with a force that takes his breath away. After that, he knows no more.

*

Jan opens his eyes and blinks in the darkness. He has no idea where he is. The air is suffocating, thick with the stink of unwashed bodies, decay and death. He's lying on his back. He puts out a hand and is surprised to feel a reasonably soft mattress. Overlaying the smell of death, there's a hint of disinfectant. He'd recognise that cocktail anywhere. He's inhaled it often enough.

He must be in the hospital, or what passes for a hospital. He tries to sit up but a sudden stabbing pain in his chest forces him back down with a groan. Whoever is lying on the mattress next to him grunts in his sleep and rolls over. What has happened to him? How has he ended up here? His mind's a blank, but then it comes to him – Sowa, the barricade, the shooting. He was going to shoot a German, and then something hit him. Was he shot? Then why isn't he dead? His chest hurts, that's for sure. He examines the spot gently with his fingertips. The flesh feels bruised, but there's something not right. Something is missing. Where's his wallet? The photograph of his family? A moan escapes his lips.

Footsteps come running, and then in the light of a carbide lamp, he sees Weronika kneeling down beside him. With the light illuminating her features in the dark room, she's never looked so beautiful. She leans over him now and places a hand over his forehead to check his temperature. The younger Weronika would have been brisk and bossy. But this Weronika touches him gently, and leaves her hand there longer than is strictly necessary to check for the presence of fever.

'You're awake,' she says. 'I'm glad.'

'What happened? How long have I been here?' He has so many questions, he doesn't know where to start.

'You were shot,' says Weronika. 'Sowa carried you here.'

'Sowa carried me?' The idea of Sowa carrying him makes him laugh. Sowa struggles to lift a sack of barley. 'Is he all right?'

'He's fine.'

'But… but why aren't I dead? If I was shot?'

Weronika removes her hand from his forehead and reaches into the pocket of her uniform. 'Your family saved you.' She hands him his wallet.

'I don't understand.'

'The leather wallet with the photograph of your family took the impact of the bullet. You're the luckiest person I know. If it hadn't been for this wallet, that bullet would have killed you.' She dips her head so that it's in shadow, and he can't be sure, but he thinks she wipes a tear from her eye. But then she smiles brightly at him. 'The wallet is a bit damaged. Look, you can see where the bullet hit here' – she points at a hole surrounded by a scorch mark. 'It's made a hole in the photograph. I've been waiting for you to wake up so that I could give it back to you.'

'Thank you for looking after it.' He reaches for her hand and gives it a squeeze. 'And thank you for looking after me.'

'Just doing my job,' she says, but he knows she'll have done more than that for him. Much more.

It must be getting light outside, although it's still dark in the makeshift ward in the basement, because he can hear people moving around. The prone bodies on the other mattresses start to stir.

'I have to get back to work,' she says. 'But I'll come and see you soon. I promise.'

Reluctantly, he lets go of her hand. Then he closes his eyes and drifts in and out of sleep, his hand clutching the wallet containing the photograph of his family.

CHAPTER FIFTY-SIX

It's over. Warsaw surrenders at the start of October. An eerie silence falls on the city. The dust settles.

When the Germans enter the hospital, they ask, *'Hier alle Soldaten?'* Is everyone here a soldier?

'Yes,' replies the nurse.

Lying on his mattress, Jan savours that moment. The Germans are calling them soldiers, not bandits. They will be treated as prisoners of war, not shot as insurgents. That's something, at least.

They are taken to a nearby apartment block where a German general says, 'Pity you lot didn't fight the Bolsheviks. We could have done with you on our side.'

Although his chest hurts like hell, Jan is determined to leave Warsaw on his own two feet and not have to be carried out on a stretcher. He joins what is left of his Home Army unit as they prepare to leave the city for the last time. The city they fought so hard to defend. Their home.

Wearing their red-and-white armbands and their White Eagle badges, they line up six abreast in long columns, heads held high. Jan stands next to Sowa, without whom he might have died on the battlefield. They embrace awkwardly when they are reunited, in the way of teenage boys.

The column of soldiers starts to move slowly forwards. Jan puts one foot in front of the other with a heavy heart. He's looked everywhere for Weronika but can't see her. He supposes she's with the ranks of women carrying first-aid kits and radio equipment.

At the checkpoint they pass German soldiers and officials who watch silently. Some even take photos. *'Sie sind alle noch so jung,'* says one as they pass. Even Jan can understand that. They're all still so young. And it's true. Most of them are in their teens or twenties. They should be at school or university. Instead, they've been fighting a war. Many of them haven't survived. They've all had to grow up so quickly. Jan would be offended if anyone called him a child. He's a man now. He fought like a man, suffered like a man. He'll carry the wounds in his heart forever.

*

Weronika isn't remotely surprised to find herself in a cattle cart. If anything, it validates her status as a legitimate member of the Polish Underground. And now she's a prisoner of war. It doesn't get any more legitimate than that.

If she'd been a boy she would have learnt how to shoot and fight and set explosives. She thinks she'd have been rather good at it; she's always had a steady hand and calm nerves. How she envied Jan the opportunity to take up arms. As it was, she had to content herself with medical duties. Not that nursing isn't without its rewards. She's saved lives, she knows she has. She did her bit to prolong the fight. And she cared for Jan when he was brought in, unconscious. That was the only time her nerves nearly failed her, seeing him lying there, wounded. He could have died. She squeezes her eyes shut and pushes that thought firmly from her mind. He survived, and so did she. But where is he now? Will she ever see him again?

The cattle cart rattles over a set of points and the women, who are packed in shoulder-to-shoulder, elbow-to-elbow, jostle against one another. They've been hours already. How much further?

They must be going to a concentration camp, but no one knows where. Somewhere in Germany. At the transit camp in Pruszków, she and her colleagues were quickly separated from the other women, the civilians, and kept under armed guard in one of the repair sheds. As if they posed a threat to the Germans with their supplies of bandages. They weren't allowed to keep those, of course. She's got nothing useful with her now. Nothing that she could use to help those in need. She feels bereft without her first aid kit, like a soldier without his weapon.

She must have been dozing because suddenly there's a squeal of brakes and her eyes snap open. Funny how you learn to sleep anywhere in wartime, she'd never have believed it. The train stops and there's a clanking as the bolts are drawn back outside. Wherever it is, they've arrived.

At the orders to disembark, the women pour from the train onto the platform. It's a real crush. Weronika expected them to be brought somewhere bigger, not this provincial little station. *Fürstenberg*, she reads on the sign. Where's that?

She also expected the German guards to be more frightening, but they're young, almost half-hearted, like they've given up and are just going through the motions. A couple of them look drunk. Still, they're the ones with the rifles and the barking, snarling dogs straining at their leads. Best to do what they say.

The women line up in rows of five as instructed and then begin the march through the town. Even here, in this quiet little German backwater, Weronika sees how the war has taken its toll. Broken shutters which no one has bothered to repair, potholes in the road, empty shelves in the bakery, dead-eyed people on the streets. The Germans are losing this war and they know it. But the thought isn't as reassuring as it should be. People who are losing become desperate, and desperate people do crazy things.

She rubs her arms against the autumn chill. They pass a

lake and then walk along a cobbled path through a forest. A beautiful place, really. But there's a funny smell in the air, and a haze of smoke hangs overhead. It reminds her of the smell, that time, when a building in Warsaw was hit with a rocket strike and dozens of bodies burned to a cinder. That was one of the worst days in the fighting. There was nothing they could do for those poor people. And here it is again, that same smell. Burning bodies.

They round a bend in the road and the camp comes into view. High walls, barbed wire, and the stench is even stronger now. Inside, rows and rows of identical blocks; thin, sexless women dressed in blue and white striped dresses; a feeling of chaos and despair. At the sight of women pushing a handcart piled high with corpses, Weronika's natural sangfroid nearly deserts her completely. In her naivety, she'd thought she might be able to put her nursing skills to use in a concentration camp. But this place is beyond saving.

The Germans march the new arrivals through the camp, past a brick building belching out smoke, and on to an area of swampy ground, in the middle of which stands a giant tent looking like it's about to collapse. Trenches around the tent are overflowing with excrement.

Inside, it's a scene from hell. Women are crammed into every available space, sitting, lying, moaning, groaning, nursing babies, scratching at lice-ridden heads. The stink of unwashed bodies and human waste is indescribable. And where on earth are the new arrivals supposed to go?

Weronika steps gingerly over legs covered in sores – that one looks gangrenous – until she finds a small space to crouch down. She closes her eyes. Even in the worst of the fighting in Warsaw, she never found herself close to despair, but this place is more than she can stand.

When she opens her eyes, she sees a young woman in front of her scratching at her scalp. She's making it bleed.

'Don't do that,' says Weronika, laying a hand on her shoulder. 'You'll get an infection. Let me help you.' She catches a louse between her thumb and finger and squashes it flat with a pop. There, it's gone. 'Stay still, I can see a few more.' She gets to work catching them.

'Thank you,' says the woman, turning to her with a smile. 'I'll do the same for you when you need it.'

This is my life now, thinks Weronika. Catching lice, and trying to stay alive.

PART TEN
END OF THE WAR
JANUARY – MAY 1945

CHAPTER FIFTY-SEVEN

The snow has turned to slush, and an icy wind blows across the flat landscape. Grey clouds hang low in the sky, threatening more downfalls of snow. Jan trudges on, weighed down by the kitbag on his back crammed with Red Cross packages.

After a couple of months languishing in Stalag-XI A on the outskirts of the village of Altengrabow, Jan and a dozen others are being sent to do agricultural labour at a farm somewhere near Magdeburg. Not that any of them have any experience of agricultural labour. Jan barely knows a hoe from a rake. But it's better than hanging around the camp, freezing to death. First, however, they have to walk forty kilometres to the train station at Dessau. It's going to take them all night.

After the surrender in Warsaw, Jan was sent to the Stalag as a prisoner of war. Sleeping in the middle of a three-tier bunk bed in a smelly stable, life in the Stalag was a never-ending round of boredom, cold and hunger. The Red Cross handed out forms for the prisoners to write to their families, to let them know they were still alive. But who should Jan have written to? His mother was no longer in their apartment, he didn't even know where she was.

Escorted by their armed guard, they pass through blacked-out villages where the residents appear to have gone to ground. Clearly expecting an attack any day now by the Red Army, each town and village has its own anti-tank barricades manned by the *Volkssturm*, a motley crew of old men and teenage boys in Hitler Youth uniforms. It's a last-ditch attempt to defend the Fatherland. They won't stand a chance when the Soviet tanks show up but you've got to hand it to them for trying.

An array of anti-aircraft guns is lined up in front of the train station. Clearly a vulnerable location, the sight is not reassuring. They board the train and Jan finds an empty corner and lies down. He's so tired, he could sleep forever.

He's just nodding off when the shriek of an air-raid siren startles him awake, followed by the crack and blast of anti-aircraft guns. Planes roar overhead and then a flash of light illuminates the dark compartment. Bombs explode nearby. The carriage shakes. The RAF, thinks Jan with a wry smile. About bloody time. How he longed, in vain, to see them flying over Warsaw in September '39. And how disappointed he was when they didn't show up. But here they are now. The irony isn't lost on him. Has he survived this long only to be killed by the British when the war is on its last legs? That would be just his luck.

But eventually the siren sounds the all-clear and the train pulls out of the station. Jan falls asleep.

*

Kommandant Fritz Suhren has a problem. There are too many women in his camp and something needs to be done about it. They just keep coming. There was a huge influx from Poland between August and October '44, and another massive contingent from Hungary in the autumn of the same year. And now more are coming from Auschwitz, which is being evacuated ahead of the expected arrival of the Red Army. This latest lot are in a godawful state. Half of them drop dead on arrival, which simplifies the accommodation crisis, although it's causing a massive backlog at the crematorium.

And now this. Sitting at his desk, he holds the order from Reichsführer Heinrich Himmler in his hand. Two thousand deaths a day, those are Himmler's orders. The reasons are perfectly understandable, of course. They need to make space and save food. *Useless mouths*, as they are termed, must be eliminated. They also need to stop large numbers of prisoners falling into enemy hands. But two thousand! Until now they've been shooting those who are ill or incapable of working, but with the best will in the world they only manage about fifty a day. This kind of work takes its toll on those tasked with carrying it out, hence the increased alcohol consumption amongst the staff. Two thousand is an impossibly big step up.

Suhren explains his problem to the two men sitting opposite him – the newly appointed chief doctor, Hauptsturmführer Richard Trommer, and Obersturmführer Johann Schwarzhuber. Suhren is hopeful that this latter may be able to offer some much-needed assistance, having arrived recently from Auschwitz where he occupied the position of *Schutzhaftlagerführer*. In a word, he oversaw the gassing of thousands of prisoners and knows what he's about when it comes to dealing with death on a large scale.

'Your gas chamber is on the small side,' says Schwarzhuber.

'It's the best we could do at short notice,' snaps Suhren. It was recently built next to the crematorium for convenience.

'No matter,' says Schwarzhuber, 'We have mobile gassing units we can employ as well. They can be hidden in the forest.'

'Even better,' says Suhren.

'The most important thing is to keep the women calm whilst we get the process underway.'

'Yes, I can see that,' says Suhren. The last thing he needs on his hands is a camp full of hysterical women. Look at the fuss everyone made over those Polish Rabbits. And what good came of it? As far as he can tell, the experiments were a failure and a waste of time and resources. Another of Himmler's half-baked ideas. The man should have stuck to chicken farming.

'At Auschwitz-Birkenau we had a system in place that worked extremely well,' continues Schwarzhuber. Suhren grits his teeth. He's tired of hearing how much better Auschwitz was in every way to Ravensbrück – bigger, faster, death on an industrial scale. He exchanges a look with Trommer. Schwarzhuber continues, oblivious to the tension in the room. 'When they came from the ghettos, we very quickly separated those who were unfit from those who could work and marched them to the gas chambers before they knew what was happening. That isn't going to be possible here where they've all been living cheek by jowl for months or even years.'

'We'll need to isolate those selected for gassing,' says Suhren. 'We can use Uckermark.' The Uckermark Youth Camp is in the forest, half a mile from the main camp.

'Excellent idea, Herr Sturmbannführer,' says Trommer.

'We should put it about,' says Schwarzhuber, 'that Uckermark is a sanatorium where the sickest will receive the care they need. Let's face it, you've got a problem with overcrowding here and that tent isn't going to stay up much longer, it's practically falling down as we speak.'

Suhren takes a deep breath and swallows the rebuke that's on the tip of his tongue. There's no need for Schwarzhuber to lord it over them. At least Ravensbrück is still standing whereas Auschwitz has had to be evacuated.

'Leave it with me,' says Schwarzhuber. 'I know what I'm doing. I've got a team of male prisoners from Auschwitz who know all about running a gas chamber. We'll need to put someone in charge of the Uckermark site.'

'I was thinking of Ruth Neudeck,' suggests Suhren. As

his deputy Kommandant, Neudeck doesn't stand for any nonsense. She keeps the women in line with her silver-handled whip.

'Just the person,' says Schwarzhuber.

'Excellent,' says Suhren. 'Then I think we have a plan.' Just as he hoped, his problem has a solution.

All three men stand, click their heels, and salute each other. A job well done. 'Heil Hitler!'

CHAPTER FIFTY-EIGHT

What's the point anymore? Lech stubs out his cigarette and grinds it into the mud with the toe of his boot. Despondency and despair have spread amongst the ranks like an outbreak of typhus. The mood in the Polish camp has never been worse.

'They can all go to hell,' says one man. He spits on the ground. Lech agrees with him. Betrayed! There's no other word for it. The politicians have betrayed Poland. And why? Because Churchill and Roosevelt haven't got the balls to stand up to their buddy Stalin. That's what it boils down to.

How different his mood is from nine months ago when he stood on the top of Monte Cassino listening to the Kraków Hejnał, tears of pride coursing down his cheeks. And it's not like there haven't been other victories since then. Monte Cassino wasn't just a flash in the pan.

After hoisting the Polish flag on top of the monastery ruins, Anders' Army advanced up the spine of Italy, and helped the Allies capture the port of Ancona in mid-July, thus ensuring supplies to secure the Allied advance.

In August, King George VI and the Polish commander-in-chief, General Sosnkowski, honoured them with a visit and morale skyrocketed. Not long after the royal visit, they joined the Allied attack on the Gothic Line. They broke into Lombardy, inching their way northwards.

And then in October '44 they were victorious at the battle of Forlì in the Apennines despite the mountainous terrain and terrible weather conditions. It felt as if they were on the homestretch. Poland was within sight.

But exhaustion and torrential rain caused them to stall on the Senio river, south of Bologna for three months over the winter.

And now, just as spring is approaching and they expected to renew the fight – one last push towards victory – news has reached them of the Yalta Conference. Is this really all the thanks they're going to get for their help at Monte Cassino, Ancona and Forlì?

The news that has made them so angry is that eastern Poland is going to become part of the Soviet Union. Stalin will get to keep all the land he grabbed back in September '39.

The Germans have been broadcasting twice daily in Polish, encouraging the Poles to desert in the face of this treachery. Many of the men fighting alongside Lech come from eastern Poland, and although he's originally from Warsaw, Lech feels a special connection with the city of Lwów. To think that it's going to stay in Soviet hands! Uncle Henryk must be turning in his grave. Thank God Halina got out. He can't see her wanting to go back.

And as for himself, what's he fighting for now? Why does he continue to risk his life for the Allies? He thinks back to the moments before the attack at Monte Cassino. *Are you going to fight the Germans?* He wanted to be able to look his little brother in the eye and say, 'Yes, I fought them.' And he's done that. But now they're going to lose half their country to the Soviets. Make yourself at home, comrade, why don't you?

He shakes his head and lights another cigarette. He's come this far and he's not going to give up. He doesn't think the other men will either. But they're fighting for their honour now. That's all they have left.

*

March 1945. A *Generalappell* has been called and everyone understands its purpose. To select victims for the gas chamber.

At first, the Uckermark Youth Camp was seen as a better option than the main camp. The promise of not having to work or stand in line for morning *Appell* was tempting. It was a sanatorium, some said. In the middle of January, with temperatures at their lowest, some women volunteered to go. It was impossible to convince them that it might not be a good idea.

It didn't take long for the truth to emerge.

A Jehovah's Witness was sent to deliver a message to the Youth Camp. She returned with stories of naked, starving women left out in the freezing cold. The latrine was an open ditch. Ruth Neudeck thrashed her charges with a silver-handled whip. The Uckermark Youth Camp was the first step on the road to the gas chamber.

For Anna and the other Polish Rabbits, a *Generalappell* is especially bad news. Anyone with their legs in poor shape is likely to be selected. The reason is obvious. The Germans will try to evacuate the camp before the Red Army arrives and anyone not capable of walking miles across country will need to be dealt with by other means. Other selection criteria include grey hair and wrinkled bodies. The selections are led by Kommandant Fritz Suhren and his side-kick, Ruth Neudeck.

The order is for everyone to line up outside their blocks. No exceptions.

'Hey, Polish Rabbits!'

Anna turns at the sound of the familiar voice. Irmgard has lost weight – food has been dwindling for months now – but she's still a formidable presence.

'You need to get out of here,' says Irmgard.

'Where can we go?' asks Anna.

'Follow me. Quick!'

Holding on to each other for support, Anna, Jadwiga, and the other rabbits follow Irmgard behind the block, through piles of stinking rubbish, to a disused block.

'In there,' says the Blockova. 'When I ran a brothel in Hamburg, I always looked after my women. I won't let them take my Polish Rabbits.'

Anna wants to hug her, but there isn't time. Irmgard is already returning to her block, doing her duty. The rabbits hunker down inside the empty block and wait until it's safe to come out.

They hear Soviet guns in the distance.

*

21 April 1945. The Polish flag flutters in the breeze over Bologna. They've hoisted it atop the highest tower they could find. White and red against the clear blue sky.

Once the weather improved, the Allied spring offensive got underway. They pushed through the Argenta Gap, up the Po valley, and, after some tough battles, finally entered the city of Bologna. The Germans are expected to surrender any day now. It's all but over.

Lech squints at the flag, disappointed that he doesn't feel happier about their victory. It's been such a long road to get here. They've slogged their way up through Italy, they've seen off the Germans, they've won. But this isn't like that moment on the top of Monte Cassino. Monte Cassino wasn't just a moment of victory, it was a moment of hope. Back then, they still had hope that their country would be theirs. They knew what they were fighting for.

The Yalta conference in February changed all that. Eastern Poland will never be theirs again. They should be looking forward to going home, but for many, home no longer exists.

Lech knows he can never return to Lwów. He also has

no idea what state Warsaw is in. There is only one thing he knows for certain. He will find Halina and they will make a home together. She's his family now.

CHAPTER FIFTY-NINE

Burning words. First, they destroy people. Then they destroy the evidence. Tons of paper and millions of words go up in smoke, the ashes dumped in the lake.

Anna stands in the middle of a long line of women stretching from the *Schreibstube* to the pyre burning brightly on the shore of the lake. They're passing piles of paperwork from hand to hand, destroying the evidence of the Nazis' crimes. Lists of names, those selected for the *Sondertransport*, details of medical experiments, those sent for gassing, falsified death certificates and condolence letters full of lies – all of it must be destroyed before the Soviets arrive. Nothing incriminating must remain.

As the precious documents pass through her hands, Anna thinks of all the names she herself typed. Thousands of women killed by the Nazis, and their names are blowing over the camp in a thick column of smoke. Their bodies burned to ash in the crematorium and now their stories will never be known. Their families will never know the truth.

'*Schneller!*' shout the guards. Faster!

Fear is making the Germans even more short-tempered than usual. Anna can see the panic in their eyes. The eyes of animals that know they're being hunted. Dorothea Binz marches up and down the line, brandishing her whip, but she's losing her good looks with the stress of it all. Her hair, normally curled so meticulously, is unwashed and messy. She looks as if she can't believe it's come to this. Couldn't they have foreseen this would happen one day? Did they really think they would get away with their crimes forever?

It's an open secret that the Red Army is coming. They can't be that far away now. Red Army prisoners are walking tall with smiles on their faces, hardly able to contain their excitement. It's just a matter of time.

*

Time is running out. Kommandant Suhren paces his office, unable to sit still. The Soviets are approaching by the minute. You can hear their artillery, like a distant thunderstorm. Apparently, they're on the outskirts of Berlin already. They could be here any day now.

Meanwhile, he's still got too many women on his hands, but what can he do?

He sent over three thousand to Belsen – children, babies, mothers, pregnant women. Probably took them days to get there, the state the railways are in, what with the air raids and everything. He doesn't suppose there were many still alive when they arrived. Anyway, not his problem anymore. He's got his hands full worrying about the women still at Ravensbrück. And there's the camp infrastructure itself to sort out. He's had the children's block cleaned and painted ready for the Soviets' arrival. Everything spick and span, just the way it was always meant to be. But there was never time for improvements in the camp's heyday. Not his fault.

That damn tent has gone too. God, the mess those women left behind, it turns his stomach just thinking about it. Anyway, they've planted saplings on the patch of ground, so you'd never know what was there before.

The Führer has insisted that no women are to be left

alive in the camp when the Red Army arrives. They're gassing as many as they can every day, especially anyone who looks as if they won't be able to keep up when the evacuation starts, which will be any day now. They're not going to sit around and wait for the Soviets to arrive. That would be suicidal.

If he could just be allowed to get on with his job in peace, things wouldn't be so bad. But now the Swedes, of all people, have started interfering, wanting to take away busloads of prisoners. Suhren would never have believed it, but a fellow called Count Folke Bernadotte has managed to persuade Himmler to let him take Scandinavian prisoners out of the camps. At first Himmler wouldn't allow the count's White Buses to go to Ravensbrück, but then he gave the go-ahead. Another example of the Reichsführer's right hand not knowing what his left hand is doing, in Suhren's opinion.

He's had to have the gas chamber dismantled because its existence would have been too incriminating, but there are still thousands of women to dispose of so they're having to make do with mobile gassing units in the forest which can be driven away as soon as they get the order to evacuate.

The Youth Camp at Uckermark has been one of his biggest headaches. Getting that place cleaned up and shipshape has been a mammoth task. But Ruth Neudeck told him this morning that if you looked at it now, you'd want to spend your holiday there. Personally, Suhren has plans to get as far away from Germany as possible.

Everywhere you look, his staff are cleaning and tidying, painting and mending broken windows. So much easier to do these jobs now that the women are out of the way. They're having to burn excess bodies in ditches because even with their own crematorium and the one in Fürstenberg working around the clock, they just haven't got enough furnaces.

Schwarzhuber's Auschwitz men who've been running the gas chamber have all been locked up in the bunker.

Really, they ought to have been shot. You can't trust men like that not to throw themselves at the feet of the Soviets and blurt out everything they know.

He had orders to kill the Polish women who were experimented on, but with everything else going on, he never got round to it. At least that's his excuse. In truth, he knew that killing those particular women would cause an uproar, something he could well do without. And thank goodness he didn't kill them, because he's now received a contradictory order from Himmler to keep them alive. What's the Reichsführer's game, Suhren wonders? He's probably got some political motive up his sleeve – maybe he plans to use the rabbits as bargaining chips with the West. Who knows what goes on in the head of that man?

The problem is, the rules keep changing. One minute they're filling out transport lists just like they've always done, the next minute orders come through to burn all the lists and documentation. Pretty Dorothea Binz was black with smoke the other day as she frantically burned everything in sight. *Make your minds up,* Suhren wants to say to those in charge. He's supposed to be the one in command here, but he's realised in these last days of the war that he's just a cog in a much larger machine. And the machine is breaking down.

He walks over to the map on his wall and reminds himself, for the umpteenth time, of the route the evacuation will take when the time comes. The plan is to walk eighty kilometres northwest to Malchow. Not that he intends to walk. He'll be taking a car. SS wives and families have already left Ravensbrück because everyone knows the Red Army is a bunch of degenerate rapists. But he's still got thousands of prisoners on his hands and what's he supposed to do with them all?

He's heard nothing from Berlin for days. The Führer is, by all accounts, holed up in his bunker. He's tried contacting Himmler but had no luck there. It's every man and woman for themselves now. If anything, that makes things easier. It puts him back in charge.

*

One foot in front of the other, Anna tells herself. Just put one foot in front of the other. The damaged muscles in her right leg protest at this unexpected exertion, but she has to keep going.

Ahead of her stretches a mass of women, as far as the eye can see. The order to evacuate the camp came early that morning. They streamed out of the gates and have been trudging across frost-hardened fields ever since. When the low-flying Russian planes roar overhead, they throw themselves on the ground or hide under leafless trees.

Jadwiga and Krystyna limp along beside her. She can see from their clenched jaws that they're suffering too, but none of them are going to give up. Not now, when freedom is in sight. They can collapse later, but they mustn't fall behind. If you fall behind, they shoot you.

Kommandant Suhren roared past them at the gates in a black Mercedes, leaving behind a cloud of exhaust fumes in his wake. Dorothea Binz and the other guards have also driven away in a convoy of trucks and cars, even horses and carts, whatever they could lay their hands on. But they must realise they're playing a desperate game of cat and mouse. The only question is, who will catch them first, the Americans or the Soviets?

Most of the guards are old conscripts with antique weapons. The SS executioner at the rear deals swiftly with stragglers.

A roar of aircraft engines overhead, and the women scatter in all directions.

'This way,' shouts Anna. They hobble as fast as they can towards a line of trees, ducking undercover just as the first fighter plane strafes the ground in a hail of machine-gun fire. More planes follow, tearing up the ground where only moments before they were walking.

'This is impossible,' groans Jadwiga. 'We're going to die out here. Don't the Russians know we're prisoners?'

To have survived this far and then to die at the hands of their so-called liberators, thinks Anna, would be the cruellest irony of all.

There's a crunch of dead twigs behind her and Anna feels a hand on her shoulder. She turns and looks into a face – red hair, green eyes, freckles – she seems to recognise but can't place. And then a memory flickers of handing out cups of water to her neighbours hiding in the basement in Warsaw whilst German planes dropped their deadly bombs.

'Anna Nowak?'

She nods. She hasn't heard her family name for so long, it's like a distant echo from across the years.

'I'm Weronika,' says the young woman with a smile. 'Jan's friend.'

At the mention of her brother, Anna grabs Weronika's hands. 'Do you know where he is? What's happened to him? Is he…?' She dares not ask if he's alive or dead. She searches Weronika's face for any sign of bad news. But Weronika is still smiling at her.

'He was fine the last time I saw him,' she says. 'Your photograph saved his life.'

Before Anna can ask what she means, Weronika scrambles to her feet and runs to the edge of the trees. 'Look,' she says, 'the planes have gone.'

It's true. The air is still.

'And what's more,' says Weronika, 'it looks as if the guards have gone too.'

'What? They can't have!'

'I don't see anyone,' says Weronika. 'They weren't doing a very good job anyway, those old men. They knew it was all over. They were just waiting for an excuse to flee, and the Russians gave them one.'

Slowly, they make their way back to the field. Other women are emerging from the trees. Bodies lie in the churned-up earth, the unlucky ones who didn't get out of the way fast enough. But Anna and her friends have survived. She says a prayer of thanks. Somewhere a blackbird sings.

CHAPTER SIXTY

May 1945. It promises to be a day just like all the others in the last three months. Jan rises at five with the other men assigned to work on the farm, and breakfasts on chewy bread and tasteless, ersatz coffee. They're about ten miles northwest of Magdeburg, in flat, open countryside. They live in a wooden barracks surrounded by barbed wire, and a guard escorts them to work each morning and back again in the evening. At night they're locked in to prevent them escaping. Such is the life of a slave labourer. But things could be worse. The weather is getting warmer, and no one expects the war to go on for much longer.

The farmer, a surly bastard named Schulz, doesn't appreciate the work they're doing on his behalf. The Poles toil alongside French and Russian prisoners of war, planting potatoes and mucking out the cowsheds, whilst Schulz looks for every opportunity to shout at them, hitting the ground with his cane, making them jump. He accuses them of being lazy, even though Jan has never worked so hard, day after day, in his life. Schulz's problem, Jan has realised, is that he doesn't trust any of them and suspects sabotage at every turn. Jan keeps his head down, quite literally, and spends many backbreaking hours in the potato field, his nails clogged with the dark brown soil. The game is just to survive another day and pray that the Americans get here before the Soviets do.

Today, as they trudge to work in single file, their armed guard bringing up the rear, there is noticeably more traffic on the road. Jan counts no fewer than ten trucks and ambulances and four Mercedes packed with German officers, all of them heading east, which can mean only one thing. The Americans must be on their way. If the Germans feared the arrival of the Soviets, they'd be legging it in the opposite direction. Will today be the day they've all been waiting for? Jan is wary about getting his hopes up, but he can't control the flutter of excitement in his stomach. He'll throw himself at the first American he sees.

When they arrive at the farm, Schulz is in a worse mood than ever. Cane in hand, he's stomping about the yard, shouting abuse at anyone within earshot. He staggers slightly and Jan suspects he may be drunk. Jan opts to work in the potato field rather than the cowshed so he can be as far away from Schulz as possible.

He's on his knees in the muck, weeding the potatoes, when he hears the first shots. The rat-a-tat-tat of machine guns followed by the boom of a larger explosion. He leaps to his feet and scans the horizon. A tell-tale cloud of smoke about a mile off is rising into the sky. Absurdly, he wants to shout and wave his hands in the air. *We're over here! Come and rescue us!* More explosions follow, but the response is half-hearted. The Germans must know the game is up. They've lost. Why don't they just surrender?

The earth vibrates through the soles of his feet. He can just make out a line of tanks heading along the nearest road. The other workers have downed tools and are pointing too.

'Come on,' says someone. 'What are we waiting for?'

Jan doesn't need telling twice. He runs through the field, back through the farm and towards the road. Schulz is practically having a nervous breakdown, but that's his problem. He can wave his cane in the air and rant and rave for all he likes. He'll be lucky to avoid a lynching.

A never-ending column of tanks, armoured vehicles and square, open-topped cars is passing along the road. The tanks have white stars on their sides and helmeted soldiers crouched around the turrets. The soldiers hold up two fingers in the 'V' for victory sign and Jan's heart swells to bursting. Schulz's wife, Jan notices, has hung a white sheet from an upstairs window. Sensible woman.

'Long live America!' he shouts until he's hoarse.

*

Later, when they're chatting with a group of Americans and Jan is chewing his first ever piece of gum, one of the soldiers asks in Polish, 'When are you going home?' He's a tall, good-looking young man with a strong jaw and bright blue eyes. He's particularly pleased to have liberated some Poles because his grandmother is Polish and he tells them he's always wanted to visit Poland. His accent is laughable, his grammar stilted and old-fashioned. But his question is perfectly sincere. 'When are you going home?'

He looks at them expectantly. The Poles fall silent and shuffle their feet.

It's then that Jan realises the gulf between them. This American has a home to go back to. Probably a girlfriend waiting for him, parents, a family, a house, friends.

What do Jan and the other Poles have? A country that has been laid to waste and is now in the hands of the Soviets, never friends to Poland.

Jan wanders away from the group, his hands in his pockets. He has no home to go back to. He's a long way from Warsaw, which is nothing but a heap of ruins anyway. And what of the rest of his family? He can only pray that his mother was sent to the countryside and that she's survived. Lech was last heard of in the Soviet Union, God help him. He doesn't know what has happened to Anna in the concentration camp. And where is Weronika? He takes the photograph out of his pocket. It's more crumpled than ever, but it saved his life and he'll treasure it until the day he dies. No, he isn't going home, but he knows what he must do. He will find everyone he loves. He will find his family and they will build a new home for themselves, somewhere, wherever that may be.

EPILOGUE

London, 2005

The wake for Anna is over. Jan shakes the hand of the last mourner to leave and closes the door of his Highgate home. When he goes into the living room, Weronika, his wife, is waiting for him. They've been married fifty-five years. Sowa was the best man at their wedding.

Weronika is just as beautiful as ever. She's been retired for twelve years now, but she achieved her ambition to become a nurse, rising to the rank of matron. By all accounts, her wards were always the most efficiently run in all of the many hospitals she worked in. Jan has no doubt that the experience she gained in the heat of battle stood her in good stead, and he's proud that she got the chance to practise on him first.

'I'll put the kettle on,' she says.

'Good idea. Do we have any biscuits?'

'I think there are a couple in the tin.'

Jan and Weronika have both become thoroughly English in their habits.

Whilst Weronika puts the kettle on, Jan takes a plate of biscuits into the living room where a reproduction of a

Turner painting hangs above the mantelpiece.

After the war, Jan took up Churchill's offer of 'citizen and freedom of the British Empire' to those who did not wish to return to Poland. It wasn't such a difficult decision to make. Following the defeat of the uprising in Warsaw and the evacuation of its civilian population, the Germans razed what was left of the city to the ground. Stalin had already installed a Communist puppet government in Lublin and there were well-grounded fears that future elections would be fraudulent. There was also alarming evidence that the NKVD was arresting members of the Home Army and sending them to Moscow for trial. The Soviets had kicked the Germans out of Poland and then moved in themselves.

Lech, who passed away five years ago, was of the same opinion when it came to settling in Britain. As his brother explained to him over a glass of warm English beer when they were finally reunited in 1946, only a tiny handful of men from Anders' Army opted to return to Poland when given the choice.

'They were all new recruits,' explained Lech, shaking his head. 'None of them had been exiled to the Soviet Union so they didn't know what they were letting themselves in for. We tried to warn them, but they wouldn't listen, the silly buggers.'

Thanks to the efforts of the United Nations Relief and Rehabilitation Administration, Halina joined Lech in Britain in early 1947 and introduced him to his son, named Emeryk Henryk for both of their fathers. Lech and Halina married on a cold, winter's day in 1947.

The Polish Resettlement Corps, set up by Clement Attlee's government, accommodated thousands of Poles in camps and facilitated their transfer to civilian life. Jan threw himself into the task of learning English with far more enthusiasm than he'd ever had for learning French. For the first time, there was a reason for him to learn a foreign language, and he discovered, to his amazement, that it wasn't so hard after all. He applied to study architecture and went on to help rebuild London, some parts of which, especially in the East End, had suffered at the hands of the Luftwaffe almost as much as Warsaw.

With the assistance of the Red Cross, Jan and Lech tracked down their sister and mother. It turned out that Anna had had a lucky escape from the Ravensbrück death march when their column was attacked by Soviet planes and the guards – a useless bunch of old men, according to Weronika – took the opportunity to abscond. When Jan learned that Weronika was with Anna, his joy knew no bounds. He didn't know what had happened to her after the surrender in Warsaw, but he did know that she meant everything to him. Maria and Agata had left the transit camp at Pruszków and spent the last months of the war on a farm. It had been hard work, but Maria's unflagging generosity and kindness had won her the affection of their hosts. When the women joined Jan and Lech in London, Jan showed Anna the photograph she'd taken in August 1939. 'You saved my life,' he told her. They wept tears of joy and sorrow.

Maria lived to the ripe old age of ninety-one and was never happier than when looking after her grandchildren and great grandchildren. She was laid to rest in Highgate Cemetery and the stone marking her grave reads *Kochana Mama i Babcia* – Beloved Mother and Grandmother – an epitaph of which she would have been justifiably proud.

Agata married a teacher and has two children and five grandchildren. She and her husband live quietly in St John's Wood and are frequent visitors to Highgate.

When Churchill made his speech about an Iron Curtain descending across the continent of Europe, Jan knew there was no going back to Poland. Throughout the Cold War, his heart ached for Poland, a satellite of the Soviet Union. It wasn't until the rise of the Solidarity movement in the shipyards of Gdańsk in the early eighties that he began to have hope for his country again. In 1984, President Jaruzelski unveiled a memorial to the uprising. And in 1994, for the fiftieth anniversary of the Warsaw uprising – when Poland was once again a free nation, following the collapse of the Soviet Union – Jan and Weronika visited Poland for the first time since the end of the war. In Warsaw they heard the German President, Roman Herzog, ask for 'forgiveness for what has been done to you by Germans'.

Afterwards, they travelled to Treblinka and laid flowers in remembrance of Wiktor and the thousands of other Polish Jews who had been murdered there.

Weronika brings in a tray with a teapot, cups and saucers and sets it on the coffee table. Then she pours, putting the milk in first, and hands him a cup. He takes it with trembling hands. It's been such a long day and he's tired. Old age is catching up with him, even if in his heart he still feels like a young man. Weronika must have noticed because she says, 'I know what you need.'

She goes to the CD player, inserts a disc and presses play. All at once the jaunty, rhythmic opening of Chopin's Polonaise in A major, the 'Military', transports him back to September '39. He's eleven years old again and he's digging anti-tank trenches with Anna by his side. He smiles at the memory.

MORE BY THE SAME AUTHOR

GOODBYE TO BUDAPEST

Budapest, 1952. When Katalin and her father, Márton, are woken by the ringing of the doorbell in the dead of night, it can mean only one thing. The Secret Police have come to arrest him on charges of subversion. But Katalin knows her father is innocent.

In a communist society where ordinary people live in fear of the dreaded Secret Police, suspicion and betrayal are rife. Whilst Márton endures the injustice of being wrongly accused, Katalin must find out who amongst her friends and acquaintances she can truly trust.

But there is a glimmer of hope in the darkness. The death of Stalin is a spark that ignites a fuse. For the first time it seems that change is possible.

In October 1956, a student-led demonstration soon turns into a bloody battle to overthrow the hated communist regime. Confronted by Soviet tanks, young and old take to the streets, armed with Molotov cocktails, bravery and cunning.

Katalin and those she loves must fight for freedom. They must fight to survive.

Packed with authentic historical details, *Goodbye to Budapest* is a panoramic novel of courage, sacrifice and the indomitable human quest for freedom.

ORANGES FOR CHRISTMAS

Berlin, 1961. Sabine can't imagine a life separated from her beloved brother. So when the barbed wire goes up overnight to divide East and West Berlin, she and her mother begin to plan their escape. But Sabine is living under the shadow of the secret police known as the Stasi. She'll have to tread carefully as the network of civilian spies closes in around her.

Dieter would risk everything to free his family from the oppressive East German regime. He joins a rebel group with plans to hatch a daring rescue. As the situation grows dire across the wall, Dieter must be painfully patient. A single misstep could get him and his family killed.

The Stasi have eyes everywhere. Can Sabine and Dieter reunite against incredible odds when anyone could be a spy?

Oranges for Christmas is a heart-wrenching historical fiction novel set in Cold War Germany. If you like authentic historical details, tenacious characters, and stories of hope in the face of tyranny, then you'll love Margarita Morris' emotional page-turner.

THANK YOU FOR READING

I hope you enjoyed this book. If you did, then I would be very grateful if you would please take a moment to leave a review at the retailer where you bought it, or on Goodreads. Thank you.

JOIN MY MAILING LIST

If you would like to receive news about new books, promotions and giveaways, please join my mailing list via the link on my website. Thank you.
http://margaritamorris.com

OTHER BOOKS BY MARGARITA

Goodbye to Budapest
Oranges for Christmas
The Sleeping Angel
Scarborough Fair
Scarborough Ball
Scarborough Rock

ABOUT THE AUTHOR

Margarita Morris was born in Harrogate, North Yorkshire. She studied Modern Languages at Jesus College, Oxford and worked in computing for eleven years. She is married with two children and lives in Oxfordshire.

ACKNOWLEDGMENTS AND SELECT BIBLIOGRAPHY

Thanks as always to Steve for his insightful comments, unwavering support and for holding the fort at home whilst I travelled around Germany and Poland by train. Thanks also to Josie for her proofreading skills.

I am indebted to the following sources:

Rising '44: The Battle for Warsaw by Norman Davies, Macmillan, 2003

Warsaw Boy: A Memoir of a Wartime Childhood by Andrew Borowiec, Viking, 2014

The Eagle Unbowed: Poland and the Poles in the Second World War by Halik Kochanski, Harvard University Press, 2012

Story of a Secret State: My Report to the World by Jan Karski, Penguin Classics, 2011

If This is a Woman: Inside Ravensbrück: Hitler's Concentration Camp for Women by Sarah Helm, Little, Brown & Company, 2012

The Diary of Mary Berg: Growing Up in the Warsaw Ghetto by Mary Berg, Oneworld Publications, 2018

The Pianist: The Extraordinary Story of One Man's Survival in Warsaw, 1939-1945, by Władysław Szpilman, W&N, 1999

A Memoir of the Warsaw Uprising by Miron Białoszewski, Ardis, 1977

The Secret Army: The Memoirs of General Bór-Komorowski, by Tadeusz Bór-Komorowski, Frontline Books, 2010

First to Fight: The Polish War 1939 by Roger Moorhouse, Bodley Head, 2019

Chronicles of Terror website - https://www.zapisyterroru.pl/dlibra